BLOODWOOD CREEK

Kerry McGinnis was born in Adelaide and at the age of twelve took up a life of droving with her father and four siblings. The family travelled extensively across the Northern Territory and Queensland before settling on a station in the Gulf Country. Kerry has worked as a shepherd, droving hand, gardener and stock-camp and station cook on the family property, Bowthorn, north-west of Mount Isa. She is the author of two volumes of memoir and eleven novels. Kerry now lives in Bundaberg and was awarded the Order of the Outback in 2022 for her work in promoting the bush.

KERRY McGINNIS

BLOODWOOD CREEK

MICHAEL JOSEPH
an imprint of
PENGUIN BOOKS

MICHAEL JOSEPH

UK | USA | Canada | Ireland | Australia
India | New Zealand | South Africa | China

Michael Joseph is part of the Penguin Random House group of companies
whose addresses can be found at global.penguinrandomhouse.com.

Penguin
Random House
Australia

First published by Michael Joseph, 2023

Cover photograph: © Magdalena Russocka/Trevillion Images
Cover design by Louisa Maggio Design
Typeset in Sabon by Midland Typesetters, Australia

Printed and bound in Australia by Griffin Press, an accredited
ISO AS/NZS 14001 Environmental Management Systems printer

A catalogue record for this
book is available from the
National Library of Australia

ISBN 978 1 76134 048 2

penguin.com.au

MIX
Paper | Supporting
responsible forestry
FSC® C018684

*We at Penguin Random House Australia acknowledge that Aboriginal and
Torres Strait Islander peoples are the Traditional Custodians and the first
storytellers of the lands on which we live and work. We honour Aboriginal and
Torres Strait Islander peoples' continuous connection to Country, waters, skies
and communities. We celebrate Aboriginal and Torres Strait Islander stories,
traditions and living cultures; and we pay our respects to Elders past and present.*

For cousins McKenzie and Willow Rose.
Live well and follow your dreams.

1

Deeply disappointed, I stood before the reception desk at the police station wondering what to do next. If it hadn't been for Aunt Fee I wouldn't even be here, searching for my cousin, but it was no good telling the constable that. And Aunt Fee, being dead, no longer cared.

'You're quite sure?' I asked, heaving a sigh. 'Maybe there's been an accident? You must know if ambulances attended a road victim – don't they report that sort of thing?'

'Look, Ms, er . . .' The young man sneaked a look south where he must have made a note of my name, but I broke in impatiently.

'It's Fisher, Emily Fisher.'

'Yes. Well, Ms Fisher, Darwin is a big place, with a large population. We cannot possibly know who might or might not be in the city. We've had no report on your cousin being missing—'

'Well, I'm making one now,' I interrupted, watching him roll his eyes in exasperation at my persistence. 'Aspen was in Alice Springs. I know that for a fact. I found where she was staying and the manager at the motel identified her. And she said that Aspen definitely told her she was coming to Darwin. Well,' I amended honestly, 'was heading north and—'

'You do know'—it was his turn to break in—'north doesn't necessarily mean Darwin? She could have stopped off in Tennant Creek or Katherine, or one of the national parks. If it comes to that,' he said wearily, 'who's to say she didn't cut back east from Tennant? She could be anywhere in Queensland by now. Just because you can't find her doesn't mean she's missing. Or that she's in Darwin. Now, if there's nothing else . . .'

'There is,' I said firmly. His attitude had nettled me. 'I wish to make a Missing Persons declaration, or whatever you call it. It's four months since Aspen vanished. Her flat's been abandoned, she hasn't been in touch with friends or family in all that time, and if I had some way of checking – which you lot do – I'd wager her bank card hasn't been used either. Give me a Missing Persons form to fill out, or take down the details and I'll leave you in peace.'

I got my way in the end and an interview with a more senior police officer than the man on the front desk. For what seemed like the umpteenth time, I went through it all and produced the much-shown photo from my purse. Sergeant Conner, dressed in plain clothes – did that mean he was a detective? – pursed his lips in an appreciative whistle that he didn't permit to escape.

'Quite a looker then.'

'Yes,' I said shortly. Aspen was beautiful, always had been, a golden blonde with fairytale blue eyes and perfect features. 'So that should make her easier for you to find, don't you think?'

'And you're her cousin?' His glance swept over me. 'Yes, you're very alike. How come the parents aren't the ones looking for her?'

'Her mother died last month, her father has dementia and she has no siblings. So I'm her closest relative apart from my parents, who are farmers and aren't free to chase around the country after her.'

'I see. I'll need the parents' names then, and an address.'

'Why? The house is on the market and Uncle Rich is in an aged care facility. He doesn't even remember having a daughter.'

'All the same, Ms Fisher.'

'Oh, very well.' Crossly I supplied them. 'Richmond and Fiona Tennant, late of 12 Crow Street, Grafton, New South Wales. Uncle Rich is in the Taylen Care Centre in Grafton. And no, Aspen didn't live at home. She hasn't done so for years.'

'And she's how old?'

'Twenty-three in August.' It was April now and as far as I had been able to ascertain with my limited resources, neither friends nor neighbours had set eyes on, or been in contact with, her since January. I told Sergeant Conner this, adding, 'Surely that's cause enough for worry?'

'Not necessarily. She's an adult with, presumably, her own vehicle – and if not, still free to go where she wishes. What's her employment?'

I hesitated. 'It changes. I couldn't say at the moment. She was a model, then she worked in retail. I haven't seen that much of her lately. She'd ring occasionally and we'd talk, but she was in Sydney and I work in the New England area of New South Wales. I'm a vet,' I explained, 'and I have a pretty full-on schedule. And before my degree I was studying with no time left for socialising. I guess we've sort of drifted apart over the last year or so.'

His gaze examined me. 'Yet you're the one looking for her. And come a long way from home to do it. What about a boy-friend? She must've had one, if not a dozen.'

'I don't know,' I said baldly, adding after a moment as he continued to watch me and wait, 'As I said, I haven't seen much of her lately. So there's only me to search.' Besides, I added silently, my wretched aunt had as good as made finding her a deathbed command, which I couldn't in all conscience ignore.

'Well, we'll keep an eye out and I'll forward the details on to our outlying stations, but I have to be honest, Ms Fisher, if she's chosen to drop out and she's travelling, or even just living under another name, there's not much chance of locating her.'

'Why would she do that?' I asked and he shrugged tiredly.

'You've no idea the things people do. Or she could simply have married, or hooked up with someone, a good-looking woman like her. Did you think of that?'

I hadn't. 'She wouldn't get married without telling me.'

'You said yourself you're no longer close.'

'I just meant we hadn't seen each other much lately, that's all. We *are* close, but even sisters live separate lives, you know. And besides . . . *marriage*? Of course she'd tell me. We shared everything growing up. She'd never get married without tell-ing me.'

Even as I spoke I realised this wasn't strictly true. We had shared when my much younger cousin was lonely, or fighting with her parents, or just lost in the insecurity and misery of adolescence. Four years her senior, I was her go-to comforter and problem-solver, the one who never had time herself to feel the drama Aspen seemed able to inject into every rebuff or set-back in her young life. When things were going well, though, she had no problem ignoring my existence for months at a time. As far as friendship went there was little reciprocity on her part. I had never really known the cause of her frequent moodiness. And all the girlish confidences in our relationship had come from me.

Aspen, my mother had once tartly told me, had the prob-lems of the beautiful – life was made so easy for them that every little disappointment they suffered became a three-act drama eclipsing all else. There may well have been something in that, I thought. On the other hand, my mother was younger, plainer and had married a poorer man than Aunt Fee had, and as I grew older I sometimes wondered if an unadmitted jeal-ousy, or the pique of the moment, had prompted this diagnosis.

But Aspen was my cousin, and I knew that her childhood, compared to mine, had been one of benign neglect. Aunt Fee had been a socialite to whom a young child seemed a hindrance. There had been no shortage of money or advantages – in fact she had showered her daughter with them, but always at arm's length. A succession of live-in au pairs had delivered the young Aspen to music and ballet and tennis lessons, and had overseen her homework and provided her meals. Uncle Rich had been the unseen presence shoring up their entitled world with a constant supply of money to pay for it all. He had worked all hours and was seldom home. I remembered Aspen saying bitterly once her father was just a voice in the night; she wouldn't recognise him if they ever chanced to pass each other in the street. Even allowing for teenage exaggeration this carried the ring of truth, making me mindful of my own luck in the parents stakes. Mum mightn't have been as pretty as my aunt, and Dad was a simple, hardworking farmer, but they had always been there for my brother and me – and still were.

Thanking the sergeant, I exited the police station for the bright humidity of the outside world. For me, born and raised in the northern range of the New England country, Darwin in April was hot. I donned sunglasses against the glare and wondered what to do next. I had taken a fortnight's leave from the Armidale veterinary practice where I worked, flying and bussing it via Alice Springs to the Top End only to draw a blank in my search. Naively I had imagined Darwin as a small town and that the first hotel, or possibly the first cafe, I entered would hold Aspen. I had seriously underestimated the city's size and population and the hopelessness of my quest was suddenly driven home to me.

My mother, well aware of Aunt Fee's failings, had said, 'It was most unfair of Fiona to lay that on you, Emily. You're not your cousin's guardian. They've both always expected too much of you in that regard. It's nothing less than blackmail, playing on your better nature. Aspen's old enough now to take responsibility for herself. Something she's never done in her life.'

That was certainly true of both mother and daughter, but the advice hadn't stilled my nagging conscience. I had wondered if Aspen even knew that her mother had died. If she'd been out of contact since January, as Aunt Fee's directive had maintained, it was highly possible she didn't. They had never seemed particularly close, so would she even care? I couldn't begin to guess. Despite my assertion to the sergeant, I had had very little interaction with my cousin since she had left home at seventeen to become the face of the big department stores, modelling clothes and cosmetics for those who could afford the luxuries of life.

We had met, more by chance than design, only occasionally since. Most of our news of Aspen had come through effusive missives from Aunt Fee, suddenly proud to be the parent of her much-photographed daughter.

Mum had not been impressed. 'I notice she wasn't the least bit interested when *you* were modelling,' she said, snorting as she flicked disdainfully at the letter. 'To read that, you'd think the girl had invented penicillin or something.'

'Your green eyes are showing, Mum,' I had chided. 'I was just a catalogue model, and there's nothing fancy about that. You could see me on the back of a bus, not the cover of *Vogue*. And you have to admit that Aspen is truly gorgeous, and more photogenic than I am. She'd never have got the contract in New York if she wasn't good at what she does.'

'So are you gorgeous, love,' Mum had replied. 'But handsome is as handsome does – and looks don't last forever, as Aspen will discover. Never forget that you are doing something worthwhile with your life and that's far more important.'

And so when I'd rung home to tell them I was going to the Territory and why, Mum's opinion of her sister and niece hadn't changed, and Dad, who was the silent rock of our family and seldom ventured opinions outside the farm, had surprisingly agreed with her. 'You've no obligation to either of 'em, Emily. If you've time off, come home, love. We all miss you.' The 'all' included the dogs and the horses, I knew, and it was very tempting to picture myself back at the old place, riding across the beautiful range country away from city din and bustle, but the nagging memories of a younger, more dependent Aspen kept intruding.

I sighed into the phone. 'I can't, Dad. But this shouldn't take more than a few days. Lord knows what she's doing, but once I've seen her I'll be back like a shot. She probably doesn't even know Aunt Fee's dead.'

'And whose fault is that?' he rumbled. 'All right, love. We'll see you when we see you,' he said, then adding as he always did, 'Stay in touch.'

'I will. Love you, Dad. Bye.'

And so here I was at the far end of the country, mission unaccomplished and with no idea how to proceed. There was a cafe across the street. I entered and ordered a flat white, which I drank while considering my options. The visit to the police station had brought home to me the difficulties of my quest. How could I have been so naive as to think I would just bump into my cousin on the first day of looking? How *did* the police and private investigators go about finding people?

I had no idea what sort of vehicle Aspen drove. The woman in Alice Springs had only said she thought it was red. Dead easy, right? One red car of unknown make out of how many hundreds of thousands? On the other hand, was it possible that the sergeant was right? Maybe she *had* married and was perhaps even now on her honeymoon. It would explain her being in the Territory – remote, exotic and the very antithesis of the city life that was all Aspen knew. The one thing I was certain of when it came to my cousin was that no scenario concerning her was too improbable.

Aspen's teenage years had been tempestuous. Aunt Fee had removed her from one school, claiming that 'undesirable elements' had made it unsuitable. Then a few months later Aspen had been asked to leave a second institution. Which, at the time, my mother had waspishly claimed, sounded better than admitting she had been expelled. I knew Aspen had experimented with drugs, but she wasn't the only youngster ever to do so. Just because I hadn't didn't mean it wasn't fairly normal teenage behaviour.

So, what should my next step be? The first and most obvious thing was to hire a vehicle. The Territory was just too big to be without one. No doubt by 2040 or thereabouts, I thought, the spaces between the far-flung little settlements that held the area's population would have shrunk, but now, in 1995, there was still a vast amount of distance separating the points of habitation.

Hopeless as my search seemed, I wasn't ready to give up quite yet. With a vehicle I could make my own way back to the Alice, as the locals here referred to the little central Australian town buried in the MacDonnell Ranges. And that way, I thought, screwing up the sugar sachet and dropping it into my empty cup, I could check out the many little tourist lodges, tropical orchards and truck stops en route. I could take my time with the search, and enjoy a bit of sightseeing along the way.

Standing with renewed purpose, I nodded my thanks to the waitress and stepped back out into the street to begin the hunt for a suitable set of not-too-hideously-expensive wheels, regretfully consigning a visit home to some future break.

2

I ended up with a new-looking blue Getz, a compact automatic with a minuscule boot and tinted windows, allegedly light on fuel.

'Leaving Darwin?' the dealer asked and when I cautiously agreed, expecting a list of restrictions, he simply said, 'Well, see you travel with water. A lot of my clients are southerners. Always tell 'em the same thing: you come up here for a holiday, not to perish yourself in the bush.'

'Thank you, I will.' I took the keys and followed his advice by going to a supermarket to pick up a generous supply of bottled water, before heading back to my hotel to collect my gear.

It was just on noon when I left the outskirts of Darwin, having stopped off at a 7-Eleven to buy sandwiches and fill my small thermos with coffee. The Stuart Highway stretched ruler straight before me, the country through which it ran lit brilliantly by what back home would have been an autumn sun. I had already learned that only two seasons applied to the Top End, the Wet and the Dry, with a minimal temperature difference between them – a matter of mere degrees. "Less there's a blow on,' a cheerful chap who'd briefly shared my table in a crowded dining room on my first day there had explained. 'She can get a bit chilly then. Where you from, anyway?'

I told him and he nodded. 'Ah. No danger of cyclones down there, then.'

Right now it was impossible to believe they ever occurred here either. Ragged-looking paperbarks grew in the swampland I passed, where placid waterholes dreamed in the soft shade, their surfaces strewn with pink and blue water lilies. The grass stood green and waist high through boggy areas, but further on the coastal look changed to miles of semi-open dry bushland furred over with pale-yellow grass and a mixture of timber. I recognised wattle and what I thought might be a species of box, but the rest was unfamiliar to me. There was none of the black sallee or native apple that grew in the ranges back home, but, I thought, slowing to stare, neither did we see a string of brolgas stepping along, stately as a moving frieze, by the roadside.

A little later I pulled into a rest stop to consult my new map and eat my lunch. The day was perfectly still and in the silence after the motor died I heard the buzz of insects and the distant cawing of a crow. I waited, listening to the tick of the engine as it cooled, then pushed the door open and got out. There was a shelter roof above a picnic table, rubbish bins and public facilities, and a large fire hazard warning.

I ate my lunch attended by, of all things, a pair of sparrows who arrived near my feet with the inevitability of gulls at the seaside. I flicked them a crumb or two, then gifted them the last piece of crust, wondering what on earth they did for water out here. Perhaps there was dew? The parched-looking ground gave no indication of it. Finishing off my coffee, I studied the map. The town of Bloodwood Creek, situated on the banks of the Adelaide River, was the first stop on the road. From there one could branch off into a national park, to several widely scattered station homesteads or to a place simply called 'The Jump-up', though the map gave no indication of what it was. A hill? Staring around at the flatness in all directions it seemed unlikely. If it was a town I'd never heard of it, so perhaps it was another station, or possibly the out-station of a property, which might amount to nothing more than a hut and a set of yards with no permanent residents. Well, that's what I was here to discover. Placing the detritus of my meal in the rubbish bin, I switched on the radio for company and continued on my way.

I hummed along to the music, which faded and returned intermittently until the news came on. It was the first I'd heard in a couple of days for I'd been too tired to bother last night and hadn't wanted to wait in for it that morning. Nothing much had changed in the world, I discovered. Somebody was banging on about unemployment, there was a segment on the dire consequences of rising sea levels and the police still hadn't caught the man who had killed a woman in western New South Wales. He was believed to have travelled into Queensland and there was an all-states alert out for a white Toyota. *Good luck with that*, I thought. Half the drivers in the Territory seemed to have them. A bridge came into view, white rails above a forest of ti-tree with a glimpse of water between. I half caught the name, Blood something, on the sign as the radio voice disappeared again and with the glimmer of an iron roof appearing ahead I reached down to switch it off, slowing my speed as the whole of Bloodwood Creek hove into view. Ah, so the town was named for the creek I'd just crossed.

The green was the first thing that struck my eye. Mown grass and watered trees fronted a building set well back from the highway. *Bloodwood Creek Pub* was blazoned the length of its long verandah. It seemed a very Top End statement; no pretence. *If you were looking for a fancy hotel then keep driving, mate.* I grinned at the thought, picturing a landlord in stubbies and thongs, and swung into the car park. Here, lush tropical growth outlined a spacious area holding a half-dozen vehicles. A sealed road ran away behind it, where other roofs making up the rest of the little hamlet could be glimpsed, along with a large millhead and a truly enormous concrete tank. The town water supply, I assumed.

The pub building seemed extensive, a low, sprawling single-storied complex with separate cabins dotted around it like chicks around a hen. I parked, picked up my bag and went inside. If accommodation was available, this would serve as a base to explore the adjacent national park. It was a natural place to begin, I told myself. There would be campgrounds within it and although I couldn't imagine Aspen in a tent, one never knew. And there might be cabins.

No stubbies-clad man was visible as mine host. Instead a middle-aged woman with a short, no-nonsense haircut and a practised smile, dressed in blouse and shorts, heard my request for accommodation in the bar where several men were chatting over cans of Fourex. She shook her head. 'Pub's full, but there're cabins, all self-contained.' She looked behind me. 'Travelling alone?' And at my nod, 'A single then. Eat in our restaurant or cook your own. Store's near the swimming pool. There're crocs in the river – big 'uns. They like the taste of tourists. This way, I'll get you a key.'

I followed her through to a small office, where I signed the register and was handed a brochure containing a local map, the restaurant menu, a leaflet about the national park and a key with a wooden tag big enough to fuel a small fire. 'Fifty bucks penalty if you lose it,' she informed me briskly. 'This way.'

Back on the verandah she directed me to cabin number fourteen. 'Staying long?'

'I don't know. Depends. Two days maybe – is it a problem?'

'Nope. Most reckon they'll see it all in a day then learn different. You're on Territory time now. Dinner's at half six. Breakfast from six. They'll do you a cut lunch too, if you want.'

'Thank you. And you are?'

'Maggie. Enjoy.' She pointed in the direction of my cabin and went back inside.

Number Fourteen was small but comfortable, with an air-conditioning unit, a mini deck out front complete with squatter's chair, and an ensuite that catered for the slim. I doubted an obese customer could have made it into the shower cubicle, let alone turned around. There was a well-sprung three-quarter bed, a four-hanger wardrobe, a wall mirror and an easy chair. Tucked in behind the bedhead I found a collapsible metal luggage holder. There was a tiny bar fridge containing milk capsules and complimentary bottles of water, an electric jug, a mini hotplate and a tiny sink to represent the self-contained component. It came with washing-up liquid and a tea towel, two saucepans, a teeny frypan and a bowl of teabags, coffee and sugar sachets. On the bed was a stack of towels and a laminated card printed in red about the habits and dangers of estuarine crocodiles.

I found a tray of crockery and unpacked my toilet bag and night things while the jug boiled. Carrying my cuppa out to the squatter's chair, I read about the tourist-loving crocodiles, and resolved to give the Adelaide River (only a short stone's throw from where I sat, according to the town map) a wide berth. The national park seemed less dangerous – though it did host the occasional buffalo – with waterfalls and pools where one could swim, and hiking trails and a large camping area, where there were slide shows and talks provided by the rangers. I still couldn't see any of that interesting Aspen, but I would need to check it out.

I turned next to the screed about Bloodwood Creek itself, learning that it was an anabranch of the Adelaide River and took its name from *Corymbia polycarpa*, the long-fruited bloodwood, a tree native to most of northern Australia. The local area was mainly known for its World War Two history. A historic airfield lay behind the town and a war cemetery within it. I would check it out tomorrow, I thought, finishing my tea. For now I needed to find the store and the pool. If they had bread and a few basics I could make my own lunches and breakfasts. And with my body pricking with perspiration from the tea, even the thought of a swim was cooling.

The pool was large and refreshing, blue-tiled with a low diving board and a few slatted chairs set back under shade sails for those inclined to loll about. A middle-aged couple occupied them and only a single person besides me was making use of the pool. When I finally climbed out, he swam another lap then, ignoring the ladder to one side of me, put his palms down flat on the tiles and lifted himself bodily, swivelling to sit on the edge as I was doing, with the water lapping his feet. He grinned across the metre or so of space separating us.

'G'day. Beats working for a living, eh?'

I nodded and gave a small smile in return. People were friendly up here but I wasn't in the mood to be picked up by some flirtatious stranger. As if reading my thoughts, he thrust out a hand, saying, 'S'okay. They know me here. I'm perfectly respectable. Name's Sam Novakoski. You staying long or just passing through?'

'Emily.' We shook hands. 'Just a day or two. Are you a local then?'

'In a manner of speaking.' His ponytailed hair, black as a crow's wing, dripped water and he reached behind him to wring it out. 'I'm from the national park – work as a ranger there. I always stop off for a dip in the pool here when I'm passing.'

'Oh.' I thought rapidly. 'I've been thinking of visiting. The brochure says you can camp. Are there cabins or does that mean bush camping, with tents?'

'Tents, a coupla cabins or your own van, though that's gotta be an off-road model to make it in. Or you can just bring a swag.' He shrugged, the muscles of his broad chest moving smoothly under skin that was surprisingly pale, though his neck, face and forearms were burned teak brown by the sun. 'Yeah, worth the trip. Where are you from, Emily?'

'New South Wales.'

'First visit?' He had a strong, tanned face, more rugged than handsome, with dark brown eyes, very good teeth and large lobed ears. There was nothing but friendly regard in his gaze and I relaxed a little. Of course with his job he'd be meeting and greeting strangers all the time. Taking an interest in them was probably just habit now.

'Yes. It's beautiful – but a bit scary. There's nothing more dangerous than the odd snake back home, which is more than you can say for the Top End. I've been reading about your crocs. They scare me to death and I'm a vet, for heaven's sake! Though I haven't actually seen one yet, not in the flesh.'

'You'll be fine,' he assured me. 'Just keep away from the riverbanks. Save your swimming for places like this – though there are springs in the park where it's quite safe. There're always idiots who think they know better, though. Mostly southerners or foreigners, and that gives the old croc a bad rap. But they *are* dangerous. They'll have you in a flash if you give 'em the chance.'

'Well, I certainly won't.' I picked up my towel and wrapped it around my body, self-conscious. 'Maybe I'll make it out to the park. Nice meeting you.' I walked off, feeling his gaze following me. It didn't mean anything. I wasn't as beautiful as my cousin but I knew myself to be quite attractive, something that had served me well in my modelling days. Aspen and I shared similar features and colouring, and I was resigned to the fact that men liked to look. I could almost hear the voice of my friend Phoebe, the practice nurse at the clinic, saying, 'Go on, girl. He's a real hunk. Live a bit! It's not like you've anyone in your life.' Except, I reminded myself, I had a task to fulfill and it didn't include dallying with tall dark strangers. Finding Aspen was all I was interested in.

It was late afternoon by then. I showered and dressed coolly in shorts and a singlet top, and bought a few supplies in the little store beyond the pool. After taking them back to my cabin I set off on an exploratory walk, during which I located a service station and a short street of houses where sprinklers threw lazy patterns over front lawns and a late breeze rustled through towering mango trees and clumps of tall bananas. Somewhere a cock crowed, and children's voices chased each other through a small park with swings and a slippery slide, the shadows tinged with the violet of coming evening.

I came to the hedged front of the war cemetery but the gates were locked, the caretaker having gone for the day. Peering through the ornate bars I saw a peaceful area dotted not with crosses but small raised squares of stone in a sea of luxurious lawn. Trees edged the cemetery, throwing the day's last shade across the graves and the rows of flowering shrubs. The air was still and heavy with the scent of blossom above the quiet dead, and I thought that nothing could be further removed from the chaos of war than this serene aftermath.

Sometime after seven, with the air cooling off, I swapped my singlet for a short-sleeved blouse and wandered over to the restaurant to see what was on offer for dinner. The side verandah was lit up, its tables filled by a surprising number of people enjoying drinks. I remembered then that the pub's rooms were full, and so was what I could see of the car park. Either they had come back from a day's sightseeing, or were new arrivals.

I crossed the wooden verandah to the restaurant, a large plain room with many tables, serviceable chairs and bain-maries fronting the kitchen where three cooks toiled. It was a do-it-yourself arrangement, I saw. One paid at the bar, then moved into the line to collect one's plate and cutlery on the way to the bain-maries, there to indicate to the servers what you wished to eat.

I watched for a little while as people came and went amid a babble of sound and laughter; the bar was busy and horse-racing was showing on the large TV fixed to the wall behind it. Mounted buffalo horns and the tanned hide of a very large crocodile was splayed above a line of bottles; I gulped at the size of it. The card in my room had informed me that crocs were protected, so this monster, which looked to be the grand-daddy of his race, must have been there for years.

'So we meet again.' Sam was suddenly at my shoulder, looking very pleased at the encounter. 'How 'bout I buy you a drink? We could have dinner together. I'm all alone, so company would be nice.'

I stifled a sigh, knowing how this would go if I agreed. My time was limited and I didn't want the distraction. Better to kill his interest now than to be seeking again for excuses tomorrow.

'That would be nice, Sam,' I said, 'but I doubt my husband would be pleased if I were to agree.'

His face fell. 'You're married.' I saw him glance down at my bare hands. 'But—'

'I did warn you about not wearing my ring,' a well-remembered voice spoke in my ear.

Truly startled, I swung about so suddenly the room reeled. 'Ben?' His name came out in a strangled squeak. I gulped and recovered, saying angrily, '*Don't* sneak up on me like that. When— what—?'

Ignoring me, Ben thrust out his hand to Sam, saying firmly with a hint of warning, 'Bennett Grier. Sorry to ruin your plans but my wife and I have matters to talk about, so if you'll excuse us.'

Sam, looking dazed as well he might, shook hands, muttered something and left. Ben took my elbow in a firm grasp and steered me to the bar.

'What are you doing here?' I hissed furiously, unwilling to cause a public fuss.

'Looking for you, of course. For God's sake, have you no sense at all? I thought you might've grown up a bit by now but plainly I was wrong. Sit.'

He yanked a spare stool out from the bar and, shaken, I obeyed. He was angry, I saw, his jaw a hard line beneath the smiling face he presented to the bartender. 'I'll have a beer, thanks,' he said, and as the young man opened his mouth to enquire what kind, flipped a careless hand. 'Surprise me. And a lemon, lime and bitters for the lady.'

Having him appear in such a sudden and unexpected fashion was as disconcerting as that moment when your foot misses a step. Studying him covertly, I cringed mentally at the excuse I had used on Sam, wishing I had said almost anything else. My husband's debonair appearance hadn't altered much, I noted, save that the usual suit and tie ensemble had been exchanged for a polo shirt (monogrammed), jeans and flat-heeled riding boots – what the city considered a country look. His face seemed not to have changed at all; maybe his hair was worn shorter but no flecks of grey marred its blackness. But then, I reasoned, he would only be thirty-three, and though his expression was decidedly bleak, that had more to do with the wintry light of his grey eyes and the lines bracketing his tight lips than the extra years since we'd parted.

When the drinks came he jerked his head at me. 'C'mon, we'll find a table on the verandah.'

I said mutinously, 'What if I don't want to? You haven't told me yet how you knew I was here.'

He leaned towards me, saying curtly, 'Well, I can yell at you here just as well, if that's what you want. I thought you'd rather not cause a scene.'

He had judged correctly, as usual. Fuming, I followed him out and, as most of the guests were now dining, we found a table near the railings where we could quarrel unheard. Night had come and the flying foxes were active among the trees, squalling and swooping between us and the stars.

Ben set his untouched beer down with a bang and yanked out my chair. He would remember his manners, I thought, on his way to be hanged. He waited for me to sit, then slammed his own chair back, saying furiously, 'Just what the hell do you think you're playing at, Emily?'

3

Refusing to be cowed, I said stubbornly, 'Who told you I was up here?'

'Who do you think? Your father, of course.'

Dad? I felt betrayed, and then angry on my own account. 'Why? Why would he do that? He knows we're not together any more.'

'He also watches the news.' Ben's words came in a restrained bellow. 'Jesus Christ, Emily! There's a killer roaming the roads and you're out here on your own, picking up strangers. Just asking to get your pretty little throat cut.'

I blinked at the barrage and went immediately on the defensive. 'I was not picking up Sam.'

'So that's his name, is it? As good as any to kill by. You know he's a bikie, don't you? I saw him ride in. Didn't take him long to latch on to you.'

'Oh, shut up,' I said wearily, 'or talk sense. He's actually a ranger from the national park and if he rides a bike, so do thousands of other men. Are they all suspects in your fantasy too? Anyway, who's been killed?'

'Who hasn't?' Ben said grimly. 'A woman in New South Wales, a traveller in southern Queensland, two backpackers the guy found on the road going north to some Godforsaken little town back there.' He waved angrily into the eastern darkness behind the cabins. 'That was a week ago. The press have dubbed him the Outback Killer. The police think he's heading for the Territory.'

'Really?' I was shocked. I had heard about the killing in New South Wales, but that was two states over and somehow I didn't expect murderers to travel, though, actually . . . I halted my wandering thoughts. Ben had always been exasperated by what he called my inability to stick to the point. 'Well, all right, I've missed a few bulletins. But I'm perfectly safe among all these people.'

'Yes, but on the road? A young woman by herself. I don't think so. You'd best travel back with me tomorrow.'

I stiffened. 'Not going to happen, Ben. I run my own life now and I'm not leaving until I've done what I'm here for – and that's finding Aspen.'

He groaned. 'I might have known it. Your damned cousin. Just tell me why you choose to take responsibility for that flaky little bimbo. She's a user – and I don't just mean drugs.'

'That was years ago,' I said hotly. 'And I do it because there's nobody else. Her mother's dead, her father's as good as, and nobody's heard from her since January. That's four months! She's *family*, Ben. There's only me and my parents, who you know are needed on the farm. And Stephen's in the UK, so he's hardly in a position to help. She could be in all sorts of trouble.'

'Yeah,' he agreed. 'She's probably holed up somewhere off

her face again. When will you learn, Emily? You can't save those determined to destroy themselves.'

'She was young,' I protested, 'with a high-stress lifestyle. She had no-one in her corner back then. It's no wonder she went off the rails for a bit. I should've been there for her then, and I wasn't. Something's wrong now, I know it, so I have to find her.'

'Well, you're not going to,' he said in his best don't-argue-with-me manner, a style I recalled only too well from our short, disastrous marriage. I flushed angrily and opened my mouth to rebut his assumptions and, seeing it, he added swiftly, 'Not alone. If you're set on it we'll find her together. If I can't rely on your common sense, and it seems I can't, then I'm coming too.'

'Oh, don't let me put you out,' I flared. 'I'm sure there's money not being made and girls going unromanced while you're wasting your precious time with me.'

He grinned nastily. 'And I expect there are dogs missing their shots and worming powder because of your stupid damned fixation. Shall we go into dinner now?'

I stood with great dignity, wondering how he could possibly know about my new career. I hadn't spoken to him since we'd parted seven years ago. 'Do what you please. I'm not interested.' As if to draw attention to that lie, for in truth I was famished, my stomach chose that moment to rumble, further mortifying me.

He laughed and held out his hand. 'Oh, come on, Em. Let's not wrangle. Come and eat.'

'No, thank you. Goodnight,' I snapped, and walked past him down the steps to the grass and back to my cabin, feeling his eyes on me every inch of the way.

Safely inside, I splashed cold water on my hot cheeks and damned him under my breath. I was shaking with anger and half of it was aimed at my father. To go behind my back like that! He must also have been the source of Ben's knowledge about my work. How could he! And as for Ben – I smarted at the memory – as if any fool couldn't give a dog a worming tablet! My stomach growled again but there was no way I was going back to the restaurant for dinner – I'd sooner starve. Fortunately, thanks to my visit to the store, I had eggs and bread to toast, and there was coffee. Only instant but it would do. It was a good thing that, unlike Aspen, who breakfasted on air and a spoonful of yoghurt, I shared my farmer mother's belief in the benefits of a hearty breakfast.

Slowly the night wound down; the distant noise from the dining room faded until only the racket of the flying foxes remained, and the last vehicle whose driver had somewhere else to be roared out of the car park. In the resulting quiet I grew aware of the faint, monotonous thumps of a diesel generator, which seemed so much a part of the night that I hadn't previously noticed it. The pub would need a lot of power, all those fridges . . . And the rest of the town. The servo I had seen for instance – the pumps would be electric . . .

'Damn, damn, damn!' Rolling over, I punched my pillow. Ben was right about my wandering mind. I could picture his pained look as if he was in the cabin with me, privy to my thoughts. Why had he come? We weren't divorced but our ways had parted scarcely eighteen months after the wedding. My mother had been against the relationship from the start but I had been so blindingly in love – or fancied myself to be – that I had ignored her counsel to wait and all attempts to persuade me that a longer engagement would be fairer on us both.

'You're so young, Emily,' she had pleaded. 'And this is all so rushed. You've known him barely three months. That's too soon to base a lifetime's choice on. If you really love him and he loves you, he'll still be around next year. Girls your age, they fall in and out of love . . . It doesn't mean because you fancy him now that he's necessarily the one for all the years ahead. Just wait a bit, lovie. If he's really the one, he won't mind. He's older – he'll see that a year isn't so unusual a period for an engagement.'

Waiting, however, was too great a risk; I had been sure of it. Ben was far too eligible, too good-looking and clever for all those beautiful girls in Sydney to ignore. I had fallen for him to the point of pain, and though I knew myself to be an unworthy choice of partner for a man so wonderful, unsophisticated country girl that I was, that hadn't mattered – or not enough. Love was everything. All the poets and songs said so. I would make him mine in orange blossom and lace, and we would walk together into a future of dreams and stars.

So much for the notions of a nineteen-year-old, I thought now disgustedly. I hadn't known any better, but that didn't excuse Ben's part in the deal. He should have seen that underneath all the glamour and high-end clothing, the poses and smart repartee, there was nothing but a pretty innocent out of depth in his milieu. Only the gift of genes had given me the face and body that gained me entrance to his upmarket world – a place I no more belonged than did the muddy gumboots I'd left behind at the farm.

So we had married, he the high-flyer in the financial world and me the country girl turned small-time model. And six months later the defects in our relationship had begun to appear in tears and slammed doors and rows. A dreary year had followed as our sheer incompatibility became obvious. For me, a picnic in the park or a walk by the river was far preferable to Ben's choice of a smart restaurant or another cocktail party. He began to go alone to such events and to absent himself at weekends. I raged and cried and in my unhappiness made myself unavailable for one too many shoots and was told I wasn't the only pretty face in town. Jobless, I mooned about our ultra-modern apartment with only the TV for company, and by year's end the whole charade of our marriage was over.

My parents had had the decency not to say I told you so, and had instead taken me in and helped me pick up the pieces and plot a new course for the future. Just as I was finding my feet and had enrolled for my veterinary degree at the University of New England, Aspen followed my previous course to Sydney, only with much greater success. Younger – she was not yet eighteen – and with a natural beauty the camera loved, she shot quickly to the top of the local modelling scene and then, inevitably, to overseas catwalks. Her face was on TV and magazine covers, she strutted her slinky model walk through showings of bridal gowns and evening wear and was photographed at parties in the company of much older, dinner-jacketed men. She looked to be and was treated as a sophisticated twenty-year-old, not the wilful adolescent she still was.

Modelling is hard work: the hours are long, you must always look your best and you are expected to perform whenever the camera is present. Aspen, stressed and unsure of herself behind the smooth facade of her beauty, and wishing to please those in command, took the wrong path. She swallowed the pills she was given by a helpful cameraman because they made her shine, she said. They took away the anxiety and boosted her confidence. They made her brighter and more energetic – or so she told me much later when it had all come crashing down and she had returned home, a haggard, twitchy wreck, addicted to the magic substance in the drugs that had ended her short career.

I visited her in the expensive rehab centre where Aunt Fee had stashed her to be 'cured of her little problem'. Aspen swung between moods of manic gaiety and depression and I never knew beforehand which version of my cousin would greet me – or not, if the depression was really bad. Then I would find her curled in a corner hunched into herself, unwilling to look up or utter a single word.

Meanwhile Aunt Fee had let it be known among her circle of friends that her daughter was resting from her demanding lifestyle and then, some time later when the cure was judged complete, that Aspen had decided to give herself a year away from the travel and stress of being a topline model. It was even possible that she believed it, I had thought at the time. That following what she saw as a little hitch in her daughter's calling, Aspen would sail back into the modelling world and regain her old success.

It didn't happen. Fragile and unmoored, and now unwilling to continue her reliance upon me, she ignored my calls and invitations and drifted into and out of a succession of retail jobs. And I, burdened with my own regrets and overwhelmed by my studies, had let her go. I learned that she had left home again and was in a relationship with somebody on benefits (Aunt Fee predictably beside herself at the news).

We'd last met at a friend's wedding three years after her rehab visit. I was surprised to see her there until I learned that she was now with the man taking the photographs. She was thinner and looked older, but I supposed that I did too. Still smartly dressed and wearing on her elegant wrist the broad gold band she had had since her early teens, there had been a suspicious brightness to her eyes that had nothing to do with seeing me. That, coupled with her febrile manner, had finally prompted the question that ended our conversation: 'You're not using again, are you, Aspen?'

'Little Miss Goody,' she'd sneered. 'You *would* think that. "*Why aren't you more like Emily?*"' she parroted suddenly in obvious imitation of Aunt Fee. '"*She's not giving her mother grey hairs.*" Well, why don't you mind your own bloody business for a change? What *I* choose to do is mine. You're so wholesome and so clever with your university degree, but you can't even keep your man. How long did you stay married for? I forget . . . Was it a whole year?' She turned on her heel and stalked off with her long model's stride, and we hadn't spoken since.

4

I woke from a restless night of broken sleep and strange dreams to the blue sky of another perfect day. There was the Wet, I reminded myself, and the Dry – and this being the Dry it didn't rain. I showered and dressed in shirt and jeans, for the morning air was cool, and activated the toaster, which took forever to brown a piece of bread. I was sitting out on the deck, watching the birds fluttering through the sprays that had started up on the lawns, and finishing my morning coffee when Ben sauntered over from the pub.

'Good morning.' He smiled and the quick, glad hiccup of my heart reminded me again of his almost indecent good looks. 'Those damn bats are something, aren't they? Kept me awake half the night. You ready to roll? No hurry of course if you're not.'

'Good morning, Ben,' I said punctiliously. 'And actually I'm not. I have to clean my teeth and cut my lunch yet.' I kept my voice cool. What was over was over, and I would give him no reason to think otherwise.

He flashed a smile and leaned against the deck railing.

'I'll wait, but don't bother with lunch – I've organised that. Incidentally I spoke with your dad last night. He was very relieved I'd caught up with you. He sends his love.'

'Does he?' I said shortly. 'Well, I still have to clean my teeth. I'll meet you in the car park.'

'Take your time. I'll wait right here,' he replied cheerfully as, my teeth firmly gritted, I retreated inside.

His vehicle was a silver station wagon, a Prado with a Territory number plate, therefore hired. 'A bit over the top, isn't it?' I asked sweetly as I buckled my seatbelt. 'You're not exactly Crocodile Dundee taking on the wildlife.'

'You think? How far off road do you imagine that little Getz of yours will take you? There's a reason four-wheel drives are preferred up here. Once you leave the highway there's not much in the way of sealed roads. So, where do you want to start – the national park?'

I nodded. 'Though I can't really see Aspen there. But if there should be a sort of wilderness lodge with all mod cons, then maybe.'

'Mmm, a safari-type lodge with personal service . . . I could see that.' He looked both ways, then pulled out onto the highway. 'She never struck me as a sleeping-bag-and-tent sort of person though. Still, if we draw a blank we can see the sights and enjoy a picnic lunch. I believe there're waterfalls and a pool sans monsters where we can swim. And after that?'

I said mulishly, 'I'm not here to enjoy myself, Ben. After the park there's something called the Jump-up. I'm not sure what that is. Then there are one or two cattle properties within reach of the bitumen. She might've gone there.'

He looked sceptical. 'Why would she?'

'A job?' I hazarded and he snorted.

'Yeah, doing what?'

'I don't know, do I? Cooking, perhaps.'

He raised his brows at that, an eloquent enough comment on the suggestion.

'Or,' I continued, 'one of the police I spoke to in Darwin suggested she might've married. Maybe she met a rich grazier and that's why she came north. I thought of it before I left and rang a couple of retreats outside Darwin that take honeymooners, but she wasn't in either.'

'If she'd married she'd have a new name,' he pointed out.

'Which won't change her looks. Believe me, she'd be noticed and remembered.'

'And speaking of names, I notice you've dropped mine.' His words hung in the air between us. Not accusatory, more as if he was curious as to why I would do so.

'Yes. These days I'm who I am, not who I was pretending to be.'

'You never have to pretend with me, Emily,' he said mildly, just as the national park sign loomed ahead. 'Right, turn-off coming up.'

It was an hour's drive into the park headquarters and the freshly graded road, if dusty, was perfectly fine, at least until we reached the first flowing creek. The Prado negotiated the steep banks and almost knee-deep water without trouble. Amazingly Ben held his tongue while I silently admitted that this was the point at which I'd have had to turn back. Holiday vans made this trip; I remembered Sam saying so, but he'd added that they were off-road models, which meant they had a much higher clearance than ordinary caravans possessed.

Unaccountably piqued by my companion's forbearance, I finally burst out, 'All right, you might as well say it: the Getz wouldn't have got me in here.'

'Did I open my mouth?' He smiled at me. 'Relax. There's no need to be defensive. You weren't to know.'

'Well,' I muttered disagreeably, 'you've changed your tune.'

'We all make mistakes,' he said. 'And I deeply regret mine. Can't we just be friends for now? What do you think of the country? I find it sort of impressive since we've left the flat ground behind. More rugged and jungly, if you like.'

'It's certainly tropical,' I agreed. 'Plenty of palms. For me, jungles conjure monkeys and liana vines. Oh, look at the flowers on that tree!'

He slowed. 'You want to stop?'

'No, it's fine. They're just so bright.' The tree itself was a weedy-looking specimen but its branches were studded with brilliant yellow blooms without a leaf in sight. It shone like a beacon against the riot of green and greyish foliage that filled in the ridge up which we were driving. 'It's getting steeper – and stonier,' I added as the Prado lurched over a rocky bar the grader had apparently failed to remove. We drove mostly in shade and just then, between the scrub, I glimpsed ochre walls rising off to the right. 'Is that a gorge over there?'

'Could be. Em, have you worked out what you're going to do if Aspen *is* here? You want to find her, I get that, but to what end? Have you thought that if she's come all this way to escape, she's not going to be very pleased to see you?'

I frowned at him. 'What do you mean escape? From what?'

He shrugged. 'Whatever made her run. So have you?'

'Well, I . . . No,' I confessed. 'I mean, I just assumed she was unhappy; maybe she broke up with her current boyfriend, or was deep in debt. You know she's not good at facing up to things. I blame her parents. Uncle Rich always paid the bills she ran up, even when Aunt Fee refused to, but once the dementia got him that was over. So it *was* quite out of character,' I added slowly, thinking it through as I spoke, 'for Aunt Fee to be so worried about her. But months without a word, not even an attempt at getting money . . . I do think that shows something is wrong, that she's in some sort of trouble.'

'So what's your plan if she's here?' he repeated.

'I won't know till I've seen her. Maybe she's broke or, like I said, owes a big sum of money. Maybe she's had a break-down?' I thrust my hands through my hair in frustration. 'How can I say till I've seen her?' It niggled at me that he had used the word 'escape'. 'What makes you think she's running from something, anyway? What do you know that I don't?'

He grinned, which made his face look more boyish than his thirty-three years warranted. 'Now how can I answer that modestly?'

'Don't fool about, Ben,' I said sharply. 'I'm not in the mood. If there's something, tell me.'

He took a hand off the wheel to change down. We were approaching another creek, this one much wider, the water sliding slickly between black stones that had the vehicle lurching from side to side. Driving one-handed, he rubbed his jaw and looked across at me. 'Okay, but don't get mad. Aspen's actually been gone from circulation longer than you think. She spent December and most of January in rehab, at my expense.'

'What?' I stared at him in utter bemusement and then dawning suspicion. 'Why? What's she to you?'

He smacked a hand against the wheel and drew an exasperated breath. 'There you go! Honestly, if there's anyone alive who could get the wrong end of the stick quicker than you, I've yet to meet her. Aspen is a pain in the arse, that's what she is. But you'll go right on believing she must've been my mistress, won't you?'

'Well, those places cost a bomb.' I narrowed my eyes, jealousy and fury warring within me. 'Why would you pay if she means nothing to you?'

'Because of what she means to you! Why else? She was off her face when I ran across her one day in the street. She was a total wreck, shacked up with some lout. She wanted money. I blew her off, so she came to the office a couple of days later looking for me. At least she'd cleaned herself up a bit. She offered to leave without a fuss if I gave her a thousand. I arranged to meet her twenty-four hours later with the cash and spent the time finding a placement for her. They're not easy to get, you know. There aren't that many with room – the government subsidises some, run by various charities, but they're always full. So it was a private clinic. And it took some talking to get her to agree. I had to promise to see her after, which,' he said firmly, 'I had no intention of doing. Anyway, she was making strides, they told me, then in late January she just walked out. And that was the last I heard of her until Keith phoned to say you'd come up here with some crazy idea of finding her.'

I had misjudged him. Remorse flooded me. I said, 'I'm sorry, Ben. You did a very generous thing and I—'

'Don't worry about it,' he cut me off. 'Did you know she'd gone back on the drugs?'

'No. I haven't seen her since we met briefly at a wedding, ages ago. She seemed very together and as beautiful as ever but I did wonder . . . and then we had a bit of a row because I asked . . . Anyway, she stalked off and I haven't seen or spoken to her since.' And, I thought, remembering her spiteful parting shot, I had been quite happy not to. Guilt stabbed me. If I'd made more of an effort . . .

He shot me a look. 'Keith had some garbled story about your aunt wishing this quest on you. How was that, then?'

I sighed. 'When she went into hospital, Aunt Fee rang and asked me to visit. I knew she'd had the heart attack and it had been touch and go, so I went down. She was beside herself about Aspen and made me promise I'd find her. She was quite agitated, so of course I said I'd look. I thought she'd recover – I never dreamt she'd die – and do it herself. Hire a private investigator most likely, because naturally she wouldn't dream of involving the police . . . But she never left hospital; the second heart attack killed her.' I sighed. 'And then after the funeral, I found she'd left a letter for me with her solicitor, reminding me of my promise.'

He nodded resignedly. 'So, equally naturally, you took off on this little escapade.'

I lifted my hands helplessly. 'Well, I'd given my word, and she'd got me worried too. I mean, months and months with no phone call, the flat re-let . . . Apart from her model-ling days, I doubt Aspen ever earned enough to live the way she wanted. Which was where Uncle Rich came in. But once he was sick, you had to wonder how she was managing.

The rent on that flat, central as it was, must've been expensive. Aunt Fee was fretting about that, said in hindsight they should have bought it for her and that without it she could be living on the streets. I didn't really believe her at the time. She was worried and getting things out of proportion because she felt helpless, I thought, but once I started trying to locate Aspen I got worried too.'

But it was more than concern on my part; there had been guilt as well. I had washed my hands of my cousin at the very worst time. If I hadn't known she was back on drugs, I had suspected it, and I should have followed up, not let her words drive me away.

Ben shook his head. 'It's a big country. What made you think she'd come north?'

'The size of my phone bill.' I watched the furry shape of a wallaby bound over a scrubby, boulder-strewn ridge. 'I rang everybody – her landlord, travel agents, car-hire places, even service stations once I'd pinned down the highway she was on. When I was fairly certain she was making for Alice Springs, I took a fortnight off and flew there myself. Then I got a list of every place offering accommodation and set out to visit them all.'

Ben raised his brows. 'You could've phoned them.'

I shook my head. 'I had her photo to show, so I could be sure. That's how I learned she'd headed north, and Darwin seemed the obvious destination.'

'How certain are you she's not there?'

'As certain as I can be.' I shrugged. 'If she's staying with a friend or camping in a van in somebody's backyard, then I've missed her. But half of Darwin's been shown her photo and nobody bit. And they couldn't *not* remember someone so beautiful.'

The road had levelled out again and we came suddenly around a corner to find ourselves at the reception area of the park. There was a long, low building painted a dull green and fronted by a bull-nosed verandah, the whole thing constructed from galvanised iron. There was a car park, the Territory flag on a pole, and set back behind it various outbuildings, water tanks and a residence. Painted signs pointed the way to walking tracks, the campground, public facilities and a shelter shed, while a large, garish map gave a rough overview of the layout, a red arrow at the bottom announcing: *You are here.*

'Well,' Ben said, standing before the board, and glancing at his watch, 'let's see what they know, shall we? Then it might be time for a coffee while we decide what to do.'

'Ben,' I said, reflecting that he really was a city boy, 'I doubt they serve or sell cappuccinos here.'

'Really.' He raised his brows. 'It's a good thing I've brought our own then, isn't it? Come on, time waits for no man – and not very many women either.'

5

There was nobody about so we entered the building, where a stocky woman wearing a dark-green shirt with the park's emblem of a brolga on the breast greeted us. She looked to be in her forties, with a tanned, friendly face and thin dark hair pulled into a knot on her nape.

'Good morning. Here to register, or just for the day?'

Caught unprepared, I said, 'Um . . .' and Ben stepped forward.

'Just a day visit, please. Thought we'd look over the campground and see what's on offer, maybe come back if we like it. Is camping do-it-yourself, or are there cabins?'

I glanced around at the displays and leaflets while the woman went through what Sam had already told me. There were prints of Aboriginal art and the usual t-shirts and tea towels for sale, and a lot of postcards and stubby holders embossed with the park's logo. Enlarged photos of wildlife – birds, wallabies, a massive python and the furry faces of flying foxes – decorated the walls, the pictures reproduced on table mats and coasters.

I tuned back in to the conversation in time to hear Ben receiving directions to the gorge. 'So, just to clarify,' he said with the smile that used to make my knees weak, 'it's safe to swim there? My wife's afraid of crocs,' he added in an indulgent tone.

'That's very sensible of her,' the woman said. 'I wish more tourists were. But yes, they don't come above the falls so it's perfectly safe.'

'And is there another road out, or do we come back this way?' He was tracing a finger over the laminated map on the counter. 'It seems to be a dead end, but my map shows a road running on from here. I thought it might lead back to the highway.'

'That's the old Jump-up track.' She shook her head. 'We don't advise people to use it. It's very basic, a lot of dicey creek crossings. Easy to get into trouble and of course it's not well travelled.'

'So what's there? Is it part of the national park?' I asked.

'Well, it's a bit of an anomaly. Nobody here seems to have decided whether it's really station, park, or Aboriginal land. As to what's there – well, I suppose you'd call it a commune.'

'So people live there? What do they do?' I pressed.

The woman shrugged. 'The boys call it Hippyville. It's a communal farm of sorts. They grow stuff and keep hens and goats – a back-to-nature movement kind of thing. That's just what I've heard, mind. I've never visited, so I'm really just guessing. You'd have to ask one of the boys.'

'And they are . . .?' Ben cut in.

'The rangers. There'll be one at the gorge and you'll very likely see Samson at the camp. They know more about it than I do. This is my first season here. I know they've had to rescue a couple of tourists who tried the road and came to grief. Confidentially,' she said, lowering her voice, though we were the only ones there, 'I think the tourists were after drugs. Rumour has it the commune grows a bit of marijuana.'

Ben nodded. 'Well, I daresay they've plenty of space. And no close neighbours, no cops.'

The woman laughed knowingly. 'I expect we'd all be surprised at what some people, not just the hippies, get up to out here. You could hide a plantation, never mind a few plants, and honestly, by all accounts – if it's even true – that's all they have. I gather it's a pretty hand-to-mouth existence, especially in the Wet.'

'The wide open spaces, eh?' Ben said genially. 'Well, we'll let you get on. Thanks. As I said, we're just here for a look around today.'

'Enjoy.' She turned away and we left, replacing our sunglasses as we stepped back into the brightness outside.

'What do you think?' Ben pulled out the keys and glanced at me.

'That we should go look at this commune.'

'Really? I wouldn't have thought the back-to-nature thing would be Aspen's choice.'

'What if it isn't?' I said slowly. 'I never thought till just now, but what if somebody's taken her? It doesn't have to be for ransom,' I hurried on, growing more appalled as the idea took root. 'There's white slavery and the sex trade. I mean, she's so beautiful, so blonde. Aren't the men in some countries supposed to have a thing about blondes? So what would she be worth? We know that sort of thing goes on. And I've read about rich families overseas paying for young women to keep as slaves – maids and nannies – in their homes. They confiscate their passports and keep them locked in so they can't escape.'

'Whoa!' Ben said. 'I don't really think that's likely. Apart from anything else, they'd get a pretty bum deal with Aspen. I can't see her shining either at cleaning floors or looking after kids.'

'It's not funny,' I said furiously.

'No.' He sobered. 'Of course not. I didn't mean to . . . but it's important not to let your imagination run away with you. I agree it's worrying. Maybe she has run off the rails in the past but there's no need *yet*'—he stressed the word—'to think it's that bad. Shall we go down to the camp and find a spot to have our coffee while we work out our next move?'

The camp was in a clearing beside a flowing creek fringed with spiky pandanus and graceful palms. It was well laid out with a large expanse for tents and caravans grouped around a central amenities block, a covered barbecue and eating area, and a couple of communal clotheslines. There were two cabins at the far end, each facing away from the other to afford some privacy. Canoes for hire were lined up next to the small ranger's hut, and behind it sat a much larger locked building that, I assumed, would be for tools and equipment. Everything was tidy, the ground was raked around the buildings and the rubbish bins had been recently emptied.

Ben pulled up near the barbecue area, parking in the space designated by yet another painted board. 'Keen on signs here,' he commented. It was true. Other fingerboards pointed to the

Gorge Walk, Reception (back the way we had come), Theatre, Swimming Hole, Boat Launch and Ranger's Office.

The kitchen at the Bloodwood Creek pub had provided a slab of fruit cake and a thermos of delicious coffee, with just the right amount of sugar and milk. I had forgotten that we both took it the same. Ben poured with a flourish, handed me mine and looked about him at the campers and various vehicles. We were far enough away from them to observe without having to interact, and my gaze skipped across the female half of them, looking without avail for height and blondeness.

'Of course that would be too simple – finding her here, I mean.' I sighed.

'Well, it's a nice day to do our looking,' Ben soothed me. He smiled and patted my hand. 'Have some cake, then I'm game if you want to start quizzing the customers.'

'Or,' I said, nettled by his playful attitude and noticing a tall form coming our way, 'there's Sam.' I stood up and waved. 'Bit of a shortcut. Hi, Sam. Can you spare a minute for us?'

Ben looked less than pleased and an unworthy part of me was glad. That would teach him not to jolly me along. It maddened me that he was simply going through the motions with no real belief in the need for it, or of Aspen's possible danger.

'Emily!' Sam smiled. 'I see you made it. How's it going?'

'Very well, thank you. It's certainly a pleasant spot; you must enjoy your work. What's the creek called?'

His wide smile flashed. 'It's Bloodwood Creek. The one the town's named after. It heads up on the plateau and runs into the Adelaide just shy of the pub.'

'Oh, I see.' I looked dubiously at its sparkling waters. 'Are there crocs in it?'

'Not here but lower down, below the falls. It's quite safe to swim and boat if you want to take a canoe out.' He looked at Ben. 'Sorry, I've forgotten your name. Were you thinking of doing so? You'll have to sign in first up at the office.'

'Ben.' He reached to shake hands. 'Not at the moment. My wife's more interested in your campers.'

'Yes. I'm trying to find someone, Sam – are you really Samson? The woman at reception mentioned it. I'd just assumed you'd be Samuel—'

'Em.' Ben nudged me and I flushed and stopped, annoyed with myself. God! Why did I always do that? 'Sorry, back to business. I have a photo . . .' I pulled it out. 'My cousin. Have you seen her at all? She was coming north and I haven't run across her yet. I thought maybe she was taking a break somewhere. It's certainly peaceful enough here for her to appreciate it.' That wasn't true – I couldn't think of a place less likely to appeal to Aspen – but it was all I could come up with just then.

Sam took the picture and studied it, pursing his lips in a silent whistle.

'Now her I would remember,' he said reverentially, glancing up at me. 'Cousin? She could be your twin. You're very alike. Sadly I haven't seen her.'

'Are you quite sure? She might have had a companion. Do you do bush camping?' I waved a hand at the immensity of landscape around us. 'Could someone just drive into the park and camp?'

He shook his head. 'No way. The only road is the one in. Of course, there's a few that branch out behind us'—he jerked a thumb west—'but you've gotta pass the camp to reach 'em.'

Disappointed, I retrieved the photograph, thanked Sam for his time and turned dispiritedly for the Prado.

'So you don't want a canoe?' Sam asked.

'No, thanks, but we'll take a look at your gorge.' Ben picked up the thermos, fished out the keys and nodded at the through road. 'We just follow that, do we? How far?'

'Five kay. Have a good day.' Sam put his hands on his hips and stood watching us, his image growing smaller in the mirror as we drove slowly away.

6

The road followed the creek, which, owing to the thick growth along its banks, was mainly hidden from sight. A pair of wedge-tailed eagles tearing at the carcass of a roadkill took wing as we rounded a bend, and the high walls of the gorge loomed ahead, ochre and orange in the strong sunlight.

'There it is,' I said unnecessarily. 'How do we get to the Jump-up? Which side of the creek is it on?'

'The other,' Ben replied. 'So there must be a crossing place somewhere. I don't imagine there'd be a bridge.'

'Hardly. So what's the plan?'

'Seeing we're here'—we were rolling into a car park, which is to say an area cleared of bush where three other four-wheel drives were parked, as he spoke—'we may as well see the sights. We could have a swim and some lunch, then head on to this commune. What do you say?'

'A quick look around then. I daresay I won't be back this way again. I didn't bring a suit, so forget the swim.'

'It's hardly crowded. We could find a quiet nook and clothing wouldn't matter. We *are* married. I've seen you naked before.'

'Well, you won't be seeing me that way today,' I said firmly. 'I just want to get on and find her. I've got a really bad feeling about this, and if you dare to mention female intuition I'll clout you one.'

'I wasn't about to,' he said mildly. 'Come on then, let's see what's to be seen and get moving again.'

He didn't seem too disappointed by my refusal. Perhaps he was finally coming to realise that I was in deadly earnest. The anxiety I felt on Aspen's behalf had grown incrementally over the last twenty-four hours and the task I had initially undertaken out of a vague sense of duty and guilt had, in my own mind, now morphed into a race against time.

The gorge was beautiful, its walls hung here and there with ferns and creepers that seemed glued to ledges and cracks in the sheer-looking rock. Its shaded waters were so clear one could see the bottom and the darting forms of the fish that swam there. We saw one couple in the water and another pair kayaking up the gorge, the droplets from the occasional spray their paddles kicked up like liquid diamonds in the sunlight.

The park had amenities – a waterless toilet block painted a dull green set back amid the bush where it was hardly discernible, and a modest shelter roof with benches and tables. There were rubbish bins and a sign about littering and fires, but otherwise the place was pretty much as nature intended and I sighed out a pent breath as I watched the little birds flittering around, unconcerned by our presence.

'What are they?' Ben asked, following my gaze.

'Finches. It's certainly peaceful here, isn't it? Like God was the last visitor.'

'Yes, very restful.' He unpacked the cold box containing our lunch and another thermos, then settled himself on the bench across from me. 'So, how're things at the vet practice, Em? You enjoy the work there?'

'Yes.' I felt a stab of irritation at the question. My father had obviously given him chapter and verse on my life. 'You know I've always had a feeling for animals.'

'True.' He smiled at me. 'I've never seen another woman keep as calm as you when faced with a snake. And a deadly one at that.'

Which didn't mean much, I thought. The serpent in question, encountered on the one bushwalk I'd ever got him to undertake, was very likely the only snake he'd ever seen. I said tartly, 'Well, we simple country girls, you know – we learn that sort of stuff.'

He winced. 'I do truly regret that remark. I was a fool not to see you were always more than that.'

'But I'm not,' I said honestly. 'Just older than the simpleton I was. Forget it. It's history now. So how's the city world of pressure and big business? Still as frantic as ever?'

'I wouldn't know.' He selected a sandwich and bit into it, adding when he'd cleared his mouth, 'I've left all that behind. And the city. I'm based in Armidale with my own small business now.'

'Armidale, really?' Well, that was a surprise, but it was a large city. 'Small, eh? How many employees does it run to?'

'Three. Me and Joe – he's my partner – and Nina, our receptionist. Nine-to-five days and free weekends. I like it.'

I hid my amazement. Talk about leopards turning in their spots for checkerboard! Ben had been the ultimate high-flyer during our marriage, Mr Cool himself, with the money and sophistication to support his position. I remembered the parties where I'd been so out of my depth, the liqueurs I hadn't known the name of, his fancy Ferrari, and Patek Philippe watch . . . Glancing surreptitiously at his left wrist I saw an ordinary-looking stainless-steel watch case on an expandable strap. So he'd either lost it, sold it or decided it was a bit over the top for a rescue mission – if that was how he saw his present occupation.

Well, it was none of my business and never really had been, I reflected with painful honesty. My role in our marriage had been to fit in with him, and I had fallen so heavily for his glamour and charm that initially it had been my pleasure to do so.

Enough time had elapsed during my wool-gathering that he must have taken my silence for a lack of interest, as he changed the subject, nodding behind me. 'Think this could be the other ranger? What did that woman say he was called?'

My mind blanked. 'I don't think she did.'

It didn't matter, for his first words told us. 'G'day. I'm Eric, park ranger. You folks just in for a visit?'

'That's right,' Ben said easily. 'Beautiful spot you've got here. I've been looking at the map and I see the track crosses the river – whereabouts would that be? I thought we might take a drive that way, see a bit more of the country.'

'Well, it does cross over, but I wouldn't advise it. The track's pretty rough. You could get yourself hung up in a creek.'

'Oh, I'm not risking anything,' Ben said breezily. 'If it looks too bad I'll turn back. Where would we find the crossing?'

Reluctantly Eric told us, issuing a further warning that Ben promised to heed, adding, 'I heard there's a settlement of some sort out that way. What's that about, then? Experimental station is it, or a ranch?'

'No,' Eric said, 'and we call them stations out here, not ranches. It's a bunch of New Age nutters getting back to nature or some such rubbish.' I could see him filing us away as a sub-species of those same nutters. 'Well, on your own head be it. But I seriously wouldn't advise it, mate.'

'Warning duly noted.' Ben piled the detritus of our lunch back into the cold box. 'We're staying at Bloodwood Creek. If we get through, I'll give the park a ring tonight to let you know we made it back, okay?' He shook Eric's hand and a few moments later we were back at the vehicle and ready to roll.

The crossing place was knee deep and the far side a stiff climb. Ben engaged the four-wheel drive and left it in as we headed cautiously down the track, veering away from the river towards the range of which the gorge had been a part.

'It doesn't look like the country would grow much in the way of veggies,' I said. 'It's all stone.'

'Pretty rough,' he agreed, wrestling with the wheel. The track was truly awful; half the time we were canted over and when the vehicle was level it lurched from rock to hollow, bottoming out now and then with a teeth-jarring crash.

'Eric wasn't exaggerating,' I observed, adding hopefully, 'Perhaps it gets better further on? I forgot to ask about the tree, too.'

'What tree?'

'The pretty one we saw, way back, with the yellow flowers? I pointed it out,' I said in response to his blank look. 'Whoa!'

I'm sure my face blanched and Ben slammed on the brakes, then whistled, as we both stared into the deep gully below the rise we were on. The track had developed a wide gutter down the centre so there was literally only the wheel tracks left to drive on, while on the far side the bottom half of the gully had been cut away, presumably washed out in the past Wet season.

'That settles it,' Ben said. 'Sorry, Em, but we could do an axle or get the back end hung up trying to get over that. I hired this vehicle – I don't want to end up having to buy it if we wreck it. We'll have to turn around. There's got to be another way in, and we'll find it, but not today.'

My nerves burned with impatience at the hold-up, but I could see that he was right. It would be folly to push on. I nodded. 'How are you going to turn around?'

'I'll back up till we find more room. Cheer up, tomorrow's another day. Now could you stick your head out and watch the sides, tell me if I'm going to hit anything?'

We arrived back at Bloodwood Creek just on dark. The ranger, Eric, hands on hips, had spotted us returning over the crossing and watched our retreat, responding to Ben's wave with no more than a nod.

'All he needs is a sign saying, "Told You So",' I said sourly.

'Come on, he wouldn't have been doing his job if he hadn't tried to stop us,' Ben replied. 'I expect they get all sorts of gung-ho types out here, running themselves into trouble. And I could've been one of them, because I've just realised we don't even have a shovel aboard. I'll have to find one before we head out again. If we'd got stuck today . . .'

'Well,' I said grudgingly, 'at least you admit it. I should've checked that myself.' On the farm every vehicle had its permanent shovel, and woe betide anyone who took it off and didn't return it.

The lights were on at the pub and the car park was almost full. Like the previous night, there was a crowd scattered among the verandah tables, stubbies and wineglasses in hand, and more heading inside, presumably to eat.

'Ready for dinner?' Ben asked.

'I need a shower first.' I remembered then that I'd walked out on him last night. 'Look, you go ahead if you're hungry. I'll be over a bit later. And thanks for coming along today. You're right about needing a four-wheel drive. I should've thought of that.'

His eyes crinkled as he smiled. There seemed to be a few more lines about them than I remembered, but time did that. 'My pleasure,' he said formally. 'There's no hurry. You want me to walk you to your cabin?'

'I'll be fine, thanks.' I picked up my hat and hurried off, wondering at this new, patient side to him. Ben had always been in a hurry before, bored by inactivity, always looking for the next thing.

In my cabin I found a fresh top and a pair of tailored shorts and took my time washing my hair and showering while pondering the difference between the man I had so disastrously married and his counterpart today. Had he simply mellowed in the seven years we had been apart, or was the tree change he'd made in his life at the root of the amazing tolerance he was now displaying? I dabbed a touch of perfume on my throat before mentally chastising myself for the action. I was over him, I reminded myself. But I was also, I decided, over second-guessing every move I made while in his company. If I wanted to wear perfume I would; it didn't mean it was for his benefit.

A quick glance across the tables when I entered the restaurant showed no sign of Ben. He must already have eaten and gone. I scorned myself for the disappointment that followed the thought. Then, as I grabbed a tray from the dispensary and lined up at the counter, he materialised beside me.

'Mmm, something smells nice.'

'Ben.' I felt myself flush. 'I didn't see you there.'

His left eyelid drooped into a wink and he gave me the ghost of a grin. 'Must be the roast taking your eye. Can happen, I fancy a bit of what I see, too.'

My husband was flirting with me. I gathered my defences and ignored his words. 'I think I'll try the fish,' I said primly, and to the server, 'The green salad, please, and the fish. No, just the one fillet. Yes, and the tartare. Thank you.'

Half the tables were still occupied. Ben led the way to an unoccupied one in the corner and pulled out a chair for me. 'They do a pretty good job for a place as isolated as this, don't you think? I've ordered lunch again for tomorrow, and I found a shovel at the servo. Bloke there said he's been asked for some funny things but that was a first. It comes from his garden. Said he'll refund the money if I bring it back. How obliging is that?'

'It makes sense,' I observed. 'He's not out of pocket if you take off with it, and he can still dig his garden if you don't.'

There was fondness, I thought, in the smile with which he responded. 'That's my practical Em. You haven't changed a bit.'

'Really?' I said flatly, busy with my fish. 'Tell me something, Ben. If you've left the city, how did Dad know where to get hold of you?'

He shrugged. 'I've kept in touch. Keith's still my father-in-law. If he wanted help, he knew he only had to ask.'

I stared at him. 'He never mentioned that to me.'

'No? Well, moving on.' He pulled out a folded map he'd tucked into his pocket, and pushed his plate to one side. 'I've found the other route into this Jump-up place. There's nothing to say how far, but it's maybe sixty, seventy kay? Hard to guess. The track winds about a fair bit. I asked at the bar. They reckon it'd be pretty rough but passable. Apparently somebody out there drives a beat-up old combi van and they make it out occasionally. And presumably back again.'

'Did you ask them about Aspen? I showed her picture around yesterday but nobody admitted to seeing her. They must work shifts though, so that doesn't mean she hasn't been here. One of the others might've noticed if she'd stopped off for a drink or a meal. I don't think she's been a guest though. I'm sure the woman who checked me in would've remembered her.'

'I asked,' Ben said, 'but travellers are anonymous here.' He absently speared half a potato with his fork. 'I mean, why give your name if you're just after a meal or a drink? I said she'd probably be travelling alone but there again, a girl comes in to order, doesn't mean she's alone. A companion could've gone for a slash, or be pumping fuel. They'd have to watch her leave to be certain she was here by herself.' He waved at the busy-ness around him. 'Look at the staff. They're flat out. They're not going to notice who gets into what vehicle. I bet all they see is the customer in front of 'em at the moment.'

However depressing, it was the truth. I sighed. 'It just seems so hopeless on every front. Because if somebody *has* taken her, of course they'd have her tucked away under a blanket or locked in a van or something . . . Those long-distance trucks, for instance – they have a bunk in the cab and they're too high up to see into from the road, or even from another vehicle. She could have been tied up in one of them and driven right past us and we'd never know. On the other hand, if she's running way – from debt, or a man, or whatever – she'd be trying for anonymity, maybe even using a false name.'

'You're not wrong.' Ben reached over to give my hand, which was lying on the table, a gentle squeeze. 'We'll find her, Emily. How was your fish?'

'All right.' I'd eaten it without registering either taste or texture. 'I wonder where they get their veggies from?'

'Tinned, I expect. Coffee? Or something sweet to finish?'

'Just coffee,' I decided. 'But I'll come—'

'It's okay.' He stood. 'I remember. Same as the thermos today. One sugar, dash of milk.'

'Yes, thanks.' I settled again, absently eating an overlooked cherry tomato on my plate. The lettuce had tasted bitter and I'd left most of it.

Ben returned bearing two chunky mugs and a packet of chocolate cream biscuits. 'Morning tea tomorrow if you don't fancy them now.' He gave me my coffee. 'Sorry about the mug. They don't do cups.'

'It's fine.' I stirred the liquid with the handle of my knife and the man who'd walked across the room behind Ben paused beside our table, pulling out the spare chair.

'You mind, folks? Got a minute? Saw you at the bar,' he said to Ben. He had a handful of leaflets and he dealt us one each. 'Linc Tetrill from Crazy Creek. I run Outback Experiences – you mighta heard of it?' Our blank looks must have convinced him otherwise, as he immediately continued. 'No, well, you dunno what you're missin'. Only fifty kay to the Creek from here and it's the genuine article. Station life in the nineties. Camp in a swag, ride in a helicopter, or on a horse if you'd rather. Campfire meals, billy tea, watch the cattle bein' worked, or dive in and try your hand at it yourself. We got safe swimmin', tennis courts and a workin' bar. End of the day you can watch the sunset from the verandah while supping the brew of your choice. Chance of a lifetime to experience the real outback. What d'you say?'

'It sounds interesting,' Ben said politely. 'But our itinerary might be a bit full already. You get many takers?'

'Yeah, yeah. Lot of city types wanting to find the real thing.' Linc gestured expansively. 'They come out to the Creek thinking it's like the cowboy films, you know? So a few days in the saddle, or maybe just joining the ringers for a drink after work and hearin' their yarns, puts 'em straight. So, what're your plans? Heading for Darwin or the Alice, are we?'

'Just looking around at present,' Ben replied. 'We're actually hoping to meet up with someone. I don't suppose she's been out to this dude ranch of yours? A blonde girl in her twenties, very striking looks. You got her pic handy, Em?'

'It's a workin' station,' Linc corrected, glancing down at the photo I produced. 'That her? Can't say I've seen her but'—he laughed—'end of the day, everybody covered in dust, a man wouldn't necessarily recognise his own sister. What's her name, this friend of yours?'

'Aspen Tennant.' I watched hopefully for a reaction but he was already shaking his head, his dark eyes squinched thoughtfully at the corners. He had crooked front teeth and almost lobeless ears.

'Nothin' in the files up here,' he said, tapping his handful of leaflets against his temple. 'Well,' he said, getting up, 'you find you can fit in a visit, you can make a bookin' here at the pub. If your friend turns up, bring 'er along too.' And nodding to us both, he left.

7

'Dude ranches out here – who'd have thought?' I said, watching Linc stop at the next table. 'Still, it's another place to look.' I lifted my mug for a final mouthful. The coffee was too strong for my taste and I pulled a face. 'I can't really see Aspen doing the cowgirl thing, though. She came to the farm often enough as a teenager but she hardly ever stirred from the house. She was afraid of the horses, didn't like dirt, or the smell of cow manure. It just seems crazy to me that she'd leave the city at all.'

'So we must assume she had a good reason to do so.' Ben set down his mug. The room was emptying out now that the servery had shut. One of the staff was resetting the tables for breakfast, and I could see somebody else mopping out behind the bar.

'They'll be wanting to close.' I stood up. 'Thanks for dinner, Ben.'

'You don't fancy a stroll round the town to settle the meal?'

I shook my head. 'No, thanks. They've got about three streetlights here and a billion mozzies. Besides, I'm tired. I'll see you at breakfast. Good night.'

'Night, Em,' he said. He accompanied me to the verandah and I was conscious of him standing there watching me
as I walked to my cabin, smacking at the first of the billion,
roughly the size of a small wasp, that had homed in on my
bare arm. They didn't do things by halves in the Territory,
I reflected. Even the insect life was over the top.

I hadn't lied, I was tired. There was nothing like racketing over
bad roads with your muscles constantly braced to exhaust you.
Disappointment also had an enervating effect. I told myself
that tomorrow we'd make it into the commune, where I was
now convinced Aspen would be, and once I'd talked sense into
her we could all go home. Aspen's welfare aside, I needed for
this to be over. I was all too aware of the draw of Ben's personality. I had loved him madly and been plunged to the nadir of
despair because of it; my heart had never truly recovered and
I had no wish to imperil it or myself again.

The cabin was pleasantly cool. There was no screen door,
but the bathroom had a small screened window, high above
the sink, and this I had left open to the breeze, which was
picking up. I could hear the sough of it through the tree foliage, a sound like gentle rain. It made me think of home, and
I remembered Aspen sharing my room one summer when she
was about thirteen and had come for a visit.

She had been a difficult companion that year, moody and
distant one moment, then frenetically cheerful, showing off
to Mum, boasting of the places she had been with her parents.
My uncle and aunt were seasoned travellers, making annual
trips to ski in the Victorian Alps or to attend the tennis in

Melbourne. They had been to the Gold Coast and Cairns and were planning to attend the next Olympics in South Korea – something my mother, who rarely got a holiday of any sort, couldn't even dream of.

'I'll go too, of course,' Aspen had declared smugly.

'Well, you're a very lucky little girl,' Mum replied. 'By the way, should you be wearing that bracelet around the farm, dear? It looks expensive. I'd hate for you to lose it. A gift from Daddy, was it?'

Aspen's right hand moved to clutch the broad mesh band of gold on her left wrist and the gaiety fell from her like a cloak. 'I always wear it.' She hugged the arm possessively to her body.

'Can I see?' I reached a hand towards it and she jerked away.

'No. Don't touch it, it's mine. I don't have to share with you. You're just jealous because you haven't got anything half so nice . . .'

'Aspen!' Mum said sternly. 'Emily was simply asking—'

'Well, she can't!' Aspen yelled, reverting instantly to spoiled brat mode, a side of her my parents seldom saw, then she burst into tears and ran from the room.

Mum threw up her hands. 'Well, what in the world was *that* about?' She shook her head. 'There's something seriously wrong with that child. Moods and tears – she's a roller-coaster of emotions.' She sighed, prodding a spoon at something in a pot on the stove. 'Go after her, love. See if you can find out what's troubling her.'

My less than sympathetic attempt to do so had got me nowhere. An uncommunicative Aspen had snarled at me from the bed, where she was actually lying on her braceleted arm as if protecting it from all comers. I had left her to her sulks and escaped to saddle Soldier. There had been far more interesting pursuits to occupy me, and why should I worry about my bratty cousin? So I had reasoned, and she had slipped easily from my thoughts.

Now, rolling over and hitching the pillow into a more comfortable position, I regretted my seventeen-year-old impatience. Mum had had the truth of it. There'd been something wrong with Aspen. Yes, puberty could lead to difficult behaviour, but hers bordered on irrational. Perhaps if I'd tried harder that day, had gained her confidence, it might have helped. Her drug dependence had started only four years later with the meteoric rise and subsequent crash of her modelling career. I had been her closest . . . I hesitated over the word 'friend', since Aspen had not seemed to have any, at least during her teens. I couldn't ever remember her hanging out with girl-friends. Plenty of boys, but nobody to invite for a sleepover, to gossip with into the small hours, or with whom to share the secrets of her heart.

And now she had vanished. Ben's revelation about the rehab clinic added to the mix of worry I felt for her safety. It had been an enormously generous act on his part for he had never really liked Aspen, though he had seen little enough of her during our brief marriage. But the fact that she had abandoned the treatment meant the strong possibility she had begun using again. Why? What was so terrible about the privileged life she had enjoyed that she would so ardently seek her own destruction?

And Ben . . . He had done it for me, he said. My heart bled at the thought of how things could have been. But he had changed . . . No, I told myself sternly. However much I mourned his loss, one mistake of that nature was enough for a lifetime. Leaves tapped intermittently against the roof like rain, and I fell asleep to dream of wet paddocks and the dimpled gleam of falling showers as the sun broke through onto wet pastures.

I woke groggily with the whiff of smoke from my dream still in my head. There had been a bushfire on the northern range, and Soldier and I were racing home with the news. The bay gelding was sure-footed but his nostrils were wide with fear and his ears laid back to the noise of the fire. He was on the brink of bolting, which would likely maim us both . . .

Heart racing, I sat up, aware of a persistent beeping, unsure at first of where I was. Memory returned with a rush and an overpowering smell of smoke. A tiny red light blinked above me like a red eye, keeping in rhythm with the shrill beeping emanating from it, as I jerked upright in bed, then fell into a fit of coughing.

It was no dream; the room was full of smoke. I scrambled out of bed, my hand plunging for the lamp switch, but nothing happened. The power was out. I couldn't locate my shoes and, abandoning the search for them, grabbed my bag, still only partially unpacked, and swept my purse into it. I left everything else and, pulling my pyjama top over my nose, blundered towards the door.

It wouldn't open. With trembling hands I checked the lock, pushing it both ways, then rattled it furiously but without result. The door seemed to be immovably jammed. Dropping my bag, I set my shoulder to it, yelling in frustration until another coughing fit choked me. Terror bloomed as my heart raced. The smoke burnt my throat, stung my nasal passages and filled my lungs so that I gasped for air. What had been a distant crackle in my dream was now urgent and near. As I watched, the bathroom window filled with an orange glow and the screen and surrounds fell in with a blazing crash as the fire spread to the walls.

I could hear shouting above the increasing roar of the fire and I beat frantically on the barrier between me and life itself, screaming and coughing and screaming again, yelling, 'Help! I'm in here! Help! Open the door!' I doubted I would be heard but surely somebody would remember the cabin was occupied? Getting air had become a desperate battle and I slipped to the floor, feeling the beginning of unconsciousness stealing over me. The heat of the fire from the walls beat against my body and I dimly heard a *whoosh* as flames engulfed the bed. Then abruptly the door tore open and Ben was there, wearing nothing but a pair of boxers, reflected firelight turning his face and torso ruddy.

'Emily!' He scooped an arm around me, dragging me bodily from my burning tomb. 'Jesus! Come on, I've got you. Where are the bloody sprinklers?' he roared furiously, reaching back to snatch my bag clear and throw it unceremoniously over the deck. A flaming panel fell with a crash behind us as the bathroom wall went and then we were in the open air and I could breathe again. He stooped and grabbed me under the knees, half running with me to a clear spot on the lawn. I tried to speak and choked, then fell into a fit of coughing until I almost passed out from the effort. When reason returned I found myself propped against his leg as he knelt beside me. He held a wet cloth in one hand and a bottle of water in the other and applied both gently. 'It's okay,' he said, mopping my face. 'You're fine. Have some water – slowly, or you'll start coughing again.'

He held the bottle to my mouth and I took a cautious sip. 'I couldn't get out, Ben,' I said. My voice was hoarse and my hands were shaking as I took the bottle from him. 'I was so scared! The door was stuck or maybe I locked it, but I don't remember—'

'It wasn't locked. The squatter's chair was jammed up against it. The wind must've blown it across and wedged it between the railing and the door. You'd have died in there,' he said grimly. 'Everybody was running around screeching about hoses and extinguishers and the last thing they were thinking of was their customers' lives. Witless lot of bastards! There should have been a sprinkler system . . . Jesus Christ!' he exploded. 'Timber built, surrounded by trees . . .'

My gaze went beyond him to the remains of the cabin and I shivered; the walls were burning down and the roof had partially collapsed. There were three garden hoses playing on it. What sounded like a chainsaw roared somewhere in the night, and then a heavy limb from one of the overhanging trees, whose foliage was already burning, collapsed into the remains, fuelling a brief upsurge of flame.

'Where's the bloody fire brigade?' Ben demanded. His jawline was hard in the partial light, his bare torso patched with shadow. His feet, I could see, were bare. He must've come straight from his bed.

'Oh, Ben!' A somewhat hysterical laugh was strangled by renewed coughing. When I could speak again I gasped, 'What a question! The nearest brigade would be Darwin. What's the point of ringing them?' I struggled up, the dew-damp grass cool under my feet, suddenly conscious that I wore only a flimsy top over short pyjama pants. 'I've got no clothes, no shoes. And I left my watch in the bathroom. I—'

'Don't worry about it. I'll get you another one. Your bag's here; it was by the door so I grabbed it. We might have to go back to Darwin for the footwear though.'

'No, it's okay.' I remembered that I had a pair of sneakers in my bag. 'How did the fire start?'

'I don't know.' He glanced around at a ring of half-visible figures in night attire – guests from the other cabins, I assumed, drawn out by the commotion. 'C'mon, let's get you to my room. No more cabins. I want you where I can see you.'

I felt too wretched and shaken to object. Carrying my bag, and with a solicitous arm under my elbow, he ushered me into the pub. The place was deserted. Everybody not actually sleeping must be out at the fire. I wondered how long it would be before somebody remembered that Cabin 14 had been occupied.

Ben had a twin room with a small but adequate ensuite. The radio clock on the chest of drawers between the beds showed three-thirty, so it was either very late or very early, depending on your viewpoint.

'I need a shower and something to wear.' It was an effort to think. I was trembling and a great lassitude filled me. I wanted nothing so much as to curl up and sleep, but the overpowering smell of fire from my hair and pyjamas was too much. I shuddered and had to swallow hard to prevent the sobs breaking through. I needed to get rid of the ash and dirt and do something about my hands, where the skin was broken from my assault on the door.

Ben dug out a t-shirt from a drawer, and found the second towel and soap. 'Will you be all right in there?'

I nodded, teeth chattering, and he said worriedly, 'Watch the hot water. It's damn near boiling. There's shampoo on the shelf. Take your time and sing out if you need help – if you feel faint or anything. Is that dirt or a bruise on your hands?'

'Bit of both. I'm fine really, just a bit shaky. You saved my life, Ben. Another few minutes and I'd have died in there.'

'Yes.' A muscle in his jaw clenched. 'And by God won't they hear about it in the morning.'

Shampooed and showered, the clothing I'd removed laced with a generous addition of shampoo and left soaking in the basin, I drank the overly sweet tea Ben produced once I'd emerged from the bathroom, then crawled into the second bed. I lay for a long time counting my breaths as I tried to relax and at some point slipped into unconsciousness. Against all odds I slept dreamlessly, exhausted by a mixture of terror and spent adrenalin, and woke to daylight and an empty room. When I checked out the window I found the sun well up; the clock radio showed it to be eight-thirty am. I had missed breakfast then, but I felt rested and well, apart from my bruised and scraped hands.

There was a pair of jeans, a shirt and underwear in my bag. I sniffed them and was relieved to find the smoke hadn't penetrated through the nylon covering. The sneakers were there too, and I blessed my tidy habit of keeping things together. The bathroom basin no longer held my pyjamas, but I found them drying, spread over a towel on a chairback. Ben. On the thought, there came a soft tap on the door and he entered carrying a tray.

'Good, you're up. How are you feeling, Em?'

'Morning, Ben,' I said. 'I'm fine. Thanks for hanging out my washing. Don't tell me they do room service here.'

'They don't,' he agreed, 'but I've had a word. Anything you fancy night or day is yours for the ordering. They're falling over themselves after what happened. So, breakfast. I ordered the lot just in case. You have cereal, eggs, sausages, tomatoes, toast, fruit juice, tea, yoghurt and a banana.'

'Good Lord!' I said, horrified. 'I wouldn't eat all that in a fit.'

'Well, just have the bits you want. I doubt they'll complain.'

'Ben,' I said worriedly, 'you haven't been threatening legal action, have you? You can't blame them for what was an accident. We don't want to be asked to leave, because we haven't finished here yet. There's nowhere else to stay.'

His eyes sparked combatively. 'If it comes to that we could always try the dude ranch place. And they *were* at fault. Nobody remembered you were there! The woman who booked you in—'

'Maggie,' I recalled.

'Whatever. She doesn't live on the premises, and of those who do, nobody took the time to check the register. Hotels have a duty of care towards their guests. You could have died, Emily! In fact, you were meant to.' His lips pressed into a thin line as I gawped at him, the spoonful of cereal I had been raising dribbling slowly back into the bowl.

Cold invaded my veins. 'What do you mean?'

'The fire was deliberate. Whoever started it wanted you dead. It was attempted murder, Em! The manager's sent for the police – they should be here about ten.'

In denial, I said, 'No. No, that can't be . . . What makes them think . . .? I could've got out, if it hadn't been for the wind and the chair. The smoke alarm woke me early enough for that.'

'If the door hadn't been jammed, you mean.' He nodded. 'But it was. We've been experimenting while you slept. There's about fifty ways the wind could've blown that chair – if it was lighter than it is – but it took the manager and me a good ten minutes at the next cabin to get it wedged just so to block the door from opening. Human hands did that. And the bloke who does the grounds found the tin used for the accelerant. Whoever did it brought petrol to the job, then chucked the tin into the shrubbery.'

I said, 'No,' again forlornly and fought the urge to cry. 'Who would . . . Why would anybody want to kill me?'

'I don't know, Em.' He sat beside me and put a comforting arm across my shoulder, and the temptation to lean against him and just let him carry the weight of worry and stress, and the new load of fear that now settled upon me, was overwhelming. 'But we will find out. I think we have to assume it's something to do with Aspen's disappearance. And if that's the case, if somebody doesn't want her found, then it proves you're right. If they don't want you nosing around, then something's definitely happened to her. It's the only thing that makes sense.'

'So you believe me now?'

'I do. We'll finish what we started and from now on you're sharing this room. I don't want you out of my sight.' He must have felt me stiffen, as he removed his arm and said equably, 'Purely platonic, and for your own safety. You're my wife, Em, my responsibility. Besides it's good sense. The guy is hardly going to burn down the pub to get you. In any event, seeing the cops buzzing round might give him second thoughts. Now eat up, you've hardly touched your breakfast.'

I pushed the food away but poured myself a mug of tea from the miniature steel thermos. 'Funny that,' I said tartly. 'Hearing there's a hit man after me has quite killed my appetite.'

8

The police arrived, a woman with dark hair flattened into a bun and a lanky older man with flaky, sun-damaged skin and a long face scarred by a shiny patch on one cheek from, I surmised, a healed burn or possibly a skin graft. He talked to the manager, while the woman poked around in the cabin's ashes. The staff had managed to save the porch, and the rather scorched squatter's chair, but the rest was gone, charred beams, crumpled iron from the roof and bathroom detritus all that remained.

I wandered over to watch, wrinkling my nose at the smell and the floating ash her boots stirred up. 'Sergeant Corrie Bader,' she said, glancing over to where I stood hugging myself. 'You the one who was booked in here?'

I nodded. 'Emily Fisher. Yes. The fire alarm woke me.'

'Well, at least they had that,' she grunted, opening her hand to show me a fused metal watch case. 'Yours? Where'd you leave it?'

'Bathroom – ledge above the basin. I took it off to shower.'

'Figures.' She slipped it into what I assumed to be an evidence bag.

'They're saying it was arson.' I shivered and rubbed my arms. 'Can you actually tell that, now it's all burnt?'

'Oh, yes. There's no doubt it was deliberately started, and that's without the empty fuel tin.' I must have looked sceptical, because she added, 'I was a fire investigator before I became a cop. I'm hoping there'll be prints on the petrol tin. So, who wanted you dead, and why?'

Her partner, who introduced himself as Detective Phil Ashton, wandered over just as she finished asking the question, and added, 'You got any enemies, Mrs Fisher?'

'It's Ms. None that I know of, and certainly not up here where I'm a stranger.'

'Ms? I understood from one of the residents that you were married.'

I felt a flash of irritation. He must have spoken to Sam.

'We are,' Ben, who had joined me and overheard, confirmed.

'We were,' I corrected. 'We're separated. I use my maiden name.'

'But you're travelling together?'

'Yes,' Ben replied uninformatively. 'Look, this is going to sound crazy but we're here to find my wife's cousin, who's either disappeared or done a runner. And our theory – *my* theory,' he corrected, 'is that last night is down to that.'

The detective blinked thoughtfully, his eyes boring into Ben for a long moment. 'Yeah? So this cousin, who doesn't want to be found, tried to knock off your wife, is that what you're saying?'

'No, of course not,' I broke in impatiently. 'But something's happened to Aspen. That's her name – Aspen Tennant. We can't find a trace of her anywhere and we know she came up this way. So she's been kidnapped, or . . . something. I don't know. And whoever's responsible must be trying to stop me from learning the truth. It's the only way the fire makes any sense.'

'Riiight.' Detective Ashton looked unconvinced. 'And you've reported this? She's officially listed as missing?'

'Well, if the police have done their work, she is,' I snapped, deeply annoyed by his attitude. 'I went to them in Darwin. *"It's a big country. She's of an age to go where she wants. People sometimes just need to get away, especially from family,"*' I quoted. 'That's the sort of response I was met with.'

'It's true all the same, Ms Fisher. Who is she, this cousin? What about her might make her a target for abduction? If'— he stressed the word—'that is what has occurred.'

'Aspen's a model – or she was. Very beautiful and quite well known a few years back. She was in all the fashion magazines. A tall blonde girl with a degree of fame – not quite *Elle* but getting close when she gave it up.'

'And why was that?'

'She had a breakdown. It's the lifestyle. The long hours, the exposure, the need to always look your best. It's hard on the young and she was only seventeen when she started. The stress . . .' I shrugged. 'I did a bit of modelling myself and you need a good stable upbringing to ground you for that life. I was lucky, I had that. Aspen didn't. She got into recreational drugs and has been drifting ever since.'

'So, an addict.'

'No,' I protested. 'She used recreational drugs for a time, then stopped.' I didn't think it would help to mention her more recent addiction. 'And then she just dropped out of things. She worked jobs here and there in Sydney – that's where she's from, but I haven't seen much of her lately, so I don't really know how she was managing. But nobody's heard from her in months and I'm worried. You read about white slavery, and girls sold into prostitution, mainly in Europe—'

'Don't you believe it,' Ashton broke in. 'Scores of young Filipina girls get smuggled into brothels right here in Oz. And others from Vietnam, Malaysia. They're here illegally, the pimps get 'em hooked on drugs and they never get out of the life. I gotta admit, your cousin being a user makes your story more likely though.'

I wanted to insist that Aspen no longer took drugs, but lying wouldn't help. I knew I should tell them about the recent rehab clinic she'd walked out of, but a missing 'respectable' Aspen would raise more concern than a known addict.

Ben ended the speculation with a forthright question. 'So what are you going to do about last night?'

'We'll investigate, Mr Grier. We'll check the guest list here, question the staff. If there're prints on the container, we'll look at those, but unless the culprit's already in the system . . .' He shrugged. 'Arson's easy enough to prove these days but catching those responsible is another bucket of fish. In the meantime, just in case there's something in your theory, I'd advise you to take precautions.'

'Such as?' I asked.

'Clear out,' he said firmly. 'Just go home. Leave it to us to locate your cousin. The details will have been circulated and we're better resourced to find people than any member of the public.'

'Except,' I pointed out, 'you haven't done so yet. And before you say it's only a few days, I reported her missing in New South Wales too – weeks ago.'

'Her and five thousand others. We're not magicians. Now, I'll be getting on. Like I said, you'd best go home. Attempted murder is a serious business. Who knows? Next time you mightn't be so lucky.'

His blithe assumption that there would be a next time was, for me, enough to end the interview. I swallowed dumbly and nodded.

We did go, but only to seek the commune at the Jump-up. The kitchen had come good with the lunch Ben had ordered and while he was stowing it in the vehicle I had a visit from the manager, as regretful as if he himself had inadvertently lit the fire. He was cancelling my accommodation charges, he said, and the money I had already paid would be refunded to my card as some small recompense for the material losses and fright I had sustained. And he couldn't sufficiently apologise for my overlooked presence in the burning cabin . . .

By the time he was through, I was almost ready to accept that the whole thing was somehow my fault. Thanking him, I wore his gift of a genuine Akubra from the pub's range of souvenirs ('a small token of our concern for your unfortunate experience and really quite essential equipment up here') out to the car park, where Ben's Prado sat next to the police vehicle.

'Ready?' he asked. 'I've fuelled up. Where'd you get the hat? It suits you.'

'The manager here. It was very thoughtful of him. Mine went in the fire.'

'Least he can do,' Ben growled, shutting his door with unnecessary force. 'Right, we've food, water, hats, a shovel and I've left word where we're going. Anything else?'

'That should do it,' I agreed. 'You sound like you were a boy scout. Isn't their motto "Be Prepared"?'

'I am trying,' he said somewhat stiffly, 'to cover our bases. Seeing you seem to think that city-born equals idiot.'

'Sorry.' I was surprised it bothered him. The Ben I remembered was too self-assured to notice criticism, let alone worry what anybody thought of him. 'And of course you're right. Also we have a map. So we're ready for anything.'

But probably not for the road that faced us once we reached the dirt track that turned off the bitumen. It was trafficable – just. And calling it a road was a drastic overstatement. Mule track would fit the bill nearer, I reflected, hanging on to the grab bar as we lurched and bounced from gutter to hole and back again. The trouble was that most of the holes were layered over with bulldust. Past traffic had ground the soil into a pale red, talc-fine sediment that rose in choking clouds about the vehicle, while the deep drifts of it obscured the shape of the bedrock beneath our wheels.

Ben swore beneath his breath but persevered until we were through the worst of it. We hit a relatively straight and even patch, before plunging into a bone-jarring section of corrugations that seemed to stretch forever. When it ended, Ben pulled in to a patch of shade and consulted the map and then the clock on the dash.

'Two choices,' he said. 'I make it about twenty, twenty-five kay from here. Time enough to get into the ranges.' He waved at the windscreen. 'You can see the ridgy country starting out way over. So we can push on, could be another hour or more at this rate, and eat when we get there, or we could have lunch now. It's nearly two o'clock.'

'Let's have lunch. I'm perishing for a drink anyway.' Pouring liquid while being thrown around the cab wasn't possible. I pushed the door open. 'Dear Lord, I'll be stiff as a board tomorrow from all that jolting.'

The meal was a welcome break. When we'd eaten I found myself yawning and wishing for a nap but settled for conversation instead. 'What do you suppose makes people live at the end of a road like this? There must be other places with easier access where you can get back to nature, if that's what they want. Imagine having to evacuate if you had an accident, or were a woman in labour.'

'If it's a proper commune, they've probably got their own health system,' Ben said. 'Midwives with herbs and magic chants, and maybe some sort of healer. Also, the poor access might be deliberate if they really want to opt out of the world. Or it could be a cult of some sort, and not a commune at all – true believers and those who wish they weren't.'

A trickle of unease ran through my veins. 'Really? Like Waco? That ranger Eric didn't say it was.'

'He didn't say he'd visited either.' Ben got up and began stowing the cold box.

'Only way to find out is to get there. You ready?'

'Of course.' But turning over his words and feeling the disquiet they brought, I was no longer so sure.

The country got steeper, the scrub giving way to rocks and

low shrubby bushes. We crossed a running creek, then ran parallel to it for a distance until the road diverged around a steep-sided plateau, only to return again to its palm- and pandanus-grown banks.

'It's hard to believe you could be self-sustaining in country like this,' I said, clinging to the grab bar; the track now was really just the flattest area of stone rather than a made surface. 'Cactus might thrive here but I can't believe vegetables would.'

'Yeah.' Ben was peering ahead. 'I guess that's the jump-up. Looks pretty steep.'

I gulped, ducking my head to see the top of what I had previously thought of as a low cliff. 'Do we have to go up that?' It looked pretty sheer to me, a wall of rock, maybe six metres high. Somewhat shrilly, I said, 'You can't drive straight upwards, Ben. Not even with four-wheel-drive.'

'I'm not about to.' He'd stopped and was looking around. 'Ha, over there – see it? The track goes off to the left.'

It wasn't marked in any way, just an uncleared opening between the shrubby growth with only two wheeltracks to show its use.

'Are you sure?' I asked doubtfully. 'Somebody could've just backed up there and out again.'

'Road's gotta go somewhere.' Ben edged into it and after a hundred metres or so, I saw he was right. The road took us back down to the creek and eventually out into more open bottom lands, a spreading valley with taller timber, the largest of which I recognised from tourist leaflets as bloodwoods by the pale lemon clusters of flowers standing proud of the canopy. And then, quite suddenly, we had arrived.

It took a moment, and the sight of the old blue combi van

parked in the lee of a thicket of smallish trees, to realise that we'd reached our destination. The dwellings were a mixture of crude unpainted huts, bough sheds and lean-tos. They blended so well into the natural background that at first only the rising smoke from cooking fires allowed the eye to pick them out.

'Well,' Ben said, pulling up and switching off, 'no barricade, no stroppy, hairy types brandishing guns. Looks like it's a commune after all. Let's go see what they know about our girl, if anything.'

9

Naturally our arrival had been noticed. The first to appear was a thin, wiry-looking man in bib overalls with a cloth hat and what looked like homemade sandals. His long beard and hair were both grey and he could have been fifty. He was wiping his hands on an oily rag and, apparently satisfied with their cleanliness, thrust one at Ben.

'G'day, I'm Kil. How can I help you?'

Ben shook his hand. 'Ben Grier.' He raised a brow. 'You did say Kill?'

'Kilmet.' He smiled with a flash of horsey teeth, gapped on the right side. 'Don't ask. My old man.' A woman of a similar age and stringiness of build had appeared behind him. 'My wife, Sal. And you are?'

He was looking at me. 'Oh, I'm Emily – Emily Fisher. I have to say yours is not an easy place to get to, Kil.'

'That's the idea.' He didn't smile.

I nodded to his wife, who was silently eyeing us, and after an awkward pause Kil stuck the rag in his back pocket and jerked his head towards the blue van.

'Well, come on over. We'll put on a brew while you tell us what you're doing here.'

Civil, I thought, but not friendly. Perhaps it would be truer to call him wary. I didn't imagine that the locals, used to the hard, practical life that the land demanded, would have much sympathy for airy-fairy greenies with their ideas of cosying up to nature with herbal teas and a belief in the influence of celestial bodies.

I could have been doing Kil and Sal a disservice but I thought of old Tom Sylvester, a neighbour of Dad's, who the authorities had moved into a nursing home some months before his death. He was estranged from his only son and had muddled along alone after his wife's passing, losing his grip on both life and the farm. According to the squatters who'd come to take over his paddocks, he had given them a lease in the interests of the land. They claimed to be Gaia-ites, devoted to a sustainable ecology and the worship of all living things. They were also, Dad reported, a grubby, unkempt lot, driving clapped-out rust buckets, and their children would have been the better for a good boot up the backside.

The kids had stolen from the surrounding farms, set fire to hay bales, and vandalised anything they couldn't carry off. Their parents were no better, the leased paddocks a disgrace, the fence lines littered with rubbish, the once-lush grazing a hotch-potch of tin and plastic shelters and dug-over ground that failed to produce much in the way of vegetables. Probably the reason, I thought now, that the kids were always into the neighbour's chook pens and orchards.

When old Tom had finally died, his son lost no time in evicting the group, who turned out to have had no right to be there in the first place. And the police had burned the large crop of wacky weed that had been doing nicely in one of Tom's old sheds.

This lot at least looked to be better organised, judging by Kil and Sal's place. Their van was their kitchen, kitted out with a sink, gas stove and fridge. It stood before a shed built from bush timber and iron, with a thatching of spinifex held down by what I took to be a trawling net. The thatch, and the fact that the ground had been selectively cleared to leave plenty of shade trees, would mitigate the dreadful summer heat on the iron roof. It had a floor of hardened antbed and a selection of bush-built furniture: halved tree trunks for benches, a table made from a collection of rails adzed flat and joined together, and cupboards converted from packing boxes.

'Take a seat.' Sal waved at the benches and table as I glanced around to see where the men had got to. They were off to one side deep in talk. 'It's simple, but it's home.' Her skin was sun-damaged but seeing her up close, I mentally removed eight or ten years from my first guess of middle age. There was grey in her thick, dark hair, which looked healthy, as did she. The stringiness of her frame was actually lean muscle. She looked strong and fit, and radiated a calm competency, devoid of any self-consciousness.

'You've made it very pleasant.' A string curtain made from thousands – maybe tens of thousands – of giant eucalyptus nuts threaded onto nylon lines cut the back area from view, and I marvelled at the industry that had gone into making it.

'The natural world has most of what man needs,' she said. 'It worked before plastic was invented. Also, it's my belief that nobody should want more than they actually need.'

'So how long has your group been here? I can see the attraction,' I admitted. 'It's a beautiful spot, but it can't be an easy life. I shouldn't like to travel your road too often, for instance.'

She smiled, ducking into the van as the kettle shrilled, returning a moment later with the teapot. 'We don't. Our group's quite self-sufficient. We grow most of our own food, keep goats for milk and meat. There's fish in the creek, and seasonal bush tucker. It's a healthy, satisfying existence. No stress, no bills, no traffic fumes.'

'And you're all of the same mind? Is it a big group?' I glanced across at the men now inspecting something under a small lean-to. I wanted to get a look at the rest of the commune but apart from a child playing under a tree I could only see the back of a seated woman bent over some task. The various camps or dwelling places I glimpsed looked to be similar in design to this one, but most were screened by the natural bush so it was hard to estimate numbers.

'Not so many as to be unworkable. We're a diverse lot, which helps too. Tea?' I nodded and she poured a pale greenish liquid that had me wondering if I should have said I only drank coffee. 'I'm a botanist,' Sal continued. 'Kil's an electrician. We have an artist and a cabinet maker, among other trades. We all bring our own skills to the mix, and learn from each other.' She poured for herself, replaced the pot and folded her thin, ringless hands. 'So, big, flash four-wheel drive, expensive-looking sunnies – you're not about to join us. What brings you here?'

'I'm looking for somebody. She's disappeared and I wondered if she'd come this way.' I took a cautious sip, my lips puckering at the bitter taste. 'What is this?'

'Bush tea. Don't worry, it's quite safe. Have some honey

with it.' She pushed a pot towards me. I picked up the whittled wooden spoon beside it and helped myself. The next sip was nicer, the liquid now sweet with a lingering nutty flavour.

'Better?'

Surprised, I nodded. 'It's quite good. Do you keep bees too?'

'We don't have to, it's sugarbag honey. From a native species.'

'I see.' I handed her Aspen's photo. 'This is my cousin. If she has decided to opt out and live here, that's her business. I'm not going to interfere, I just need to speak with her, see that she's okay.'

Sal was already shaking her head. 'Sorry. She's not one of us. Why would you think she was?'

'Because she came north and frankly I'm running out of options. She's officially missing and I'm worried that something's happened to her. So you haven't seen her?' I pressed.

'I told you.' Sal's tone hardened. She twisted on the bench to call her husband. 'Kil, tea's made. Does our guest want some or not?'

The men came over and Ben accepted a cup with a word of appreciation. I pushed the honey towards him, nodding at it as he lifted an eyebrow. 'Ah,' he said after sampling a mouthful, 'that's different. But refreshing. So, how do you find living off the land? I'm a city boy myself, so I don't understand the attraction. My wife, however, is a country girl.'

'What do you do then?' Kil asked.

'Accountant. Minding other people's money. Not something you'd have to worry about, living off the grid. I see you've got power though.' He nodded at the single bulb hanging from the shed roof. 'How's that?'

'Solar,' Kil said. 'It runs our water pump too. If government had any sense, solar would be the whole country's power source. But no, convenience is the urban god these days—'

'Kil,' Sal interjected sharply. 'They're not interested. He's a money man, she's looking for her friend. I've told her she won't find her here, so we'd best stop wasting their time.'

'Right.' Kil drained his own cup. 'Seems you've had the ride in for nothing. It'll take you a good coupla hours to get back, so we won't hold you up.'

'That's all right,' Ben said, replacing his cup as I rose. 'But seeing we've come this far, would a quick tour be out of the question? I have to admit I'm fascinated by the idea of life without a supermarket.'

I could see neither of them was keen on the idea but Ben seemed oblivious to their wishes, and sheer good manners on Kil's part prevailed. Sal, I thought, would have refused outright but he had already muttered, 'It'll have to be quick then,' and turned to lead the way.

Left to Kil we would have been out of there in fifteen minutes, but Ben refused to be hurried. He wanted to see and ask questions about everything. We toured the extensive vegetable garden, where sprays were playing over the vegetables, and the man who couldn't tell kale from potato plants was suddenly interested in every shoot. We saw the goat yard, the water tank raised to a modest six feet on timber piles, the fowl house and homemade incubator, the pigsty, the composting system and the extensive workshop without an electric tool in sight . . .

And, despite their apparent unwillingness to socialise, quite a few of the people going about their daily work. We received a few reserved greetings, a nod or two, and a glimpse of half-a-dozen children in an airy open structure using the type of slate my mother had probably practised on in first grade at school. The youngsters showed the most interest in us, grinning and waving until they were called back to attention by the woman in charge.

When we were finally back at the Prado, Ben shook hands and heaped effusive thanks on our reluctant host.

'Well, you haven't made a friend there,' I remarked as we drove away. 'He was itching to get rid of us.'

'Oh, you noticed?' He tutted. 'You looked as if you wanted it over too. Still, if Aspen was there we might've clocked her. And nutters or not, they're an ingenious lot. It's like a glimpse back into the middle ages before machines were invented.'

'Discounting the solar pump,' I agreed dryly.

'Yes. Though they missed a trick there. Their tank could've been raised higher and gravity would've given them better water pressure for the garden.'

'No,' I said. 'Not without a bigger pump it wouldn't. Pumps,' I quoted my father, 'can push water for miles but they can only lift to a certain height, which is governed by their size.'

He slanted a look at me. 'Really?' he murmured. 'You do surprise me, Em. How do you know that?'

The surprise, I thought, was because he'd never taken me seriously enough during the period of our short marriage to be interested in my background, who I truly was. Not the fresh-faced young ingenue he'd fallen for, but the real me with experiences outside his own urban life. It put a bite of remembered irritation in my tone. 'Oh, we country girls, you know . . . I think you're right, though. Aspen isn't there, but did you get the impression they were acting like they had something to hide?'

'Or maybe they were just naturally defensive,' he suggested. 'I mean, those outside the mainstream must get sick of having their beliefs rubbished. Maybe when people come calling they feel like exhibits in a zoo. You know, *Step right up, look at the weirdos.*'

'Mmm. Or it could be a question of their tenancy here,' I mused. 'Unless it's freehold land? But I'm sure I read somewhere that the stations are crown leases. Perhaps they're squatters and any visitor could be the authorities come to chuck them off?'

'You might be right. She was pretty quick to ease us out once she knew my occupation. She certainly didn't want to talk about what they were doing, or why.' The steering wheel bucked under his hand and he turned his attention back to the road.

'As to that,' I said, 'I thought you were a trader. When did you become an accountant?'

'A while ago.' He glanced at me, then swore as his momentary inattention had the front wheels jarring into a gutter in the track. 'You weren't the only one who studied. And numbers are my thing.'

It was a long, slow journey back to the pub and dark had fallen well before we arrived. I got stiffly out of the vehicle in the unlit car park, groaning as I bent to pick up my hat and sunnies from the floor, where they'd fallen during the ride.

'I feel like I've spent all day in the saddle. Shall we try the dude ranch place tomorrow?'

Ben yawned and sighed. 'I need a drink and a hot shower and dinner – if there's any left. It's damn near eight o'clock. Let's leave plans till the morning, eh?'

'You always did exaggerate.' I grabbed his wrist and tapped his watch. 'Seven forty. Why don't we eat first? The kitchen probably closes early.'

'Okay. I'll just dump the stuff in our room first.'

'Yes . . . About that – I think I should get my own. Last night was different but there's no need for us to share now.'

He shrugged as we climbed the steps to the verandah, the cold box he carried lifting with his shoulders. 'You can try. Mine was the last they had, but maybe someone's left.'

I muttered a heartfelt 'Damn!' and stopped off at reception only to find that he was right. I washed my hands and face in the rest room and tidied my hair, then waited for Ben to return, which he did in company with the female police officer. Carrie, I thought – no, Corrie. Sergeant Corrie Bader. What was she still doing here?

'I thought you'd have gone,' I said on greeting her, and she gave me an odd look.

'I must say, Ms Fisher, that you take attempted murder more lightly than we do. Or have you forgotten that someone tried to kill you?'

I hadn't, but I had deliberately refused to think about it. Because if they wanted to kill me just for looking, what did that imply about the object of my search? What, I wondered despairingly, had Aspen got herself into it?

'Em!' Ben said urgently, jerking me back to the busy room where we stood. 'Did you even hear me?'

'Sorry, what?'

'I said, your tyres – on your car,' he added as if I were an idiot, 'have been slashed.' He nodded at the policewoman. 'So she tells me. All four of them. That's it. I've had enough. We're heading back to Darwin tomorrow.'

10

Of course I argued against it over dinner, but Ben was adamant and, as he pointed out, he had the only transport. Unless I wanted to be stranded at Bloodwood Creek or start hitchhiking, I was going with him.

'It makes sense,' he pleaded. 'You can shop, replace the stuff you lost in the fire. Report the vandalism to the hire company – you don't want to be up for a new set of tyres, but most importantly, you'll be out of the firing line. Emily, you came very close to dying. And,' he added, as my mouth opened, 'it doesn't mean we're abandoning the search. Just regrouping. Isn't that what the army call a strategic retreat?'

'How would I know,' I said huffily, then sighed. 'All right, damn it. You're right. I can't stay here without a vehicle.'

Worn out from the terrible road, I had a shower and went straight to the twin bed I'd used the night before. With my back turned to the room and my eyes closed, I heard Ben moving about, the muted sound of the TV turned low and, later, the bathroom door closing behind him. I was asleep before he returned, falling into the billowy softness of my pillow where

Aspen's face waited, her long blonde hair draped artfully about her perfect features. I tried to talk to her but she turned her head, moving slowly away with her long, graceful model's stride.

'Just tell me!' I shouted. 'Where are you?' *Are you? Are you?* the echoes mocked and I saw that I'd entered a tunnel where all light had died. Panicking, I stumbled to one side, feeling for a wall, which, when I touched it, was red hot. I yanked my burnt hand back with a cry of pain and all at once I could smell the smoke. There was no flame to give light, just the sense of choking and the wreaths of smoke like fog filling the spaces I couldn't see. *Get low! Crawl!* screamed some atavistic instinct, but which way was low? There was no up or down, just the enveloping panic that seemed synched to the mad beating of my heart. I shouted, losing precious breath, and tried to run but iron bands were holding me back.

'Em! Em, wake up! You're dreaming.'

I opened my eyes on a sob, then drew a long, shuddering breath against Ben's restraining arms and let myself sag onto his chest.

'Oh, God! I thought— I dreamed— The fire, I couldn't get out. Aspen was . . .' The details of the experience were fading along with the dreadful trapped feeling as my heart settled from its frantic pace.

'It's okay.' He rubbed my back. 'Delayed shock or something. Shall I boil the jug, make you a drink? There's coffee or chocolate powder.'

'No, I've cleaned my teeth. But thank you.' I was still trembling, the memory of the dream fire and the real one intermingled now in my head. 'I can't . . . Just come onto the bed and hold me for a minute, will you? Please.'

'Come here.' I lay back and he pulled me against his chest, spooning my body with the sheet and cotton blanket between us, and his chin on my shoulder. 'I've got you, Em. You're safe. You can sleep now and I'll keep the bad dreams away.'

It was nonsense, of course, something you'd tell a child, but I believed him. There was comfort in his solid warmth, in the firm weight of his arms. He was fond of me still, I thought, and my treacherous heart mourned the lukewarm nature of that regard, even as I was grateful for his presence. My quest to find Aspen had taken an ugly turn from the sunny uplands of curiosity to the dark woods, where something far more dangerous lurked. I had gravely underestimated the risks I hadn't known existed, and was immensely grateful to feel him there at my back.

The following morning saw us on the road, heading back up the bitumen. Ben had settled up the room account while I was showering, and the manager had come through with his promise about not charging for my stay. Ben had kept the shovel he'd hired, packing it firmly apart from the luggage, along with a carton of bottled water; he was learning something from his enforced venture into the outback, I thought.

'We'll make a bushie of you yet,' I said lightly, checking that I had the keys and paperwork for my own car hire.

He flashed a smile, looking undeservedly handsome in the clear morning light. There was a chilly touch to the air, along with the scent of wattle blossom under a sky that stretched forever. 'That's as may be. So, you never really got around to telling me, Em. How's the vet business doing? Are you happy in the work?'

'I love it.' I pushed my hair back, settling my new hat in place. 'I do the small animals mostly and Pavel – he owns the clinic – handles the big ones, mainly horses, but cattle and alpacas too. I give him a hand sometimes, if he needs it. Lots of farm animals, as you'd expect in that area, but pets as well. They're the worst ones to lose. Especially children's. The kids often don't understand that life is finite, even for a beloved pet. That's hard.'

'Well, it seems to suit you, though it's not something I'd have pegged you for.'

His prolonged gaze was embarrassing me and I said more sharply than was warranted, 'I'm not just a pretty face, Ben. That's something you never understood about me.'

'Maybe you're right,' he said, opening the driver's door, and the rueful tone was as big a surprise to me as the actual words.

Back in Darwin, we went first to the car-hire place and when everything had been explained and sorted and the keys returned, our next stop was accommodation. We found a quiet hotel on the edge of the business section and took two rooms on the second floor. Ben argued for adjoining ones but none were available, so he compromised by selecting two contiguous room numbers instead.

'I'd feel happier if you were where I could see you,' he grumbled as we rode the lift up.

'For heaven's sake. You think someone's going to try to burn this place down? I'm perfectly safe here.' Still, his concern was warming and I relented, giving his arm a gentle squeeze.

'My trusty knight. Truly, it'll be fine. I can always thump the wall and yell if I'm in trouble.'

Having dumped our belongings, we found a corner bakery that boasted a few pavement tables and a coffee machine for lunch. It was unexpectedly relaxing sitting beneath the umbrella watching the casually dressed crowd pass by. Thongs and shorts, singlets and sandals, Akubra hats, flashes of brilliant florals in shirts and dresses. It was said that all races met in Darwin, where the cuisine was as varied at the nationalities of its people, and it seemed to be true. I heard Irish accents, the thick vowels as well as the clear precision of English spoken as a second language, rapid Chinese and the broad twang and casual profanity of my own country.

As if he had picked up on the thought, Ben said, 'Seeing we're here, we ought to go to the night markets. They're supposed to be something special.'

'We haven't come to sightsee,' I reminded him.

'No, but we still have to eat. Why don't you go and shop for what you need, and I'll meet you in an hour or two back at the hotel? That long enough? I'll get the geography of the place in my head and hunt up the venue for the markets. If they're on, that's where we'll get dinner. And it could be just the sort of place to attract Aspen. Some of the regular stall holders might have seen her.'

There was enough truth in the observation to convince me. I said doubtfully, 'Aren't they held only one night a week?'

'I'll find that out too. Just leave it to me. Go shop, Em. You got enough cash or do you need a loan?'

'Thanks, but I'll manage.' In truth, I would have to watch my spending. Long distance travel had been more expensive than I'd reckoned on and I still had to get home, though I knew I could always ask Dad. But that was a last resort – well, second last. My last would be to owe Ben. I might love the man, hopeless and useless as I knew that to be, but I was damned if I would be beholden to him as well.

Taking my time, I sought out the cheaper shops and made frugal replacements to my clothing – a couple of t-shirts, some cotton shorts, undies, toiletries and a length of soft blue jersey sprinkled with glitter across the top, which, the sales-girl demonstrated with a deft wrap and twist or two, became a sarong. It would replace the skirt and tops the fire had taken, and be suitable for hotel dining rooms or anywhere requir-ing something other than shorts. And because it was there and cheap, a cotton shoulder bag with a draw top and cord strap.

That done, I explored a little, as interested in the people surfing the pavements as in the entertainments on offer. There was a museum exhibit dedicated to Cyclone Tracy, a place where you could view (and even swim in a tank with) croco-diles, and multifarious touristy shops spilling Aboriginal, Asian and Indian wares onto the pavements.

I found a leaflet on a cafe table and read through it while I hydrated with a cold drink. There were harbour cruises one could take, day trips to the Katherine Gorge or Litchfield national parks, and offers of guided walks through historic sections of town. The Overland Telegraph had ended in Darwin and was later joined to the Undersea Cable to link Australia to the world. There was a military museum, historic airfields from the war and regular festivals and art displays. I wondered which, if any, of the options might have taken Aspen's eye, and slumped a little at the thought of doing the rounds of such places to show her photo and ask if she'd been seen.

I'd forgotten about the two hours Ben had stipulated as a meeting time. It had long passed, and when I returned to the hotel I found him sitting in the poky little lounge with his eyes on the door.

'Oh, there you are,' he said, getting up and eyeing my various bags. 'Find what you needed then? I'd forgotten the length of time it takes your sex to shop.'

I felt a twinge of guilt. 'I had a bit of a poke around as well. Watched the people for a while. You never know, if she *is* here, spotting her on the street would save us a lot of hassle.' But it wouldn't make sense of the attempt to kill me, I thought. And come to think of it, that also negated the need to traipse around the attractions asking questions. I hadn't considered that before. 'Have you been waiting? I'm afraid I forgot about the time. What about the markets?'

'All sorted. They're on tonight. And there's a sort of young travellers' place I found, about twenty kay out, called Groove and Grove. I thought we could have a look there tomorrow. It's an orchard and a backpackers' lodge. Cheap rent, food and transport supplied, and the guests work for their keep. Seems popular with the young kids.'

'I must've missed it.' Doubtfully I added, 'It doesn't really sound like Aspen's cup of tea though.'

'Depends how broke she is,' Ben said calmly. 'Worth the half-hour to take a run out and check, I thought.'

'Yes.' But once again, if she was blamelessly working as a shed hand or picker, how did that square with the attack on me?

Ben looked at his watch. 'Not much else we can do today. I thought we might drive to the beach about six-ish while it's light enough to see. I understand they're quite large markets, so we'll need time to work through them. If we go a bit early the regulars are more likely to take the time to talk to us.'

'That's true. Okay, seems like a plan. I need a shower anyway.' And five minutes off my tired feet. I must've tramped for kilometres about the shops. 'I'll meet you down here at six . . . Oh.' I looked down at my wrist, remembering the molten lump that had been my watch. 'Well, the radio will have a clock.'

'You won't need it. Here, I got you this.' He handed me a velveteen-covered jeweller's box, open to display a dainty wristwatch. Its expandable band was decorated with pearl shell.

'It's beautiful!' I said. 'Thank you, but you shouldn't have. If I'd thought of it I could've picked up a cheap one somewhere.'

'Now you don't need to,' he said. 'Go rest. And if you should drop off to sleep, I'll bang on your door when it's time.' He stood up, gathering my parcels together. 'I like your new bag, by the way. Come on, I'll walk you up.'

There was a soft glow to the evening sky when we parked at the beach. The bay looked silver in the fading light, the sky a mellow gold with the black silhouettes of the palm trees like giant cut-outs on a tropical stage. There were already dozens of vehicles lining both sides of the street and the car park was nearly full.

'Seems we aren't alone in wanting to be early,' I said. I could smell grilling meat and onions, and other more exotic cooking aromas. The market appeared to stretch forever, a grid of sorts with tented booths on either side of narrow lanes. Music blared, the beat of drums overlaying the sweeter sound of a busker with a saxophone. Lanterns shone palely in the dusk, while a huge white arc light on a tall pole blotted out all shadow within its range.

'God, what a mob!' Ben sounded startled. There were people everywhere, strolling, eating takeaway food, crowded about the stalls, standing watching the live performances on display. I caught a glimpse of slender Asian girls all brightly gowned, performing a dance, another of a juggler throwing clubs, then spun around with a start to the sudden thunder of a whip-cracking artist somewhere behind us. 'Looks like we should've got here an hour ago,' Ben said. 'Let's do this by the numbers then. Up one side and down the other, then move on to the next row. I don't rate our chances with the stall holders though. They're pretty busy.'

The brochures hadn't exaggerated the pull of the markets. Within minutes I'd almost forgotten our purpose in being there. I kept close to Ben and after a while, to avoid being separated, linked my arm through his as we worked our way from stall to stall. There was everything one would expect of a market, but with a tropical twist. Some of the colourful fruits and vegetables I couldn't put a name to. What on earth was an icecream bean? I wondered. Bitter melon I had heard of, but jojoba, sapote? There were stalls selling plants, homeopathic remedies, fancy soaps, exquisite needlework, crystals, treen, art on silk, on wood, on glass. There seemed to be acres of filmy clothing and cheap jewellery, as well as leatherwork, polished and unpolished gemstones, stalls selling fried food, ice cream, coconut milk and sugarcane syrup.

Most of the stall holders were far too busy to chat. I found one arranging t-shirts on a rail and whipped out the picture of Aspen. 'Excuse me, please. Have you seen this woman at all?'

She spared one quick glance from the photo to my face. 'Her and a million others. You're kidding, right? I see who buys and forget 'em just as quick.' Her gaze dismissed me for a man fingering the shirts. 'See anything you fancy, love? That black 'un would suit you a treat.'

The lights brightened as the colour leached from the sky and the stars came out, faint and pale above the market's illumination. Now and then I caught the distant murmur of the surf through the sounds of the music and the noisy throng. Stilt-walkers wore flowing cloaks despite the warmth of the night. A guy with dreadlocks and a vivid vest and headband was thumping out a calypso tune, and I noticed figures cloaked in the fantastic masks of devils and tiger faces capering through the crowd. The leading tiger, in boots instead of the sneakers the others wore, carried a stick of balloons, one of which brushed against a palm frond and punctured with a bang. I jumped and Ben patted my arm.

'What about we eat? I'm starving.'

We bought dishes of satay from an Asian food stall and cans of Coke from an ice-cream vendor, finding a spot on the grass between the beach and the market to sit and eat. I plumped my shoulder bag on my lap to use as a table and tore into the tender meat with appreciation.

'Here.' Ben had acquired a handful of paper napkins. I took some gratefully and wiped my mouth. He had always been thoughtful that way. He pulled the tabs on the drink cans and handed me one. 'I'm glad we came, though I don't think we'll get much help from the stall holders. I doubt even Aspen would've made an impression here.'

The stilt walkers went past again and I saw more masked figures, or possibly the same group. This time, instead of balloons, the tiger with the boots carried a hand of bananas. Somebody was playing an accordion. I glanced around to locate the sound and heard a long 'Ahh' from the crowd as first one and then several rockets shot skywards, exploding in whirling patterns of scarlet and gold.

'It's all happening here.' Ben stuffed the remaining napkins into his empty dish and rose, holding out a hand to me. 'You ready? Let's get back into it then.'

11

We had done perhaps two thirds of the markets, I thought, as we plunged down another booth-lined lane. The food and clothing section had given way to more interesting art and whimsy, and I found myself frequently stopping to browse. There was a stall selling calligraphy performed while you waited, a silhouette artist cutting the profiles of his customers from black art paper, then pasting them onto a white background – all done within two minutes. At twenty-five bucks each, he was making himself a fortune. There were gem collectors, crystal sellers and artists working on silk. The jewellery was no longer tat; this was the expensive end of the market. I eyed paintings bearing prices of four and five figures, and handmade cards with pop-up dioramas, perfect in scale and detail. The pace here was slower, the customers fewer but with more genuine buyers among them. However, the stall proprietors, if more inclined to listen, had no help to give.

'Sorry, love.'

'Nope, not that I recall and I reckon I would. She's some looker – your twin, is she?'

A shake of the head, 'Can't help you, sorry.'

I turned to the next tent, which a sign declared to be Mystic Meg's Cave. It resembled a grotto, filled with rails of tinkling crystals lit by one of those fancy muted lamps with a coloured-glass shade that threw winking lights on the moving stones. The air was quite still. Puzzled, I glanced around at the gently spinning merchandise, then saw that the woman – Meg herself, I assumed, with long dark curls and a froth of floaty clothing cinched in with a wide tasselled belt – had a treadle near her foot that she intermittently tapped, causing incremental movement in the bamboo poles from which the crystals were suspended. It was a clever piece of marketing. A tent opened to one side where you could purchase a 'psychic reading' and have the crystal of your choice aligned to your personality. Whatever that meant.

Without much hope, I dug in my bag for the photo just as she gasped and grabbed my arm. Something stung my skin and I jerked back, even as reason explained it to be static electricity. The same unpleasant prickle that heat in a car door could cause, or, I thought, a cheap nylon carpet. Glancing down, I saw just that underfoot. Perhaps the sand got into the treadle mechanism, or maybe the carpet simply added to the cave effect. I could smell incense and was suddenly aware of the woman's dark eyes fixed on my face.

'Be careful, my dove.' She had an accent, vaguely British but neither posh nor Cockney, which was really all I could recognise. 'Danger is close. Very close to you. Be wary this night.'

'What? Look, I'm sorry, I'm not here for a reading. I wondered if—'

'Go.' She actually pushed me. 'She is not here.' Panic poured off her; she was pale and panting, her eyes wide. She looked terrified and I felt my heart lurch in empathy for her fear.

'What do you mean? How do you know what—?'

'Leave!' In her agitation she stepped heavily on the treadle and the hanging crystals set up a mad dance. 'Death is close, dove! Flee while you can.' She vanished into the other tent, the flaps fell behind her and the large metal zip ripped downwards, sealing her in.

'Well, for God's sake! Of all the loony . . .' Throwing up my hands, I turned and found Ben peering in at me between the crystals.

'There you are! Thought I'd lost you. Any luck?'

'Of course not,' I said crossly. 'The woman was batty. I think she was trying to scare me into a reading. I couldn't even get her to look at the photo. She said she wasn't here, then bolted into the back tent there.'

'Who wasn't where?'

'I don't know. *She* certainly wasn't all there. Look, we may as well face it, this is all a waste of time.'

'Probably, but it's interesting.' He slanted a look down at me. 'Have you had enough? We can leave if you want.'

'It's getting late but I suppose we may as well finish this row first. Oh look, a juggler. Oh, my God! He does actually have a chainsaw and a cat!'

'Not a live one,' Ben assured me as we paused on the edge of the circle that had gathered about the performer. The man was good. He pedalled a unicycle in small circles, juggling madly as he rode. A ring of fake flambeaus threw light on his brightly coloured costume and the objects he manipulated. The chainsaw was half-sized, a kid's toy, the cat a floppy battery-operated imitation with a lifelike yowl. He also had a bowl of plastic daisies, a soccer ball and a large grapefruit. His hands, I thought, must have had minds of their own in order to catch the disparate objects as they flew around.

There was a hat upturned on the ground and Ben had his wallet out. I bent to add a modest scatter of change to the note he was extracting and felt someone bump me from behind just as I moved. I staggered a little and felt my bag, which for safety's sake I had slung crosswise over my body, slip.

My first thought was robbery. I grabbed onto the strap as the bag dropped, and swung around just as an anonymous hand shot out to steady me.

'Whoops, love!' somebody said. 'You right?'

'Who was it? Did you see?' I shouted at my helper.

'See what?' He was jovial, red-faced, a tourist enjoying the markets.

'Someone tried to rob me. There!' A man was running, eeling through the crowd. I saw his back, his boots and, just before he vanished between two tents, a side glimpse of a tiger mask. 'Him! It was him.'

But my assailant was gone. Ben turned then and saw my agitation.

'What? What happened?'

'A thief. He tried for my bag. Look—' I held out the severed cord, then stared down stupidly at the gaping folds of the sarong, their edges stained red.

'Is that blood?' Ben grabbed me. 'Here, lean on me. Jesus, Em! You've been stabbed! Sit down.' He seized a stool from within the nearest tent and pushed me onto it. 'Let me see. Oh, God! You need an ambulance.'

'No.' Shock at sight of the blood had left me feeling faint and sick, but the wound was shallow, more like a cut. Blood welled from it, hot against my skin and tickling as it ran. I dragged a handful of tissues from my bag and clamped them against it; it didn't hurt much, just a sting like a cut finger when the knife slips, though it might throb later on. 'I think he must've just missed. I bent over to put the coins in the hat. My moving must've ruined his aim.' Blood was seeping onto the tips of my fingers. Realisation hit me and my teeth began chattering. 'It wasn't a robbery. He was after me, not my bag.'

Nobody else had noticed, glued to the performance before them. I heard a long 'Ahh!' of expectation as the juggler nearly fell, but apparently the wobble had been deliberate and the unicycle steadied again, the objects continuing to fly.

The tissues were soaked. I lifted them, relieved to see that the flow of blood had dried to a sluggish trickle. Replacing them with another handful, I stood up, clutching at the sagging sarong. 'I only bought this today. It's ruined. Let's go back to the hotel.'

Ben fretted around me, looking helpless. 'You sure you're okay? Can you make it to the road, do you think? We'll go to the hospital.'

'No, please, Ben. We'd just sit around for hours and truly it's not that bad,' I said, though my side smarted as the pain started to make itself felt. 'Besides, the hospital would call the police, so we'd be there half the night. Let's just go back to our rooms.'

'But we have to report the attack. You've been *knifed*, for Christ's sake.'

'In the morning then.' I felt frustrated enough to scream. 'I wouldn't recognise the man anyway, so what good would it do? He only has to take the mask off and he could be standing right beside me, ready to have another go. So can we please leave before he decides to do just that?'

It was the wrong thing to say. 'You *saw* him?' Ben's eyebrows climbed and his voice hardened. 'We have to report it, Em.'

'Phone them if you must.' I sagged against him. 'But I just want to go back to the hotel and lie down.'

My words – or the sagging, only half of it pretend – did the trick. Once back at the hotel, Ben keyed the door to his room and helped me inside. Reaction had set in by then and I felt trembly and weak, appalled by the narrowness of my escape. As soon as I sat, my teeth began to chatter again. Ben grabbed the cover off the bed and wrapped it around me, then rattled through the stash of bottles on the minibar and decanted one into a glass. 'Here, drink this. I'll boil the jug.'

I swallowed the liquid, grimacing at the taste and coughing as it burned its way down, but its heat served to drive some of the cold from my body and stilled the shaky feeling. Ben, who must only have put a cup of water in the jug, brought me coffee with an extravagant amount of sugar stirred into it.

I pulled another face. 'God! That's ghastly.'

'Drink it, Em. Sugar's good for shock.' He frowned at me. 'Let me see now.' His hands were gentle as he peeled back the tissues. The bleeding had stopped. 'It's clotted nicely but I still think you should have a doctor see to it.'

'It's just a cut. No different to slicing your finger, and you don't need medical help for that. Look, there are some band-aids in my clothes bag. Get them for me, would you? I'll give it a wash and it'll be fine.'

Ben went one better, bringing cotton wool pads from the bathroom, a roll of paper tape and the soap dispenser. He helped me remove the ruined sarong, used the cotton pads moistened with the soap to wipe around the torn edges without disturbing the clots, before taping another pad across the cut.

'Where did that come from?' I indicated the tape and caught a sheepish look on his face.

'I carry it. Surgical tape. Good stuff.'

'You do? Why?'

'I've got a bunion,' he admitted with a scowl. 'I layer the tape over it to protect it from knocks. It's not funny,' he added at my barely suppressed amusement. 'How does that feel?'

'Much better, thanks.' It throbbed the way cuts do, but paracetamol would help that. I relaxed my taut torso and was suddenly aware of my state of undress, hastily gathering the folds of the sarong to drape over my panties and bra. Wrapping it around me so that I was halfway decent, I pulled my room card from my bag and got up. 'Thanks, Ben. About the police, I'm too tired tonight. Maybe tomorrow – but what can they do?'

He frowned at me. 'Nothing if you don't tell them about it. Obviously the two attempts are connected, which means whoever set the fire followed us here.' He shook his head, saying firmly, 'It's time to quit, Em. We should head home tomorrow, or as soon as I can get us flights out of here.'

'And what – forget about Aspen? I won't do that, Ben.'

'She's not worth your life. Whatever she's got herself into, it's not your job to rescue her.'

'Then whose?' I asked wearily. 'Look, it's late and I don't want to argue. I'll see you in the morning.'

He came with me into the corridor and watched until my room door closed behind me. I immediately felt less safe, which was ridiculous. The room was secure; nobody could get in. To prove it to myself, I switched on every light and toured the space, yanking the cupboards open to find a fridge, a broom closet and a hanging area complete with ironing board and iron. I investigated the bathroom but stopped short of checking under the bed, because nothing short of a cockroach would have fit there, and anyway it hurt to bend.

Moving slowly, I took my night things from my bag and got ready for bed, switching off the lights one by one. The curtains were tightly closed, the air conditioner sighed softly and I lay rigidly in the double bed, feeling the throb of my wound and imagining footfalls and shadows where my reason told me there were none. I eventually dozed off, only to wake with a thundering heart and a gasp of terror from a dream of pursuit where I was the prey.

I grabbed my abused bag (I would have to find some way to reunite the severed cord tomorrow) and, peering both ways first, scuttled to Ben's door and knocked urgently on it. When he opened it, I almost fell into his arms.

'I'm sorry,' I said, my teeth chattering, my breath coming in gasps. 'Can I stay in here tonight? I'll sleep in the chair.'

'Don't be silly.' He swept me in and closed the door. 'Take the bed. No argument. You're hurt, you need your rest.

And a hug – you're shivering. Come here.' He wrapped his arms carefully about me and held me close for a moment, his burgeoning whiskers prickly against my neck. 'Go on, into bed with you. I'll sleep outside the covers if it'll keep you happy.'

I nodded dumbly, despising my need but grateful for his presence as the terror that had gripped me gradually abated. I could have died. A surer thrust on the would-be killer's part, a smaller movement on mine . . . But I was here, safe and protected, and tomorrow would be soon enough to find my courage again.

12

In the morning, my side was stiff and the beginning of a large bruise showed beyond the padded cut. It hurt to bend and I caught my breath as I pushed myself up from the pillow and gingerly raised my pyjama top.

Ben, lying beside me on the queen-sized bed, lifted his head. 'How is it? Did you get much sleep?'

Surprisingly I had. Deep, dreamless rest, secure in the knowledge of his nearness. Doubtless – though I had taken care not to know – there had been other women in his life after me, but I had slept alone since leaving him. Last night didn't count. He had kissed my head as if I was a child when he'd said goodnight, then turned his back and reached for the light switch and I had drifted off as comforted as if I had been in my own bed at home.

'I did, thanks,' I said. 'It hurts a bit, but so do paper cuts. I expect it'll be tender till the bruising comes out. I'll meet you down in the dining room for breakfast, shall I?'

I thrust back the covers and got carefully to my feet. My side pulled at the movement and I grimaced. The dull throbbing had gone, replaced by a general soreness. I wouldn't be turning cartwheels for the next little while, but I'd live. Collecting my bag, I made it back to my own room to shower and dress, then headed downstairs to find coffee and something to eat.

Over a meal of fruit and toast and despite my half-hearted protests that it would do no good, Ben insisted we make the police station our first stop. So by half past nine I was entering the grim-looking building with its reception area protected by a heavy perspex shield and a keypad-operated inner door. I asked the officer manning the front desk for Sergeant Corrie Bader. 'It's about an ongoing matter,' I said. 'She attended the recent fire at the Bloodwood Creek pub.'

'Take a seat,' he said, 'and I'll see if she's here.'

We sat watching the passing foot traffic, black-clad officers going in and out, one with an amorous drunk he was holding at arm's length while the man, whose smell was truly appalling, blew kisses at him. When the officer paused to key in the door code, the man slid in close and got an arm around the officer's neck. The cop promptly kicked his captive in the shin and the man fell away with a howl of outrage. 'What you do that for? I lurve ya, baby.'

'Well, I don't bloody love you.'

They disappeared inside and the next visitor was a tearful woman whose dog had gone missing. By the time she'd been convinced that the police weren't there to locate missing pets, Bader had arrived.

She inclined her head at us as she opened the door. 'Mr and Mrs Grier. Come through.' She showed us into a stark room with a water cooler and a scatter of uncomfortable-looking chairs. 'What's this about? And before you ask, no, we haven't made an arrest for the arson attack.'

'So there were no prints on the petrol can after all?' I asked.

'Oh, yes. Two clear ones, and the rest smudged but enough for identification purposes.'

'So?' Ben said impatiently.

'They belong to William Judd, Willy to his mates. A small-time crook from New South Wales, who was probably hired for the job. He was picked up for a break and enter as a young-ster, and he did a short stint inside five years back for attempted arson – same method, only he was caught that time. He's kept his nose clean since. Unfortunately, he's long gone but there's a warrant out for his arrest. We'll find him sooner or later. They said you asked for me – so what's the trouble now?'

'Exactly that – trouble,' Ben said tersely. 'Last night some-body tried to knife Emily. Pure damn luck they didn't kill her.'

I went through it all again: the market, the crowds, seeing the masked mummers and noticing the tiger's boots. Then the fortune teller's booth, at which point I stopped with a gasp, staring wide-eyed at Ben.

'She warned me! I'd completely forgotten. I thought it was just the usual gypsy-type patter they use to draw you in, but she said evil was close, that I should flee – I think that was the word she used – while I could. Then she pushed me away and ran into the other tent. I remember now, she looked really frightened. Then you came back to find me and we stopped to watch the juggling, and that's when he attacked.'

'But you're not hurt?' Bader enquired. I thought she sounded sceptical and wished that I'd left the crystal seller out of it.

'She damn well was,' Ben said. 'If she hadn't ducked down just as he struck, she'd be short a kidney. As it was, the knife cut through clothes and skin only.'

'See?' I pulled up my blouse to display the taped padding below my ribcage. The cut was covered, of course, but seen in daylight the nascent bruising was quite plain. I winced as I touched it, fingers feather-light on the discolouring skin. 'I didn't feel it at first. It was very crowded. I thought I'd just been shoved. Then my bag fell, because he'd sheared through the cord handle when I moved. That was when I turned and just glimpsed the mask and his boots as he vanished into the crowd. It has to be the same person who lit the fire.'

'That, or hired by the same person.' Corrie Bader nodded. 'Which brings us back to the interesting question of why somebody wants to kill you.'

'I don't know!' My voice rose in mounting exasperation. 'Don't you think I'd tell you if I did?'

'Are you sure of that? Seems to me somebody is taking a lot of trouble, if you were followed back to Darwin. You must have *some* idea, Mrs Grier. It usually takes a lot to move someone to murder.'

'The only possible reason I can think of,' I said slowly, 'is that he doesn't want me to find my cousin. That's why I'm here in Darwin. I don't know a soul in the north, so how can anyone know me? It has to be about Aspen's disappearance, and I'm the only one taking that seriously.'

'That's not true,' Bader contradicted. 'The police take all matters reported to them very seriously indeed.'

'Well, what are you doing to find her then?' I asked.

'We're making enquiries,' she said stolidly. 'Perhaps you

should worry more about yourself. I repeat what I've already said: go home, leave the search to us.'

'We plan to,' Ben interjected. 'I'm booking our plane seats today.'

The fact that we hadn't discussed it beyond his announcement of intent the previous evening annoyed me and I said flatly, 'You might be, but I'm not. Can't you see that the very fact somebody is trying to stop me finding her means she's in desperate trouble? How can I not keep looking?'

'I can't make you leave,' Sergeant Bader said. 'It's a free country. But if I'd had two attempts on my life, I wouldn't be risking a third. Your statement will be typed up and printed. Please sign it before you leave. And if you're really staying on, Mrs Grier, leave a contact number at the front desk.'

'Very well. And I go by Fisher, not Grier,' I snapped. Snatching up my bag, I marched from the room.

As I strode out of the station, Ben, hurrying behind, caught my arm. 'Tell me you're not really going to stay. It's madness!'

I pulled away. 'I guess you'll just have to call me mad then. I was shaken up last night and you were kind, but today it's clearer than ever that I can't just leave. She's somewhere here. Or,' I said starkly, 'maybe she's already dead. Either way, I have to know. But there's no need for you to delay your plans on my account.'

'Don't talk bloody rubbish,' he snapped. 'Of course I can't leave you here alone. All right, get in the vehicle. We'll go visit this orchard I told you about. Of all the pigheaded, wilful idiots in the world . . .'

There was more in the same vein muttered half under his breath as he stalked to the Prado, leaving me to open my own door as he got in and slammed his. He peeled out of the parking space and headed out of town, bullying his way through the traffic, his face set in a heavy scowl. I held my tongue, more grateful than he would ever know that he was sticking with the search. To myself I admitted that yes, I was scared, but I clung to the thought that whatever had befallen her, how much more terrified must Aspen be?

Groove and Grove Orchard and Accommodation was easy enough to find, tucked in some little distance behind Palmerston at the end of a long metalled road that wound through acres of mango and other trees, most of which I didn't recognise. The feathery shapes of palms filled the space around the accommodation and working areas, which consisted of large sheds – for packing and machinery, I assumed. There was a central office and residence for the owner or manager, and a string of cabins set on low blocks, presumably for the guests/help. Ben pulled into the parking area and we sat for a moment taking in our surroundings.

It was lushly green and the place looked neat and well cared for. A tractor rumbled somewhere out of sight and I could see a stack of pallets by the open roller doors of the packing shed. A small fenceless garden had been created about the central residence. I recognised hibiscus, bird-of-paradise and a glossy-leafed multi-coloured shrub very popular with Darwin gardeners. Banana plants towered over the rest and a single mango tree provided a black circle of shade.

'Shall we?' Ben asked brusquely. Sunglasses covered his eyes, masking his expression.

'Yes.' I pushed my door open and climbed out, hoisting my bag with its knotted-together strap under my arm.

'It's not the sort of place I can see her,' he said, marching ahead of me. 'When did Aspen ever do any physical work? The whole idea is codswallop.'

I stopped. 'Ben,' I said, 'if you're going to stay, and I'm not making you do so, will you just leave me to ask the questions? Please? You go in there with that attitude, nobody's going to tell you anything. Let me handle it.'

'Suit yourself,' he said huffily.

The electric door sighed open at our approach and a woman behind a desk looked up with a bright smile. 'Good morning.'

'Good morning.' I glanced around at the uneven white-washed walls and the timber-edged windows set deep into them. Bright posters broke up the expanse, adding a touch of colour. 'This is a bit different. And very cool too.' I looked for a fan or air conditioning and could see neither.

'Isn't it?' She beamed. 'There used to be a government experimental station here in the pioneer days. This building was their office. As you can see it's made of mud brick on a base of stone. The bricks were manufactured from powdered termite mounds, which sets like concrete. Great insulating properties too, which accounts for the temperature. And cheap, convenient materials.'

'What about the monsoon?' Ben asked gruffly, intrigued. 'Doesn't wet weather dissolve the mud?'

The woman shook her head. 'We don't get flooded here, and the overhang of the roof protects it from direct rainfall.

Now, how may I help you? You wish to book in as guests or workers?'

'Actually I was after information.' I fished Aspen's photo out of my purse.

'I read about this place and I wondered if this young woman had been here? We were supposed to meet up,' I said, inventing freely, 'but we missed each other and I think I remember her saying something about the Groove and Grove. Have you seen her at all?'

She pursed her lips as she studied the picture and my heart sank as she shook her head. 'No, sorry. Nobody like that's been through in the last couple of weeks.'

'What about earlier? Could you check as far back as late January?' That was when she had purportedly left Alice Springs. 'It was a very loose sort of arrangement,' I ad-libbed. 'Her name's Aspen Tennant. Perhaps somebody else took her booking?'

'Would she have been coming here for work? We'd still have been picking well into February.'

I hesitated. 'Probably not, but I really don't know.'

'Well,' the woman said, clicking away on the computer, 'we do get heaps of backpackers through, especially during the mango crop – not so many now, but— oh, wait.'

I leaned forward. 'You found her?'

The woman nodded. 'Way back in February – she was to join somebody already here on the fifth, but she never showed, and it lists the other person as leaving the next day.' She raised an enquiring eyebrow. 'February. It seems you've missed your friend by quite a margin.' There was a question in the observation.

'Oh.' Disappointment swamped me. 'Well, who was he or she? Do you have a name?'

'No. The room was booked for two in her name, so presumably he arrived first and paid for it. Cash payment, not card, which isn't so unusual out here with the backpackers.' She sat back in her chair, hesitating. 'Is there something wrong? You seem . . . It's rather late for it, but should I have called the police about her no-show?'

'I've already done that.' I hesitated; perhaps the truth would serve me better after all. 'Look, she's actually my cousin and she appears to have vanished. I'm trying to find her, so thank you for your help and your patience.'

She got up, looking concerned. 'That's all right. I'm sorry I can't tell you more. I hope she turns up, especially with that monster on the loose.'

'Sorry, what?'

Suddenly flustered, the woman repeated, 'I'm sorry too. That was thoughtless of me, but of course it'll be nothing to do with him . . . I mean, he was nowhere near here then, anyway. I'm talking about the Outback Killer. I heard on the news this morning that he's crossed into the Territory – well, that makes it scary for us all, doesn't it? He held up a roadhouse south of Katherine. That's how they know where he is, you see,' she explained.

'God, yes!' I'd forgotten all about him and had a moment of horror until common sense kicked in. 'Really? But as you say, we're talking two months back, so I think we can rule him out. Thanks again for your time. Bye.'

13

Returned to the vehicle, Ben sat for a moment without turning the key. 'We should get back in touch with the cops, Em.' He glanced across at me. 'You've got a definite time scale now from when she was in the Alice to the day she was expected here. That gives them something solid to work with. It might also move her out of the "Pending" basket, where I'm pretty sure they've stuck her, into an active investigation.'

'So you believe me now?' Relief gusted through me.

'Yes,' he said soberly. 'I mean, I did before but I also thought you were panicking needlessly. You have to admit that Aspen was always unreliable.'

It was true. My cousin thought nothing of standing someone up. She would make plans to meet you, then ignore them, without a word, if she was offered something better or she had just changed her mind. She had never cared much for the convenience of others.

I sighed. 'I know. I realise that she could have simply decided not to turn up but—'

'Agreed.' He keyed the motor. 'But this is not country to

take chances with, and maybe she didn't realise that. How empty it is, I mean. It's not like you can call somebody or phone a taxi if there's trouble. And whoever she was going to meet – what happened when she didn't turn up? We know there was no report to the police, so whoever it was must have just scarpered. And didn't take long to do it either – they left the very next morning.

I chewed my lip. 'I just wish I knew why she was up here in the first place. Okay, so back to the cops. They'll be getting very sick of us at this rate.'

At the police station Corrie Bader had finished her shift and gone. I dictated a message to be delivered to her while Ben went off to buy lunch. He returned with two coffees and an overnight booking at the pub back at Bloodwood Creek.

'I thought,' he said, pulling a map and a folded paper from his back pocket, 'we could work our way back to Alice. I've got a list. It has the names of every orchard, roadhouse and tourist venue along the Stuart Highway. I never knew there was so damn much to do up here with pubs and national parks, even a reptile farm—'

'We can strike that off,' I interrupted. 'No way would Aspen go there. Creepy-crawlies gave her the screaming ab-dabs. I've seen her hysterical over a sleepy lizard.'

'Okay.' He looked up and down the street outside the station. 'There's a bench over there in the park. Let's eat and get moving. How much time have you got off work?'

'I've got as long as it takes,' I said grimly. I actually had ten days, five of which had passed, and Pavel was going to be very annoyed with me if I overstayed. We were a busy practice, but family came first. If it came to it I would just have to talk him around. 'You?'

'I'm the boss,' Ben said simply. 'If Joe gets overloaded, my customers' tax sheets will simply have to wait.'

It was cool under the tree, some sort of massive fig, I thought, which threw a dense black shade. With its many aerial roots forming supplementary trunks, the tree was almost as large as the park, which was really just the space between where two streets met. There was a standing water tap and a concrete dish where dog walkers could get their pets a drink, and beyond that the brilliant sunlight where colourfully dressed passers-by languidly strolled the pavements. Nobody seemed to hurry, as if time in the north was expanded or of no moment.

'Peaceful,' Ben commented, crushing the plastic boxes the sandwiches had come in. 'See a bin anywhere?'

'Over there.' I pulled my sunnies down and stood up, feeling a tug in my side as I did so. A reminder that however relaxed the surface appeared, it would pay us not to forget there were darker undercurrents beneath and that somebody wanted me dead. Back in the vehicle, I said, 'Where next then?'

'The list is there.' Ben nodded at the map resting in the space between our seats. I picked it up and glanced over the dozen names. 'Mango Magic? What's that? And Old MacDonald's?'

'An orchard, apparently. Worth a look. Seems a lot of these places have a second string putting up tourists. They run dorms for the workers during the picking season and rent them out to travellers the rest of the time.'

'I see. Only not during the Wet, obviously. And the other? Not a Big Mac, I take it?'

'Nope, another touristy joint, as in Old MacDonald had a farm. I gather they grow a few tropical fruits and keep animals. You can milk a goat, ride a pony, feed the chickens and collect the eggs, that sort of thing. Popular with young families. Then there's Litchfield National Park, and Crazy Creek, the dude ranch place, and some roadhouse . . . I figure we can knock off the mango joint and MacDonald's this arvo. Stay the night at Bloodwood Creek and carry on south tomorrow.'

'It's a good plan. Thank you, Ben.' I eyed his profile, adding, 'I'm glad you stayed and I'm very grateful for your help. I know you think it's foolish of me to continue with this, but I have to. And yes,' I confessed, 'I am scared; I'd have to be stupid not to be after what's happened. So having you with me means a lot.' Trying to lighten the mood, I added, 'There. I've actually admitted there are some things I can't handle alone. My boss would fire me if he knew.'

'That's okay. I would never not help if you needed it. I just wish I knew what the hell that cousin of yours has been up to. It has to be something bloody serious to warrant attempted murder.'

'But we don't know she did anything,' I protested. 'She's the victim after all, the one that's vanished.'

The dark glasses turned my way. 'And if it's by design? Look, Em, I know you never saw it, but I always thought there was something a bit off about Aspen. In some ways she was too knowing for her age. She manipulated people – you, and others. She was cold and controlling, everything was just a means to an end with her.'

'You're wrong.' I straightened indignantly. 'You hardly knew her! You met her, what, half-a-dozen times? I've known her all my life. She wasn't cold, just not very demonstrative, but given her parents . . . It doesn't mean she didn't *feel* things. And what do you mean by *knowing*, anyway?'

'Sexually aware. She was like a cat in heat, right from the first time I met her – which was on our wedding day, if you remember. She came on to me then, with my bride in the next room. And she still in her teens.'

I gaped disbelievingly at him and he nodded. 'And don't say it was just harmless flirting. I saw it happen with other men too. If you'd been a little more worldly you'd have noticed yourself, but you still thought of her as a kid.'

'That's rubbish,' I said hotly. 'You imagined it! She was a model, Ben. They're trained to look and act desirable. It doesn't mean anything.'

'This was before she started modelling, remember?'

I did; Aspen would've been fifteen that year.

He hesitated. 'I wasn't going to tell you, but that thousand bucks she wanted? It wasn't to be a gift or a loan. "I'll earn it, Benny boy," she said. "You'll get your money's worth." She'd just put her hand on me when she said it.'

There was no mistaking his meaning. I was speechless. In the silence that followed his words I felt his glance but, shocked to my core, I could find nothing to say to repudiate them. It couldn't be true, I told myself. I *knew* my cousin. But I knew Ben too, and why would he lie? He and Aspen had never hit it off and in our short time together we hadn't seen much of her. Was this why? A blistering rebuke for her action, or even just turning her down – something life had not accustomed Aspen to – would make her into an enemy. She had still gone to him when she needed money, but when it came to feeding their addiction, addicts had no shame or, presumably, memory of past rebuffs.

In the end I said, 'I wonder if Aunt Fee knew she was back on drugs. If Aspen was constantly wanting money . . . Maybe that's why her mother was so worried when she disappeared.'

'It's possible. Wouldn't she have told you, though?'

'Ha! You didn't know my aunt. Respectability was her god. She would *never* admit a daughter of hers was an addict.'

'Pity. Intervention at the start might have saved us all a lot of trouble.' He was slowing down. We drove through a gate and gravel crunched beneath the tyres as he came to a stop before a complex of buildings, backed by an orchard set out in shady rows and seemingly stretching to the horizon. He switched off and pulled on the handbrake. 'Well, here we are.'

Mango Magic was one of the larger orchards in the Top End and among the first to see the advantage of opening its doors to tourism. The reception area, all glass and tiles, extended into an expensive boutique with all things mango, from dishes shaped to hold the fruit and cutters to de-seed it, to a bewildering array of chutneys, pickles, jams and mango-scented soaps. There were carry bags, tea towels and t-shirts imprinted with the image of the fruit, which was also available dried and bottled for out-of-season visitors. One could take a tour through the orchard aboard open-sided carriages pulled by a tractor, sign on as a worker/guest in one of the cabins, or – if one's finances permitted – opt for the luxury of the chalet with its in-ground pool, spa and nine-hole golf course.

The curved glass display counter holding jewellery, scarves with mango motifs and expensive pens was presided over by a pleasant-faced, middle-aged woman who greeted us with a smile. 'Good morning. How may I help you?'

'Well, I don't know if you can.' Glancing around, I saw that we were the only customers. 'Do you get many people through? And are you always here?'

'Quite a number, yes. Workers, guests and drop-ins.' She smiled again. 'Which lot are you? And to answer your question, I'm here most days. Why?'

'Oh, we're just drop-ins, and I was wondering . . .' I paused to bring out the much-shown photograph and handed it to her. 'Have you seen my cousin? She's missing and we have reason to believe she was up this way. She's about four years older now, and maybe she wears her hair differently, but she'd still be tall and very pretty – quite unmistakable.'

I waited hopefully as the woman really studied the picture, tilting it this way and that and pursing her lips. My heart leapt as she looked up, those same lips tightening.

'Missing, you say? Any reason?'

'Not that I'm aware of.' I hesitated. 'Drugs, maybe. Have you seen her?'

She shook her head sorrowfully. 'Girls like her? About a thousand times, my dear. Spend long enough working with them and you can read it in their eyes. She was abused as a child, wasn't she? It kills something in them and you come to recognise it. Ask any youth counsellor – that's what I was until the job got on top of me. You never forget their eyes. I'm sorry. You think she's at risk? Judging from this, I'd have to say you're right, but she hasn't been here. I'm good with faces – you had to be in my old job. I'd remember if I'd seen her. She looks like she could've been a model.'

'She was.' I felt lost suddenly and bewildered. 'You really think . . .? I mean, if that happened . . . Why wouldn't she tell someone?' Aunt Fee would have denied it to her last breath, I thought wildly, but she could've told my mother – or me.

The woman regarded me sympathetically and patted my hand where it lay on the glass counter. 'You didn't know? Well, that's not unusual. Shame keeps them quiet, or it could be fear. Did she cut herself?'

Horrified, I said, 'You mean hurt herself?'

She nodded. 'It's not unusual. They hide that too. Did she tend to keep her arms covered?'

'Well, yes, but that was for her skin; she was very fair and in her job . . .'

'Uh huh. Or to cover the scars. She could've been cutting to let the pain out. Sometimes they just pick the one area that can be easily hidden . . .'

Her words faded as I was transported back to the farm kitchen and the memory of Aspen's hand shielding the wide band of her bracelet, refusing to let me see it. Was that the reason? But no, it was ridiculous . . . Not knowing what to think, I surfaced again in time to hear a question from my interlocutor.

'Did she leave home early?'

'What?' The question was so unexpected that it took a moment to sink in. 'Well, yes. Seventeen. That's when she started modelling.'

'Mmm. I'd look close to the family then for the culprit. Father, uncle, neighbours . . . And frankly, dear, I'd be worried for her too. It can sometimes catch up with them later in life. They have a bad run, get depressed . . . My advice would be to involve the police.'

Ben, silent till now, said, 'We've reported her missing. It hasn't helped.'

'No, well,' the woman said, her shoulders lifting, 'I hope you find her, but sometimes there's nothing anyone can do.'

14

Back in the vehicle, we sat for a little while digesting this bombshell. I was shocked to realise that I believed what I had heard – it rang too true to allow the luxury of doubt. I felt a sort of queasy disgust, coupled with a horrified sympathy for my cousin. I hadn't known Aspen's parents well. Mum had not got along particularly well with her sister, and Uncle Rich had been a nebulous figure, a self-satisfied voice in the background, too busy to interact with children.

When I had stayed at their place, I was seldom aware of his presence and, looking back, I realised how little Aspen had spoken of him. She had described him once as a voice in the dark. At the time I had taken it to mean that he returned from work after she was in bed, but now I wondered sickly if she had meant something entirely different. Had it been an attempt, an opening remark that would have led to the truth, which I, in my ignorance, had let slip past?

'If it was Uncle Rich,' I said, 'it can never be proved. He's so far gone with dementia he can barely speak, and when he does it never makes sense. Chances are he no longer even knows who Aspen is, never mind what he might have done to her.'

'Em, you don't know it even happened,' Ben protested. 'The woman could've been talking through her hat. She gets all that from a photo? What is she, psychic?'

'I know,' I said miserably, 'I've told myself that too. I'm not entirely gullible. But it does make a sad sort of sense. Aspen definitely had issues – at home, at school. She was very moody and unpredictable in her actions, never a happy kid. And it was you who said she was too sexually aware for her age. Too practised, if you like. And she,' I added, with a nod back at the building, 'wasn't putting it on to impress us. She looked . . .' Sorrowful, I thought, heavy with the knowl-edge of the evil that had wrecked too many young lives. 'Too unhappy about it,' I continued. 'She believed what she was telling us. And I think she was on the money.' I told him about the incident with the bracelet. 'I never saw Aspen without it. If she was cutting herself, that gold mesh was broad enough to cover a lot of scarring. Was she wearing it when she looked you up?'

He frowned, then shook his head. 'I don't remember. I just wanted to be rid of her. I wasn't paying much attention to her jewellery.'

'Keeping a secret like that, having it fester inside you, would explain the drugs. Anyone would have thought she had everything going for her with the modelling – I mean, she was a natural. The camera loved her and with her looks she could've been the world's best. But I expect if you feel used and worth-less, then none of that really matters.'

'Maybe.' He turned the key and the engine caught. 'Well,

it's one more down. Old MacDonald's next then? See if you can find the turn-off on the map.'

We backtracked to the bitumen, and then it was another thirty kilometres to the garish sign on the verge and the gravelled road leading in to the farm.

We weren't the day's first visitors; family groups were scattered across the various pens and tiny paddocks, and licking ice creams in the shade of several huge mango trees planted about a grassy area in front of the homestead and restaurant. There was a playground of bright plastic cubes, a small lagoon and a plethora of animals, from a friendly collie to an aloof pair of alpacas; also ponies, a donkey, calves, lambs and baby goats. An emu paced a small enclosure, beak at the ready for whatever it could snatch from the visitors, and a variety of waterbirds paddled and poked about the water's edge next to the picnic tables and shade trees there. There was a kiosk and a barn, whose open door showed hay bales and some sort of wheeled conveyance, probably pulled by the two big brown horses in the far paddock.

'You want an ice cream or a coffee?' Ben asked, getting out and gazing around.

'A coffee would be nice, but in a minute. I'll have a look around first.'

The collie came bounding up, its tail waving a furious welcome, and I bent to pat it before it transferred its attention to Ben. 'Must be the official greeter. Shall we?' I nodded at the alpaca pen. 'Seeing we're here.'

'Why not?' He reached back into the vehicle to hand me my hat. 'Looks like the place does good business. It's early still, but the car park's half full. It's a wonder there isn't an entry fee.'

As it turned out, there was. A thick unbreachable hedge and a reach of unobtrusive fencing led us to a gate where a small booth protected a turnstile blocking entrance to the complex. Ben paid for two tickets and we spent ten minutes wandering about, looking at the animals and reading the signs, which offered hay rides and an opportunity to feed the ducks, milk a goat, take a pony ride or bottle-feed the lambs and calves. One woman with an impatient youngster in tow said rather helplessly, 'What would you like, Sammy? We could go and feed the ducks – there might be baby ones, too.'

'No. I wanna ride a pony,' the boy declared.

'Oh, I don't think so. It might bite, darling. Why don't we see the little lambs instead and give them a bottle? That would be fun, wouldn't it?'

'Wanna ride!' The boy stamped his foot. 'Don't wanna feed the stupid lambs, that's sissy stuff. Wanna gallop.'

The woman looked so distressed I said, 'Oh, they won't allow that, you know. They just lead the ponies around.'

'Are you sure?' she said doubtfully. 'I don't think . . . It's not really safe. Ponies bite and kick. He could fall off. No, Sammy, we'll do something else. It's too dangerous, darling.'

My farm background wouldn't let that statement pass unchallenged. Honestly! City people hadn't the least idea. From the corner of my eye, I saw Ben's infinitesimal head shake but I said crisply, 'It's perfectly safe—' and she turned on me like a tigress.

'It is not!' she snarled. 'Nothing up here is. I wish we'd never come. There're crocodiles everywhere, and snakes. Even the mosquitoes can kill you, with all sorts of diseases. And if your car breaks down you'll die! We're at risk every single day. I wish we were home. I just want to go home.' The last words were muffled by sobs and I put a tentative hand on her shoulder.

'Come on, it's not that bad, really. I mean, people live up here, don't they? I'm sorry if I upset you, but really there's no risk in letting your little boy have a ride. Kids just love ponies, you know.'

'No,' she said hysterically. 'And as for living here, they die here too. What do you think happened to the people in that abandoned car on the highway? It's a horrible, horrible place and I wish we'd never come!'

'Oh, for pity's sake, Elena!' I turned at the man's voice and he, obviously the husband, thrust a takeaway cup at her. 'Here's your drink. Stop mollycoddling the kid, for Chrissake!' Taking her arm, he dragged her off, the child clamouring beside him, 'Daddy, Daddy, I want to ride the pony.'

Ben was shaking his head at the retreating pair. 'I'd say she's a bit out of her comfort zone. You ready for that coffee now?'

'I suppose so.' I glanced around and he nodded back the way we'd come.

'There's a sign pointing back to the building. Cafe and gift shop for a bet, with living quarters behind. Why on earth would you get involved, Em? I thought that woman was going to eat you.'

'Because she was talking rubbish. That sort of ill-informed generalisation is the bane of a vet's existence. They're either trying to turn their animals into human babies or they act as if everything on four legs is Godzilla. Why would a business keep a pony that was going to savage a kid? Fat lot of profit that would turn. All the poor little beggar wanted was a ride.'

'Well, he'll plainly have to wait till Mum's not around.' There was a glint of a smile in his eyes. 'I should like to watch you handling your customers. I imagine all the compassion in the world for the animal and a brisk "Pull yourself together" for the owner. Am I right?'

I laughed ruefully; his guess was truer than it needed to be. To change the subject I said idly, 'What abandoned car was she talking about? I bussed up and I don't remember seeing any on the highway.' But I could have been asleep. The coach's motion had been soporific and we had made few stops.

'Probably got there since. Do we get a stamp or something?' he asked the attendant at the gate. Instead, the man slipped paper bracelets around our wrists.

'There ya go,' he said, pressing the release on the turnstile, and we passed through and headed into the building.

There were five or six couples already seated at the scatter of tables. Ben pulled out a chair for me and raised an eyebrow. 'Just a coffee, please,' I said and sat gazing around as he went to the counter. The cafe was geared for crowds and on the thought, the door opened again to admit a family of five, followed by another couple and a man wearing jeans and a dusty Akubra, who looked vaguely familiar.

A TV was on, barely audible over the clatter of voices, the scrape of chairs and an exasperated, 'Stop it, Charlie!' from the mother of the family group. When Ben returned, I nodded at the man in the Akubra. 'He looks familiar. Have you seen him before?'

'Yeah.' Ben folded his sunnies into his shirt pocket. 'He's the chap from the dude ranch, remember? Looks like he's touting for business here too.'

'Of course. Crazy Creek. Do you remember his name? Because I think he's coming over.'

The man arrived on the heel of my words. 'Well,' he said, flashing a smile, 'we meet again. How're you travellin' then?'

Ben clicked his fingers. 'Outback Experience, wasn't it? Sorry, I've forgotten your name.'

'Linc, mate, and you're Bill – Bob . . .?'

'Close. Ben.' He offered his hand, adding, 'We're thinking of dropping by your place in a day or two, so no need for that.' He nodded at the stack of leaflets the man was carrying. 'Few other spots to visit first.'

'I'll tell 'em to expect you, then.' Linc turned his attention to me. 'How're you finding it all? Most visitors feel the heat, even at this time of the year.'

'Well, it must be thirty degrees outside,' I said. 'That's warm for me. My friend hasn't turned up in the meantime, has she? The blonde girl?'

''Fraid not. Still, it's only been a coupla days. How did you like Darwin?'

'It was interesting.' I wondered how he knew we'd been there, but it was where the bitumen led, after all. I glanced up to see a girl heading our way with a tray. 'Ah, here's our coffee coming.'

'I'll leave you to enjoy it, then. See you at the station.' He turned to the family table and I heard him trying to spruik the attractions of the dude ranch over the quarrelling children and the mother's insistent warnings to Charlie.

The news signature sounded then and I glanced automatically at the TV. The lead story was of a supposed sighting of the now infamous Outback Killer, who had reportedly been filmed filling up at a service station in Tennant Creek. Silence descended on the room as the information filtered through the hum of talk. There was a grainy black-and-white photograph of the back view of a tall figure at the pump, beside a white four-wheel drive. He hooked up the handpiece as we watched, slapped the fuel cap back on and pulled the cab door open. Then, without once facing the camera, he slipped into the vehicle and roared out of view.

The scene was immediately played again, the newsreader commenting on the mud-encrusted numberplate with only two digits legible. Staff at the service station had, he announced, been fortunate in losing only the fuel. Given the killer's past activities, it could have been their lives. The public was asked to report any sightings of the man or vehicle immediately and warned not to approach either one. *Armed and dangerous* read the caption running underneath the picture.

'Well, we'll be giving all white Toyotas a wide berth,' Ben said. 'Do you think it's worth checking out the caravan park at Bloodwood Creek? There're two apparently. One's in town and the other's on a lagoon about ten kay down the road.'

I glanced at my new watch. 'It'll be a bit late by the time we get there. First thing in the morning? People will have heard the news, and nobody will want visitors after dark.' And young Sammy's nervous mother, I thought, would now really have a reason to freak out. Life had suddenly become more uncertain for everyone in the area.

15

It was just on dark when we reached Bloodwood Creek, the evening sky marbled in fading shades of gold beyond the timberline, where the flying foxes in their thousands were streaming out to feed, leathery wings blooming open above us.

The same woman – Maggie, I remembered – met us with a hearty, 'Back again? Well, you know the drill about the pool and the dining room. I've got you in room twenty-one.'

I lifted my brows at Ben as he greeted her in turn and received the key.

'Enjoy your stay.' She turned aside to another guest.

'One room?' I queried, following him down the long hall-way. 'Why not two? I don't think—'

'It's a twin,' he interrupted, dumping our bags to open the door he'd stopped at. 'Safety in numbers. I am trying,' he said with a weary sort of patience, 'to keep you alive, not to inveigle you into bed, if that's what's worrying you. Your virtue is safe with me.'

I flushed at the bite in his tone. Of course he wasn't; he'd been quick enough to lose interest in me once we were married.

I cringed inwardly at the thought. I had my pride and whatever my heart might want, I would not again willingly suffer that rejection. 'I appreciate it,' I said stiffly. 'I'll pay my share.'

The room was stuffy and a carbon copy of the previous one. I sank onto the nearest bed with a sigh, holding my ribs as they twinged in protest, while Ben activated the air conditioner. 'I'm going to shower,' he said, dropping the TV remote onto my bedside table. 'Catch the news or have a nap. How's your side feel?'

'It's okay, thanks. A bit tender. You get on, I'll just lie here for a bit. I want to process things – try and make sense . . . If Aspen truly was a victim of sexual assault as a child—'

'We've only that woman's opinion on that,' Ben said, gathering up fresh clothing from his bag.

But it rang true, I thought as he disappeared into the bathroom. And it could explain so much. I heard the shower come on and moved my head deeper into the pillow, closing my eyes to picture the face of the woman at Mango Magic. I wasn't imagining the resigned recognition I had glimpsed there. Whatever the truth of it, she had been convinced of what she said. I thought back to childhood, remembering how eager Aspen had always been for my visits. We had shared her bedroom but once I arrived she had been a poor companion, more interested in her own pursuits than anything I might care to do.

It wasn't the way I had been raised. A guest's wishes came first, my mother always told me. And so they had when Aspen came to the farm. If I wanted to ride or be with the animals, Aspen always had other desires and, however unwillingly, I had concurred – because she was the visitor and that's what a good hostess did.

'It doesn't work when I go to hers,' I had grumbled, and I could still hear my mother's voice: *You're responsible for your manners, Emily, nobody else's. You needn't be rude just because Aspen is.*

Looking back now in the light of this new suspicion, I wondered if it was my presence rather than my company that Aspen had craved. Had my being there kept her molester away? Had her visits to the farm come about solely to avoid him? Once there, she had evinced no desire to join me in my daily activities, boasting instead about her belongings, like the fancy western boots bought for her week's visit, even though she scarcely stepped outside the door. Or the gold bracelet she always wore, and the expensive puffer coat I had envied, knowing my parents could never have afforded the like for me.

There had been endless tales of outings with her mother to restaurants and fashion shows once she was old enough to have an interest in clothes. And extra lessons for everything: ballet, music, elocution, swimming. She had learned French from the age of six – 'For when I go on European holidays,' she had once said grandly. I would sooner have had a new saddle and told her so. She had shrugged, bored by the ordinariness of my aspirations. 'So tell your father. That's what I do. It's how I got this.' She had touched the bracelet – I could see it in my mind now, her slender fingers moving over the supple mesh. Aspen had the most elegant hands. I shivered a little, remembering her words: *just a voice in the dark . . .* Were they guilt gifts or bribes for her silence? And in either case, how could Aunt Fee not have known?

*

When Ben and I reached the dining room, the conversation was mostly focused on the Outback Killer. People had angled their seats where possible to watch the TV, where the Imparja channel was replaying the film from the service station and giving brief news updates – or, as Ben said, 'best guesses' as to the man's current whereabouts and intentions. A senior police officer told viewers that roadblocks had been set up on the highway either side of Tennant Creek, which elicited a snort from the staff member serving me.

'Yeah, like he's gonna stay on the bitumen.'

'Of course he won't,' I said to Ben as we found an empty table and settled to eat. 'There must be plenty of backroads he can take.'

'I suppose it depends what he's trying to do.' Ben quartered a baked potato.

'Well, get away, I imagine.' I twiddled the fork in my pasta.

'That too, but he could have a destination in mind, which might drive him in a certain direction. He probably thought going bush was a smart move. In his shoes I'd have headed for Sydney – better chance of losing yourself there.'

'More police,' I pointed out.

'And more crime to spread them among. How's your meal?'

'Not bad. Not as good as Mum makes, but she's had the practice.' Spaghetti bolognese had been a childhood favourite of both Stephen's and mine.

As if the thought had leapt from my mind to his, Ben nodded. 'Your brother. Heard from him lately?'

'It's Louise who keeps in contact. They're okay. The company's moved him again so they're in Leith now. The boys are in school there. I daresay by the time they come home they'll both have Scottish accents.'

'Your parents must miss their grandkids.'

'They do. But if they were over here, then Louise's people would be missing out instead. Stephen says they're planning on Christmas at the farm, so Mum and Dad are hanging out for that.' Abruptly I changed the subject. 'About tomorrow. Do you think it's safe for us to be heading bush – with him around?' I jerked my head at the TV, where the service station film was showing yet again.

'Realistically?' He shrugged. 'We'll be one set of travellers among many, and with the hunt up he should be keeping his head down. Do you want to stop looking, Em? We've given it a pretty fair crack of the whip.'

'We can't,' I said starkly. 'If she's anywhere in the north he's as much danger to her as he is to us. And surely they'll be drafting cops in from all over the Territory to catch him.'

He shrugged. 'The caravan parks tomorrow then. Do you want coffee?'

'Please. And then I think I'll have an early night.' My side hurt and I was suddenly weary. Things always looked better in the morning, my mother maintained. I doubted they would, but I still hoped that she was right.

The following day there was time for a quick look at the war cemetery before we visited the town caravan park. The walled enclosure, with its lawns and tidy rows of flat marker stones, was an oasis of peace, the dew still lying on the clipped sections of lawn and the hush broken only by birdsong.

Considering those who lay there had died in battle storm and terror, I thought they could not have had a better resting place. They had faced great challenges and were now beyond all strife and fear, as one day I should be too. It might have been a morbid thought, but it heartened me. Closing the gate carefully behind me I looked back and Ben, once again divining my mood, if not my thoughts, said, 'Nice. There'd be worse places . . .'

'Yes. I'm glad we came.'

The road was lined with trees. Whether they had been planted or just left when the road was pushed through I couldn't tell, but it was pleasant strolling in the shade into the freshness of the new day. The caravan park was only a short walk away and we arrived to find it full, its customers moving about their vans and in and out of the amenity blocks, some eating a late breakfast, others readying their vehicles for a day excursion. The manager was a leathery-skinned man of middle age wearing only thongs and stubbies, the grey hair on his chest glinting in the bright morning light. He pursed his lips appreciatively at Aspen's picture and shook his head.

'Not like I'd forget her, but hang on while I get the wife. She mighta seen her while I was off somewhere.' He stuck his head through the office door and yelled, 'Di, can you come here a minute, love?'

Di, an improbable redhead of the same vintage, studied the picture, glancing from it to me. 'Nope, sorry. Your sister, is she?'

'My cousin.' I hadn't really expected any other outcome but my discouragement must have shown, for Di patted my arm with a sun-freckled hand.

'Sorry, love. Try the other park out by Fishers. Maybe she went there.'

'Fishers?' Ben lifted an interrogative brow.

'Fishers Lagoon. Ten kay outta town. The turn-off's marked.'

'That was to be our next stop,' I said. 'Thank you.'

'Best of luck,' she called after us as we left.

Back in the vehicle Ben turned south onto the highway. The hamlet of Bloodwood Creek – it scarcely warranted the name of town – vanished behind us and there was just the bitumen, with the odd cow or roo carcass dotted like litter along the verges and the wide sweep of the land under its never-ending sky. A wedge-tail abandoned a dead roo at our approach, its powerful wings hauling it skywards, and a half-dozen brolgas stood by a flooded borrow pit, where prickly bushes provided shade.

Because I'd been thinking about it, I asked, 'What made you leave the city, Ben? And why Armidale?'

'The opportunity was there,' he said as he reached to adjust the driving mirror. 'A business already established. Too good to turn down, really. Better hours, my life was my own, less stress. The trading floor . . . It used to excite me, but it takes its toll. I was burnt out, so why wouldn't I change?'

'But you weren't an accountant.'

He grinned. 'I am now. As I said, you're not the only one to retrain.'

'No, well.' I stared at him as if seeing him anew. 'You're different,' I said frankly. 'I don't feel that I know you at all.

You never used to be so reasonable. I mean, actually listening to me. I'm not trying to score points here,' I added hastily, 'but you have to admit that you rarely considered my take on things before. You always knew best.'

He glanced sideways at me. 'I regret that, Em. Maybe I thought so because you were so young.' He grimaced. 'I was an arrogant fool. I treated you like a child and I shouldn't have.'

The admission floored me. I said honestly, 'It wasn't just you. Mum thought I was too young too. She begged me to wait. Looking back'—I recalled the stormy, tearful, door-banging months that had led to the breakdown of the marriage and my intemperate departure—'we were a catastrophe waiting to happen, we . . . What's that up ahead?'

His foot eased on the accelerator. 'Accident? No, it's the roadblock. That's a police car off to the side.'

'And a wreck.' I eyed the sedan resting on its roof on the far side of the table-drain, its glassless light wells winking in the morning sun. 'Maybe there *was* an accident.'

'An old one,' he murmured, coasting to a stop before the barrier, and I saw that he was right. It must be the one the woman at Old MacDonald's had spoken of. It had been there a fair while, its crumpled red duco showing rust stains, the bare axles witness to the wheels having been souvenired. 'Got your passport?' Ben quipped facetiously as he slid his window down to speak to the approaching officer.

We weren't held up long. The female officer asked where we were bound and, upon learning our destination was Fishers Lagoon, shrugged and waved us through. 'Well, we know Gorblin's not *there*,' she said, 'but be aware he's around somewhere.'

'Gorblin?' I leaned forward. 'Is that his name?'

'Martin Gorblin,' she confirmed. 'The one the media are calling the Outback Killer. We'll catch him, don't worry. But in the meantime watch yourself.'

'Will do,' Ben said, as he drove on.

'I believe they have this saying in the Middle East: Trust in God but tie up your camel,' I said. 'I don't know about catching him. They've had two states to do it in already.'

'It's a big country. They've probably more chance here – fewer roads, unless he really takes to the back blocks. I guess the farmers are all on high alert.'

'Graziers,' I corrected. 'They aren't farms. Some of these properties are as big as small countries.'

'Oh, yes?' He slanted a look at me. 'Name one, then.'

'Monaco,' I said promptly. 'Haiti, Luxembourg . . . You can check it out when we get back. Look, that must be the lagoon.'

Fishers Lagoon was a crescent-shaped stretch of peaceful water hosting a garden of pink and white lilies, their pads stretched like a green coverlet over its surface. The sturdy forms of ti-trees, with their soft, greyish-white bark, formed a shady ring about the adjacent grassed complex where perhaps thirty caravans were parked, the windscreens of the vehicles flashing in the morning light. There was a brick office near the open entrance gate with a three-car park beside it and a riot of magenta bougainvillea, as well as a kiosk advertising Coke and ice creams.

The office was small, its walls plastered with racks of leaflets and posters of past and future attractions coming to the area. A quick glance showed a rodeo, a race meeting and a circus. There was also an enlarged photo of a truly enormous crocodile, mouth opened so that he seemed to be grinning evilly at the photographer, against a background of river bank and shadow.

'Can I help you?' asked a voice from behind a computer screen. 'If it's a berth for the van, I'm afraid we're full up.'

'Morning,' Ben answered. 'That's okay, it's just information we're after. Nice place you've got here. Does the kiosk do coffee, by any chance?'

'Yep. Camper comforts and hot drinks.' The man stood up, disclosing a bald head and a sun-wrinkled face. 'So heading north or south? What did you want to know?'

He hadn't seen Aspen. I was unsurprised by the fact, having reached the point where abduction by aliens would have seemed a reasonable alternative theory. The hope went out of me; we weren't going to find her, I realised. The whole thing had been a mistake . . . Maybe she was never here to start with. She could've lied to the woman at the motel in Alice Springs and headed south or west instead of north. She could be in Perth or Adelaide or, for all I knew, have flown overseas. She'd been short of funds, though, I thought – based on her attempt to get money from Ben. As for the booking at Groove and Grove, that could have been her laying a false trail. Which begged the question: why do so? And why the attempts to kill me by parties unknown? Even if she was no longer in the Territory she was manifestly in trouble.

Overwhelmed by it all, I thanked the man and turned listlessly to leave. 'It's hopeless,' I told Ben. 'We might as well give up. It's plain we're not going to find her.'

16

I thought – perhaps I had half hoped – that Ben would leap at the chance to call the search off. Instead he touched my elbow lightly, steering me to the side, and said, 'Let's take ten, see what sort of coffee they serve, eh?'

It turned out to be instant, but the kiosk had a sparkle to match the smile of the teenage girl who served us. 'There you go,' she said as she slid the coffee cups onto the table, each saucer holding a napkin and a tiny wrapped biscuit the size of a twenty-cent piece. 'You Mexicans or Queenslanders?'

Ben's eyes crinkled up. 'Neither, we're from New South Wales. You get a lot of Victorians, do you?'

She grinned. 'Yep. Soon as it gets cold down there. I suppose fuel's cheaper than heating bills. Your first time up here?'

'Yes.' I stirred my coffee. 'Do your parents own the place?'

She laughed. 'Lord, no. I'm just the help. Darwin born and bred. Bet I get to work quicker than you do though, if you live in the city.'

'That's possibly true,' I said, liking her. 'And the drive should be safe enough now. Did you know the police have set up a roadblock on the highway, in case the murderer they're after heads north?'

'The OK?'

I had a mental pause working out what she meant as she swept on regardless.

'Really? Whereabouts? 'Cause I didn't see it when I came out this morning.' She plucked a chair from the next table and straddled it, arms along the back, dark hair falling to her hunched shoulders, a lively interest on her face.

'Right next to the car wreck,' Ben said. 'What happened there? Looks like it rolled.'

'Oh, that was months ago. It was stripped ages back. My boyfriend came out in March, I think it was, looking for some part for his old bomb, but he said everything had already been scavenged.'

'Was the driver hurt?'

'Dunno. Happened over a weekend and I saw it there on the Monday. Even the coppers had gone by then.' She shrugged. 'Accidents on the Stuart aren't rare, you know. Mostly they hit something, a roo, a cow since the roads aren't fenced – or they just fall asleep. The bitumen sort of hypnotises them. So where are you heading?'

To my surprise Ben said, 'Oh, we heard about this dude ranch place, thought we'd see what that was about. You know it?'

'Crazy Creek, yeah. Haven't been out there but the customers seem to like it.'

Ben lifted an eyebrow. 'But . . .? You don't sound convinced.'

She flushed a little. 'I don't mean to bag the place – people genuinely enjoy the experience. But it's just that Linc who runs it, he's a bit of a lech, you know?'

'Thanks for the heads-up.' I smiled at her. 'I thought he was a little smarmy myself.'

She nodded. 'Watch his hands. He's a great toucher. You ask me, a good smack in the chops is long overdue there. Whoops, here's the boss coming. I'd better look busy.'

'Thanks.' I rose, pushing the cups together. 'It's been a nice break.' I looked at Ben. 'Crazy Creek it is then.'

Back in the car as we headed off down the road I said, 'Thanks, Ben.'

'Yeah? For what?'

'Not listening to me when I said we should quit. It was just a weak moment, but you could have taken advantage. I know you don't want to be here.'

'You've got that wrong, Em,' he said quickly. 'I don't want you at risk – an entirely different thing.'

'Well, whatever.' We were back in flat country with a scatter of timber and a nice stand of yellowing feed carpeting the red earth. There was a fence just ahead with a sign beside the grid reading Crazy Creek. 'This must be the boundary.' I reached to touch his arm and smile. 'After everything, I'm glad we can still be friends.'

He cleared his throat. 'About that— Jesus Christ!' He yanked violently on the wheel as the strident blast of a horn sounded and a dark station wagon shot past towing a dense trail of dust that cut visibility to a few feet. For an instant the car seemed a mere hand's width away from Ben's window. I grabbed the handhold and let out a muffled shriek of fright as Ben stood on the brake. Then the vehicle canted down the road verge and came to a rocking rest less than a metre from the solid grid post, the Crazy Creek sign filling the windscreen through a thick veil of drifting dust.

Ben was swearing, his hands still locked to the wheel. Hardly able to breathe, I stared dumbfounded at the sign. If we had been half a car's length closer, or Ben hadn't pulled off the road . . .

I said faintly, 'What sort of an idiot tries passing when . . . He must've seen the fence!'

'Not through our dust. It's why I didn't notice him. Are you all right?' The hand he raised to swipe over his face was trembling.

'I've just lost ten years of my life,' I said shakily, 'but yes. Is the car okay?'

'Maybe a few scratches. God almighty! Talk about road-hogging Henrys . . . If I get my hands on him . . .' Ben took a deep breath, restarted the vehicle and backed up, swinging the wheel about until we were facing the road once more.

'Unless he works on the station, he must be a visitor like us. The road doesn't go anywhere else, does it? Are we actually going to stay the night here, Ben?'

'Do you want to?' He drove carefully up the verge and across the grid, which was only wide enough for a single vehi-cle. I shuddered inwardly. My brother had hit a grid post in his first car as a teen and almost died. It had taken months in hospi-tal and then a rehabilitation facility before he'd walked again. I'd been ten at the time and could still remember the terror on Mum's face when she opened the door to see the policeman who brought news of the crash.

'I don't think so. Unless we can't speak to anybody without

actually booking. Surely we can stroll around and look at the place first?'

'I would imagine so. See how we go anyway. You're not missing the saddle and pining for a ride, are you?'

I pulled a face. 'Tourist horses? Spoiled nags with ruined mouths – not likely.'

The Crazy Creek complex was laid out beside the creek of that name, so that the homestead and various sheds and guest quarters were backgrounded by the crowns of palms and the spears of thickly clustered pandanus. There was parking off to one side, a glimpse of rails where the stockyards stood, a huge overhead tank with the station name emblazoned around its girth and some half-dozen horses in a small paddock at the back of the yards. Ben pulled up, killed the motor and nodded to an individual rolling a tyre into one of the sheds.

'There's a place to start.'

'Yes.' I spied a dark vehicle on the far side of the car park. 'And there's the road hog.'

'One thing at a time. Got your pic?'

The mechanic, if that's what he was, looked middle-aged and unhelpful. I thought he probably got tired of tourists asking foolish questions. He looked up at our approach and nodded briefly. 'G'day.' He jerked his chin at a sign. 'Office's that way.'

'Thanks,' I said. 'I was wondering, have you been here long?'

'Yeah.' He straightened up from the tyre and put a hand to his back. 'Why?'

'Six months?' I pressed.

'Six years, more like.' He needed a shave and his teeth were tobacco stained. *Concentrate*, I told myself, *you don't even know if he smokes.* 'What's it to you?'

Definitely unfriendly then. 'This.' I handed him Aspen's photo. 'I'm trying to find her. Can you tell me if she's been here, please? It's very important.'

He studied the image, interested despite himself as he sucked at his lower lip. 'Nope. If she was here I ain't seen her, an' I would've, me being the jack of all trades round the damn place. "Saddle their horses, Bill. Build the fire, Bill,"' he said bitterly. '"Cart their bloody luggage" – like a man hasn't got enough on his plate already without nannying a bunch of—' He broke off, possibly remembering he was speaking to two more of the bunch. 'Sorry. Can't help you there. You booking in, then?'

'I think not.' I looked to Ben for confirmation but his gaze had shifted to the car park.

'Hang on here a tick, Em. I'll just be a moment,' he said, and went striding off.

He was heading for the man whose back end was protruding from the vehicle that had run us off the road. I said, 'Oh, dear. Do you know whose is that dark station wagon over there?'

He craned his neck. 'Yeah. Boss's runabout. One he drives when he's not doing the cowboy thing in the LandCruiser.' He handed me back the photo. 'Good looking sheila. What's the story?'

I sighed. 'My cousin's missing – four months now. I'm afraid that something must have happened to her.'

'That's too bad.' He held silent for a moment, eyeing me, then said awkwardly, 'Sorry I was a bit short before. Bloody tourists, you know. They might be the boss's livin' but they ain't mine.'

'I know,' I said sympathetically. 'People wear you out.'

'Ain't that the bloody truth.' He fished in his pocket to produce a tobacco tin. 'So what makes you think she mighta come here, your cousin?'

'We're checking every place along the highway,' I said simply. 'Where the backpackers work, fruit farms, roadhouses, touristy joints. We haven't tried the stations yet, but it might come to that.'

He licked the paper on the cigarette he was rolling. 'Four months, you said? It's a big country, she could be anywhere by now.'

'I know.' I sighed. 'Thanks anyway, Bill.' I turned away to the car.

'Try the Jump-up,' he called after me. 'You never know. I heard there's lotsa drop-outs shacked up there.'

I waved to acknowledge the suggestion; no point in telling him we'd already done so. Ben, coming back just then, jerked his head at the vehicle and I climbed in. He was fuming.

'So, did he apologise?' I asked.

He snorted angrily. 'Fat chance. "*Yeah, well, that's how we do it out here,*"' he quoted furiously. '"*You're not in Pitt Street now, boy.*" Bloody idiot! He could've killed us. If the vehicle had rolled . . . Another dead end then?'

'Yes,' I said glumly, 'not that I could really see her coming here. So where to now?'

'Katherine? We could stay overnight, look over the town. If she came north at all she must've stopped somewhere.

Granted, she could carry her own food and water, but she must've bought fuel. And the highway is the only place she'd get that.'

'Of course. It's a pity that woman in Alice Springs didn't notice more about her vehicle than the colour. There must be thousands of red cars about.'

'Oh, no.' He shook his head. 'We are not chasing red cars, Em. Blondes are bad enough, but cars – that would truly lead to madness. There're too many of them. I read a study that reckoned red is twenty-five per cent more noticeable on the road than black, silver or blue.'

'I wasn't suggesting it.' I sighed. 'Well, petrol stations it is then. What about lunch?'

'It's packed in the esky,' he replied. 'We can stop any time you like.'

Half an hour later we did stop, pulling in to a rest area where a picnic table and bench sat under a tin roof. 'The Territory does this well,' I remarked, eyeing the nearby facility with its waterless composting toilet.

'They've only one main highway.' Ben had pushed up his sunnies and was investigating the sandwich fillings. 'It's not like they have walking paths or emergency road assistance phones.'

'No,' I agreed. 'If you broke down out here you'd really be in trouble. There'd be no hiking your way to the nearest garage. As for crashing, it'd be a long wait for an ambulance.'

'Egg or meat?' he offered. I took the egg and he added, 'I hear you. Your best hope'd be for someone to stop and help. Speaking of which, somebody's about to – stop, that is.'

I glanced up to see a police car that had been travelling north power down and cross the road to turn into the rest area. It pulled up behind our vehicle and two officers, one of them a woman, got out and strolled over.

'G'day. You travelling okay?' the male cop asked.

Ben had stood at their approach. He said, 'Yes, we're fine. Just stopping for a meal. Is something wrong?'

The woman flashed a smile. 'Not at all, sir. We're checking on travellers, that's all. You are aware there's a wanted man somewhere in these parts?'

'Gorblin,' I said, 'yes. We spoke to a colleague of yours back at the top roadblock. But he couldn't be *between* the road-blocks, could he?'

'We don't know,' her companion answered. 'There are plenty of tracks leading into the properties out here. He could've taken one of them, so we're advising people not to stop if they come across a stationary vehicle. You saw the TV footage from the servo?'

We both nodded.

'Well, don't assume he'd still be driving the same model. Dead easy to get another vehicle out here. If you can believe it,' the man said disgustedly, 'station people garage theirs with the keys still in 'em. Just begging to have 'em nicked.'

'I'll bear it in mind,' Ben said. 'We're heading for Katherine. After that, might be we'll have a look to the west. Isn't there a national park out there?'

'Gregory Park,' the woman agreed. 'It's a good way over, near Timber Creek. You want to carry plenty of water if you're heading out there, and leave word with someone on your ETA. Even without Gorblin, it's no country to take on unprepared.'

'We'll be careful,' I promised. Ben's declaration surprised me. By now I'd spent a lot of time with a Territory map, and Timber Creek was more than halfway to Kununurra in Western Australia. Surely a light car would never survive the trip – unless the road was bitumen, which didn't seem likely.

I stowed the lunch rubbish in the bin provided as the police car resumed its cruise down the highway and we got underway again ourselves.

'It's a very long way to Timber Creek,' I said. 'Why would Aspen even think about a place so remote from – well, anything? Shops, people, life as she knows it.'

'Your guess is as good as mine.' Ben shrugged. 'Maybe we should just head back to the Alice and start again from where we know she actually was. We've been acting like blind men blundering around on a football field looking for the goalposts. And with about as much chance of success. It's all too hit and miss, Em – and a great deal more miss than hit.'

'Perhaps you're right. I was so sure she'd be in Darwin that I never thought of checking along the way. Not that I could've. The bus only made a couple of stops, and none of them very long.'

'So, Katherine first, then onto plan B?'

'Which is?'

He flashed me a smile. 'We'll work it out.'

There was something very comforting about that *we*. I said impulsively, 'Looks like I'll have to forgive Dad. I wasn't best pleased before, but now I'm really glad you're here, Ben.'

'That's something then.' A numbered post flashed by. 'Not far now. Maybe,' he added hopefully, 'Katherine'll give us the clue we need; we're well overdue for one.'

17

In Katherine we booked in to the Gorge Motel, then did a slow cruise through the streets, getting the layout of the town. The motel provided breakfast but had no dining facilities, so we looked first for a restaurant and then began canvassing the service stations. While Ben filled up, I went inside to show the photo and ask my questions, drawing a blank at both Mobil and Caltex. But as Ben had said, we were overdue for some help and it was delivered at our third stop on the southern side of town.

'Yeah,' the man behind the counter mused. 'I remember her. Way back in January, maybe? The run-down old heap she was driving had blown a tyre. No wonder, it was damn near baldy. Somebody stopped and changed it for her. She asked if we could fix it. Like, hello? The side was ripped clean out of it. Sold her a retread instead.' He smiled a little self-consciously. 'I even filled her tank for her and I haven't worked a pump in years. Pretty thing she was, but helpless. Shouldn't have been alone on the highway.'

I felt limp with relief. 'What sort of vehicle?' I asked. 'And did she say where she was headed?'

'Old model Datsun,' he said positively. 'A 240, maybe.' It meant nothing to me as he added reflectively, 'Yeah, just mighta been the first ever made, it was that old. Lot of miles on the clock, more rust than red.'

'Oh, that's great.' I beamed at him. 'We know what we're looking for now. Did she happen to say where she was going?'

He shrugged, bemused. 'Well, Darwin? It's where the road leads.'

'And can you remember how she seemed? Was she upset, worried? She's missing and we're trying to find her.'

'Well, she was a bit put out about the tyre. 'Specially when I gave her the price of a new 'un. Maybe a touch nervy, you know – pacing around, though I told her there was a chair and a fan in the office and she could wait in there. I put the retread on the front 'cause the tyre there didn't look too good, neither.'

'Thank you!' I said fervently. 'You've been a great help. Nobody else we've spoken to has seen her. Or if they have they've forgotten.'

'Must be blind then.' He glanced down at the picture in my hand. 'She's kind of hard to forget, know what I mean?'

'I do. We think she's in trouble. So, I know it's long odds but if you remember anything else, we'll be at the Gorge Motel tonight.'

He eyed us both. 'You cops?'

'No. Family. Thank you for helping her out.'

He waved a dismissive hand. 'It's my job.' But I could see he was pleased all the same.

*

'So she got this far,' I mused as we drove off, 'but where did she go from here? We'll have to turn back and I think we should try the first turn-off out of town, see where it takes us. She has to have left the bitumen, or surely somebody else would've seen her.'

'Worry about it tomorrow,' Ben said firmly. He pulled suddenly into the kerb before a low-set house whose front yard was strewn with toys.

'Why are we stopping here?' I turned to him but his gaze was on the driving mirror. A vehicle drove past and turned the corner. 'What's going on, Ben?'

'I think we're being followed. That Toyota – it was behind us on the highway and I've seen it twice since. The driver was fuelling up while you were speaking to that fella, and now he's behind us again. After the fire and the market and, yes, being run off the road – though I hadn't counted that before – it's maybe a coincidence too far.'

'But that was just road-hogging,' I protested.

'Maybe. And if the vehicle had rolled and we'd broken our necks, whoever was trying to kill you could chalk it up as a success, even if he wasn't behind it.'

'You must be mistaken . . . There are hundreds of Toyotas, and most of them that beige colour. It might not even be the same vehicle.' I desperately didn't want it to be true.

'It is. Unless they all have the same numberplate.' He eased back onto the street. 'I think we'll not try the night-life here. How about eating in tonight? Fish and chips okay?'

Shaken, I nodded. 'They'll do.'

We reached the motel's entrance without sighting the Toyota again. The entrance made a dogleg into a square car park hedged in by a riot of bougainvillea, and as I depressed the door handle, Ben stopped me. 'Slide down a bit in your seat,' he said, and as I obeyed he got out and made a stooping sort of scuttle over to the hedge to peer through it into the street we'd just left. A few moments later he straightened and returned.

'Did you see him?' I asked. After my recent experiences I really didn't like the idea of being spied upon.

'Yeah. He musta been hanging back. Just drove past, so he knows we're here. Checking us in for the night, I expect.'

'Maybe we should just wait until it's properly dark, then hightail it out of here.'

'And go where?' he asked practically, scooping up our bags. 'I don't fancy sleeping on the side of the road with a murderer on the loose, Em.'

He was right of course. Sighing, I followed him into the motel.

Nothing disturbed our night. Ben went out for fish and chips while I showered and boiled the jug for his return. We watched the news; there had been a sighting of the Outback Killer's vehicle at the Three Ways, a roadhouse north of Tennant Creek. It was a positive identification so far as the vehicle went, though the witness admitted he hadn't seen the driver. 'One less worry, that's miles away,' Ben observed, and we spent a little time with the map examining our options for tomorrow. The fact that someone had actually encountered Aspen, even if it was four months ago, had energised us both.

'I should have thought of checking more of the service stations,' I said, 'though I did ring one in each town. Of course, the Darwin ones see far too many customers to remember any of them. What are you doing?' I asked as Ben upended his bag onto the bed and began sorting clothes.

'Need to wash some socks 'n' jocks. I'll give them a splosh in the sink. It's not like we've time for a laundromat.'

'Very domestic of you.' During our life together, I couldn't recall ever seeing him use a household appliance beyond a jug or toaster, and he had never helped with the dishes or picked up after himself.

'You'd be surprised,' he said mildly. 'I've got quite handy in the absence of my wife.'

'Good for you.' I folded the map, briefly considered my own wardrobe and decided I could manage for another day. The twin room was small, the beds uncomfortably close together, and though I was grateful for the protection his presence offered, I wasn't about to trust myself with him in the more intimate space of the bathroom. I said abruptly, 'I think I'll ring my parents. Mum's probably worrying.'

'Tell them hello from me, then,' he called and I heard water powering into the hand basin.

The phone rang only three times before Mum picked up. She sounded pleased to hear from me. 'Are you all right, Emily? We've been very worried, with that murderer on the loose up there. Where are you?'

'I'm fine, Mum. In Katherine tonight. That's on the Stuart Highway, nice little town.' I chattered on, not mentioning Ben, but asking after their own activities on the farm.

'It's been a week – I thought you'd be in Darwin by this point. Dad's into the mustering. And I'm doing the same old stuff. When are you coming back?'

I said, 'I've been up to Darwin, now I'm working my way back. We've got a hired vehicle and I've still got a few days left. I expect I'll book my flight when I get down to the Alice.' Pointless worrying her with details. 'How's Dad?'

'He's fine – here, I'll put him on.' The phone was passed over, I heard Mum say 'Emily', and then my father's voice was there, slow and firm as always, the steady heartbeat at the core of my life.

'Emily, love. Glad you called. So how's it going?'

'I'm fine, Dad. But annoyed with you. You had no business telling Ben where I was.'

'Ah, so he found you. That's a weight off my mind. Tell him g'day from me. I'll put up with your anger just so long as you're safe, love. I've been out in the top paddock today, took the quad because it's a bit boggy still on the low ground . . .' He talked on, telling me about the country's condition and the muster, his slow country drawl bringing it alive for me. I almost wished myself back there and was about to ask after the dogs and Soldier when he abruptly asked, 'So, have you found your cousin?'

'Not yet, but we're on her trail. Dad, will you ask Mum if she ever had any suspicion that Aspen was . . . that Uncle Rich interfered with her?'

There was a brief silence and he said, not disguising his surprise, 'You mean sexually? Why?'

'Just something that's come up. I wondered.'

There was a brief confab between them, too muffled for me to hear properly, then Mum was back, sounding aghast. 'Whatever gave you that idea, Emily?'

'I met a youth worker, a very experienced one, who I showed Aspen's photo to . . . And I've been remembering back to times I spent with her, those sleepovers, things she said, and I'm starting to think that maybe he did. And Mum, looking back, I think she may have been self-harming. Cutting herself. Remember how she was about that bracelet she always wore? Never taking it off. She wouldn't even show it to me. It must've been five centimetres wide – that'd cover a lot of scarring.'

'But her father gave it to her. Richmond doted on that girl!'

'Well, maybe it was guilt. You yourself said, one time she was at the farm, that there was something amiss with her. It would explain such a lot. Her coldness, her tantrums and unhappiness. You could never get close to Aspen, you know that. Nobody ever seemed to. Maybe that's why.'

I had really shocked her. She said in a troubled tone, 'But I can't believe that Fiona wouldn't have known if . . . How could she not? If it happened, why wouldn't Aspen have told her?'

'Maybe she did and Aunt Fee didn't believe her?'

I thought about my aunt. Would she have known and done nothing? Balancing the shame of it all coming out against her daughter's safety and wellbeing? I didn't want to believe it, but appearances were all with the Tennants. I heard Mum draw in her breath as if she'd had the same thought.

'I don't want to believe it,' she said wretchedly, 'but if it did happen, why didn't the poor child tell me?'

'If – *when* I find her, I'll ask. I'd better go, Mum. Take care, love you both. Bye.'

18

In the morning there was no sign of the Toyota. We ate our continental breakfast, checked out and visited a little bakery to buy our lunches. I'd filled the thermoses at the motel and we still had plenty of bottled water. I searched the streets diligently as we drove through the town, checking the numberplates on the several Toyotas I saw without spotting the one that had followed us.

'He's given up,' I said optimistically. 'Maybe he thinks we have too, that we're heading for the Alice?'

'Could be. Or he's waiting for us out on the highway,' Ben said.

A little shiver of fear went through me at the thought. There was something so inimical about the idea of someone sitting in ambush, prepared to do us harm. Why else follow us? Unless . . . I said, 'What if they're trying to find Aspen too? And they think following us is the best way of doing it?'

'Then why the attempts on your life?' Ben asked practically.

'I don't know. Maybe,' I hazarded, 'they've since rethought things? What if she's got something they want? Or, it could be just that she's seen something they did – she's a witness to a crime, say – and it's her they want to silence? So first'—I warmed to my theme—'they try to stop me from reaching her, because they don't want anyone else finding whatever it is she's got or knows, and when that fails they let us do the work of tracking her down. Perhaps they reckon we'd have an edge, being family. What do you think?'

'It makes as much sense as anything else,' Ben admitted. 'And if it means you're no longer a target, then I like it. But we don't know it for a fact.'

'But if it's true,' I fretted, 'and we lead them to her, then we're putting Aspen in danger as well.'

'*If* it's true, which it may not be.' We had reached the outskirts of Katherine and he increased his speed. 'On the other hand . . . Keep your eyes peeled. If he is waiting for us and has any sense, he'll be planted in the scrub and let us pass before he follows. He wouldn't want to flag his intentions. Maybe we can make the Notting Hill turn-off before he sees us.'

Notting Hill was marked on the map but it gave no clue as to what it was. We had dismissed the idea of a cattle property, and it could be anything from a mining camp to a flower farm, but as it would take us off the highway and the turn-off was a scant five kilometres out of town, Ben reckoned it was worth the detour, particularly as taking it could lose us our pursuers.

The road was a narrow stretch of gravel that hadn't seen a grader for a good while, and I released a pent breath as we sped along it. The only vehicle we had met on the highway was a huge road train with three loaded trailers, the sun glinting blindingly off its duco, and a tail of three cars behind it, none apparently willing to pass the swaying trailers. Not that they needed to at the speed the road train was going. There was nothing behind us; twisting in my seat, I watched the receding bitumen without catching so much as a flash of light.

'We seem to be alone,' I said, facing forward again. 'Are you sure this isn't a dead end? It doesn't look like it gets much traffic.'

'Not according to the map. It wanders a bit but it heads broadly north and eventually leads back to the highway.'

'I see. How much fuel do we have?'

He slanted me a look. 'Enough. It's a diesel so we're getting good mileage, and there's a spare jerrycan in the back. You might give me a bit of credit – I'm not quite as clueless as you seem to think.'

'Just checking. You can't be too careful.'

He nodded, went to say something and swore instead. 'Shit!' The front wheel crashed into a hole and he slowed to engage four-wheel drive. The road had deteriorated, the former gravel now a two-wheeled track with a ribbon of grass up the middle. The country had changed from flatness to a series of gentle ridges that grew progressively rougher, the far ones topped with crenellations of rock that stretched into the distance. They weren't high but they looked very rough.

I said uneasily, 'Maybe we should turn back. If anything was to happen, nobody would know where we were.'

'It fine, Em,' Ben said. 'We'll be careful. Four-wheel drives were made for this. We'll just take it slowly. Can you remember the distance to this place?'

'Fifty kay, I think.'

'Right, well we're about halfway there. Look, there's more of your trees.'

'What? Oh, so there are.' The bright yellow blossoms I had noticed on the day we'd visited the national park were again on display across the stony slopes, bright shouts of colour against the drabness of the rock. 'I never did find out what they are.'

'You should buy a book on the local flora,' he murmured, peering fixedly ahead. 'The tourist places are bound to have one.'

'What are you looking at?'

'Over there to the right – that dark patch. I hope to hell it's not a gorge, because we might be turning back if it is.'

I stared where he indicated. 'Hmm, hard to say at this distance. A cave, maybe? Or perhaps a spring. There's a lot of growth, like there could be water there. Maybe that's what Notting Hill is – a spring?'

'Bit unlikely. With the Katherine Gorge in the locality, who's going to bother putting a mere spring on the map?'

He had a point. I watched the distant shadow darken and grow as the vehicle lurched and scrambled forward, aware that Aspen couldn't have come this way; a Datsun could never handle this road. The first ten kay had established that, I thought, but there was still the matter of our pursuer, and if the detour threw him off, we weren't wasting either our time or fuel. Then we were close enough for the shadow to gain definition and suddenly it made sense.

'It's a cave – a big one. But the tracks don't look to be going there.'

'No,' Ben agreed, eyes on the odometer. 'If the map distances are right, we're still eight kilometres short of Notting Hill. Well, onwards and upwards. I don't really think we've time for a closer look.'

'It'd be interesting but I'm not sure I want one. It's probably full of bats, and that means snakes.'

'And you a vet.' He raised his brows. '*Tsk*. Isn't your calling supposed to be for all creatures great and small?'

'Maybe. Doesn't mean I want to treat a skunk or a raging bull.' I watched the cave disappear slowly as the road descended into a broad flattened area, then abruptly and bizarrely stopped before a rusty chain-link fence about two metres high.

'It's an old airfield!' I said blankly after a moment. 'Good Lord, whoever would've thought . . .?'

There were no buildings, just a broad tarred strip with grass growing through the cracks and the dilapidated fence rattling forlornly in the wind. The chain links stretched away, unbroken, in both directions for, I guessed, a kilometre or more. There was a sagging metal gate secured with a rusting chain and padlock, and a faded noticeboard on which I could just make out the words NOTTING HILL, despite half the letters being missing. There was something about authorised admission only and 'property of', but time and weather had obliterated the rest.

'Relic of the war. Could've been the Yanks,' Ben mused. 'Somebody obviously scavenged the buildings afterwards. You'd probably find Nissen huts scattered across the stations round about. The literature says there're old wartime airfields all across the Top End. It does explain the state of the road – I guess this isn't on many tourists' lists.'

'No,' I agreed. 'Does the road continue, I wonder? I'll bet there's one going to that cave we saw.'

'How's that?'

'Think about it. Hordes of young men stuck out here for months on end with nothing to do, of course they're going to explore the country. Bet they started with a look at the cave.'

'You're probably right.' Ben backed up and began driving cautiously around the airfield's perimeter. 'There must be another gate. Let's see where its road takes us.'

There was a second entrance situated on the far side of the fenced rectangle that delineated the airstrip. The road leading from it looked to be in much the same condition as the track we had arrived on. I got the map out and we spread it on the bonnet, arms touching to hold it down in the wind. A dotted line ran away to the north-west, curving slowly back eastwards. Placing a finger on a patch of green, I said, 'It seems to meet up here with a track into the national park. I don't recall there being another way in except the one we used.'

'There must be more than one road. It's probably not advertised though, so the rangers can control the traffic in and out,' Ben reasoned. 'What do you think – shall we risk it? If we head back to the highway, there's always the chance that Toyota could pick us up again.'

I weighed it up, staring around at the blowy space of sky and the rocky folds of range, ochre and dun in the morning light. The scrub was olive-grey, with brighter patches of green spinifex and the glitter of red gravel across the ridges. Ben was obviously keen to go on, but the road was abysmal. I said hesitantly, 'And if we run into trouble, get stuck, do a tyre? How much food do we have?'

'Our lunches. Plus chocolate – a full block – some protein bars, a bag of nuts, and a couple of tubs of instant noodles. Enough for dinner if we run out of time and don't make it back tonight – not that we're booked in anywhere. Also we've plenty of water, a shovel, spare tyre, billycan, matches and'— he patted his jeans' pockets to produce a chain holding a house key and a small pocket knife—'there's this. All contingencies covered.'

'Oh, great.' I rolled my eyes at him. 'If a bear turns up you can kill it.'

'So, we go then?'

'I suppose so. If we've slipped our tail, let's not make it easy for him to find us again. If we ever catch up with Aspen, I swear I'll wring her neck.' I lifted my head then and inclined it. 'Listen! Do you hear something?' It had been very faint, more a thrumming against my eardrum than an actual sound.

'What?' I watched him as he stood, jaw pushed forward and mouth a little open, straining to hear. He was, I thought, still unfairly good-looking, though many men in their thirties were starting to grow jowly. 'I can't hear anything.'

'It's gone. It was pretty faint. Might have been a plane, I suppose.'

'Onward then.' He folded the map and we resumed our seats and headed off, climbing slowly on a trek that, judging by our present speed, was going to last all day, if not longer.

Some time after twelve, we stopped for a quick lunch eaten in the vehicle. Quick because we hadn't made much mileage. We'd seen wallabies and a little mob of wild horses, all blacks and browns with long unkempt tails and muddy hides, as if they'd been rolling in a shallow waterhole. Once we'd had to stop while we both got out to clear the track of the limbs of a fallen tree; later we had been forced to tumble rocks into a washed-out gully to fill the hollow there. I was having second thoughts by then about the wisdom of our actions, but these impediments seemed only to increase Ben's determination to follow through on our decision. Men! I could see he was getting a kick out of testing his driving skills and having an actual need for the low-range gear never used on the open road.

Starting off again, we found that beyond the ridges the land flattened obligingly into lightly forested red country where the track was almost lost in wheel-high grass, where nubby anthills lurked. After hitting the first one Ben slowed to a more cautious pace, grumbling, 'You'd think the bloody things'd have more sense than to build on a road.'

'The fact that they did just shows how long since it's been used,' I said. 'How's the fuel going?'

'It'd get us to Darwin, no problem. Don't worry, Em. Everything's fine.'

I bristled immediately. 'Because you say so? Don't patronise me. I'm in this too. I don't need to be patted on the head while the big man looks after things I couldn't possibly understand.'

'Hey,' he protested, 'that's not fair. I just don't want you to worry unnecessarily. I'm being protective, not patronising. There is a difference.'

'I can protect myself.' The words were scarcely said before I had an inconvenient flashback to that night in Darwin when I'd scuttled into his room in fear of nothing more than shadows. 'Well, most of the time,' I admitted grudgingly, and saw by the little smirk that he had remembered too.

I said abruptly, 'Why did you really leave the city, Ben? What happened? You loved the job, the life. I can't actually picture you in some little two-person show.'

'Three. You're forgetting Nina, our recept— Well, *that* wasn't on the map.'

As the vehicle came to a sudden stop, I saw that we had come to a fork in the way with another track leading off at right angles to the north-east. Ben killed the engine and we both sat for a moment staring at the choice before us.

'A signpost would be handy right now,' he grunted as he got out.

I reached into the side pocket for the map and followed him to spread it on the bonnet. With my fingers, I walked the track from Notting Hill, following the winding dashes that marked the way, but they simply continued without an offshoot. 'Perhaps it's an old station track?' I hazarded. 'Could have been made after the map was. The cartographers wouldn't necessarily include property access roads, would they?'

He frowned, staring both ways as if seeking inspiration. 'Anybody's guess. I'm a bit inclined to take it. What do you think?'

'Why? We've no idea where it leads.'

'Yes, but it is heading where we want to be, which is back on the highway. The other way, even when we reach the national park, is still a couple of hours' drive from there to the bitumen.' He consulted his watch. 'It's past three already and I'd really rather not be trying to find my way in the dark. Not on these tracks.'

'I— Listen.' I tilted my head and this time there was no mistaking the steady throb in the air.

Ben heard it too; he straightened and began to fold the map. 'A vehicle. Must be a local, we can ask—'

I practically screamed, 'Ben, are you crazy? No local's used this road for years. Remember the anthills? It's that Toyota. He must have worked out where we'd gone.' I rushed for the cab. 'Come on! We have to get out of here.'

My panic convinced him, and a moment later he was behind the wheel, tapping his fingers impatiently as he waited on the glowplug. Then we took off, taking the offshoot, which had the advantage of running down a gravel incline that was momentarily clear of grass. Not until we'd sped a full kilometre and he was forced to slow to negotiate a series of bends through ti-tree scrub did my heart rate slow, to be instantly raised again as he spoke.

'You know, we could be mistaken about this. It mightn't be our tail at all. Because *he*'s still out here somewhere, that bloke the cops are after.'

'The Outback Killer? He's way down Tennant Creek way, isn't he?'

'Unless the sighting was wrong, or he's managed to swap vehicles. Actually, he'd only have to swap the plates. How many drivers automatically check their numberplates?'

It could happen, I supposed, and I felt numb with horror at the thought of him on our tail. 'You really think?'

'I don't intend finding out,' he said reassuringly and shot me a look. 'And at the risk of sounding patronising, I guarantee it will be okay, Em. I'll never let anyone hurt you.'

19

We didn't stop to discover whether the stranger was behind us or had taken the other road. Never before had I wished so much for speed, but the track made anything beyond a pedestrian ten and occasionally fifteen kilometres an hour impossible. More worryingly, we came to and crossed a number of small, flowing creeks. The water was only shallow but we needed low-range to negotiate the banks where the track had degenerated into channels gouged by the rains; still, we crossed them easily enough. They weren't the problem, but the larger watercourse into which they must flow surely would be. If we couldn't get across that, we would have to turn back.

Then the whole issue became superfluous. Just as dusk was falling, the vehicle came to a stop as if a giant hand had grabbed it. Ben engaged the lowest gear and revved the motor, but the vehicle remained stationary.

He swore in a tone of extreme irritation and climbed out.

I followed him, saying worriedly, 'What is it?'

'Oh, that's just bloody lovely,' he exploded. 'We're hung up on a rock.' He sighed out a breath and killed the motor.

'All right. Of course it had to happen just when a man can scarcely see the bastard thing, but we can fix this. If we jack it up, I should be able to shift the rock, or at least lower it. It's not catching by much.'

'How come the front axle cleared it?' I wondered aloud.

'Twist of the wheel, or Blind Freddy's luck.' He was rummaging in the back to produce a jack. Fitting the two pieces of the handle together, he said, 'Can you chock the front wheels?'

I did so, checking the vehicle was in gear and the handbrake on, as he stretched out on the rocky ground to push himself under it. The last of the daylight leached through the scrub, the birds and the flies were still and the only sound was the scrape of Ben's body against the earth and sough of a little breeze. *The only sound* . . . With a jolt I remembered the other vehicle and listened with all my being, relaxing only when the night remained silent. Well, thank God for that. Raising my voice, I said, 'He's gone, Ben! I can't hear a thing.'

An irate 'What?' came from under the car. I repeated my words and he grunted.

'Good. Can you take a look in the glovebox? See if there's a trouble light there. It's as black as the inside of a bloody coffin under here.'

We were there for hours. With the small bright light fixed to the chassis, Ben worked and swore at the rock, grunting as he wielded the shovel and tyre-lever, attempting to lift it out of its bed and then, when that failed, to scrape away the rubble surrounding it to lower it enough to clear the axle. Lying on his side, it was impossible for him to bring his full strength to the task and when he had shifted what he could, he lay back with a groan.

'It's bloody hopeless! Em, see if there's a screwdriver in the tool kit, will you? A big 'un. And something to hit the damn thing with.'

I switched on the headlights to examine the roll of tools, located a sturdy screwdriver, settled doubtfully on the largest spanner, then swapped it for the wheel brace. 'Here. What about this?'

'Great. Can you get me my sunnies, please?'

It seemed a strange request but once he started chiselling away at the top of the rock and I heard the chips zinging off the metal of the chassis, it made sense. Finally he tossed the tools out and slid forth, bringing the light with him. His face was covered in stone dust, there were stone nicks on his neck and he was favouring the little finger of his left hand.

'What happened there?' I went to inspect it but he brushed me aside.

'Never mind now. Let's see if that's done the trick.'

I held my breath as the vehicle, headlights spearing into the dark, slid slowly forward over the rock and onto a patch of level ground. Ben switched off and came back to where I was gathering up the jack and other tools.

'Thank God for that! But we'll have to spend the night here, Em. We've food and water, and we can sleep in the vehicle. Sorry, but it's too big a risk otherwise. That rock could just as easily have holed the sump, so I'm taking it as a warning.'

I was more relieved than worried by his words. To continue was to ask for trouble and it wasn't as if I'd never camped before. 'We've got a billy,' I said. 'Do we have any tea?'

''Fraid not. Can you switch on the headlights again? I'll scrounge some firewood. We need to heat water for the noodles.'

This was accomplished. He built a small cairn of sticks, hesitated, then passed me the matches. 'You're probably better at this. I looked but we have no paper for starters.'

'We don't need it.' I had gathered a handful of dried leaves to poke under his structure and the moment I struck the match, the evocative smell of burning eucalypt scented the air. The flames licked and caught, burning blue at the edges, then rushing into golden tongues of fire. The shadows drew back and we were held in the comforting circle of light. Ben emptied two bottles of water into the billy and handed it to me, then brought the carton of ill-matched edibles from the vehicle.

'Pity about the tea,' he said, 'but I found this.' 'This' proved to be a poly-backed picnic blanket that I had assumed was part of the back seat. 'Something to sit on,' he said, spreading it.

'Good. We'll need it for warmth later on.' The nights were cooling rapidly as the dry season got into full swing. 'Can you get the lid off those noodles without wrecking the pots?'

The fire, having served its purpose, sunk to a glow of embers as we ate our noodles with the plastic spoons provided. 'Not the best meal I've ever had, or the most comfortable circumstances in which to dine,' Ben murmured, laying his empty pot aside, 'but I can't fault the company.' He kept shifting about, unused to being on the ground. 'I could just about murder a cup of coffee.'

'Have some chocolate instead.' I handed him his share of the block of Cadbury I'd broken in half. 'We'd better save the protein bars and the nuts. We'll need breakfast and who knows? Maybe even lunch.'

'God forbid!' he said fervently, lying back on the rug. 'Man! Will you look at those stars.'

It was past midnight by then with a cloudless sky and very still; the earlier fitful breeze had died with the coming of darkness. Overhead the Milky Way resembled a beach – one on which every grain of sand was a glittering light. Venus had long since sunk, and the Cross was high, while the Big Dipper shone as if polished. A curlew's wailing call rose suddenly from the dark and I felt Ben jump.

'It's just a bird,' I said. 'Have you never camped out before?'

'Only once, in the backyard when I was about eight.'

'What happened?'

He made a rueful sound. 'Mum and I put up the tent and she made me a bed in it. She said she'd leave the back door unlocked in case I changed my mind about staying out there. What I didn't know was that she'd also left a sheet on the line. I got into bed, but it was so quiet I couldn't hear anything but my own blood thundering in my ears. Maybe ten minutes passed, though it felt like hours. It was pitch black. I mean it couldn't have been, the streets and houses were lit up, but it *seemed* pitch black to me, which was crazy because there were shadows on the tent walls. Real spooky stuff. They got to me. I could see them moving about. The wind in the shrubs, I suppose. I imagined all sorts of monsters coming for me. I lay there shaking like a leaf, but I wasn't going to give in to my fears.'

He chuckled quietly, rising up on an elbow, and I caught the gleam of his teeth in the dim glow from the coals. 'After a bit I got up very slowly. I told myself I wasn't scared, I'd just go inside for a pee, and come straight back – even though I knew I wouldn't. Anyway, the wind had been increasing steadily all the while and the moment I crawled out of the tent, the sheet blew off the line and came straight at me. Jesus! I can still feel the way my heart all but leapt from my chest. I thought it was a ghost come to get me. I ran straight through the screen door, yelling my head off. Result: one busted screen, no more camping.'

'That would certainly put you off,' I agreed. I had never heard the tale before. I had met his parents, Marg and Charlie Grier who lived in Brisbane, at our wedding, but had not seen them since. They had seemed a little tentative, as if they hardly knew the adult version of their son, and swamped by the smart crowd and fancy surrounds of the restaurant where the wedding feast was held. I had had little chance to speak with them. Marg had eyed me and told me I was very pretty, and Charlie, whom I had addressed as Mr Grier, had said we must come and stay after the honeymoon, but we had never done so. I regretted that now, though at the time I was so besotted with my new love I hadn't given the invitation another thought.

Following the memory, I said, 'How are your parents keeping? Do you see much of them?'

'More than I used to. Dad's got a bit of a heart problem but it's under control. Mum worries about him.' He leaned forward to poke the coals, saying quietly, 'I'm a bit more . . . grounded now than I was in my Sydney days. Less self-centered, I hope. I neglected them then and I regret it.'

I said, 'We all make mistakes, and it's better to regret than not even notice your actions.'

He turned to look at me, the light from the dying coals casting a shadow across his eyes. 'I know I was guilty of that with you, and for what it's worth, I'm sorry, Em. I'm trying to do better these days with everyone I hurt. To be a nicer person.'

So he was here with me not just from his own sense of obligation or simply at my father's behest, but to tidy up an old relationship? Did that mean that he was seeing somebody? The sudden certainty of it lodged in my mind beyond dispute and I berated myself for not seeing it before. Of course he was. Some woman, smarter and much cleverer than me, had changed him. I swallowed what felt like a mouthful of glass and shrugged, affecting unconcern. 'It's history. Which I've always found pretty boring. We were mismatched from the start. I daresay there's plenty I could apologise for too – I wasn't very mature back then. What we have to do now though is not rake over what's finished and done with, but work out our next move in finding Aspen.'

'Any ideas?' Was he relieved that I had moved the conversation on? He had responded so quickly that it seemed likely. Drawing up his feet to clasp his knees, he added, 'Well, apart from getting off this track, which is a given.' The words sounded forced, as if to cover what could have been an awkward pause, then the curlew cried again from the darkness, an eerie wail that split the night's stillness, and put the hairs up on my neck.

'That'll be a start,' I agreed. 'After that I'm out of ideas. What we *do* know is that she made it to Katherine, so logically she must be north of there. Unless,' I frowned, picturing the map with a memory of a road turning westward from the town, 'she really did head over to Kununurra? But that seems unlikely when she already had a booking at Groove and Grove. Besides, we know she was having trouble with her car.'

'If she did go west, we can't chase her that far,' Ben protested.

I sighed. 'I know. I have to get back to my job. Anyway, if she is in WA it would mean she's okay. Obviously nobody's looking for her there.' I stood up, tidied away the remnants of our meal and looked without enthusiasm at the vehicle.

'How far back do the seats recline? I suppose we had better try and get some sleep.'

It was a forgettable night as far as comfort went. Ben, being taller and constrained by the steering wheel, had the worst of it. I lay breathing evenly to mimic sleep, very conscious of him a mere arm's reach away. I watched the stars through the windscreen, stifling the desire to cry, though it didn't prevent tears from leaking silently down my face. What had I expected? That because I loved him Ben would stay true to me? We had separated after a blazing row, but the strain and unhappiness wrought by his expectations and my inability to meet them had been accumulating for months.

Mum had been right, I reflected. I might have loved him, but it was as an encumbrance, not an equal partner, and that was how he had seen me, once the novelty of my innocence had worn off. We had separated at my instigation, and in the interim he had moved on, found somebody else. It was the natural, obvious – if heartbreaking for me – thing to happen and all I wanted, as I slipped in and out of fitful sleep, was for this night to be over so that we could finish our quest and part again. I would give it just two more days, I resolved, bleary-eyed and wakeful as I heard the first bird herald the grey light stealing through the trees, then remove my shattered heart from the constant pain of his presence.

The raucous cry roused Ben too. He sat up, pushed his door open and scrubbed a hand through his hair. 'Not even a coffee to wake up with,' he grumbled. 'How did you sleep?'

'Is that what you call it?' I groaned and stretched, throwing off the picnic rug that had covered us both. 'I suppose the ground would've been harder, and colder. I spent a night in a stable once with a foaling mare, but last night was far worse.'

'I thought hay was supposed to be soft. People roll in it, don't they?'

'Not when it's in bales,' I replied tartly. 'Then it's much the same as bricks. Let's eat and get going. I want a shower and a cuppa and a proper bed tonight.'

We breakfasted on energy bars and a handful of nuts and, even more than a cup of tea, I wished for the wherewithal to clean my teeth. I did what I could as far as ablutions went with the hem of my t-shirt and half a bottle of water, but we could spare no more. We'd fill the empty bottles at the next creek but heaven knew when we'd reach it. I wished now that, tail or no tail, we'd stuck to the highway. I was more convinced by the moment that we had no hope of finding Aspen – in which case, I thought, let the Toyota's driver tail us to China and back. I wished him joy of the task!

20

The track didn't improve. It wound through ridges and belts of scrub and eventually, as I had feared, we came to the pandanus-fringed banks of a substantial creek. There would be no crossing it, I thought, glimpsing the gleam of water between the spiky growth; we might as well turn back now. But just as I was about to suggest this, a natural gap appeared in the thick growth and the track tipped down to a crossing place.

Ben pulled up and got out. I scrabbled the empty water bottles together and followed.

'What're you doing?'

'I'm going to fill them. You?'

'Just checking the depth and the far bank. I'd feel happier if we had a winch.' Hands on his hips, he eyed the creek, then took the filled containers I handed him as I scrambled back up the bank. He reached into the side pocket for the map, which he folded to the section he wanted and studied for a bit. 'Got it,' he said. 'I figure we're somewhere here and this is Crossways Creek.'

I swiped my hair back and leaned over his shoulder to see as he tapped the name printed along the blue line.

'So,' he continued, his finger tracing its course, 'it runs past the Jump-up, which means we're likely heading for the general vicinity of the commune.'

I was surprised. 'Have we come so far? It doesn't seem like it, for all the time it's taken.'

'I've been keeping track of the mileage and it's pretty close. Depends how high up the creek we are, of course. No way of knowing that, but there're ridges ahead, and the commune's in the ranges, so we're maybe not all that far away.'

Remembering our previous visit there, I said dryly, 'I daresay they won't be that thrilled to see us again.'

'We don't have to stop. Well, we probably should,' he amended. 'To check if that vehicle we heard came through, and who was in it.' He settled himself behind the wheel and handed the map across to me. 'Looks okay.' He nodded at the creek. 'I can see the bottom – it's gravel, so we should be right to cross.'

We chugged over in first gear, the diesel note deepening as we climbed the far bank and picked up the track. Ben grunted with satisfaction as it ran parallel with the creek for a kilometre or two, then frowned as it bore away east again.

'It could just be a detour around broken ground or particularly rough country,' I pointed out, seeing him tense up and the frown deepen.

'It's not that.' He was staring through the wheel at the dash. 'The engine's heating up.' He stopped, pulled the bonnet control and got out.

I unclipped my seatbelt to follow and heard him swear. 'What is it?' I came to his shoulder and peered past it. 'Oh, that's not good. How long . . .?'

'A while, obviously.' He rubbed a hand over the back of his neck as we both eyed the top radiator hose. The heavy rubber was perished at one end and had peeled away from its coupling. Ben swore again and kicked the front tyre. 'It'll cook the goddamn motor. Jesus! What happened to vehicle inspections before they're leased out? Any mechanic worth his pay should've picked that up.'

'Can we . . . Have we got anything to patch it with?'

'Like what exactly?' he demanded, then his glare vanished and he said penitently, 'Sorry. Sorry, Em. Not your fault. I doubt it though. Basic tool kit and one spare tyre seems to be the go for hired vehicles. But I'll take a look in case . . . Even a bit of wire would help. If I took a twitch around the hose, it might hold it together a while longer.'

'The handle of the billy?' I suggested, and he brightened.

'It could – yeah, worth a try, anyway.'

A search of the vehicle provided us with the canvas roll of tools, a plastic tube containing a chamois leather, and a tyre pressure gauge. I pulled the billycan from the carton that served as our tuckerbox and eyed the handle, which seemed too stiff to be useful.

Ben, meanwhile, had tumbled the tools out of their holder and was busy folding the stiff fabric about the damaged hose pipe. 'Might work for a bit,' he muttered. Using the pliers, he detached the billy handle from its lugs, straightened it out, then seated it around the canvas-wrapped pipe and twitched it tight, teeth bared with tension as he waited for it to snap. It didn't, and I let out the breath I'd been holding. He topped up the radiator and closed the bonnet.

'What're the chances it'll work?' I asked.

He shrugged. 'I'm no mechanic. If the motor heats up again, we'll stop. Every kay we make is one less to walk, and it could come to that, Em. I'm sorry. I should've stuck to the highway. I just hope to Christ I'm right about the track and there's someone at the end of it.'

'It's not your fault. We made a joint decision,' I said. 'And if we don't know where we are, neither does our tail.'

'Or anyone else,' Ben said heavily. 'Don't forget that. Hop in.'

A nerve-racking couple of hours followed. Our repairs seemed to be holding up, although the canvas leaked water persistently, but not to any great degree. We stopped twice to check things and poured another two bottles into the radiator. As time inched towards noon, I no longer noticed the road or our surroundings, and Ben kept an eye constantly on the temperature gauge, watching that the needle stayed below the danger level. It came as a surprise, therefore, when I glanced up and saw the rockface looming ahead.

'Is that the Jump-up? It doesn't look the same.'

'It's the back side of it,' Ben said tersely. He slapped the wheel. 'Damn it, we're all the way round behind it, with no way through. The commune's on the other side.'

'But this track must link up to another one,' I said. 'It makes no sense to have a road to nowhere.'

'I hope you're right. Otherwise we'll have to hoof it to the camp.'

'Then what?'

He sighed harshly. 'A lift back to Bloodwood Creek? Unless they've got some way of messaging the town. Maybe the mechanic at the servo would come out? Or there might be one at the commune.'

He changed down for a bend and I glanced worriedly at the stark line of the ridge against the sky. It wasn't quite per-pendicular; the incline was towards us, which is why it had looked so wrong to me. In our first sighting the rock had leaned away from us, but now, approaching from the west, the face it showed was in shadow, lending it a forbidding aspect. The scrub huddled below it, as though cowed by its looming menace. Something caught my eye. The briefest flash, there and gone again, and I leaned forward, searching the shadows. Then I saw it.

'There's a roof – a building, Ben! There! Under the tall trees – and a fence too.'

'I see it.' He sat forward in his seat. 'Well, hallelujah!' Then he sobered instantly, saying, 'If there's anybody there. Might be abandoned.'

'It isn't. There's smoke, look! Well maybe don't.' I was giddy with relief as we swept down a bank into a shallow creek, the crossing roughly flagged with slabs of stone. Ben, obeying, dropped his gaze and braked abruptly, then took it at a slower pace.

On the far bank we broke through the last bit of scrub and saw a dwelling of what appeared to be adobe, with a cor-rugated iron roof overhanging its walls. It was set – nestled, really – amid a grove of trees and fronted with a low verandah. The fenceposts I had spied surrounded a netted veggie garden and I got a glimpse of more corrugated iron and a ramshackle-looking yard made for some smaller animal like sheep or goats tucked away in the scrub.

'Is it a station, do you think? A homestead? It's not marked on the map,' I said.

'Pretty downmarket if it is,' Ben replied disparagingly. He pulled into the shade and stopped. 'All looks a bit secondhand, doesn't it? No paint, no frills, and that bloody road . . . Well,' he said as he pushed the door open, 'let's go see who's home and if they can help. There's a shed back there. A place this remote, you'd think they'd have a few spare parts on hand.'

Despite the thin column of smoke spiralling from a chimney set towards the back of the small house, the place appeared deserted. Anybody there must have heard our approach but nobody came to meet us. A peewee called on a high insistent note from among the trees that, now I was closer, I realised were part of a small orchard. There was mango, paw-paw, avocado and, crowded towards the back, the rustling green flags of a banana patch. A stand of bamboo sighed in the little breeze where Rhode Island hens scratched and clucked.

The vegetable garden was a busy section of earth, with a plethora of closely planted greens and root vegetables interspersed with marigolds already in flower. To control the nematodes, I thought, trying to overcome the unease the silence bred. Maybe the commune was closer than we thought and this was the home of another member, an outlier from the main camp?

When we were close enough to the verandah, just unlined iron over bush timber rails with a floor of roughly matched stone slabs, Ben sang out, 'Hello, the house! Anyone home?'

'What d'you want?'

The reply was so sudden, I jumped. The top half of a man had emerged from behind a metal cylinder set on a stand abutting the house. It was a tank, I realised, presumably for hot water, judging by the copper piping. The man was shorter than Ben and older. His neatly clipped beard showed grey at the edges, though his hair, under a battered and dirty felt hat, was still dark, as were his brows, presently drawn together in a scowl.

There was an unfriendly rasp to his voice as he spoke again. 'This is private property. And that'—he jerked his head at the way we'd come—'is a private road.'

'Sorry, mate,' Ben said. 'It's not signposted, so we didn't know. We're not intentional trespassers. Actually, we're in a bit of strife and that's why we stopped to see if you could help us out. I'm Ben Grier and this is my wife, Emily. We took the road into Notting Hill to have a look, you know? Then sort of followed the track on and our radiator hose quit on us. It's a hire vehicle and the damn thing's split – the rubber's perished. I reckon we were lucky to get this far. But there's just no way we'll make it back to Bloodwood Creek without a replacement.'

'We're really sorry to have to bother you,' I put in. 'We were actually making for the commune over the way. We visited them before and thought maybe they would be able to help, or could send a message into town for us. I know they've no phone, but do you know if they have a radio?'

'Yeah, they do.' Either Ben's explanation or my presence had allayed his initial grumpiness or suspicion, and he came fully into view, stepping onto the verandah to reveal muscular brown legs in shorts below a t-shirt and – I gulped at the sight – a rifle carried negligently in his right hand. He saw me looking at it and set it aside. 'Can't blame a man for taking precautions.' He spoke gruffly. 'There's a murderer on the loose. Heard it on the wireless this morning.'

'The Outback Killer? He was supposed to have been seen near Tennant Creek.' I hesitated before continuing, but he deserved to know, in case the sighting had been wrong. 'We heard a vehicle behind us yesterday, but we didn't see it and whoever it was took the other track where it forks. Has anyone else come through?'

He shook his head. 'He's either lost then, or turned back. Nobody's come by here.'

'It's very isolated,' I remarked. 'Are you all alone out here, Mr . . .?'

'Rick'll do,' he said. 'Nope, there's me and the wife. We like the quiet. Well,' he said, rubbing his hands together as he came forward, 'let's see the problem then. I dunno that I can help, but you'll be wanting to get on.'

A pretty strong hint, I thought, that he'd appreciate it if we left and the sooner the better. Ben led the way and as I turned to follow him I saw movement in the shadow of the doorway. The wife, I thought. I had a ten-second glimpse of a thin scarred face half veiled by long black hair before the figure dodged out of sight, leaving the impression of a dull-coloured dress above a set of slender ankles emerging from work boots.

'So what brought you out here, Rick? Wherever here actually is,' Ben asked chattily. 'Does the place have a name?'

'Yeah, it does. It's the Jump-up block, a homesteader's lease. Six hundred and forty acres – you can put that into hectares if you want. Used to be an old mineral field till it was granted as a lease to the original owner. Freehold, in case you think I'm squatting,' he added truculently. 'It takes in the valley where

Kilmet's mob are. The locals reckon we're nuts, but we're just a like-minded group sick of the way the world's going and wanting out of the rat-race.'

'Fair enough,' Ben said pleasantly. 'I guess you can't get much further out of it than you are here. So what was the field about then?'

'Copper. Bit of lead too. Distance killed it, and bigger and better finds elsewhere.'

We reached the vehicle. Ben popped the bonnet and both men stood looking at the repair job. Rick grunted and tugged at the edges of the canvas to reveal the crumbling lip of the rubber beneath.

'See what you mean. Come on then.' He jerked his head at Ben. 'We'll have a fossick in the shed, see what we can find.' He headed off at a tangent to the house and finding myself not included in the invitation, I wandered slowly around the garden area, though it was less that and more a gradual blending of bush growth into orchard. There was nothing ornamental to be seen apart from the bamboo and I knew from articles I'd read that there were a hundred uses for that, while the green shoots were edible. The Jump-up was plainly a survivalists' paradise. The far yard held a goat placidly chewing its cud, so Rick and his wife obviously had milk and possibly cheese and meat. The scratching hens would supply eggs, the garden patch vegetables, and the orchard all the fruit they could want. I spied the cactus limbs of a dragon fruit halfway up a shade tree near the house, and passion vines swarmed willy-nilly over anything they could reach.

Investigating further, I found that the goat pen was con-structed from palm logs, hauled, I assumed, from the creek

where their feathery tops could be seen. The goat bleated at me
and I wandered over to scratch her face. One front leg seemed
to have been broken; it was splinted and bound in sacking,
plainly the reason for her captivity. A cut-down drum beside
her was filled with leafy greens and bits of scrub. The rest of
the flock (it was quite a spacious yard) must be out bush.

Movement caught my eye in the vegetable garden. The
woman was crouched there, half hidden behind young tomato
bushes as she watched me. The moment our eyes met she
dipped her head, letting the dark hair mask her face. I caught
only a glimpse of the scar and felt an instant pity for her. It
bisected her brow and the outer corner of one eye, giving that
side of her face a slight droop.

Smiling, I took a step towards her just as her head rose,
then she shot to her feet and ran for the house. I stood there
in the open watching as the nose of a vehicle appeared, revving noisily as it breasted the creek bank. Ben and Rick had
just emerged from the tree shadows, both carrying something – tools and, I hoped, the spare part we needed. Seeing the
approaching vehicle, Rick dropped his load and followed his
wife at a dead run to the house. I can only put it down to the
fact of the others' presence at the Jump-up that I didn't follow
Rick's example. It was our tail, I knew even before I noted the
vehicle's colour and numberplate, for who else would be on
that road? So we had been found, but it no longer seemed to
matter so much. It would give us a chance to front the driver
and learn who had sent him and why.

'Did you find something?' I called to Ben.

'Yeah. Perfect match.' He started towards me, stepping
quickly as the vehicle surged forward without slackening

speed. The driver must have been caught flatfooted; he hadn't expected either the dwelling so skilfully disguised by the trees, or to find us there in the open, observing him come. He would scurry away, his cover blown.

That's what I thought, but then his foot went down, the engine roared into overdrive and I had a split-second glimpse through the windscreen upon which the sun was dazzling, of a felt hat, a stubbly face and the sudden flash of bared teeth as the vehicle came at me like a charging bull. Ben's voice howled my name in sudden terror but all I could see was the monstrous shape of the bull bar tearing towards me.

'Run!' my brain screamed but my legs wouldn't move and there was no time anyway. The steel smashed into me, and I felt an immense force scoop me onto the bonnet, roll me across it, then throw me off. The ground rushed at me like a brick wall. The enormity of the impact drove the breath from my body, and I heard something crack like a whip in my ear as my head slammed into a tree trunk. My last muzzy thought was that the bull had got me. Then the world went away.

21

I woke to the frantic repetition of my name. Everything was blurry. There was dirt in my mouth and my eyes. Somebody was making piteous noises, a repetitive 'Uhn ahh' in time with the waves of pain, and Ben's face, white as bone, hovered above me, his lips moving soundlessly. I felt myself fading and tried desperately to tell him, before it was too late, that I loved him but pain stopped the words. There was a background roar of noise as the world went red, then I spiralled down into a little black hole, while my words were still blocked behind my useless tongue.

After that all was confusion. Noise and the frightful agony when I was moved. Ben's face coming and going and, weirdly, a black-haired woman with a hand hiding her mouth and her eyes stretched wide, who bobbed into my sightline and out again accompanied by a brief vision of the young ranger Sam from the national park, his boyish face aghast. He said, 'How you doing then, love?' and held my hand gently, and I blinked and his face changed back to Ben's before it too vanished. Some ragged hold on reality told me that I was dying. It had to be why the faces of those I had recently met kept appearing. But it didn't seem to matter. Nothing mattered beside the pain, not even the idea I weakly grasped at, that death might provide the answer to where Aspen had gone.

The jolt of being carried, like a corpse on a bier, dragged me back to life, but the blackness kept rolling over me with dreams of my mother and the farm. Dad said, 'You saddled up then? Ready to go?' and I sprang joyfully onto Soldier's back. Aspen watched from the garden. 'You should come,' I said. 'It's fun.' But she turned away and faded into the mist that had rolled down from the range. It damped our shoulders as we rode and made the scrub drip, cloaking the trees in strangeness.

'Are you sure, Emily?' Mum said. 'You're so young. If you would just wait a year . . .' But consumed as I was with the pains and ardour of first love, how could I bear to do so? Ben and I danced out onto the balcony amid the potted palms and he kissed me by the railing with the city lights below us like fallen stars. The good cheer and laughter of the wedding party dimmed to nothing in his embrace. We were honeymooning in Fiji and I smelt the brine of the endless Pacific and the toasty warmth of the sun on my bikini-clad body.

A stranger pushed into my space to squeeze my hand, dissolving the beach. He frowned down at me as I stared at his moustache. 'Emily, can you hear me? We're taking care of you.'

Then somebody said, 'We've got her, doc.' And the light was so bright I moaned and turned my head, letting the black wash over me again.

'You're all right dear,' someone said, and I felt the sea lap over my hips and laughed as Ben grabbed me up in his arms.

Of course I was! I had my love and was the happiest girl in the whole world.

I woke eventually to a weariness I could never have imagined. I dimly knew it wasn't the first time. There had been hands that pulled and lifted me often before, and the muted earlier glimpse of quiet rooms, but this time I was waking up myself. It was the work of Hercules to open my eyes, and when that was accomplished I saw a dim light and the profile of my father's face. My vision was blurred. I moved my lips but only a croak came from them. It was enough, however, to alert him. His head turned and our gazes met, even as my lids began to droop and close.

'Emily! Sweetheart, you're awake. I'll get—' But I didn't hear the rest, drifting off again, though I was comforted by the knowledge of his presence.

The next time I surfaced I was more aware: of pain, and the oxygen tube irritating my nose, and a swelling that half-closed my left eye. I murmured 'Ben?' and the nurse doing something at the foot of my bed smiled brightly and said, 'Oh, you're back again. How do you feel?'

'Hurts,' I croaked. 'Thirsty,' and she came and wrapped my lax hand about the morphine pump attached to my chest. 'Press that when it hurts. I'll get you some ice chips and tell them you're awake, shall I? They've been waiting for ages. I told them they should leave and come back but they refused.'

'Where?' I asked muzzily. She wrote something on a chart and hooked it over the bed-end, clipping away the pen she'd been using.

'. . . are you? Hospital, dear. In Armidale. The doctor will be along soon. He'll tell you all about it.'

My mother was first through the door, Dad crowding on her heels. Mum clasped my hand, saying, 'Oh, thank God, Emily! We've been so worried . . . We were frantic when Ben called.' She touched my hair and cheek with gentle fingers. 'Oh, your poor face, sweetheart. But you'll get better. That's the main thing.'

'Ben?' I asked, and Dad leaned forward to kiss my brow, the scent of him bringing tears to my eyes.

'Waiting outside,' he said. 'Only two visitors at a time, and only for five minutes, they told us. He'll come later. Everyone's been asking after you. The phone hasn't stopped since the news got round.'

'Does Pavel know?' It was the first time I had thought of him, or my old life. 'Shorthanded.' My brief burst of strength was spent. 'So tired,' I murmured. '. . . wrong with my eye?'

'Your cheekbone's broken,' Mum said. 'Go to sleep, love. We'll be here when you wake. And don't worry, you'll heal up ju—' The rest of the sentence dissolved into a muddle of sound as I slipped into the vehicle and we drove, Ben and I, along a highway that ran forever. I laughed with delight at the antics of the brolgas performing their courtship routines, and when they changed into masked stilt walkers, I shrieked with pretended fright, just so Ben would hold me close, the way he did when we danced that night. Then I was back home, hurrying through the house, searching the bedrooms, the sleepout, the back laundry.

'Aspen!' I yelled, upset and weary of the game. 'This isn't funny! Where are you? Aspen!' There was no answer but noise grew out of the silent rooms and suddenly a vehicle burst through the lounge wall and I shrieked in terror seeing it come for me, the black metal of its bull bar an implacable wall of steel that would smash my fragile body to pieces.

I jolted awake to find Ben sleeping in the chair beside me. The light streaming in through the window had a softened look about it, though whether from the glass or because it was late, I couldn't tell. My hand seemed strengthless as I pushed it towards where his lay, but the touch was enough to wake him. His eyes fluttered open, found mine and he smiled. There was stubble on his jaw and worry lines between his eyes.

'Em.' He raised my hand, careful of the cannula that linked me to the pole at the bed's head, and kissed it. 'Oh, Emmy, I've been so worried, but they say you're going to be okay.'

'How did I get here?' I looked around at the sink and bedside trolley now pushed to one side. 'Mum?'

'Down in the cafeteria. Keith too. We've been taking it in turns. They got a chopper in to the Jump-up, lifted you out to Darwin. The Aerial Ambulance flew you to Brisbane for surgery, and when you were stable your parents had you shifted here to Armidale.'

'Oh.' I thought about it, bits of dream events resurfacing. 'There was a doctor; he had a moustache, and a woman with a scarred face.'

'That's right. He came with the chopper. The woman was Rick's wife, Marie. You remember Rick?'

I moved my head on the pillow, an action that sent a stab of pain through my face. I lifted my hand to my cheek. 'Mum said . . . broken?'

'The bone there, yes, but the swelling's almost down now. You had the blackest eye! Looked like you'd gone three rounds with a bruiser.' He stroked my hair. 'God, Em! When I saw you bounce off that vehicle I was sure you were dead. Rick shot at him, you know. The driver was backing up for a second go at you when Rick let loose with that rifle of his. He saved your life. The gun certainly changed the murdering bastard's mind. I guess they aren't so used to getting it back,' Ben said with satisfaction. 'The vehicle veered off into the scrub then and beat it. The cops were looking for him, last I heard.'

I found I didn't care. Even the why of it all no longer mattered. I said tiredly, 'How long?'

'Six days, if you count from when you were run over. It was touch and go for a bit. Your heart stopped once and you've had a few days in Intensive Care, but that's all behind you. Seeing you've stayed awake this long, they'll probably start feeding you now.'

As if on cue the curtain that shielded the door was suddenly whisked back and a nurse appeared. 'There you are, Emily,' she said brightly. 'Awake again. That's good. I'll take some obs, and we might freshen that bed up, hmm? If you'll just step outside for a bit.' She looked across at Ben, who kissed my hand again before rising obediently.

'I'll go find Keith and Beryl, tell 'em you're awake,' he said. 'Then I'll be back.'

'I'm not going anywhere,' I replied wearily. My head itched and my face hurt and my whole body was one tired ache. The morphine pump I dimly remembered using had vanished. Presumably that was a good sign, but I missed its soporific effect.

A doctor came to see me with notes from the surgeon who had operated on me in Brisbane. It had been, he said portentously, quite a serious accident. I had required five bags of blood to stabilise me en route to surgery and my list of injuries included a broken cheekbone, ribs and pelvis, but the worst damage had been internal. My spleen had been ruptured, resulting in almost catastrophic blood loss during the flight to Brisbane, where the organ had subsequently been removed. I was therefore at an increased risk of infection, but I was young and healing well, and if I kept on as I was going, I would be out of their care in no time at all. Though I must take things easy for at least a month after I was discharged.

He asked me what work I did and shook his head at my reply. 'No wrestling with large animals for at least three months,' he warned.

'Yes, Doctor,' I said meekly. I would be flat out wrestling a kitten the way I felt, but hopefully matters would improve. In the meantime I needed the bathroom, which meant the indignity of a bedpan or manoeuvring the IV stand around the bed and through a door to the ensuite, then making it out again before I collapsed. Resignedly I pressed the button for the nurse, then fought my way upright, feeling the movement cause pain at what must be the site of the surgical scar in my abdomen.

After that the days passed slowly. I slept and woke and started back on solid food, and as the long days dragged by the crack in my pelvis healed. After this I was encouraged to sit up in a chair and shower unaided. My ribs still hurt, and the scar from the operation remained covered, but the swelling around my eye gradually eased and my face returned to its normal colour, though my cheek was still tender. It was healing with a slight concavity where the bone had been pushed in. Like a special dimple, Mum said.

Ben visited regularly, coming in the evening, or the late afternoon when his office closed. I wondered at his continued attention but didn't question it for fear that it would stop. If he was seeing someone else, she must be very understanding of what he regarded as his duty, a charitable act that my present state only underpinned. I was thin and pale, without energy, and my looks had gone out the window. My skin was sallow and pasty, my hair in strings, but still he visited. The nurses were smitten, I could see, by his faithfulness – and his looks. Once he came with a bouquet of white orchids fringed with delicate ferns, the self-same bridal bouquet I had carried. He produced it with a flourish from behind his back.

'Oh Ben, they're beautiful,' I gasped, thinking of the cost. 'You shouldn't have! I have so many flowers.' The clinic had sent them with get-well cards from the veterinary nurses, as had my parents and friends, and a bunch had even arrived from Stephen in the UK.

His face fell a little. 'Have you forgotten the date?'

'What? Oh.' I had. 'Well, that's sweet of you but I tend not to memorialise that particular anniversary. And I have a few other things to think of right now.'

'Of course,' he said quickly and with a spurt of tired fury I wondered why he couldn't have been as understanding and willing to accommodate my views when we had lived together. 'Well, is there anything you need that I can get you?'

'Information would be good. Nobody ever mentions my "accident". It's like I was run down in the street by a careless driver, not someone trying to kill me. I have no idea what hap-pened between when the Toyota hit me and I woke up here in the ward. Mum and Dad don't know, of course, but the police haven't come calling, and the nurses tell me "best not to dwell on *how* it happened, dear. Just concentrate on getting better." As if that helps.'

'Okay. Look, do you feel you could make it out to the lounge? You must be tired of this room. There are comfy chairs, better than this one anyway, and I'll fill you in on what I can.'

In the patients' lounge, where a large window looked down upon the garden, he settled me with a cotton blanket for my knees and patted my cannula-ed hand.

'Well, I don't know how the bloke who ran you down expected to get away with it, because he must've seen me – maybe not Rick, but certainly me. I was right there, after all. A witness to his action.'

'Perhaps he meant to do for you too,' I suggested. 'It was all a blur. I remember rolling off the bonnet and my face hit-ting a tree.' I raised my hand to finger the damaged cheekbone. 'All I could think at the time was, thank God I didn't go under the wheels. And then it's all a muddle of noise and pain and people's faces. I remember yours and . . . call me crazy but *Sam's*? The young ranger on the bike from Bloodwood Creek? I thought I saw him, but I must've imagined that. God knows how he would've got there.'

'He was there,' Ben said. 'You didn't imagine it. The police had radioed the national park about the Outback Killer being in the area, you see, and Sam took it upon himself to alert the commune and rode the bike over. He'd missed the news

briefing about the sighting at the Three Ways. Turned out
Rick's joint was only about a kay away from Kilmet's place, so
once he got that far he rode on to pass the word there. Just as
well. He had a satellite phone with him – the park has one for
the rangers' use when they're away from headquarters. So he
was able to call in the medical team that came for you.'

'Lord, I'd forgotten all about the murderer,' I said. 'Have
they caught him yet?'

Ben nodded. 'Yeah, the cops finally got him. Nowhere near
Tennant Creek. He'd swapped the numberplates, not the
Toyota, so it was a duff sighting at the roadhouse. While the
cops were chasing that vehicle, he doubled back and snuck off
the bitumen, onto the Notting Hill track, would you believe?
Apparently he was hiding out in that cave we saw, and that's
where they finally nabbed him. His trial's coming up sometime
next year.'

'Dear God!' I said fervently. 'And we talked about not
having time to explore it!'

'Yep.' He nodded. 'You and danger, Em. You go together
like meat pie and peas.'

'You were there, too,' I protested. 'What about the man
who ran me down? Nobody's said if they caught him. Did you
tell me before that Rick shot him? Or did I dream that too?
I can't really remember him,' I confessed. 'I don't know why.'

'He shot at the vehicle because after the driver hit you
he reversed and was heading back for another go. As for the
cops nabbing him, I'm afraid not. It was a matter of timing.
Half the Territory police were probably involved in the hunt
for the Killer, so I guess it gave him the chance to disappear.
That sergeant we dealt with? I spoke to her on the phone right

after you were hit. Sam called it in, you see, when he dialled triple 0, asking for medical help and the police. She wanted an interview but there was no way I wasn't going with you. I've heard nothing from her since, so I assume the bastard's still in the wind.' He stood up. 'Come on. Best get you back to bed before the nurses come after me. I thought if it's nice tomorrow, I might wheedle a wheelchair out of them and we could go out into the garden.'

So he intended to return. Knowing it was weak of me, I said meekly, 'That would be lovely, Ben. And thank you for the orchids. Mum's coming tonight. Dad's well into the farm work now and it's harder for him to get away for such a long drive, and of course my friends are all working, though Phoebe comes sometimes of an evening. What I'm saying is, I do appreciate your visits. It helps to pass the time.'

He took me unawares by stooping to kiss my cheek. 'Don't worry, you're not getting rid of me anytime soon.'

I was still pondering those words as, having delivered me back to my boring room, he strode off down the corridor to the freedom of the healthy, outside world.

22

The following day Ben duly wheeled me down to the garden, and periodically afterwards until I walked there myself, finally free of my wheeled companion.

'Your last visit,' I said, brushing my hand over the lavender bush growing beside the umbrella-shaded chairs where we customarily sat. 'I'm going home tomorrow. Mum'll pick me up at about ten, after the doctor's been. I have a follow-up visit with my own GP next week, then I'm officially cleared to resume my life.'

'You're not going back to work yet, I hope?'

'Not for a week,' I agreed. 'But Pavel must be run off his feet, so I can't take more time than that. We were always flat out, even when the two of us were there.' Lightly I added, 'So you can get back to your life, too. And Ben, I just wanted to say there's no need for you to feel guilt about what happened to me. I brought this on myself, you know. God knows you tried to stop me often enough. And I can't claim I didn't get enough warnings that whoever this was meant business. So don't blame yourself. I've really appreciated your visits, but I don't in any way hold you responsible for what happened. I just want you to know that.'

He shook his head, compressing his lips in exasperation. 'Emily, damn me if you are not the most aggravatingly dense woman I've ever had to deal with! I'm not here because I blame myself – though I do. Traipsing daily to your bedside isn't any sort of weird attempt at atonement. I come because I want to! For a long time now, I've known what an idiot I was to ever let you go. I want you back in my life, Em. I still love you – in fact, I don't think I ever stopped doing so.' His eyes searched my face and he grimaced. 'I know, I know. Arguments got in the way and my stupid pride and, yes, maybe we were mismatched at first – you too young, me too arrogant and full of myself – but we've both changed. Can't we try again, love, please?'

Part of me was thrilled at his words but another, not so admirable, piece of me wanted to hit back at him for the pain and hurt and abasement I had suffered through all the lonely times of needing him when he wasn't there.

'And suppose I don't want to? Suppose I'm no longer willing to sit at your feet adoring you? What then? I have my own life, my own career and I don't intend to give them up to be your ornament again. I want a home and a family, not just a peacock of a husband who simply wants to wear me on his arm for his own glorification.' He winced at my description but I carried on regardless. 'I'm no longer an impressionable nineteen, you know. If it comes to that,' I added dryly, 'I'm no longer the ornament I once was, either.'

'You were never more beautiful to me than you are right now,' he said, and took my hand, cradling it in both his, his eyes penitent. 'I do know how I failed you. And I promise it will be different this time. Of course I don't want you to give up your career, I know how hard you've worked for it. I've come to realise that I want a family too – your children and mine. Sweetheart, you were always generous in your love. Won't you grant me this last chance?'

I couldn't refuse him, not when it was what my own heart had yearned for. Temporising momentarily, I warned, 'I'm not leaving my life here – my job, my patients, my family. Are you sure you're not going to want the city lights again? Because it's no good us getting back together if you're going to be hankering after the Sydney high life.'

'God, no. Those days are gone. I'm perfectly content here – at least I will be if you'll come back to me. Why do you think I chose Armidale? I could have set up anywhere. Every fair-sized town needs an accountant, after all.'

I was stunned, having assumed it was a coincidence. 'Because of me?'

'My dear girl, of course. My wanting you back is not a sudden flash in the pan. It's been a long campaign, but I never envisaged it ending in me almost getting you killed.'

'You didn't,' I said automatically.

'There is one thing,' he said huskily. 'I have to know if you still love me. It would serve me right if . . . but just tell me. There's no-one else, is there?'

'No,' I said. 'There never has been. What about you? Can you say the same?'

He shook his head. 'Nobody that mattered. I fell for you and you're the only one I want. Tell me I can come tomorrow to pick you up and take you to my place. That we can become a couple again.'

My expression must have answered, because I found myself hugged in his arms before my murmured acquiescence could possibly have registered. Almost instantly his embrace slackened as he remembered my condition.

'I didn't hurt you, did I?' he asked anxiously. 'You're so thin, Em! I can feel all your ribs.'

'It's nothing that love won't cure.' I kissed him, wishing my body was stronger, that I had the energy I needed to love him properly.

'Then you shall have it in spades,' he promised, 'in shovelfuls, and if that's not enough I'll hire a front-end loader. The past will be like a bad dream, a nightmare we've wakened from in our right minds and will never think of again.'

'And Aspen?' some contrary part of me asked, despite how precious it was to hear his words and to have my longings fulfilled.

'She's gone,' he said, 'lost. But we are here, with the rest of our lives to look forward to. That's all that matters, love. Thank you for your trust in me. I swear I'll never let you down again.'

Later that day, having hugged my news to myself in the intervening hours, I rang Mum and told her that Ben would make the pick-up tomorrow morning. She would be pleased, I thought; both my parents held old-fashioned views on marriage being a permanent institution.

'I can come,' she protested. 'I don't mind, and he'll be working.'

'Not tomorrow. He's taking me home and there'll be stuff to sort out. I won't start back at the clinic for another week, and he's having that time off. His partner can cope, he says.'

She gave a little gasp. 'You're moving back in with him? Oh, Emily! Are you absolutely sure? Your father will be pleased – he's always liked Ben – but I don't know. He says Ben's changed for the better since we first met him. And I have to admit he's shown a proper devotion ever since he went north to find you. All the same, are you certain it's the right move while you're still so weak and dependent? Are you happy, lovey? That's the thing.'

'Very,' I said tremulously. I still felt absurdly fragile emotionally as well as physically, and teetered now on the edge of tears. I sniffed. 'I never stopped loving the wretched man, you know. I've been going through the motions of living for so long, and now . . . and now—' I swallowed a sob.

'Are you crying?' I heard the concern in her voice. 'Shall I come in?'

'No, no. Don't mind me. I'm . . . it's just so strange to feel really happy again. I'm fine, Mum, truly. Love you, bye.' I hung up and wiped my eyes, fingering the dint in my cheek as I did so. It was a little tender still, but the bruising had gone, the damage repaired, as, if it were visible, would be the case with my heart.

Ben's place, my new home, turned out to be a modest two-bedroom brick veneer with a broad chimney in the living room and double-glazed windows to handle the bitter New England winters. Nothing like the huge, mezzanine palace we'd started our married life in. The kitchen was modern, with a microwave,

an electric stove and dishwasher and a huge fridge. There was
a bunch of flowers arranged clumsily in a water jug on the
scrubbed pine table. My heart melted as I looked from them to
his face watching anxiously as I took it in.

'It's lovely. Are you renting?'

'It's mine – ours. I bought it when I moved here. There's
a verandah too, nice in winter. It's closed in at one end, like a
glass box, and catches the morning sun. Great place for coffee
when there's frost on the ground. It's all a bit bare at present.
I'm not so good at the homey stuff.' He threw up his hands.
'As you can see I don't even have a vase in the house.'

'That's easily fixed.' I was opening cupboards, checking
supplies. 'I'll make a list. What have we got for our lunches?
Maybe we should shop today.'

'Not you,' he said firmly. 'Make a list and I'll pick it up, but
for now you should be resting. What about you lie down and
I'll make you a cuppa? You have to take thing easy for a bit.'

I was glad to. I snuggled into the pillows in the main bedroom, watching his image in the wardrobe mirror as he lowered
the blinds and tiptoed out. 'I'm not going to sleep,' I said, but
it was so peaceful with none of the hospital noises, like call
buttons and nurses' footsteps, that I drifted off. It could only
have been a few minutes before I was woken by the ringing of
a phone. I lay listening to the muffled tones of Ben's voice and,
in a little while, his footsteps approaching the bedroom.

I pushed myself up against the pillows as he entered carrying two mugs, a plate of biscuits balanced perilously atop one
of them. 'No tray either,' he said, apologetically.

I rescued the biscuits. 'Something else for the list then. Was
that the phone?'

'Yes.' He handed me a mug and sat down on the bed. 'A bit of a coincidence coming today, but it was the cop from Darwin, Sergeant Bader.'

'Oh, yes?' I took a sip of the tea. 'Why was she calling?'

'It's good news. They've found him, the man that ran you down – well, his body.'

Startled, I almost spilled my tea. 'He's dead? How?'

'It looks like Rick did for him after all, when he shot at the vehicle. He must've hit the driver, because they found a bullet in the corpse. From a .303, same as the rifle Rick was using. Bader said preliminary findings are that it wasn't immediately fatal, because he drove a good distance first before bleeding out. Last week the pilot of a mustering helicopter saw the vehicle nose down in a scrubby creek, way off the track. He alerted the station people and they went out for a look. So the cops are assuming he must've been in a semi-conscious state by then, got off the road as a result of it, and ended up passing out and crashing into the creek. His body was still behind the wheel when the rescue team arrived.'

'Oh.' I digested this. 'Is Rick in trouble? I mean, if he shot him, isn't that manslaughter?'

Ben shrugged. 'I expect they'll question him but he was saving your life, so I can't see a charge coming out of it. I'll give a witness statement to that effect. Apparently I can hand it in to the local cop shop and they'll send it through. I'll have to attend the inquest, but that's probably months away.' He drew a deep breath and smiled at me. 'So the good news is it's over, Em. We can forget the whole thing and get on with our lives.' He raised his brows at me as he saw my frown. 'What?'

'We still don't know why he was after me, or even who he was. Did Sergeant Bader say?'

'Yeah.' Ben snapped his fingers. 'What was it . . . Barry, Bart, Bert. Something like that. The surname was Fendon. A stranger, but she reckoned half the population of Darwin is transitory. He wasn't known to the cops. Or to me. How about you?'

I shook my head. 'Not that I'm aware of. Which makes it all the odder,' I said slowly. 'If it's not personal, then somebody must have paid him.' The realisation when it came was like a blow.

Sensing something amiss, Ben put down his mug. 'What is it, Em?'

'Well, don't you see? It means whoever's behind it is still out there, so it isn't over after all.'

23

The extra time off for recuperation that I had granted myself passed quickly. Stepping back into my marriage was like moving out of empty darkness into a warm, lighted room. Our lovemaking was intense and gentle, Ben worrying needlessly for my physical welfare; I was daily gaining in strength and my heart and body was hungry for him. I bloomed under his attention, beginning to regain some weight so that the gauntness of my frame softened and my hair, which had always been my best attribute, resumed its shine and bounce. Nothing would change the extra dimple my face had acquired, marring the symmetrical line of my cheek, but that was a small price to pay considering the gravity of its cause.

I had been lucky, I thought, remembering that hazy glimpse of the frightened-looking scarred face that had loomed so briefly above my semi-conscious self back at Rick's place. It was strange; I could remember her, though I had little memory of him. He was a shape in shorts, running – though I couldn't remember where. Ben had tried prompting me, describing him and his dwelling and the spare part they'd found in the shed, but it was as if my mind had been wiped of all but a few vivid images. I couldn't remember the night we'd spent in the car, or the days in Intensive Care in the Wesley Hospital in Brisbane. For me, life had begun again waking to find Dad by my bed.

Notting Hill had also gone from my memory. I knew we had been there, but beyond the cave, which for some reason had stuck, I had no recollection of the airfield or the road trip. The accident had caused a concussion, the doctor told me, and the lost fragments of memory could return, or conversely remain missing forever.

'What was her name?' I asked when Ben appeared with the coffee he'd gone to make. It was mid afternoon and we were on the verandah, sheltered from the wind by the closed end. 'You know, I've been thinking we should get a cat.'

'Why not, if you'd like one.' He deposited my coffee on the plank table beside the basket chair where I'd curled up. 'Whose name – the cat's? Shouldn't we get it before you start deciding on names?'

'Thanks.' I lifted my mug and sighed with content. 'It's lovely here, just warm enough, and I was imagining how nice it'd be to have a cat purring on my lap. No, I was thinking about the Jump-up and I meant Rick's wife. The woman with the scarred face. Do you know?'

He frowned. 'Oh, Marie. I thought she might be German, actually. Dunno why – I didn't hear her speak. Just one of those ideas you get. Was she scarred? I never really saw her front on, only her back. I thought you couldn't remember?'

'Bits are coming back,' I said. 'And she was leaning right above me for a moment.' My hand rose unconsciously to my own face and, misunderstanding, he suddenly put down his coffee and came to kneel by my chair.

'You are still as beautiful as you ever were, Em. I swear it. Nobody would ever even notice that little dint. It doesn't—'

'Heavens, it's not that. I hope I'm not that vain. She just came into my mind, that's all. It was a dreadful scar, right across one side of her face, poor thing. She tried to hide it with her hand, and I remember her from earlier, peering at me through the tomato plants. She seemed very shy, or maybe just terribly self-conscious. She ran as soon as she heard the vehicle coming.'

'It could have been one of the reasons they were out there,' he offered. 'People bail out of the rat-race for all sorts of reasons apart from stress and ecological beliefs. If you'd been traumatised through injury and scarring – well, you couldn't get much further away from it all than she was. Maybe Marie was the reason for the commune? Rick might've bought the land just for her sake. You'd think plastic surgery would be cheaper'—he shrugged—'but who knows?'

'I suppose.' I squeezed his arm gently. 'Sorry. I don't mean to sound neurotic. Her face just popped into my head. Mum rang earlier – she and Dad are coming over for dinner tonight. Leaving about now, so they should be here before seven. He trucked cattle off this morning, so he's got a clear half-day. Mum insisted on bringing the main course, so I've made a flummery for dessert. Could you pop out and fetch a bottle of wine? Red, I think, because knowing Mum and her drive to get some weight on my bones, she'll have made her hunter's stew, which is beef.'

'I can do that. Anything else you want?'

'Maybe a light beer for Dad? He's driving so he'll only have the one, and perhaps half a glass of wine.'

'I'm on it, Em.' He drained his mug, dropped a kiss on my hair and went to collect the keys.

I stayed curled up on the chair, hearing the car start up and drive away, content for the present to remain where I was. Much of my energy had returned but I still had times when my body relished a rest. I would be back at work in the clinic the following Monday, picking up the final pieces of the life I had left to rush off on my fruitless quest. Not entirely fruitless, I mused. I mightn't have found Aspen, but Ben and I had rediscovered each other, something that might otherwise never have happened. Or at least not so quickly. I smiled a little at the thought, remembering his patient manoeuvring: coming here, changing his job, getting my father to help him . . . So everything had worked out for the best after all. Except that my cousin's whereabouts remained a mystery, and I still had no idea why three attempts had been made on my life. And, I silently acknowledged, I probably never would.

In the meantime, I should set the table and see what I could find in our pocket-sized garden to fill the vase that had been among the necessary purchases I had made for my new home. My week's grace had been well spent; I had turned in the keys of my former flat and, with Ben's help, packed what I wanted to keep from it and disposed of the rest.

Ben returned with the wine, a sixpack of the beer my father preferred and a sturdy box, which he gave to me. 'What's this?' I asked. There were holes in the side and a sudden plaintive sound from within gave me an idea. 'What? Oh, Ben!'

'Well, you said you wanted one.' His grey eyes crinkled into a smile. 'I was passing the Pet Barn and there was a litter in the window. She's weaned, vaccinated, micro-chipped . . . There didn't seem any reason not to buy her. I expect that you can desex her yourself when she's old enough.'

I opened the lid and my heart melted. 'Oh, she's adorable.' Blue eyes, shiny black fur, a white chest and two white front feet. She gave a tiny meow and came trustingly to my hand. 'A black cat – that's lucky. Thank you, Ben.' Cradling the kitten, I reached up to kiss him, then smiled down at the perfect little bundle of cuteness I held. 'We'll have to find a name for you, won't we, hmm? And are you hungry?'

It was the first time my parents had visited. Mum took herself on a tour of the interior, while Dad, beer in hand, inspected the exterior – guttering, downpipes and the contents of the garden. I overheard him tell Ben he'd need to get rid of a clump of rats' tails before they took over, and Ben passed on the news Sergeant Bader had given him.

'Serve the bastard right,' my father grunted. 'Wish I coulda shot him myself.'

'Dinner,' I called from the back door as Mum came up behind me.

'It's perfect, Emily. I see you've kept the cushions from your old place. You'll be very comfortable here and closer to everything. Now, can I help—oh!' She spotted the kitten. 'Well, isn't he a little cutie?'

'She. Ben got her for me today. I think I'll call her Mia. Better than a dog, as she won't mind being alone all day.'

'You sure it's not too soon for you to be starting work?' She stooped to pet the kitten as the men came in.

'I'm fine, Mum,' I said. 'I'm looking forward to it, actually. And I'm quite recovered, so there's no reason not to.' We sat and I started passing plates while Ben poured the wine. Hearing a plaintive wail, I looked down to see the kitten crouching near my foot, tiny tail waving, then she made a tremendous leap that took her a good seven centimetres off the floor before falling back. Laughing, I scooped her into my lap where she curled up and promptly fell asleep. Ben, noticing, smiled across at me, his gaze warm on my face, and a feeling of ineffable joy filled me at the perfection of the moment, surrounded by people I loved, who loved me, all capped off by the absolute trust and acceptance of the tiny creature asleep in my lap.

The following morning, Ben and I left home simultaneously in our vehicles. There was only one garage, so my car was sitting at the kerb – something Ben said we would have to change, though he hadn't yet worked out how a carport could be added onto our smallish plot. He waved as he drove off, giving a little bip on the horn as I turned the key. I lifted my left hand in reply, my wedding and engagement rings that I was once again wearing catching my gaze. Behind me the house slumbered in early winter sunshine, and smiling a little I pictured the pink-tongued yawn of my sleepy kitten somewhere within it. She'd have the day to herself to explore her environs. I hoped her nose would take her to her food and that she would find the litter tray when it was needed. And be happy to see me on my return.

Humming to myself, feeling a purpose that had been missing for too long, I joined the stream of traffic, glad to be back in the bustle of ordinary life, the past months falling away like a forgotten dream.

At the clinic, eagle-eyed Phoebe immediately spotted my rings as she held out her arms for a hug, crying, 'Welcome back, stranger.' Then immediately demanded the reason for their appearance.

'Ben and I have got back together,' I said airily. 'Who's shifted my chair?'

'Who's Ben?'

'My husband.' And at her widening stare, I added, 'You knew we were separated. Well, now we're not. He came north to find me. I'll tell you all about it at coffee time. What's *happened* to this place? All my files are missing too.'

'Pavel's got them. He had your patients, so of course he needed your files. Let me just find today's list and divvy it up.' She tossed her pony-tailed head as she worked the keyboard and shot me a warning glance. 'And don't think I don't want *every* detail. Jeez, girl, you go on holiday, half kill yourself and come back with a husband? That's a tale I want to hear.'

I grinned. It was good to be back. 'I've missed you, but tales come with a price. You'll be buying the muffins.'

24

My old life settled back around me like the comfortable folds of a well-worn coat – with the addition, I thought tranquilly, of a handsome buttonhole crafted from dreams and happiness. Winter was upon us and crisp mornings were succeeded by evenings spent in front of a log fire, and frosty nights under the doona. The newness of our resumed marriage was as intoxicating as wine, our bodies as hungry for each other as if this new phase was an extension of our distant honeymoon. We made vague plans to visit Ben's parents but ended up phoning them instead. Ben's scheme of building a shelter for my car was shelved, along with the ideas I had for transforming the garden.

Instead we walked, hands linked, through the park where the fallen leaves lay soggily underfoot, and explored the city, stopping frequently to browse antique showrooms or drink coffee in cosy cafes. We laughed a lot and read by the fire, and made plans for the summer, then went to bed and made love. I began knitting him a jumper, the jerking ball of wool an irresistible lure for Mia, while Ben frowned and fiddled with the parts of a clock he was putting together for his father's birthday.

'You could just buy one,' I had suggested, but he was determined to craft it himself, carving the face and fitting the individual numbers, then attaching the actual working parts.

'Not the same. When I was a kid, Dad was always showing me how to make stuff. I'd like him to know I haven't forgotten.'

The gift would mean the world to Charlie, I reflected fondly. And tomorrow I would ring Marg again. I was slowly establishing a bond with my mother-in-law, who frankly attributed to me this new, caring version of the son she'd hardly seen in years. I was humbled by the good fortune that had brought the two of us back together.

Mia blinked sleepily beside me, her slitted gaze on the needles working through the wool. I said to Ben, 'Have you much on tomorrow? If you're free, I thought we could take a look at the show. It's People's Day, so the clinic will be closed. And it's Pavel's turn to be on call for emergencies.'

'We'll do that then. It's a half-day at the office. Joe gave Nina the day off, so we'll do a bit of a catch-up on the accounts, then head home.'

'Great.' I speared the needles through the wool and rose, shaking a minatory finger at Mia. 'Don't touch. Coffee, Ben?'

Thousands of people had turned up for the Armidale Show. Ben eventually found a park and we hiked to the entrance, passing families of excited kids. I snuggled my chin into my scarf against the chill of the wind, and tucked my gloved hand through Ben's arm.

'We used to come as kids. Stephen and I loved it. We went on all the rides – well, he did. I usually got sick after two.'

'But it didn't stop you going back?'

'Of course not,' I said. 'Mind, in hindsight I blame the fairy floss. It was always the first thing I'd buy – and see, the stall's still in the same place.'

He glanced across at it, a wheeled kiosk parked just inside the gates, and wrinkled his nose. 'You want some now?'

'No, thank you. Yuck, the things kids think are great! Dad showed cattle here, you know. It's too much bother now, he says. And one year Mum got a first with her dahlias, well, *a* dahlia. It was a beauty, a bronze, about the size of a dinner plate.'

Pavilions stretched away in every direction; we chose one at random and kept wandering, following the crowds, the families heading off to the plethora of spinning, dipping, whirling rides on offer, everything from merry-go-rounds to truly hair-raising roller coasters and something that lifted its cargo to a great height, then dropped it like a stone to the accompaniment of ear-splitting screams. We bought ice creams and a show bag, admired the cats in their decorated cages, the fascinating varieties of poultry and, for a change of venue, the truly magnificent decorated cakes. We made our way to the main ring in time for the showjumping, and spent an hour touring sideshow alley, where Ben repeatedly missed at the coconut shy but won a giant teddy bear for me at the shooting range.

'Where did you learn to shoot a rifle?' I asked, impressed.

'Cadets, at school.' He grinned. 'Plus a little psychology. I figured none of the sights would be true, so I aimed a bit to one side. Lucky I picked the right side.'

'Clever. What about a sit-down and a cuppa someplace? My feet are killing me.'

'Why not? I think we've covered most of it.' He cocked an ear to the voice on the loudspeaker. 'You don't want to stay for the judging? They're parading the champions now.'

It would mean nothing to him, I thought, and I was weary. 'I don't think so.'

'Okay, there're tables over there. Grab a seat and I'll see what I can find.'

Half an hour later, replete and refreshed, we headed back to the vehicle. The sun was setting as we turned into our street, the short winter day done. Ben clicked the garage opener and drove in as I stifled a yawn.

'What do you fancy for dinner?' I asked, collecting my teddy and the show bag, full of the usual junk. 'There's a packet of popping corn in it,' I said, not a little surprised.

'Definitely not that,' Ben replied. 'I'm not really hungry. Maybe in an hour or two I might feel different, but the tea and scones filled me up.'

'Omelette then, or a toasted sandwich,' I suggested, 'about seven? I might have my shower early while you're lighting the fire.' I hoisted the teddy. 'Mia's going to love this. Where is she anyway?'

The kitten usually greeted me at the door, but there was no sign of her as I stepped into the kitchen. 'Puss?' I called. 'Mia, where are you? Kitty, kitty.' She couldn't have got out, I thought. There were dogs next door and she was only let into the garden when one of us was out there too.

'She'll be sleeping,' Ben suggested. 'Try our bedroom.' There was a fluffy rug in there she often curled into. As if he'd read my thoughts he said, 'She couldn't have got out, Em, but I'll just check the back door.'

Dropping the teddy on the nearest chair, I went through to the bedroom but the rug was bare. Truly worried now, I called her again and was answered by a tiny mew from under the bed.

'There you are!' I dropped to my knees and she meowed again and came to me, limping, fur bristling and her ears flat. 'Oh, poor Mia, what happened? She's here,' I called to Ben. 'She's hurt herself.' She mewed with pain when I picked her up to examine her. 'You must have fallen. Did you climb too high, sweetie?'

'I doubt that,' Ben said behind me, a fistful of papers in one hand and a grim look on his face, 'but never mind the cat. Somebody's been in the house. The chances are she ran into him and got booted for her pains. Come and see.'

He used the spare bedroom as an office. His clients' papers and the folders he brought home to work on were stored in a filing cabinet, which had been tipped over, spilling its contents across the floor. The bottom cabinet, which had contained oddments like pens, paperclips, old folders, a snow globe, stray coins and old keys, had been rifled through and flung aside.

Ben retrieved his briefcase from the floor. It had been sliced open and emptied of paper, pens and his calculator. 'I had fifty bucks in that,' he said resignedly. 'Lord knows what else is missing if they were after client information.'

'But who . . .' Depositing Mia carefully on the bed, I went to the dressing table and found that the drawers, which contained spare sheets, had been disarranged, as had the linen closet, and our own wardrobe and drawers. Somebody had searched the house very thoroughly, initially taking care not to be obvious about it, but plainly growing more reckless or frustrated as the hunt continued. 'What was he after?' I said bewilderedly. 'Even the sugar canister's been emptied.' Into the sink as it happened. 'The TV's still there. And the stereo. Aren't they the first things housebreakers make off with?' My amber pendant and sterling silver bracelet, the only pieces of jewellery worth anything, were still in their boxes, and none of the portable items like the coffee maker or the set of high-quality chef's knives in the kitchen had been taken. So why empty the sugar tin?

'He must've been after something specific – information about a client,' Ben said. 'I'll have to go through everything, see what's been taken. Unless,' he said, turning his head to look at the printer, 'they simply copied whatever it was. If that's the case we'll never know.' He placed his hand on the printer and shook his head. 'Stone cold – though that doesn't mean a thing. We've been out all afternoon.'

'How did he get in? Back door?'

'It was fine, as was the front. Maybe a window?'

We checked the rooms, eventually getting a result in the lounge, where the drapes had hidden a small circle of missing glass immediately above the catch on the sill.

'A professional job,' Ben said, 'which means gloves. Bastard probably watched us drive off and was inside five minutes later.'

'Call the police, Ben.'

'I will, but it won't do any good. The burglar's long gone, and we don't know what, if anything, he took. So the cops won't sprain an ankle getting here, if they come at all.'

He was right about that. A patrol car pulled up the next morning while we were breakfasting and a constable walked through the house, viewing the missing circle in the window and the detritus in the spare room, which we had been told to leave in situ. He simply mumbled that there was a lot of vandalism about and left.

I stared indignantly after the receding car. 'It wasn't vandalism. Vandals heave bricks and smash things. This was planned. And when he couldn't find what he was looking for, he took it out on Mia.'

The kitten was currently lying in a nest of soft cloths in the corner of the kitchen. She was badly bruised, I thought, but nothing seemed to be broken. She was eating, and purring when I stroked her, and I'd fixed a light splint to her front leg in case I was wrong about the bone. If she hadn't visibly improved by tomorrow, I'd take her into the clinic for an X-ray.

Ben looked worried. 'Are you saying the office is likely to be targeted? If he didn't find whatever it was, that's the next logical step.' He half rose. 'Jesus! I should've thought of that while the cop was here, got him to drive past and check.'

I said vehemently, 'I don't think it's anything to do with your job, Ben. How would anyone even know who your clients were? Most of your work's done on the phone. I have the strongest feeling that this is to do with the business up north – with Aspen.'

Ben opened his mouth but before he could argue, I said, 'I know – why would somebody trek halfway across the country to break in and search? But why were there three attempts on my life? Don't you see? If they're prepared to commit murder, then jumping on a plane or whatever and searching an empty house, even in another state, pales in comparison. They must think we have something, that we found whatever it was they were chasing Aspen for. Could it have been drugs, do you think? Does sugar look like heroin, say, or cocaine?'

'What?' He stared at me as bewildered as if I'd suddenly turned blue.

'The sugar – they emptied it into the sink.'

'Those drugs come as powder, not crystals,' he said patiently, like someone humouring a lunatic.

I threw up my hands. 'Well I don't know my drugs, do I? Some other sort then.'

I saw the alarm grow in his face as he thought about it. 'You seriously think it's the same mob as up north?'

'I don't know,' I repeated. 'I'm probably leaping to conclusions, but is it too much of a stretch? I mean, we're not exactly poor. We've plenty of stuff a real burglar could've nicked. But all he took was some cash. So he was on a mission and just got lucky with your fifty bucks.'

Ben sighed and scratched glumly at his jaw. 'Unfortunately you're making a lot of sense.' I could see from his eyes that he was worrying over a problem. 'Look, Em, how would you feel about shifting back to the farm for a bit?'

'What? Why would I do that? No way! I can't commute that far.'

'It wouldn't be forever, love.' He took my hand, his eyes pleading. 'And at least you'd be safe. You may not be here.'

'Of course I am,' I said. 'He's been, he's searched, he hasn't found whatever he's after, so why would he come back? Anyway it's out of the question. We're busier than ever and Pavel needs me.'

'Not so much as I do – alive and unharmed. You don't know that this guy won't come back. If he's determined enough to follow us here, it must be a major deal. We can't be talking a few kilos of weed. There has to be something big behind this.'

'There always was. Nothing's changed. We could go to the police and lay it all out, but realistically what could they do? And if I did go to the farm, aren't I just taking the danger with me? What about Mum and Dad? What about you? If he can't get to me, why wouldn't he go after you? You were there too, so aren't you just as likely to have whatever it is he wants?'

We talked about it – argued – until it was time for us to leave for work. Ben insisted on following me to the clinic before heading off to his office. I had instructions to wait for him to collect me that afternoon, instructions I had to promise to obey. He was badly rattled, I saw, and though I tried to brush off his fears, I was spooked at the thought of somebody lurking about, observing us. And I was filled with hatred for the pointless cruelty inflicted upon Mia. Anybody who could hurt a defenceless animal deserved to be locked up for that crime alone.

A week passed, and then another. Ben followed me doggedly to work each morning and home again each night. We had an expensive alarm system installed at the house, along with security screens over the replaced window and the others. As an extra precaution the security alarm was linked to the police station, so even if we weren't home there would be an immediate response. These costly preparations lessened our anxiety but as the days passed and nothing happened, eventually we concluded that our burglar was satisfied we had nothing for him to find.

By the time the end of winter was in sight, we were ready to admit we had overreacted. Ben agreed to let me drive alone as long as I phoned him the minute I arrived and before I left. As emergency patients had a tendency to arrive as we were scrubbing down the theatre, this suited us both. Life went on. We made holiday plans and began to talk about starting a family.

Ben had raised the subject once before when he'd asked me to move back in with him, but I was still a little surprised. I wanted children someday, but from the start I had never been able to visualise him as father material. He had been too driven, too bent on making his mark and rising to the top of his profession. But that was the old, careless Ben, not the man with whom I now shared my bed and life.

'Are you quite sure?' I asked. 'Children take time and work – years of work – and all the love you can give. It's a big commitment, Ben.'

He stiffened, affronted, almost insulted. 'You think I'm not up for that? Our own little boy – or girl,' he added as an afterthought. 'I'd give them everything. And how could I help loving something we had made?'

'That's all right then.' I melted into his arms. 'It's just – well, you don't have any family experience do you? No siblings. You've no idea what you'd be letting yourself in for. And,' I added warningly, 'it might be more than you bargain for. Grandpa Fisher was a twin, you know. Twins often skip a generation.'

'Do they? Well,' he said, as he settled my head comfortably into the hollow of his shoulder and Mia, sensing she was missing out, jumped onto my lap, nestled down and began to purr, 'twice the value. Bring it on, my love.'

*

Then, as is often the way with fate, three separate incidents occurred that changed our lives again. The first was Pavel's announcement that we needed more room in the clinic. 'There's no room to move here,' he said, his dark eyes flashing with intensity as he used his hands to illustrate his words, exaggerating shamelessly. 'We must have more space. So, we're shifting. I've bought a sort of mini warehouse joint in Ashfield and the builders have been working on it. I didn't want to say anything till everything was ready.'

'Ashfield?' The suburb was further away for me, closer to the main hub of town. Parking would be a problem, I thought, and it would add, what, ten minutes to my commute. That was doable. A more central location, though our work mainly arose from the suburbs and the surrounding farms. I said, 'This is very sudden, Pavel. And shifting everything – the stock, the patients – will cause a huge upheaval.'

'We'll close for that, naturally.' His hands drew diagrams in the air. 'A week, ten days at most. I've arranged for Pet Haven to take any serious cases we have at the time. The removalists can handle the packing, and the staff can take a week on half pay.'

'When's all this going to happen then? And what about me?' I looked around at the familiar space, hearing the murmur of the receptionist's voice through the door and the clatter of a cage latch as Phoebe or one of the other nurses removed an animal or returned it to its temporary home. God! It would take days to set up everything again, to sterilise the new rooms and organise the drug supplies. Not to mention fielding the calls of customers irritated at being abruptly cut off from their pet's saviours. Pavel was tremendously popular with his clientele; his skill and devotion to his calling saw to that.

He flashed a smile. 'Take a holiday, Emily. Just a brief one. You work hard, so a week's break won't do you any harm. The big day's on the eighteenth, just six days from now. I'll send out the flyers tomorrow to remind our customers when we'll be closed, and where to find us when we open again.'

It was a lot to take in. I told Ben about it that evening as I cooked and he sat companionably on the low stool that lived under the kitchen bench. 'So, I'll have a week off,' I finished. 'I suppose I should have seen this coming. We *are* cramped at the clinic and sometimes the overflow has to be temporarily housed out the back, which isn't ideal when it rains – animals that need hospitalisation are pretty sick.'

'Mmm,' Ben agreed. He pulled a dish of nuts towards him and selected an almond. 'I had a phone call today from Sergeant Bader.'

'The Darwin cop? What did she want?'

'Just to pass on the date for the inquest on Fendon. She was giving me a heads-up because I'll be called as a witness. She didn't know if you would be – probably not, she said, as you were mostly unconscious at the time.'

I added a dash of fish sauce to the stir-fry I was making. 'When is it?'

'Coincidentally, the twentieth. Six days till you close, you said? I'll have to take a few days off. You want to come with me, seeing you'll be free too?' He rose to stand behind me and circled his arms about my waist, pulling me back against his body as he nuzzled my neck. 'No night markets this time. We'd fly up, hire a car for the day or however long it takes, then fly back. Maybe have a look at Alice Springs while we're at it?'

'How could I refuse? Sounds better than moping here

without you.' I tapped his hand. 'Now let me go before our dinner's scorched black.'

Events, they say, tend to come in threes, as if the universe were in love with that number. The third thing to happen was a phone call from Mum with the news that Uncle Richmond had passed away that afternoon.

I said, 'Well, I suppose it's a blessing really. Who's going to take care of the funeral? Didn't he have a brother somewhere?'

'Yes, an older one, but he'd already died,' Mum said. 'A solicitor's been in touch. Fee held a power of attorney over her husband and she'd appointed Keith as his executor, so it'll come down to your father.' She huffed out a sigh of annoyance. 'As if he hasn't enough to do! And I must say, ever since you told me about Aspen and Rich . . . well, I'm more inclined to dump him in a ditch somewhere than grant him any sort of church send-off.'

'If it's true,' I reminded her. 'I really think it could be, but we don't actually know. So apart from funeral arrangements, what else does an executor do?'

'You'll laugh,' she said without any humour at all, 'but once probate's granted, he'll have to find Aspen. Turns out that the bulk of Fee's estate was being held to finance Rich's care and now that's ended, it all goes to Aspen. Organising that is now your dad's responsibility. I suppose we'll have to advertise, ask her to get in touch.'

'Huh! Best of luck then.' The universe understood irony if nothing else. I put the thought away, and continued, 'Mum, could you do me a favour? Ben and I are taking a little trip in about a week. If we drop her off early on Sunday could you look after Mia for a few days?'

'Well, of course, Emily. Where are you going?'

I had no intention of getting into that, predicting she'd throw a fit. 'Thanks, Mum. It's just a short break while the clinic is being rehoused,' I said. 'Because that's my other news. Pavel's moving to a new location in Ashfield and I've time off while it happens. I'll give you the details later. Love you. Bye.'

25

In the end we took the full week, flying out on a Sunday and booking our return from Alice Springs for the following one. Ben had decided we would drive from Darwin and use the extra days to explore the country around the Alice.

'Great thinking,' I enthused. 'There's Palm Valley and Simpsons Gap, and lots of other places.' I racked my brain to think of some. 'I'm sure there's an Overland Telegraph station. Maybe we could even get out to Ayers Rock?'

'Might be a bit far,' Ben demurred. 'We don't want to spend all the time driving. Let's just play it by ear. But first, Trouble here'—he nodded towards Mia—'has to be delivered. Got everything?'

'I think so.' I took a last look through the house, checking window latches, power points and the dampness of my indoor pots. 'Let's go. We need to be at the airport by eleven, so it'll have to be a quick turnaround at the farm.'

We achieved this, but not without a string of recriminations from Mum for again putting myself in harm's way. 'Tell her, Keith,' she pleaded, turning to my father, then before he could do so, snapping at me, 'I don't know who's worse – you for putting yourself at risk again or you'—she rounded on poor Ben—'for encouraging it.'

'It'll be okay, Mum,' I soothed. 'Nothing's going to happen to me. We'll only be in Darwin for a couple of days anyway. I'll send you a postcard from the Alice. It'll be a proper holiday. I might even get to ride a camel.'

We stepped off the plane in Darwin into the balmy warmth of a tropical winter day. Only, I reminded myself, they didn't have winter. It must have been thirty degrees, with a gentle breeze in the tops of the palms as we rode the airport bus into the city. The brilliant crotons and bougainvillea added to the colourful backdrop of sea and sky and the vivid green of the parks. I had removed my winter coverings on arrival and was down to blouse and slacks when we were dropped off at our hotel, a modest family establishment set back from the bigger, flasher ones dotting the Esplanade.

Once we were settled in our room and I had changed into sandals and a skirt, Ben said, 'What do you want to do? I was thinking coffee and a snack. Then we could see about hiring a vehicle. And I'd better find out where the Magistrate's Court is. We don't want to be late tomorrow.'

'Coffee sounds good.' I hesitated. 'Would you mind if I didn't go to the inquest with you? I haven't been called for it. I thought I might just wander about the city. I didn't really see anything last time, apart from accommodation offices.'

'No, that's fine,' he said. 'There's no need for you to be there. Lord knows how long these things take. You amuse yourself, and I'll meet you after.'

'It won't run longer than one day, surely?'

He shrugged. 'I've no idea. Depends who else they've found to talk to. Rick, of course. The coppers who flew out with the chopper, maybe even the ranger. He was too late for the shooting but he saw the aftermath of the accident.'

'Sam, yes,' I said. 'I'd forgotten that Rick would have to attend. I wonder if he'll bring his wife with him?'

'Not to the inquest,' Ben said. 'She was in the house the whole time.'

I shook my head. 'No, I saw her – after I was hit.' Ben looked dubious and I repeated it. 'I did.'

'Well, maybe,' he conceded. 'God knows, seeing you lying there, I wasn't in any state to notice who was where. You ready then? Let's go.'

Ben hired a vehicle from the same business he had used before, a blue SUV. 'Just in case we have the urge to go off road around the Alice,' he said. That done, we had a late snack at a little bistro behind the Esplanade and eventually located the Magistrate's Court. I bought a hat from a street stall and Ben treated us to ice creams that we ate strolling beneath beach almonds and pandanus in the park fronting the wide stretch of the harbour.

'Great place to laze with a book,' I said. There were seats, picnic tables and gym equipment dotted along several kilometres of concrete path, presently used by cyclists, skateboarders and a variety of pedestrians pushing prams, walking dogs or just striding it out, dodging the runners as they passed. The day had cooled, though the light breeze was still pleasant on my bare arms. We found a seat and sat watching the afternoon light sparkle on a benign-looking sea, its blueness rippled by tiny waves.

'You'd never think there were crocs in there,' I said, 'and God knows what else that'll eat or destroy you.'

'Spoken like a true country wench.' Ben grinned, producing a handkerchief to wipe the stickiness from his hands. He was a beach lover, a surfer, when we first met, with browned shoulders and zinc on his nose, but I had never trusted the sea. He offered me the handkerchief. 'That said, it's strange to see a beach so empty. A waste, really. Shall we make our way back? We could look for somewhere to eat tonight, or dine in – your choice.'

'Let's try the night-life,' I said. 'We missed out last time.'

The following morning, just before ten, Ben set off for the court on foot, leaving the vehicle for me, saying, 'You might want to explore.'

'Only the shops.' I kissed him. 'Have fun. I'll try not to spend all our wealth.'

And in fact I found little to tempt me. I bought a handbag for Mum's birthday, which was coming up, and a colourful batik print shirt for Dad, spent an hour in a gallery featuring Top End Indigenous art and browsed the attached gift shop, where I bought a book and a string bag knotted from wallaby grass by a local Indigenous woman, to carry my purchases.

When I grew tired of the shops, I sought out the bistro from yesterday and bought a takeaway coffee, which I carried into the beachside park. There were fewer people about, I saw, but then it was a working day. A small child was playing with a dog under a truly enormous fig tree and, spying one end of a seat behind the trunk, I headed for it, not seeing until I arrived that it was already taken. The child's mother, I thought, as I hesitated, coffee in hand.

She looked up then and smiled. 'You want to sit? Be welcome. Plenty of room.'

'Thanks.' I settled myself. 'It's a wonderful tree, isn't it? And so good to be out of the sun.'

'It is that.' She had an accent of some sort, but I couldn't pick it. Vaguely British, I thought. She was middle-aged, with a friendly face, and the child was too young to be hers. Grandmother then.

'Do you come here often?' I asked.

'Only days when I have Danny. His mum works three days a week. It suits us both – he has room to play and I can get on with my handwork.' Her fingers were busy as she spoke, drawing wool from a wheeled bag at her feet. She was weaving something, stopping every now and then to add a tassel or a bead from a plastic box on the seat beside her, which also held feathers and crystals.

I watched, fascinated, and realised that she was fashioning dreamcatchers. 'That looks interesting,' I said. 'Do you sell them?'

'At the market, dove. I have a stall there.'

And with those words I knew her. I stared, unsure for a moment. Her grey hair was clubbed short and as she sat slumped comfortably on the seat, wearing a no-nonsense shirtwaister dress and a pair of sports shoes that had seen better days, she looked nothing like her former self. But her voice and her use of the word 'dove' made me positive I was right.

I said, 'You're Mystic Meg. From the night market. But your hair . . .' Of course those black flowing curls had been a wig, and the make-up she'd worn had accentuated her high cheekbones and dark eyes – the very antithesis of the homely granny she now looked. 'You warned me that night,' I said. 'How did you know?'

I had startled her. Her gaze narrowed as she drew herself up and I saw recognition spark in her eyes. 'The lass with the shadow.' She nodded and gave a little shiver, her voice suddenly hoarse. 'Dear Lord, and I felt it touch me. I . . . but you survived. How was that?'

'The knife missed. But I almost died later on. I want to know how you knew. What's your name?'

'Glennis. I was born with the gift – or the curse, if you like – of seeing. Psychic, they call it. I can't turn it off, though God knows I would if I could. I don't need the cards to see, but people are more comfortable that way. And sometimes I need to warn folk. It's as if the bad thing threatening them will come for me if I don't. I'm sorry if I scared you.' She put a tentative hand on my wrist, and for an instant I felt it pulsing there, warm against my own.

'I see,' I said slowly. 'Well, thank you. I didn't pay attention at the time, but afterwards I remembered your warning. That accent . . . Where are you from, Glennis?'

'That's Cornish, that is.' She laughed. 'Bone deep 'tis, and won't be shifted. Thirty years an' all since I left. I lost my man along the way but I have my daughter and the wee lad. Children are the blessing of life. You've none of your own yet?'

'No,' I said. She was gathering up her work, closing the box and folding down the cover of the wheeled bag. 'Are you going? Don't let me chase you away.'

''Tis time, dove.' She smiled at me. It masked her face with sweetness but now that I knew, I thought, I would always be a little afraid of the knowledge behind those dark eyes. What else did she see of the future, my future, that remained unspoken? As if she had divined the question she patted my hand and called to the child. 'Come, Danny, we're leaving. Named for his da,' she confided as the little boy ran to her. 'You could do worse with yours. A strong name never hurts a young lad.' Then she was gone, one hand holding the child's and the other towing her makings bag behind her.

26

I sat on in a daze, coffee forgotten. Had she really meant what I had taken from her words? Could I be pregnant? I cupped both hands over my abdomen as if it was already swelling with new life. Unless I had misunderstood and she simply meant the advice for a later date? Or perhaps it was another trick, like the cards. It was a fair enough assumption that a young married woman would eventually have a child, and she would have noticed my rings.

That must be it. Maybe she was a psychic and all she claimed, but she couldn't see through flesh. That was ridiculous! Then, uncomfortably, I remembered the sheer terror on her face that night as she had fled into her tent.

Almost forgetting my purchases, I returned to the hotel. I wouldn't mention the encounter to Ben, I thought, until I knew for certain one way or the other. There was nothing to stop me going to a chemist right now to buy a test, but the chance was too precious to be so quickly discounted if she was wrong. Which she probably was . . . Still, I wanted to hug the possibility to myself a little longer. My cycle had been irregular

since the attack on me and was only now beginning to settle;
I couldn't really go by dates. So I would wait, and dream and,
once we were home, find out for certain.

The inquest took most of the day. It was late afternoon
before Ben returned with little to add to what we already
knew.

'Did you see Rick?' I asked. We were seated in the small
lounge off the bar, a jungle of potted palms, overhead fans and
cane furniture, where he was enjoying a beer while I sipped
my tea.

He nodded. 'He was there. The coroner actually com-
mended his action, said it had saved a life. Of course his
findings won't be brought down for a while yet. Whole thing
seems to me to be a waste of time. We already know the how
and the why of everything, anyway.'

'Well, not the why. We still haven't a clue about the moti-
vation behind it all,' I pointed out. 'But inquests are held by
law, so I suppose it had to happen. Were you asked a lot of
questions?'

'Oh, yeah. Name, occupation, how I came to be there, that
sort of thing. He was very thorough, that's why it took so long.
The Outback Killer's input was part of it – the fact that he
was the reason your Sam was there with the phone that saved
your life—'

'He's not my Sam,' I interrupted mildly, 'even if he did.
Though actually, I guess that distinction belongs to Rick.
I'd like to see him again. Do you know where he's staying
in Darwin?'

'He isn't. He left straight after they finished with him – that's
what Sergeant Bader said when I spoke to her afterwards.'

'Oh, that's a shame. Still, we can always call in on our way south. I'd like to thank him for saving my life – or at least stopping me from being run down a second time. I wonder,' I added inconsequentially, 'whatever happened to the Prado you had. Do you know?'

Ben regarded me with the baffled look that my mental gymnastics had always produced. 'Where did that come from?'

'Do you? I never gave it another thought until now.'

'I left it to Sam to contact the company, let 'em know where it was. The insurance covered the cost of retrieving it. I wasn't in any state to care what happened to it at the time.' He burped gently into his fist. 'So what did you do with yourself today?'

I told him, including the meeting in the park with Mystic Meg. 'You wouldn't believe how *ordinary* she looked! Except for her eyes. She said the cards are only a prop for customers, and that she really is a psychic. I'm sure of it. She does know things.'

'Maybe.' It was an acknowledgement of my words, not an agreement. Ben believed in what he could see, but he wasn't going to argue with me. 'You finished?' He stood up and took my hand. 'Come on, then.'

'Where are we going?'

'Well,' he said, a glint in his eye, 'here we are with time on our hands and a comfy hotel room. We could hang out the Do Not Disturb sign and make a little whoopee.'

I laughed. 'Why not? And later we can talk properly about the inquest.'

*

I dreamed that night, a jumbled mish-mash of events beginning in an endless park where I wandered, searching for something I couldn't remember the name of, until Mystic Meg appeared. She placed her hands on my lower body. '*The one you seek is closer than you think, dove*,' she said. Then there was a baby in my arms, who began to squall before morphing into Sam, the young ranger, impatiently revving his motorbike. '*Get on if you're coming*,' he yelled. I obeyed and we went flying through scrub and rock towards the Jump-up, which seemed never to come any closer. I remembered the baby and looked down, but my arms were empty and I was filled with a great sense of loss. I clutched desperately at the leather jacket before me, screaming at Sam to stop. We had to go back, the baby would die without me, but deaf to my entreaties he roared on until, in desperation, I pitched myself off the pillion, landing with a thump and a cry that woke me.

'What?' Ben stirred beside me and sat up. 'Em, what is it?'

'Nothing,' I said dazedly. 'I had a crazy dream of riding and falling.' The details of it were already fading – something about the old woman in the park . . . I shook my head. 'You know how it is when you dream of falling. It gave me a start, that's all.' My breath and heartbeat were slowing down, and it wasn't hard to marry the inchoate memories of the baby to the psychic's words. I'd thought of little else all evening. I wanted to believe her and my subconscious had done the rest, including manufacturing a scenario of loss. All mothers, I suspected, carried fears for the young they bore, which their dreams would occasionally echo. You didn't need a psychologist to work that out. I breathed slowly and snuggled against Ben, feeling his arm come around my shoulders in response, and in a little while I drifted back into sleep.

The following morning we left Darwin, heading south down the Stuart Highway with a pale sky above us and the land stretching brown and sere ahead. The lagoons and roadside borrow pits that had been full in April were now either shrunken or dry, and fewer birds were visible. We stopped for coffee at the Bloodwood Creek pub, unrecognised by the busy staff from whom Ben ordered a packed lunch, which came in a small disposable foam box with two packets of frozen juice to keep it cool. The day was pleasantly warm but lacked the fierce humidity of our earlier visit.

'It's strange seeing it all again,' I remarked as we drove away. 'It seems so familiar somehow, the signs and turn-offs, and little places. As if we've been here dozens of times before. Perhaps it's because there're so few of them.'

'Could be,' he said. 'Plenty of traffic though.' Vehicles sped by us, towing caravans and trailers. There were motor homes, and station wagons driven by obvious amateurs in the camping game with gear bundled onto roof racks and filling the backs of their vehicles. Cars zipped past, and buses, and plenty of loaded road trains heading north to the port of Darwin for the cattle trade to Asia.

Then the turn-off for the Jump-up loomed and our speed dropped to a comparative crawl as the tyres met the inequalities of the unsealed track.

'You're sure you want to do this?' Ben asked. 'It's going to take us half a day to get in and back. And there's no saying Rick's going to welcome us. He pulled a rifle on us last time, if you remember.'

'He was carrying one,' I corrected. 'There's a difference.' In the last months my scrappy memory of events had coalesced until I now had a fairly reliable knowledge of what had gone down that day. Only one detail still eluded me. 'How do we actually reach Rick's place, Ben? Because last time we came on it from the other side of the range. Do we have to go to the commune first, then drive back?'

He shook his head. 'Unless we find a track we missed before, I guess we pull up at the Jump-up and hike around it. Can't be more than a kilometre.'

'Right.' I glanced at my feet, glad that I had chosen to wear ankle boots rather than my sandals. 'It's true what the slogan says then: "The Territory State of Adventure".'

The way seemed shorter compared to the first time we had driven it. The SUV made nothing of the track and it was only a little after one when we arrived at the foot of the massive rock wall. Ben glanced at his watch. 'Might as well eat before we set out, but first I'm having a really good look around to make sure there isn't a road in.'

I set out the drinks, now a slush of melting ice, and the sandwiches and waited for him to return from beating the bushes. 'Any luck?'

He grunted. 'Not so you'd notice. Maybe Daniel Boone could tell if a vehicle ever progressed beyond this point, but I certainly can't.'

Twenty minutes later we tidied away the remains of our meal, collected our hats, locked the vehicle and set off. At least, I reflected, there was no danger of getting lost. The great ochre cliff face was the tallest thing for miles around and all we had to do was to return to its base. I said as much to Ben, adding,

'I wonder why it's here. I mean, all the rest of the range has been degraded down to mere ridges, but neither wind nor time seems to have touched it.'

'Core of iron?' he suggested, holding back a branch for me. 'Careful on the slope – that gravel rolls under your feet. Last thing we need's an injury.'

'Right.' I caught his hand and smiled at him, feeling strong and happy in the sunshine. 'Say what you like, but our holidays *are* different, Mr Grier. Who needs to lie on a stuffy old beach when they can go trekking through trackless bush?'

'To visit a trigger-happy hermit,' he agreed. 'You have a bad influence on me. Next thing you'll be talking me into paragliding.'

'Fat chance!' Ben had a phobia about heights, something I'd learned the first time I'd ridden in a glass lift with him. He'd spent the entire ascension of thirty floors with a death grip on the handrail and a bone-white face.

After what seemed more like five kilometres than one, we came out of the low scrub to a glimpse of the well-camouflaged buildings below us to the right. The going was easier then, rock giving way to light gravel and then soil at the edge of the orchard. Ben stopped to disentangle a dead stick from his pants leg so I was a little ahead when I spied a figure moving through the mango grove. It was Rick's wife, Marie. She was hatless, dark hair streaming about her shoulders, humming to herself as she walked. There was something about her carriage and easy stride, the tilt of her head, that jolted my brain. It was like glancing at those drawings that change as you look, from young girl to old crone, and back again. A deception as plain as the ink that drew them, but very hard to see. At that exact moment she saw me and stopped dead, her right hand flying to her left wrist before she hugged both arms against her body. She shrank into herself, the dark hair cloaking her scarred face so that only one terrified eye held mine.

I put my hand out as I would to a frightened animal, gentling my voice as Ben came up behind me. 'Hello, Aspen,' I said. 'We've been looking for you all over.'

27

She froze. Ben, at my shoulder, inhaled in surprise and said, 'What?' in an incredulous tone.

'It's all right,' I said soothingly. 'We're not going to tell anyone or do anything you don't want us to. I've been worrying about you, Aspen. I even thought you were dead. I'm so glad we've finally found you.' I took a step forward, hand still out, and Rick was suddenly there, standing between us, shoving my arm away.

'Get away from her!' He was carrying the rifle again and lifted it, poking the barrel at me.

Ben yelled, 'Hey! Cut it out! What—'

'It's okay.' I lifted my hands, stepping back. 'We don't mean any harm – to her, or to you. Tell him, Aspen. She's my cousin. I just want to talk to her, to help her. That's why we're here.'

Rick scowled. His finger, I noticed, wasn't on the trigger and the rifle, an old .303 like the one Dad kept in the gun safe on the farm, hadn't been cocked.

I let out the breath I hadn't been aware of holding and relaxed a little. 'I'll give her any help she needs,' he said fiercely.

Aspen still hadn't opened her mouth, or given any sign of recognising me. I smiled at her, trying to ignore the still livid scarring on her face. 'C'mon, I haven't changed that much in a couple of years, have I? And you know Ben.'

She shook her head and looked to Rick. 'I don't . . . I can't . . . only her,' she said, frowning, and raised a finger to point at me. 'There's something.' She clutched at her head, mouth stretching in misery or frustration, the words almost a wail. 'I can't . . . There's a horse, and a woman – she was kind – and someone, but I don't know who . . .' She beat at her head with closed fists. 'Oh, why can't I remember?'

Rick folded his free arm around her, pulling her into an embrace. 'Hush, dear, don't cry. Come on, remember what we agreed? If it doesn't come back you don't need it. But you think you might know her? She's the one who was hurt here – maybe you remember her from then?'

'No.' Sniffing, Aspen swept her hair back and stared at me. 'There's something, I just can't . . .'

Ben clicked his fingers in discovery. 'Amnesia. She's lost her memory.'

'So it would seem.' I turned to Rick. 'Look, we don't mean any harm to either of you, but for our own peace of mind, can we just sit down and talk to you both? There are things Aspen – that's her name, by the way, Aspen Tennant – should know.'

He eyed us both, then grudgingly nodded.

'And could you put the rifle down?' I asked. 'You're not going to shoot us. You saved my life last time, firing at the man who ran me down. You're hardly going to undo that now.'

He looked a little startled by my reasoning, glanced down at the weapon as if wondering how it had got into his hand, then gave me an infinitesimal nod. 'Right. Well, you'd better come along then.' His arm around Aspen, her hair once more shrouding her face, he led us out of the trees, across the verandah and into the house.

First impressions had made me expect a shack, but in fact the place was quite comfortable, a definite step up from Kil and Sal's place. Here the floor was paved, the corrugated iron walls sealed, there was plumbing and, judging by the standard fan in the corner, and the light fixtures, they obviously had power, though I hadn't noticed any solar panels. The room was a combination of kitchen and living area equipped with simple pine chairs and table, a wood-burning stove and a padded bench off to one end beside a couple of hassocks, an old couch and an easy chair made with greenhide straps fixed over a timber frame. The walls were lined with shelves in lieu of cupboards, each one held up by carved wooden brackets, and a variety of handwoven baskets, used, I saw, for storage, depended from hooks fixed to the ceiling. A doorway, screened once again by a bead curtain, led off to the rest of the house – bed and bath, I thought, and perhaps a laundry.

Ben, gazing around, said, 'It looks very comfortable. Did you build it yourself?'

'Yes.' Rick vanished through the curtain with the rifle and returned without it, waving a hand at the bench. 'Have a seat.' He nudged the hassocks into a pile by the chair and led Aspen to them. 'Sit, my love. I'm right here.'

Obediently she folded her long legs and sank onto the cushions without letting go of his hand as he seated himself beside her. Brow knitted, she stared at me through her hair in silent agitation, her efforts to remember painful to watch.

I said gently, 'I'm your cousin Emily. The horse you mentioned was mine, and the kind woman was my mum, your Aunty
Beryl. And this is my husband, Ben. You came to our wedding.
When you were a kid we spent holidays together. Your mother
was worried because you'd disappeared. She asked me to find
you.' I hesitated, wondering whether to tell her that her parents
were dead, then decided it could wait. 'Does any of this help?'

'Don't badger her,' Rick said forcefully. 'If she can't remember she can't. Why'd you come back?'

'Actually'—Ben was equally brusque—'because you took
off so damn fast after the inquest. Emily wanted to thank you
for saving her life. And when we got here, she suddenly recognised her.' He jerked his head at Aspen, adding to me, 'Though
I'm damned if I know how.'

'It was her walk,' I said, smiling at Aspen. 'You've never
lost that catwalk sway. I saw it and immediately knew you.
It was as simple as that. Faces can change and hair, especially
women's hair, but not the way one moves. So,' I said, looking at Rick, 'how did she come to be here? And why are there
others looking for her? With no good intentions, I might add.
The man who ran me down? That was the third attempt on my
life since we started our search for Aspen, and quite recently
somebody broke in and searched our home. Do you know
what they're after? Because we don't.'

He ignored the last question, saying, 'I found her by the
highway. There'd been an accident. The car had rolled and she
was staggering about, covered in blood and badly concussed.'

'Whereabouts on the highway? Why didn't you take her
straight to a hospital?' I demanded.

'Between Katherine and Bloodwood Creek. What bloody

hospital?' he demanded irritably. 'She needed help right then, and the closest place was the commune. Besides, she was terrified, kept saying she had to hide. It's about all she did say. And Sal's a botanist – she knows all the healing herbs – so I took her there. She did a good job.' Tenderly he brushed the hair back from Aspen's face to expose the damage. There was a long scar across her temple and another running down through her cheek to the corner of her mouth. Once they faded they would be noticeable but not as dreadful as they looked now, though she would never model again. Even expert make-up wouldn't disguise the puckering of her skin around the corners of her eye and lips.

'Sal saved her eye, stitched up her cheek,' he said. 'But Sal couldn't do anything about her memory, or her fear. Marie's terrified of people but she can't tell me why. So in the end I brought her here.' He glared challengingly at me. 'And we're together now so here she stays.'

He loved her, I saw, his brown, combative eyes softening as he looked back at her. 'So what *do* you know about her past?' I asked. 'What can she remember?'

'Very little,' he admitted, 'but I know her. She's sweet and kind, a good woman. And she needs a protector. That's me. We're happy here, so you needn't think she's leaving with you – you could be anybody.'

'You were at the inquest. You know exactly who we are,' Ben said. 'Incidentally, before she came, was it your habit to meet visitors with a gun?'

'I don't get visitors,' Rick replied tersely. 'Except for you.'

'But you're expecting them, aren't you? On a daily basis. So what's that about?'

Ben's increasing ire wasn't helping; this solitary man would not be intimidated by temper. In an attempt to scale down the tension, I said, 'You must have lived here a while, Rick. The trees are well established and this place . . .' I glanced around at the care that had been lavished on the furnishings. 'That didn't happen overnight.'

'No.' He seemed glad of the change of subject and cast his gaze around the room. I took the opportunity to make a shushing motion at Ben, who rolled his eyes and leant back, as Rick continued. 'I acquired the lease in my late twenties, and I've been here fifteen years building self-sufficiency. Kil and the others drifted in about six years back.' He bristled, a touchy man with strongly held views, I saw. Somebody with no time for fools, or those who held opposing opinions. 'Not every-one's happy about the way our society's going, you know,' he said sharply. 'If you can't change it, you can always opt out, I say. Some might think it's the coward's way, but shutting your eyes, going along when the decision to improve matters is in your own hands – that's what does the lasting damage.'

'I know,' I said. 'We all have a duty to care for the planet, but not everybody is brave enough to leave the life they know. Nor are their temperaments necessarily suited to isolation. Aspen was a top model, you know. She travelled the world as a teenager: Sydney, New York, London, Milan. She's used to money and all it buys. How does she find it here?'

'It's safe.' Aspen's sudden interruption surprised me; con-centrating on Rick, I had almost forgotten she was there. She glared at me. 'You say you're my cousin. Why would you come looking if my parents didn't? What do you want?' Turning to Rick she said, 'Make them go away.'

Quickly, before he decided to do so, I said, 'I wanted to find you because your mother has passed away. Before she died, she asked me to do it, and since then your father has died too. He had dementia for years. Aunt Fee made my dad her executor and he needs to find you to settle their estate, which is quite sizeable.'

The news seemingly made no impression on her. I glanced at her bare arm. 'Aspen, what happened to your bracelet? The one Uncle Rich gave you. Did you lose it?'

Her eyes went wide and her right hand flew to cover her wrist. She cried, 'You can't have it!' then stared at me open-mouthed and I could almost see the tumblers falling into place. Looking down at her arm, she said blankly, 'It's gone.' And then, 'He gave it to me.'

'Who?' I asked, but she just nodded to herself, mouthing the word 'dead', then smiled. 'Good. I'm glad.'

'Do you mean your father?' I asked and got the same puzzled, blank look in reply.

'That man.' It was all she said; she really didn't remember.

I rose slowly and went to her, squatting down to her level to turn her left wrist upwards. The faint silvery scars there were barely visible beneath the tan. I said softly, 'He hurt you, didn't he? I'm so sorry, Aspen. Do you remember me from when you were a little girl?'

Timidly her hand rose to touch my hair. 'Mine was that colour too, before,' she said. 'You came to stay and it kept him away. I'm Marie now. I don't want to be Aspen any more.'

'Then you needn't be.' I squeezed her hand. 'Aspen wasn't ever happy, was she? But it's all right now. Can you tell me about Alice Springs and coming here? Or further back than that? In Sydney. Do you remember going to see Ben?'

'No.' She frowned. 'There was you and the pony and the kind woman. I remember that. She hugged me. And you came to stay and *he* couldn't do it because you were there.'

My neck hair bristled at her words. It was true then; her father had abused her. 'It's all a blank then until Rick found me and hid me. I love Rick.' She shook her dark head in sudden alarm. 'You can't take me away from him. He's good to me, he keeps me safe. You can't make me leave him.'

'I don't want to,' I assured her and tried another tack. 'Asp— Marie, how did you make your hair black?' The chances of Rick having hair dye would, I judged, be minimal.

She smiled proudly. 'My friend Sal did that. She's clever. She makes medicine and dyes from her plants, and soaps and shampoo too.' She ran her hands through it. 'It doesn't wash out. I saw you before when you were here, but you didn't know me then.'

'No.' Nor had she recognised me. I wondered how permanent her memory loss was. 'So you don't know why you were driving to Darwin alone?'

She shook her head. I ran a hand up her arm and gave her a consoling pat. 'Never mind then.' There were no needle marks that I could see. How long did an erstwhile addict retain them, anyway? It was late August, over seven months since she'd vanished, time enough for her to be clean. I wondered if Rick knew of her drug abuse. He must have seen the evidence if she was using when he found her, but I doubted it would make any difference. He seemed besotted by her, and she herself couldn't be further removed from temptation.

He glanced at me as I stood up, his gaze challenging mine. 'So what are you going to do?'

'Nothing. It's not my place to interfere with an adult's decisions. You seem a bit old for her – she's only twenty-three – but if you're her choice . . . I would still like to know why she's hiding, why my life's been at risk, but if she can't tell us then that's that.' I threw up my hands.

He stood up and, thinking it was our signal to leave, I rose also, but he was smiling down at Marie. 'What about you stick the kettle on, love? Our guests could probably do with a cuppa.'

I subsided again and as she moved away he turned abruptly to Ben. 'About these attempts on your wife's life – what happened?'

'You saw the last one,' Ben said. 'Nearly a month in hospital and she was lucky to make it that far. Damn lucky! Before that somebody tried to knife her at the night markets while we were in Darwin, and her cabin was set on fire at Bloodwood Creek. We think it happened because she'd been showing Asp— Marie's pic around.'

'After the fire'—I took up the story—'he must've started following us, to Darwin, then down to Katherine. We decided he wanted me to lead them to you. Which in the end we did, but he died, so you should be safe. Well, as safe as you were before anyway. It depends, I suppose, on why they're so desperate to get to her.' I hesitated but if he hadn't already worked it out, he needed to know. 'Marie was an addict. She's been in rehab twice. Ben paid for the last stint but she walked out and then vanished. That's when her mother asked me to find her. So all this mayhem could be down to drug traffickers. If she lost or stole a consignment, say, or . . . well, who knows? By all accounts they're pretty ruthless people. Quite ruthless enough to murder to protect their operation.'

Rick said curtly, 'She doesn't remember taking drugs.'

'She may not,' Ben said, 'but her body would've. You don't just turn off the craving because your head doesn't work.'

'I do know that,' Rick snapped. 'Sal handled it. Being a botanist she's very knowledgeable about alternative medicine. And Marie was out of it for days. I daresay the drugs didn't help, but she'd survived a car accident and was in quite a bad way for weeks. Broken ribs and her face all torn about . . .'

'So everyone at the commune knew that she was here?' I thought back to our visit. 'They could've saved us a lot of time and grief if they hadn't lied about it.'

'They were protecting her. They didn't know against what, and she couldn't tell them, but any fool could see she was terrified.' He stood again. 'Looks like that tea's ready. Come, sit.'

Marie had filled a china pot with the same brew that Sal had provided. There was a jar of honey to sweeten it and some lumpy rock cakes on a tin plate.

'That looks very nice,' I said, sitting down. 'Did you bake them?'

'Yes.' She wrinkled her nose. 'I don't think I learned to cook very well before.'

'You didn't have time. You travelled and modelled clothes, then you worked in the city selling them. Do you remember coming to visit me at the farm?'

'Where the pony was? Bits – the rain, it was so heavy, and I was afraid of the cows. But I milk the goats now,' she said proudly, 'and Rick's teaching me about the earth. Are you coming, Rick?' she called. 'Tea's made.'

'I'm here, Marie.' He came through the curtains from the back of the house carrying a flat wallet that he set on the table. Marie gave a little gasp, her hand flying to her mouth to stifle it, and he reached to put his hand on her shoulder. 'It's all right, my love. I think they should know.'

Ben half rose. 'Know what exactly?'

'The reason behind it all.' He pushed the wallet across the table. 'It's not drugs they're looking for. It's this.'

28

Ben and I exchanged a glance. Our hands crossed as we both reached for the wallet, then I pulled mine back. 'You open it.'

There was silence in the room. I was conscious of a crow's cawing from among the trees and a tick, like iron creaking, from the roof. Ben unzipped the vinyl pouch and upended it. A shower of sparkling stones fell out and rolled across the bare boards.

'Dear God!' he said devoutly. 'What . . . They can't be—'

Rick nodded. 'They are. Blood diamonds at a guess. Smuggled into the country and, seeing they were headed north, probably due to be smuggled out again, into Asia. From some warlord in West Africa, I assume. Stolen, of course. They're illegal, used to fund wars – that's why they're called blood diamonds, mostly mined by slave or child labour. It's a trade just about impossible to control.'

'They're worth millions, I imagine.' I cupped the scattered stones and pushed them into a heap. There must've been hundreds in the pile, enough to fill my two hands. 'What on earth was Marie doing with them?'

'My guess is she was the courier. She had them on her when I found her.'

'Our enquiries showed she was supposed to rendezvous with someone at the Groove and Grove – that's an orchard-cum-backpacker's place – back in February,' I said. 'The man checked in but left immediately when she didn't turn up. He didn't wait, or report her missing – now we know why. He must've been her contact, there to take delivery of the stones.'

Ben blew out a breath. 'No wonder they meant business.' He nodded at the glittering gems. 'What's a death or two to protect a fortune like that? Why didn't you call the cops as soon as you found them? They'll think any sort of delay damn suspicious, you know.'

'They would have arrested Marie,' Rick said. 'I thought about it. I thought about tossing the damn things into the creek, too, but in the end I just put them away.' He ran a roughened hand through his dark hair lightly flecked with grey, his expression haggard. 'Perhaps I always knew it'd all come back to bite us. We've been living on edge for months, waiting for someone to turn up.'

'Hence the rifle,' I said.

He nodded. 'We don't get visitors here. Very few people know this place exists, only the commune. Anyone else that's seen me coming and going would just assume I lived there. It wasn't something I planned – it just happened – but it made it perfect for Marie.'

Ben said challengingly, 'Well that's going to change, I'm afraid. We have to involve the cops. I told you our place was broken into and searched. Luckily Emily wasn't there, but suppose she had been? Suppose they come back and next time she is? They've shown they're willing to kill. The only way to stop them is if they have no reason to do so. Which means handing these in and with the utmost publicity.'

Rick came to his feet. 'And what about Marie?'

Ben shrugged. 'They can't very well prosecute somebody who doesn't remember committing a crime. Odds are she'd be ruled unfit for trial. But there's no contest, mate. Emily is blameless and I'll not risk her to shield someone who has been involved in a crime, however unwittingly. People are respons-ible for their choices, after all.'

'Ben.' I put a hand on his arm. 'Don't. There are extenuat-ing circumstances – the drugs, and what drove her to them. It's not entirely her fault.'

Marie, who had watched wide-eyed as the two men faced off, said, 'What are you talking about?'

'You were an addict before. I don't blame you,' I said quickly. 'There were reasons but if you can't remember them there's no point bringing them up now. I'm just saying you'd probably get a sympathetic hearing. There's this sergeant we met – a woman. I think if I could talk to her, explain things, it mightn't go too badly for you. Because Ben's right. We have to bring this into the open. It's the only way any of us can be safe again. It could just as easily have been you knocked down that day. Or somebody else could sneak in and pick you off with a rifle, say.'

'But if he's dead . . .' Rick began, then trailed off. 'Oh, I see.'

I nodded. 'He wasn't the boss any more than was the man who torched my cabin. Hired help, maybe part of the gang, but somebody's still directing things because the break-in at ours happened only a couple of weeks back. So no, it's not over and it won't be while the diamonds are still in play.'

Marie gasped in horror and Rick put a supportive arm around her.

'So what are you suggesting?' he asked, as I began loading the gems back into the wallet.

Ben nodded at it. 'I think we should take that straight to the cops in Darwin.'

'To Sergeant Bader,' I interposed. 'She's up to speed on what's happened so far.'

'Yeah, good thinking. And then,' Ben added judiciously, 'maybe a word to the media. "Cache of stolen diamonds found." That makes a good headline. No need to mention where or how, and we'd keep you both out of it.'

'How?' Rick scoffed. 'No journo's going to be satisfied with that.'

'Perhaps just say that the police stumbled across them?' I suggested. 'The cops can stonewall without arousing suspicion. The main thing is to get the word out so that those involved give up the hunt.'

'It might work,' Rick conceded, 'but we've no way of knowing where the ringleader is. What if he's not a local? He mightn't get to hear of it and we'd be no better off. Worse, in fact, because we'd have the cops on our backs.'

'He has to be local,' I argued, 'or at least from the Territory. The first attempt on my life came at Bloodwood Creek after I'd showed Aspen's pic around. I started doing that in the Alice, so he either followed me this far, or was already here. I even wondered'—I paused uncertainly, because according to Ben he had helped save my life—'if it could be Samson, that ranger from the park?' Seeing their faces, I continued defensively, 'Well he did try to pick me up the moment I saw him, and it was you,' I told Ben, 'who called him a bikie.'

'And you who pointed out that not all bike riders are criminals,' my husband retorted. 'I can't really see him in the role. What do you think?' He turned to Rick.

'He wouldn't be my first choice. Too helpful. Like riding all that way to warn us about the Outback Killer. Besides, he got the chopper in for you. If he'd really wanted you dead, he needn't have mentioned he was carrying the satellite phone.'

'True,' Ben said. 'Em would've died if the helicopter hadn't come. Can't be him then. But the pub was chockers that night, every room taken, so there's no shortage of suspects.'

'Mostly tourists,' I observed. 'So, someone from the town or the pub, using their job as a cover perhaps? Though how you get from West Africa to a whistle-stop on the Stuart . . .'

'Could be a local badhat acting as middleman or courier. It's not like the thief could send the gems through the post – they'd have to be transported by hand. In fact we know they were, because Marie was part of the chain,' Rick said.

Hearing her name, my cousin drooped her head. 'I just wish I could remember. It's dreadful feeling responsible for something you can't remember doing.'

'It's just as well, dear.' Rick clasped her hand, her slender fingers disappearing beneath his larger ones. 'If they're going to the cops . . .'

'But not now,' she said in something like panic. 'It's nearly dark out. They should stay, Rick. It'll be safer.'

For her, or for us, I wondered? I couldn't blame her though. Our last appearance had brought the enemy roaring to their very door. But perhaps she viewed us as some sort of protection?

'Nobody knows we're here,' I assured her. 'We should be going, Ben. In fact we should have left while it was still light enough to see that wretched road.'

'No, stay,' Rick urged. 'We're not exactly set up for visitors but we can make up a bed on the floor if you don't mind that. You're just as likely to break an axle in the dark.'

'We've no accommodation teed up,' Ben said. 'It'd mean driving through to Darwin. Well, if you're sure . . .'

In the end Rick found an old polyester tarp in the shed, which, brushed free of dust, served as the base for a bed made out of sheets of sponge, the doona from their own bed, and all the spare blankets in the house. It was surprisingly comfortable. We used the couch cushions for pillows – which were not – and I woke with a crick in my neck to the sound of butcher birds carolling on the verandah.

Rick was lighting the wood stove, his unshaved cheeks flecked grey with stubble. 'Sleep okay?'

'Mmm,' I said. 'Sore neck, but it was fine, really. What did you do, Rick, career wise, before all this?' I swept a hand around me.

'Taught geology at Sydney University.' He blew on the coals, eliciting a puff of ash, but a tiny flame rose behind it and I heard the crackle of the tinder catching. 'I was a consumer, part of the planet's problem. I came north for a holiday, and seeing the unspoilt wilderness opened my eyes. So I chucked in my job and opted to change. Became a funny bugger, a tree hugger. But there're more of us seeing the light than you might think. And not just drop-outs either.'

'I met some of your friends,' I said. 'They all seem to have their skills, and a passion for what they believe in.'

'That's right. It's not simple what we do. It takes dedication and a great deal of hard work building from nature, but at least we're not destroying it.'

'And you never married?'

'No,' he said shortly. 'If you're thinking this is just a fling with Marie, you're wrong. I'd make her my wife like a shot, but until this business is cleared up I can't risk having her seen. Our isolation's kept her safe.'

'And you didn't think her family might be worried when she vanished?'

'The state she was in when I found her, I doubted anybody cared,' he said coolly. 'She was lost, full of pain, and God only knew what she'd done to have those stones in her possession. I certainly didn't. So I kept her safe.'

'And fell in love with her,' I said gently.

'Yes, well, she needed love and care, and while I'm around she'll get it, no matter what.' His stare was challenging as he turned away from the stove. 'If you're so concerned, where were you when she needed someone?'

I ignored the impulse to defend myself, saying instead, 'It's very hard to help an addict who doesn't want to be helped. Ben tried. He paid for her rehab but she walked out of that. And she resented me, so we weren't talking. It wasn't entirely her fault. It seems pretty clear now, though we had no idea at the time, that her father abused her sexually. Hence the cutting and, I expect, the drugs. You'll have seen the scars on her wrist?'

He nodded. 'On her thighs too, but she couldn't tell me why she'd done it.'

'Well, now you know. I think from what she said that she's aware someone used to hurt her in the night when she was a child, but she doesn't seem to have made the connection – or maybe she can't bear to. So perhaps don't tell her? It's a dreadful thing to know about your own father. Luckily he's dead, and her mother's gone as well. My uncle was well off, so there's money for her to inherit. My father was appointed as their executor so she can contact him about it. I'll give you his address.'

'Yeah, well, if she's locked up there'll be no need,' he said bleakly. He took a tray from the table and, shouldering the door open, left the room.

Ben arrived back from a trip to the outside facility and jerked his head behind him. 'He doesn't seem too pleased this morning. Not having second thoughts, is he?'

'Just worried for Aspen.' She might be Marie in her new life but it seemed more natural when not in her presence to use her given name. 'I do hope we're doing the right thing. I suppose when we hand in the diamonds we couldn't just pretend we found the wallet? Leave her out of it?'

'It sounds possible,' he said, 'until you're faced with inventing believable details – and sticking to them. Not a good idea, Em, lying to cops. And with everything else that's gone on, they'd see there had to be a link. We'd be lucky if we didn't end up charged with smuggling them ourselves.'

'I suppose,' I said dispiritedly. 'But if she goes to jail, won't that push her straight back onto the drugs? Prisons are supposed to be full of them.'

'Let's hope it doesn't come to that. When's breakfast, I wonder?'

We left after we'd eaten: toast from homemade bread, native honey and fruit from the platter Rick had brought in from the orchard, washed down with the bush tea that I was developing a liking for. 'You should market this,' I said. 'It'd be a winner.'

He snorted dismissively. 'Oh, sure. And if it was a hit, the next thing would be somebody tearing up the native scrub to plant a thousand acres of it. More monoculture and degradation of the soil, just what the planet needs. Palm oil production's done enough damage without me adding to it. So when will we know?'

The abrupt question threw me and it was Ben who answered. 'We've no way to contact you, unless we can send a radio message to the park?'

He considered briefly. 'Better not.'

'No,' I agreed. 'We want the fact that the gems have been found made public – nothing else. Otherwise the bad guys might think about revenge. You'll probably have to wait for the police. They'll want to interview you.'

Aspen swallowed, her eyes flying to Rick, and as if she had spoken he moved his hand to cover hers. 'It's all right, my dear. We're in this together, remember.'

'When it's over,' I said to her, 'however things turn out, you should come home for a visit. See my family, who are yours, too, after all. Maybe consult a specialist about your amnesia – even get married if you want to. You'll always be welcome. Both of you will.'

'That's kind,' Rick responded. 'Thank you, but we can't decide anything until . . .'

'I know.' We'd finished at the table, and I stood up. 'We'd better hit the road then.' I badly wanted to hug my cousin but she shrank from my approach so I abandoned the idea, reminding myself that I was, at best, a vague memory from her past. We shook hands with Rick, thanked him for his hospitality and, with the gem wallet tucked into my bag, took our leave.

The return trip to the car was shortened by Rick showing us a foot-pad, a path made by the traffic of human feet, that led right to the base of the cliff, then skirted its edges, bringing us out, twenty minutes later, on the far side.

'There's the vehicle.' Ben pointed down slope. 'Pity we hadn't known about that yesterday. Just a walk in the park compared to that slog through the scrub.'

'True.' The elevation gave a good view over the country. 'If you wanted to drop out of sight he's got the perfect spot for it. Well,' I said with a sigh, 'that was the easy bit. Now we've got that horrendous track in front of us. Better make a start I suppose.'

Back in Darwin we re-booked into the hotel we'd left the previous day, went out for a late lunch, then drove to the police station where, I mused, we were becoming regulars. The person manning the front desk evidently thought so too.

'Back again?' He lifted one eyebrow at Ben. 'So what can I do for you this time?'

'We need to speak with Sergeant Bader,' Ben said. 'If she's

not available now, can we make an appointment for when she will be?'

'You could tell me what it's about,' he offered, 'then we'll see.'

Ben shook his head. 'No, I'm afraid it's the sergeant or nothing. She'll know what it concerns. We'll wait if necessary.'

'Our officers do have more to do than pander to the public's every little problem, mate,' he retorted, leaning hard on the last word. 'Could be she's busy with something more important.'

'I doubt it, but like I said, we'll wait.' Ben took my elbow to turn me about. 'Over there will do.' He nodded at a row of hard-looking chairs.

'Suit yourself.' The man scowled but he did pick up the phone, speak into it and replace the handset, not offering to share the result of his brief conversation. 'Might be a long wait.'

29

Twenty minutes later Sergeant Bader arrived. She greeted us hurriedly, not looking pleased as she shook hands, saying, 'I thought you'd left town.' She glanced at her watch. 'I'm afraid this will have to be quick. I have a meeting to attend.'

'I think you'll find our news more important,' Ben said, 'but I really don't want to do this in public.'

'Very well,' she huffed, 'we'll go in here.' She tapped out a code on the keypad and we entered the station proper, following her down a hallway into what I assumed was an interview room furnished with a desk, a couple of worn chairs, a mini fridge and a window facing out onto a car park. She sat behind the desk, waved a hand at the other seats and said, 'Right, what appears to be the problem this time?'

'Stolen goods – these.' I pulled the wallet from my bag and opened it, spilling its contents onto the table. 'We think – well, actually, we're quite certain – these are what's behind the attempts on my life.'

'And we want the police to advertise the find,' Ben added. 'That way the thieves have no reason to come after us again.'

'Whoa!' Corrie Bader raised her brows and then her hands. 'Not so fast. First, where did you get these? How do you know they're stolen, and why should they be connected to you? I think you'd better explain yourselves. Let's start with the basics – are they even real?'

'Well, I'd hate to think I almost died for the sake of fake ones,' I said dryly. 'We think they've been smuggled into the country – probably from Africa – and were possibly bound for Asia. Why else bring them to Darwin? It's not like it's an international diamond mart.'

'Just a minute.' Bader rose, selected several of the stones and found a tissue to hold them. 'I'll need to get these tested, see if they're real. Looks like I'm not going to make that meeting. Wait here, please. Can I get you something? Tea, coffee?'

We declined and she went out, closing the door. The moment it shut I said, 'It's going to get messy, isn't it? With Aspen? They're never going to leave her out of it.'

'No,' Ben agreed. 'We'll just have to hope she's found unfit to plead. I wonder how long this is going to take?'

It turned out to be the rest of the afternoon. Corrie Bader returned with a constable carrying a recording device and a tray of mugs. 'In case you change your mind,' she said. The constable, introduced to us as PC Holden, fetched another chair, then dug a notebook from his pocket and clicked his pen, hunching over the pad like an eager acolyte imbibing the wisdom of the ages.

We gave our names and addresses and, for what seemed the hundredth time, I launched into the tale of my search for

Aspen. I had scarcely covered the relevant family details when another officer slipped into the room, handing Bader a tiny paper bag as he murmured a brief message.

'Right. Thank you.' She dismissed him, tipped out the stones the bag held and drew a deep breath. 'Seems they are real, and top quality too. Go on, Mrs Grier, you were saying?'

It took a long time to recall everything in its right order. Ben helped, chipping in with details I'd overlooked: the night we'd spent in the car, the fear of being followed. Even the idiot from Crazy Creek who had run us off the road. It felt like I spoke for hours. I explained about the ex-social worker who had picked Aspen as the victim of abuse, the evidence of self-harm on her arm, her drug habit, and the amnesia that had followed the crash before Rick found her.

'Rick who?' Bader demanded.

I looked at Ben. 'I never asked,' I confessed. 'He was at the inquest. He took Aspen in when she was badly injured, her face ripped open; she was all messed up with the drugs too. They cared for her at the commune and she's clean now, but she can't remember a thing from before the time she woke up there.'

'He didn't report the accident,' Bader stated.

'Well, it's not like there's a phone out there,' Ben said, 'and calling their road a goat track's being generous. Besides, she was terrified and he found the diamonds, so he figured she had cause.'

'The more reason for him to contact the police,' Bader said firmly.

'Look,' I said, putting in my five cents' worth in defence of Rick, 'he's isolated himself to get away from rules and bureaucracy. So you can't expect him to get involved for no good reason. He's . . . fond of my cousin, sees her as in need of protection. What's so wrong with that? At least he's not trying to kill people. He was going to chuck the diamonds in the creek, so he wasn't planning on benefiting from them either.'

'Anyway,' Ben said, 'you've got them now and we thought if you told the media, made a fair sort of fuss about the trade in illegal stones that funds death in third-world countries, headline-grabbing stuff like that—'

'Without mentioning how or where they turned up,' I interjected, 'then the bad guys wouldn't bother coming after any of us again.'

'So what do you say?' Ben asked hopefully. 'Can you do that? I know the local rag's on sale in Bloodwood Creek because I saw copies in the service station there.'

Bader leaned forward. 'Is there something you're not telling me, Mr Grier? Why Bloodwood Creek?'

'Well, the fire. Emily had only just got there and the following night her cabin goes up? It's obvious, I'd have thought.'

Bader cocked her head, considering his words. 'So how would they know to target her?'

'I was showing Aspen's photo around,' I said slowly. 'Not to the customers – what would be the point? – but to the permanent staff at the bar, and the manager or receptionist who booked me in. And let's see . . . the woman at the shop and the ranger from the national park, Samson somebody.'

'And,' Ben put in, 'while we were away, somebody slashed your tyres.'

Bader's eyes narrowed. 'That's right, and the guy who set

the fire was long gone. Seems like you could be right, then. It had to be somebody there.'

'But not Samson. He was at the park when we arrived, so it couldn't have been him. Which only leaves the pub staff and the woman from the store,' I said triumphantly, before noticing the look on her face. 'What?'

'Or anybody they told about your search. Coupled with the fire that's news, so trust me, the story would've spread far and wide. And it's not a long drive from here to there, not by Territory standards. However, I've had an idea – if you agree, of course. I have to run it by my superiors and it would mean delaying the announcement of the gems' discovery for a bit, but it could lead to an arrest – if the ringleader is there.'

'Well? What did you have in mind?' Ben, impatient with her caveats, demanded.

Bader's eyes glinted. 'A trap to draw them out. Say you, Mrs Grier, turn up there with a few of the stones and flash them about. I'll have undercover officers among the guests and when they make a move to recover the diamonds, we'll have them.'

'You could end up nabbing one of the rank and file though,' Ben objected. 'And that won't help us. We know they're not working alone. There was the arsonist, for instance, and the dead guy in the Toyota.'

'Not to mention whoever was behind the tiger mask at the markets,' I added.

'Yeah, but would you trust a henchman with untraceable diamonds? I'm damn sure I wouldn't. Remembering that they may not even know how many there're supposed to be. No way.' Bader shook her head. 'I'd be seeing to the matter myself.'

'Won't it be dangerous?' I asked anxiously. 'We want to get them off our backs and out of our lives, but not if it's going to get me killed. Supposing they – I don't know, try to knife me again.'

Ben looked alarmed. 'No way. You're not doing it, Em.'

Bader said calmly, 'My officers will keep you safe. You'll be protected every step. There'll be a guard in your room and somebody watching your back every moment.'

I said, 'I can't do it alone, it'd look wrong, so Ben will have to come too. Whoever they are, they probably already have a good idea we've returned for the inquest, so why wouldn't we both check in at the pub? They'll assume we're heading home. Though maybe the undercover lot should arrive the day before? Then I suppose I wait for the right moment – when everyone's at dinner and the staff are all there, maybe? I can drop my bag or knock it over so the stones spill out, and then scramble around making a fuss until everyone has a chance to notice . . .' I trailed off, looked at Bader. 'Wouldn't it be better if you swapped them for zircon or glass? I don't want to be responsible for losing the real thing. And I might if they're rolling around the floor. Anybody could snaffle a couple under the guise of helping me retrieve them.'

'It's a thought,' she agreed. 'If I get permission, we'll work out a plan. Where are you currently staying?'

'We've checked out.' Ben rose, holding out a hand to me. 'Looks like we'd better reverse that.' He gave her the hotel's name and she wrote it down.

'I'll be in touch first thing tomorrow. If it's a go, we'll get my people moving immediately. Then you can ring the pub, make a booking and turn up the next day.' She grinned mirthlessly, an eager glint in her eyes. 'Once they've taken the bait, they're ours.'

'So much for our plans,' Ben said as we left the station. 'The hotel's going to think we're crazy. We're leaving, we're staying . . . Are you sure about this, Em? You could wait here and let me do it. I don't want you anywhere near that murderous bastard.'

'No way. Besides, you heard the woman – we're going to be guarded. Though I don't know about having some hulking cop in our bedroom.' The street lights had come on and the palms were black silhouettes against a red sky, from which the colour was slowly leaching. 'I hope Bader can get her hands on some fake stones. That wallet's got to be worth tens of millions.'

Ben fished the keys from his pocket and the car beeped as its doors unlocked.

I paused beside mine. 'What'll we do tomorrow? We can't sit in the hotel all day.'

'We'll think of something.' He switched on the headlights and eased out of the park. 'In the meantime, why don't we go find somewhere to have a drink before deciding on dinner? You never know, a friendly barman might give some advice on how best to spend the day.'

'Sounds good.' I leaned back in my seat, watching the anonymous cars zip by. Darwin seemed to come alive after dark, the rhythm of life quickening as the sun vanished. 'I wonder how Mia's settled in. Maybe I'll give Mum a call later.'

'Well, don't tell her about Aspen yet, for God's sake. Let's wait until we find out whether she'll be charged. The whole thing's going to be very upsetting for her – your dad too, I imagine.'

'I wasn't going to,' I said. 'But Mum's not starry-eyed about people, you know. Even family. She calls it as she sees it, and though she blamed Aunt Fee for her daughter's shortcomings, I think she's always had reservations about Aspen. She told me once she'd be a nicer person if she'd been born less beautiful.'

'Ouch,' Ben said. 'I hate to think how she views me.'

I patted his arm. 'She's coming round. And she knows our problems were half my fault. But yes, for a while there you weren't her favourite person.'

He grunted. 'Good to know where you stand, I suppose.' Indicating right, he swung into a park in front of a neon-lit sports club. 'Shall we try here? There'll be a restaurant, but we can go somewhere else later, if you'd rather.'

I yawned. 'Oh, sorry. Whatever, only let's not make it too late, hmm? It's been a long day.'

30

The phone rang at seven-thirty the following morning. Ben was in the shower, so I rolled over in bed to reach the handpiece and found Corrie Bader on the line.

'It's a go,' she said. 'Three officers will leave this afternoon for Bloodwood Creek, so you can go ahead and make your booking for tomorrow. Try for a room in the pub, rather than a cabin – we don't want any more fires. Better book for a couple of nights too.'

'Why? Surely they'll want to act immediately. After all, we could leave at any moment.'

'Yes, but if they're not in the pub when you flash the gems, they mightn't hear about it till the next day. You have to give them time to react.'

It made sense; the tale of somebody spilling diamonds all over the shop would certainly make the rounds of the town. 'Right,' I said. 'Have you managed to find substitutes for the stones?'

'It's in hand. I thought about a dozen should do it. They don't have to see the whole lot. Just remember, neither of you are to go swanning off anywhere while you wait. Stick where you can be guarded, even if it means sitting on the verandah all day.'

'Right.' I felt a nervous flutter at her words, suddenly regretting that we had agreed to participate in her plan. What had I been thinking? But there was really no alternative. If we didn't go through with it, then in six months, or twelve, or two years, we would still be looking over our shoulders. Living with fear, never able to relax or count on a future, until the bad guy was caught.

I passed the news on to Ben when he emerged wet-haired with a towel wrapped around him. He sensed my ambivalence now the plan was afoot and said, 'You don't have to do this, Em. Stay here and I'll go alone. Lock the door and sit it out until they've got their villain.'

I shivered. 'No. I couldn't bear to. Besides, better for us both to be guarded, don't you think? What if they suspect it's a trap? They could come after me, use me as leverage while you and your guards are waiting at Bloodwood Creek.' I was prob- ably gifting our unknown enemies with supernatural powers but at that moment nothing seemed beyond them. They had tracked us to the city once before, then, as if to prove their omniscience, even to our home in Armidale. 'Better if we're together. That way we can watch each other's backs.'

'If you're sure.' Ben came to take me in his arms. 'It will be all right,' he murmured into my hair. 'I won't let anyone hurt you, my love.'

'I know.' I kissed him, then moved aside. 'Do you want to order breakfast while I shower? I don't feel like facing the dining room this morning.'

*

My reluctance for the company of others persisted, and when we left the hotel later that morning it was for a leisurely drive along the coast, rather than any of the crowded tourist venues. We duly made our bookings at the pub and filled in the day with a picnic on the beach and an afternoon spent by the hotel pool. It had the novelty of difference, at least; back home it would still be too cold for swimsuits.

The following morning we spent a little while at the shops and I bought souvenirs for Phoebe and Pavel. Ben purchased a mouse on a cord for Mia, and when I teased him about being a big softie, he raised quelling brows.

'Not at all. It's a training aid. To teach her to catch mice.'

'So she has to earn her keep now?'

'Certainly. I'm only maintaining one female in the lap of luxury.' Adopting an atrocious Scottish accent, he said, 'Keep your sillae in yer sock, mon, and no be wastin' it on bawbees.'

I laughed. 'You'd be a riot on the stage. After that I feel I can handle even murderous crooks. Let's go pick up the wallet and get our instructions.'

We coasted into the car park at the pub just shy of five. Bloodwood Creek drowsed in late afternoon light, the ground painted with long shadows and the river surface a dull pewter colour. Flying foxes hung in dark clumps in the trees and I wondered how many ended up as meals for the crocs. There were ibis on the lawn and the usual scatter of holiday makers enjoying happy hour at the verandah tables as we trod up the steps and pushed open the doors.

Maggie met us at the desk with no sign of recognition, but then she would see some thousands of travellers every year, so I wasn't surprised. 'Room Eighteen,' she said, 'a double, right, for two nights? I hope you'll be comfortable. It's straight down the hall, the end room on the right. Checkout's at ten and there's a penalty for losing the key. Enjoy your stay with us.'

Ben picked up our modest luggage as she bustled off and we followed her directions to the room. I had glanced sur-reptitiously at other visitors we passed in the bar and on the verandah. They were a mixture of ages from a sulky-looking teenager with an attitude to a couple of geriatrics, one of whom had a walking frame, but none seemed likely candidates for undercover police. Bearing out my assessment, the teen-ager chose that moment to shove his legs into the path of an older, rather plump couple trying to walk past.

'Excuse me, young man,' the woman said frostily, and got a smirk in reply.

'Free country, lady.' He curled his lip at her. 'Why don't you walk round? Looks like the exercise'd do you good.'

'Mind your mouth, sonny,' the man snapped but the boy just grinned, making no effort to move his feet. Scowling, the couple stepped around him, voicing indignant displeasure.

In the room I did a quick unpack – toiletries, night clothes, something to wear tomorrow – then I looked across at my handbag sitting innocently on the bedside table. 'What now?'

'What about a swim?' my beloved asked, patting the bed beside him. 'That or a coffee? Relax, Em. Or we could go for a stroll if you like. We're supposed to be enjoying ourselves, remember?' He saw me glance again towards the bedside table. 'And we need as big a crowd as possible before you do your thing.'

I stood up. 'I don't want coffee, but a cold drink would be good. Have you spotted the cops yet?'

'That kid in five years' time?' he suggested flippantly. 'Come on, then. Maybe the walk is a bad idea – we're not supposed to go wandering off. Let's sit on the verandah with a drink and see who we recognise from last time.'

The car park had started filling as the day trippers returned. Almost the first person we saw as we stepped onto the verandah with our drinks was Sam, sitting with his feet up on the rail and a beer in his hand. He saw us and dropped his boots back to the boards to stand up.

'Hey! How you doing?' To Ben he said, 'Noticed you at the inquest. I wasn't called but I was in town so I attended.' To me he added, 'You're looking pretty amazing, considering the last time I saw you. How are you, Emily?'

'I'm fine, really.' I remembered that I probably owed him my life. 'Thanks to you. If you hadn't been there that day . . .'

'Hey, I only made a phone call. So, are you on holiday now or what?'

'Just making our way home.' Ben took over the conversation. 'Our last trip was cut a bit short. What about you – still at the park?'

'Yeah, but I've got a week off. So I took the bike in for a new engine. She's got three hundred ccs now, runs like a dream. Makes for better highway riding—'

I tuned out as the conversation turned to pistons and the engine power of respective brands of motorcycle, and looked around me. The verandah space was becoming crowded. A lamp in a bamboo holder was burning in the dusky light; I could smell citronella and realised that there were no mosquitoes. Most of the people were sitting in groups of friends or family. The sulky teenager, I observed, was sitting alone, staring sullenly at his Coke. A mid forty-ish couple, who might have been his parents, occupied the next table along with a young girl. I let my gaze wander over the rest but to the best of my knowledge I had never seen any of them before. Not even in the cop shop in Darwin, so maybe our guards were in the bar?

We stayed seated with Sam until most people left for the dining room, then Ben raised a brow at me. 'Shall we?'

'May as well. Would you like to eat with us, Sam?' With his easygoing ways and willingness to chat, he was as good a choice as any to ensure the spread of the story of the woman carrying diamonds, like loose change, in her purse. I slipped a hand into my bag to unzip the wallet and smiled at him.

'That's kind of you. Thanks, I will. So, you're on the home-bound track now?'

'With a stop in Alice Springs, maybe,' Ben agreed. Turning to me, he said, 'Why don't you grab a table, Em, and I'll get the dinners. What would you like?'

'Oh, the fish, and salad, thanks. It was very good last time, and we don't often have barramundi.' I cast a quick look over the room, searching for a central table. 'I'll be just over there, okay?'

'Got it.' He nodded approval. The table was on the edge of

the central walkway, in plain sight of the servers and the bar. 'Drink?'

'Something soft,' I said, though I was so nervous that a brandy wouldn't have gone amiss. Clutching my bag, I made my way to the chosen spot, sat down and was immediately approached by an Akubra-wearing customer. 'Sorry.' I placed my bag on the seat next to me. 'This table's taken.'

'That's fine, I'm not here to eat,' he assured me. 'Name's Linc. Owner of the Crazy Creek Experience. I've got a leaflet for you, in case you feel like givin' us a try.'

'Oh, of course.' I recognised him now, though perhaps my shorter hair and the weight I hadn't yet regained prevented him from doing the same; besides, he would see hundreds of tourists and probably remembered none of their faces. 'From the dude ranch – I heard about that.'

'Right, well, you'll know we're the real McCoy. It's a fair-dinkum Aussie experience you won't find anywhere else, so come on out and give us a try.'

I smiled and took the leaflet without committing myself, and he moved on to the next table.

'Who was that?' Ben asked as he placed my plate and his own on the table. 'Sam's bringing your drink.'

'The road hog from the dude ranch. He was here last time too, remember? Are the staff the same, could you tell?'

He shrugged helplessly. 'No idea. They probably get quite a bit of turnover here. Most of these places use backpackers, and they'd burn out pretty quickly. Stands to reason there wouldn't be enough locals in a little whistle-stop like this.'

'I suppose not.' I glanced around. 'When should I do it? Now?'

'Wait till Sam gets back. After all, he's not entirely above suspicion. Bit of a coincidence him being here again.'

'I don't know about that. He has a good reason, and he saved my life.'

'But it's got to be somebody we've seen before.' Ben picked up his knife and fork. 'Eat up, Em. Your dinner's getting cold.'

My appetite, however, had fled. 'There is no saying the bad guy's even here,' I objected, convinced in that moment that everyone present was who they purported to be. Sam arrived with his own plate and a glass of lemon squash for me. I thanked him and took it, the condensation from the crushed ice wetting my hand. In as natural a way as I could manage, I reached into my bag for a tissue and managed to upend it across the floor.

'Oh, damn!' I clapped a hand to my mouth, feeling like the biggest ham in the world, then thrust my chair back, deliberately toppling it as I got up to draw as much attention as possible. Ben and Sam both half rose from their chairs but I waved a hand at them. 'Don't bother, I'll get it.' The bag's innards were strewn across a couple of metres of floor: nail scissors and loose coins, a mini pack of tissues, another of tampons, Panadol, lipstick, comb, nailfile, library card, wet wipes and, tumbling through the rest of the collection, like sparkles of light, the stones, which had obligingly separated themselves from their wallet.

I cast what I hoped was a guilty look around at my audience and bent to scoop everything up, only to be forestalled by the sulky teenager, suddenly alert and pop-eyed. 'Holy shit! Diamonds!' His voice came from his boots and most of the room must have heard him. He held up a glittering stone. 'Dozens of 'em! Are they for real, lady?'

'Of course not.' I had no need to feign astonishment, given his intrusion. 'They're glass beads. I broke a necklace.' I held out my hand. 'If I could have them back?'

The young sister jumped up from her chair at his words, exclaiming excitedly, 'Diamonds? I want to see,' but he wasn't ready to relinquish the stage. 'Scram, brat.' He scowled at her, putting a hand on her chest and actually shoving her back so that she bumped into the chair of a young woman sitting with her partner to our right. His action drew a sharp reproof from the father, which he ignored.

'Jeez! You must be rolling in it, lady,' he said.

I snatched the stone from him, discomforted by his smirk, and snapped, 'I told you, they're glass.' I bundled everything into my bag and regained my seat, flushed and bothered, my heart thumping.

Under the table, Ben squeezed my leg. 'Pretty good,' he murmured. 'You'd have convinced me.'

'Let's hope more than that young lout feel the same way,' I muttered softly. 'His dad looked like he wanted to strangle him. I don't even know if I got all the beads back, so if the person we're after's here and picked one up, they might find out the stones really *are* glass or zircon or whatever.' Corrie Bader hadn't actually told us their pedigree. 'I was too flustered to count them.' I fretted and took a calming sip from my drink, then, without turning my head, let my eyes drift over the diners I could see. 'Did you catch anyone reacting?'

'Well, everybody looked at the kid,' he half-whispered, 'but nobody smacked their forehead and cried, "Aha! Got you!", if that's what you mean.' He winked at me. 'Relax, Em. That's the cops' responsibility. We've done our bit.' He looked across at Sam, who was engrossed in his meal. Speaking in a normal tone, Ben remarked, 'I daresay you're too young to have discovered the amount of junk women carry in their handbags? You literally would not believe the stuff they lug about with them.'

'Yeah?' Slicing his roast, Sam looked across and grinned at me. 'I'm game – like what?'

'Nothing that isn't essential,' I said with dignity. 'Ben exaggerates. Just because I have a little screwdriver and a pair of miniature pliers . . . Both of which are very helpful for cleaning hooves, or getting a stake out of them, I might add.'

'Tell the truth, you've a small vet's dispensary in there, and enough gadgets to pick a lock or perform surgery,' he teased.

I protested, pretending indignation as Sam laughed, and then, relief having renewed my appetite, I began to eat my now exceedingly cold fish.

We stretched out our time in the dining room, ordering coffee after our meal, while Ben involved Sam in a long discussion about motorbikes, and when that had run its course, his plans for the future after his time at the park.

'Who said there'll be an after?' Sam looked surprised by the idea. 'No, man, I've got it sorted. I'm where I wanna be, and I can't see any changes coming down the pike. Apart from promotion, of course. Someday I'll be in charge of my own park. It's a great job – the pay and conditions suit, and you're spending your time protecting what's precious. If it wasn't for the Parks and Wildlife mob, there'd be nothing for folks like you to come and enjoy. It's not just the land, you know. It's the fauna and flora, pristine waterways, and yeah'—he looked at me—'even the crocs. They're part of it all too. It's the chance for city folk to see what's natural and unspoiled.' He smiled and then, looking very young and suddenly self-conscious about his earnestness, cleared his throat before rising from the table. 'Hey, they're closing up. We better call it a day. Thanks for the company – been good to meet you both again. You must come back someday for another visit.'

A quick once-over of the room showed he was right. The only ones left, apart from the staff cleaning up, were the couple nearby who, with clasped hands and their heads close together, seemed oblivious to their surroundings. So much for our police guard not letting us out of their sight.

'It is late,' I agreed. 'And we enjoyed eating with you. Come on, Ben, let's get out of their hair. Goodnight, Sam.'

''Night,' he called, and we made our way down the long hall to the end room. Noticing us move off, the remaining couple reluctantly vacated their table and, hands still entwined, wandered after us, stopping a few doors short of ours. Honeymooners, I guessed, and had a silent bet with myself that they'd be kissing the moment they entered their room.

Ben opened our door and swept a hand down the wall. 'Can't find the damn light switch,' he muttered. There was a dim glow from a heavily shaded touch lamp on the far side of the bed, which one of us must have accidentally activated, but it did nothing to illuminate the room.

'Never mind,' I said. 'Put your hand around the bathroom door. The switch is right next to the jamb.'

He stepped forward, feeling his way along the wall, then pitched suddenly forward. 'What the—?!' His words cut off. He stumbled and fell, and a brilliant light dazzled my eyes.

'Not a squeak,' said a voice in my ear, 'or I'll smack him again. Harder next time. Get over here. Sit on the bed and shut up.'

'What?' I said stupidly, and then, ignoring the hissed instructions, dropped to my knees, feeling frantically at the supine body near my feet. 'Ben! Ben, are you all right?'

A rough hand gripped my arm, yanking me back onto my feet. 'You deaf?' the voice growled.

Ben groaned faintly. 'Who are you?' I demanded, but my sinking heart already knew. Terror dried my mouth so that the question came out as a gasp of fright. He was here! Where were the police? Where was the protection we had been promised? As if the thought had prompted it, I heard a thump and an inarticulate sound from the bathroom floor.

The lights came on then and with a sort of bemused horror, I took in the room. Ben, with a thin trickle of blood across his brow, lay stunned at my feet, across the legs of a securely trussed male figure at whom I goggled in disbelief. It was the teenager from the dining room, a gag across his mouth. 'What's *he* doing here?' I blurted. I looked at my captor for the first time and recoiled at the slit eyes in the black mask of his face before realising he wore a balaclava pulled over his head.

'A thief. Young fool musta fancied the diamonds for himself.' He kicked the boy and yanked me past him, ignoring Ben who, save for that single groan, hadn't stirred again. 'Your bag. Empty it onto the bed.'

I did so, groping hopelessly for a convincing lie, because a dozen stones were never going to satisfy him, not if he knew – and I had to suppose he did – how many had originally been in the wallet.

I was right. Seeing the pitiful number diminished by the broad spread of the quilt, he seized the bag, shook it violently, inspected the inside of the wallet then turned to me with a sort of leashed ferocity to demand, 'Where's the rest of them?'

'What rest?' I despised the quaver in my voice and cleared my throat. 'That's all he had.'

'Who? Where'd you get them from? And don't lie to me, woman, unless you want your face cut up. That'd be a shame, wouldn't it? Pretty thing like you?' His hand emerged from his back pocket and I heard a snicking sound as an evil-looking, narrow blade sprang into view.

The strength drained from my legs at the sight and I felt sick with fear. 'From him,' I cried in a high voice. 'The man who died in the Toyota. He knocked me down and broke my leg.' I prayed my captor wouldn't have learned the full extent of my injuries. 'Then he crashed the vehicle and killed himself, but . . . but my husband went after him. He never told the police, because he found the diamonds, you see. We were called to Darwin for the inquest and we – we thought it might be a chance to sell them. But the jewellers asked too many questions, so we didn't,' I finished hurriedly. 'Take them. You can have them.'

'Oh, don't worry. I intend to. And the rest. Why were you out there in the first place? Is that where she is – the woman you were looking for?'

'Out where?' Stalling, I feigned incomprehension. Of course the shooting would've been all over the news at the time, and the discovery of the crashed vehicle with the body in it. But I couldn't betray Aspen's whereabouts. If he found her, he would silence her. I hadn't a doubt about that. Or of Ben's and my own fate now that Sergeant Bader's wonderful plan had so spectacularly failed.

He raised the wicked blade to my eye level and touched the point to the corner of my mouth. 'How'd you like your smile widened? Don't play me for a fool.'

There was something familiar about his voice. I croaked, 'You mean the hippy commune? Because he was following us! The track we took was the only way to get off the highway. We didn't know where it went, and then we wrecked the car and had to limp into the settlement – commune, whatever – for help. And he caught up to us there.' Gabbling, I gasped for breath, mouth dried by terror. 'But somebody shot at him when he ran over me, so he wound up crashing and killing himself. When they went after him, Ben saw the diamonds – they were on floor, he said, fallen out of the glovebox. And he just grabbed them before the other man caught up. He didn't have time to think about what he was doing.'

'What man? You said your husband went after him alone.'

'I did not. I said Ben went after him. He wanted to stop him – the man had just tried to kill me! But our vehicle was wrecked, so somebody had to drive him. I don't know who,' I stuttered frantically, 'I was out of it. They had to call a helicopter to get me to hospital.'

'I don't care if they called a bloody boat! Who was this other man who drove your husband?'

'I don't know,' I wailed. 'We just got there and he – the Toyota man – came boring out of the scrub like a mad bull. I'd only just got out of the car. I never got to speak to the hippy people—'

Ben groaned again and made an attempt to stand up before falling back to his knees. 'Em?' he said thickly. 'You okay?'

'Yes.' I swallowed a sob and, ignoring the knife, ducked to his side and helped him stand. 'He's taking the diamonds,' I said urgently, hoping Ben's head was clear enough to understand. 'I've said he can have them. We won't tell anyone – we can't anyway, because we stole them from that man in the Toyota first. And he's got that kid tied up in the bathroom. And he won't tell either, because he came to rob us. So that's okay. We'll be gone in the morning and he'll never hear from us again.'

'Right.' Ben winced as he felt his head. 'There was no need for any rough stuff,' he complained and glared at the masked figure. 'Like my wife said, take 'em and be welcome. I can't sell the bloody things anyway. We're well out of it.'

'I don't think so.' It was strange how menacing the faceless voice sounded. 'I want the rest of them and it's not over till I find them.'

31

Ben staggered to the bed and sat down. 'Well, you're shit out of luck there, mate,' he growled, ''cause we didn't know there was any rest. Who the hell are you, anyway?'

I said hurriedly, 'We don't want to know, Ben. That man in the Toyota must've been working for him.'

'And stealing from me. Well, he got his comeuppance,' the masked figure said grimly. 'And so will you both if I don't get the rest of the stones. So'—he showed Ben the knife—'if you don't want to see your wife's face rearranged, you'll do exactly what I say.' He pulled something from his pocket that glinted in the light, and my heart sank at the sight of a roll of plastic tape. 'Hands together behind your back. Now.'

'If you're going to tie us up,' I said, 'I have to use the bathroom first. Only that boy's in there. Will you move him, please?'

'What d'you think?' he scoffed. 'You've got three minutes. Shut your eyes or tell him to shut his.' Almost as an afterthought, he added, 'And don't try to run. I can knife your man before you're through the door.' He began winding the tape around Ben's wrists, then paused to punch him in the ribs. 'Together, I said.'

Ben grunted but must have complied as I hurriedly snatched up the tampon pack from the bed and ducked into the bathroom.

The boy lay on his back, hands taped together, his ankles similarly secured. Above the gag his eyes sought mine as I bent down and poked my nail scissors, which had lain under the tampons, into his cupped palm. 'Free yourself. Call the police,' I hissed. 'Tell them the Jump-up. Close your eyes.' I spoke the last words more loudly. 'I'll kick you if I catch you watching.' I poked the nailfile I had also taken deep into the tampon packet, took a hurried drink from the basin tap and flushed the loo. The boy gargled something behind his gag and I said severely, 'Serves you right for trying to rob us,' then stepped over him and back into the bedroom.

'Get yourself over here,' our captor said, then, 'What's that?' as I pushed the packet into my pocket.

I pulled it out to show him. 'I need them,' I told him hardily and held my breath. Men seemed uncomfortable about the subject and I was banking on that fact to get the nailfile past him. I had no idea how it would help, or how I would reach it once my hands were tied, but it was the only weapon at my disposal. I'd have kept the scissors, but I doubted the boy would get far without them, and he was our only real hope. If he could be trusted, that was. I wouldn't put it past him to cut himself free, then just return to his room, pretending the whole incident had never happened.

Dragging me with him, our captor opened the door and affixed the Do Not Disturb sign to the outer handle. He then taped my hands in front of me but left my legs free like Ben's. Then, before I could decide whether to risk a scream, he slapped tape over both our mouths and prodded Ben at knife point towards the long drape screening the window. I had not stopped to consider how he had gained entry to our room, but yanking back the curtain revealed all. The windows, as was common, were sealed shut, and he had circumvented this by simply cutting the entire pane out. He shoved us through, Ben, without hands in front to help himself, landing awkwardly. I fared better, but Balaclava Man immediately seized my arm again and raised the knife, thin moonlight glinting on the blade as he showed it to Ben.

'Not a sound. And no heroics. Try it and your wife gets it. Head for the car park.'

They must, I thought despairingly, keep early hours at Bloodwood Creek. It was barely eleven, but the only light visible was a dim glow from the verandah as we made our way down the side of the hotel, and a solar-powered fixture illuminating the sign out front. Balaclava opened the back of a station wagon; it was too dark to discern its colour, but its shape was obvious. He jerked his head at the space within, which had been cordoned off from the front seats by a mesh barrier. Like a paddy-wagon, I thought, or a vehicle that habitually carried dogs.

'In,' he said, and when we'd complied, he slammed the door, leaving us crouching in darkness.

Moments later, the engine started with a low growl and we eased slowly out of the parking space and onto the highway. Ben and I sat crouched on the floor, knees touching, our backs pressed to the wheel wells on either side. The vehicle gathered speed and we had to brace our feet to stay upright. I raised my bound hands to my face and tried scraping at the tape across my mouth, but tied as they were, I couldn't get my nails under the edge. I rubbed the sides of my thumbs repeatedly at the one spot, stretching and easing my mouth in an attempt to loosen it, and was eventually rewarded with a slight puckering at the edge.

About then the vehicle turned off the highway for, I guessed, the track into the Jump-up and everything immediately became more difficult. Every time the vehicle lurched we were thrown off balance and a particularly hard bump while I was raising my hands again to my mouth jerked my thumb into my eye. Tears streamed from it and the pain was intense. I sniffled helplessly, reapplying myself to the task and finally, after what felt like hours, worked the corner free.

After that, with the help of my denim-covered knees, against which I rubbed my face, I managed to peel the tape away completely. Bending down to Ben's ear, I whispered my news, adding, 'Can you thread your feet through your hands, do you think? I've got a nailfile.'

I felt him nod and applied myself to the next step, which was getting hold of the implement. From the occasional clunking against the bodywork I surmised that Ben was trying to follow my suggestion. His struggles went on and on, parts of him bumped against me and I heard muffled grunts and once a noisy clang as his boot hit the vehicle's side, but the road was so rough that if Balaclava heard, I doubted he would have wondered because of the way we were being thrown around. We would be black and blue by this time tomorrow. Then I remembered that we might also be dead, and the fear came rushing to the forefront of my mind again. The familiarity of the man's voice teased at me again and I tried desperately to place it, but I had met so many people lately that it was impossible to isolate the intonations of one voice to pinpoint its owner.

Then Ben's hands thumped against me and, feeling my way up them, I realised that he had done it; they were no longer stretched behind him. 'Right,' I whispered. 'I'm going to shuffle round next to you. See if you can get the packet from my right-hand side pocket. The nailfile's inside.' I felt him nod against me and an interesting ten minutes ensued as I tried to help him slide his fingertips into and out of the pocket while retaining his grip on the slippery plastic covering. When we finally succeeded, I went to work on the tape across his mouth, but he shook his head, thrusting the packet at me.

'No time?' I whispered. 'You're probably right.' I couldn't remember how long it had taken us to drive into the commune but we seemed to have been bumping along for hours. There might well be only minutes before we arrived and our bid for freedom was discovered. In hasty whispers, I told him about the scissors and the message I'd left with the teenager, but his shrug seemed to echo my own fears about the boy's reliability.

With only our fingertips to manipulate the packet, it took forever until I felt the point of the nailfile protrude beyond the wrapping. I bent to grip it with my teeth and draw it out, then transferred it carefully to the fingertips of my two hands, pressing them hard together to maintain my hold on it.

'Put your wrists on my knees,' I whispered. It was essential that no clumsy movement in the dark knocked it from my weak grasp for I would never find it again, or pick it up if I did.

There followed an endless anxious time. With only my feeble hold to power it, I repeatedly stabbed and pulled at the tape confining Ben's hands. I must have driven the file into his flesh more than once, but at long last the perforated tape stretched enough for him to move his hands apart. They still weren't free, but he had movement enough to reach up and peel the tape from his mouth.

'Let me have it,' he whispered and a moment later had dragged the steel through his remaining bonds. 'Now yours, Em. God, woman, you're a wonder to have managed this!' He began to work on the tape around my wrists.

'How's your head?' I asked, remembering the blow that had felled him. 'And how did that little scrote get into our room? And why? If he was after the diamonds, he must've known they were in my bag.' It was something I'd only just realised.

'I'm fine,' Ben said. 'I was already falling over the kid when he hit me, so it wasn't as hard as he no doubt intended. As to the boy, maybe he planned to hide somewhere – wardrobe, bathroom? Wait for us to sleep, then grab your bag.' I could feel his warm breath on my cheek. 'Let's just hope he gets out of there and tells someone. The staff won't ignore the Do Not Disturb sign. We booked for two days, so it could be another day before anyone finds out we've gone.'

I peered out the window as the vehicle slowed, then made a lurching turn to the left. I had a momentary glimpse of stars that were almost instantly blotted out, and suddenly I recognised our location. 'It's the cliff at the Jump-up,' I hissed. 'We're almost there. He's just turned down the track into the valley.'

Ben's hacking at my bonds intensified. Then swearing softly, he grabbed both my wrists and yanked them apart. I felt the tape stretch, cutting into my arms, and bit my lip but he'd got the space he needed to pull one of my hands back through the loop he'd made and free it.

'Okay,' he breathed, slipping the nailfile back to me. 'Hang on to this – you never know. Did you see if he had a gun?'

'No. But he could have.' I clutched him. 'What are you thinking? Be careful, he's got a knife.' I shivered, remembering its cold touch against my lips. 'It looked awfully sharp. And I feel really bad about bringing him down on Kil and Sal. I was just trying to buy time.' The vehicle was slowing and, twisting about to peer through the mesh, I saw the shape of the old blue van form in the headlights. Panicked, I ducked back, hissing, 'What'll we do? We're here.'

The vehicle stopped but its headlights stayed on and the driver got out.

'Quick!' Ben whispered. 'Put the tape back on, loop your hands up again.' I scrambled to obey as Balaclava reached back into the cab for something. His footsteps sounded around the side of the vehicle and next moment a torch beam shone in on us. In its light I saw Ben, hair dishevelled, the tape crooked on his mouth, his arms apparently strained behind his back. I glanced down at the hasty cobble of tape on my own wrists, praying it would pass muster, and that the adhesive across my face, which felt far from secure, didn't choose that moment to let go. Apparently satisfied, our captor clicked off the torch and left, his boots crunching away through dried grass.

Ben stripped the tape off his mouth. 'Okay,' he said softly. 'Now we have to get out of here.'

It was easier said than done. There were no windows large enough for us to fit through, the back door was locked, and the mesh was bolted firmly to the floor of the vehicle. It felt strong enough to hold a grizzly bear. Ben seized two handfuls and tried mightily to bend it in two but he may as well have been tugging on a tree.

'God Almighty!' He slammed a hand against it. 'There's got to be some way out.' Bracing himself against a wheel well, he placed his feet on the lock of the back door and thrust against them by suddenly straightening his legs, but to no avail. The vehicle might have rocked to an infinitesimal degree but that was all. He aimed a kick with the same result. The noise boomed like a bass drum and we froze, then Ben resumed kicking.

'Stop!' I cried. 'He'll hear us!'

'So what if he does?' Ben's blood was up and I could tell that he was furious – desperate too. 'He didn't tie our legs, and he can't think we're going to sit here meekly waiting for whatever happens. At the very least the noise might alert someone in the camp. If this goddamned lock would only give . . .' He kicked again and again, but with less force each time, as the hopelessness of our situation sank in. Freeing our hands had achieved nothing. We were stuck here until our captor chose to let us out.

32

At least half an hour passed before we heard the sound of returning shoe leather. Ben picked up the discarded strips of tape and placed one tenderly over my mouth. He kissed my brow, whispering, 'Leave your hands free, just hold them together. The minute the door opens I'll tackle him. You get out and run for it.'

'No. I don't want to leave you. I can help.'

'You can't,' he said flatly. 'Promise me you'll run.'

The lock twisted. There was no time for more. In the dim starlight I sensed Ben slapping his own tape back on, then torchlight momentarily blinded me as the back door swung open.

It settled on Ben. 'Out,' Balaclava snapped. 'Is this the guy who drove you?' The light moved to take in the tall thin shape of Kil, hair ruffled and cheek reddened with a trickle of dried blood at one nostril. It was only a momentary shift but Ben used it to power out of the vehicle. He hit Balaclava mid body, knocking him backwards, and must have torn the tape from his mouth for he yelled, 'Now, Em!' as he went and

I scrambled immediately into the open. But obedience only took me so far.

I had a split second to see that Kil seemed frozen to the spot in shock. I don't suppose the poor man had a clue about any of it, but he plainly wasn't going to help by joining the fray. He just stood there, as much use, as Dad would've put it, as tits on a bull. I ran to the cab, scrabbled madly at the door and thrust my hand under the seat. There had been nothing in the back, so the tools – and there must be tools; it was the bush, for God's sake! – had to be under the seat.

My questing hand found and seized the canvas roll and I pulled it feverishly apart. The tools were only shapes in the darkness. I found the wheel brace by touch, seized it and raced back to the thrashing figures. Balaclava had dropped the torch and its beam cut uselessly into the space beneath the vehicle. Grabbing it up, I pushed it into Kil's unresisting hands.

'Shine it on them so I can see,' I ordered and willy-nilly, stammering questions I had no time to answer, he obeyed. By its light I saw that Balaclava seemed to be getting the best of it. Ben was underneath and the man's brawny arm was pressed across his throat. Both were bleeding from the face. Ben's eyebrow had split, the blood masking his right eye, while I could see red drops over the bared teeth showing through the stranger's woollen mask. I raised the wheel brace in both hands, but at the last moment I couldn't bring myself to smash it down on his exposed head. I didn't want to kill him, so I hit him as hard as I could across the shoulders instead.

He let out a roar, but his grip slackened and Ben improved his position by jabbing a fist into his face. I hit him again, aiming for the point of his shoulder. The torch beam dipped, as though its holder had flinched from the violence, and I yelled furiously at Kil, 'Well don't just stand there. Help him!'

'He's got a switchblade,' he stammered.

Ben's brief advantage had disappeared. Balaclava had the point of his elbow deep in his throat and he was thrashing uselessly, his face purpling. At that instant, with the help of the wavering torchlight, I caught the gleam of the knife lying within arm's reach of my husband's shoulder. Balaclava must have glimpsed it at the same moment. He lunged for it, snarling. Knowing he'd get there first, I used all my strength to swing the wheel brace at his straightening elbow.

It was like one of those slow dissolves you see on TV. Everything was crystal clear in the torch's beam: the drops of blood spilling from the woollen mask, the dark hair on the man's thick wrists and the silvery, graceful arc of the metal as it swung towards him. There was a roaring in my ears, masking the yammer of Kil's words.

Why didn't he just run if he was so scared? I thought furiously. Some help he was, standing there like a useless lump! Well, maybe I didn't want to be responsible for killing Balaclava, but I had no compunction about maiming him. My blow landed. His arm folded and his body followed it down before the roar of pain escaped him. Certainly broken, I thought with vindictive satisfaction, and, now the rush was passed, I took an unhurried step forward and kicked the knife far under the vehicle.

Ben, coughing and gasping, had rolled away when a figure erupted into our midst as if birthed that moment from the violence of the night. He wore a biker's helmet that obscured his face and, without pausing for explanation, fairly dived on

Balaclava, yanked his arms together and clapped a set of handcuffs on him, ignoring his yell of pain.

'Got you, you bastard,' the biker said with the utmost satisfaction.

Ben, to whose side I'd gone, coughed harshly. His voice was a strained whisper: 'So the cops finally made it.' He was holding his throat, his breath wheezing harshly. 'Better late than never, but they cut it bloody fine. I thought I told you to run?'

'Well, I didn't agree to do so,' I pointed out. My legs suddenly weren't up to their job of supporting me, and I sank down beside him. 'I feel a bit funny, Ben.'

He put an arm around me in an instant. 'It's shock,' he whispered and coughed again, the sound painful. 'I'm glad you didn't. I could be dead without your help. That's a mighty mean swing you've got. Where did the cop come from?'

'Search me.' My hands were shaking and there was a strange buzzing in my ears. 'Are you badly hurt?'

'I'll be fine.' He massaged his throat. 'Wait! Is that a bike?' I followed his gaze and made out the front wheel and part of a handlebar lying on its side in the wavering torchlight. 'I never heard it. Can you get up?'

My momentary weakness was passing. I rose with Ben's help just as the still-helmeted man grabbed hold of the balaclava and yanked it from his captive's head.

'Well, well, who do we have here?' he said. He took the torch from Kil and shone it on the man's face.

I gave a gasp. 'I *knew* I recognised his voice. That's the Crazy man!'

Ben and the cop spoke together. 'Who?'

'It's the dude ranch guy from Crazy Creek. The one who ran us off the road.' To be fair, he looked a bit different. Ben's fist had done serious damage to his nose, and one eye was swelling shut.

He scowled at my identification, snarling, 'Bitch!'

'His name's Tet— something. Tetram, Tetrill . . . That's it,' I said triumphantly. 'At least it's what he calls himself. He was in the pub last night.'

'I know it,' the cop said feelingly. He removed his helmet and began to read his prisoner his rights, the litany interrupted by my cry of astonishment.

'You!' It was the teenager from the pub. Not a youth at all, I saw now, but a man in his twenties. The softness was gone from his face, the sulky pout he'd adopted for the occasion merely a cover for the real man with his lithe, boyish body. He'd certainly fooled me. 'What were you doing in our room?'

'I wanted a discreet word. Unfortunately *he* was already there. He clobbered me while I was closing the door. Thanks for the scissors though. I dunno how I'd have managed without 'em.'

Dazed, I said automatically, 'You're welcome. How on earth did you get from there to here?'

He grinned. 'Borrowed the ranger's bike. I was talking to him earlier in the day so I knew which was his room. Showed him my ID and he came through like a champion. Gotta say it's a hairy old track though.'

Ben grunted sourly. 'You should try it trussed up. So where're the rest of your mates who were supposed to be looking out for us? Bader said we were getting protection. I didn't see much of that.'

'Should be here any old tick of the clock,' the cop replied cheerfully. 'We had a helicopter on standby.' He cocked his head to a faint vibration in the air. 'That's likely to be them now. It was coming from Katherine, so the pilot had a bit of a detour to pick 'em up.'

I thought back over the evening. 'Don't tell me – they're the courting couple. Youngish woman, older man? Had a table near ours at dinner.'

'You got it. They were watching your door, but of course he took you out through the window, so the first they knew about you being gone was when I'd freed myself. Sorry about that, but you know – best laid plans . . .'

A sudden plaintive voice broke into our exchange as Kil, standing like an unwanted extra at a photoshoot, said, 'Would somebody like to tell me what the hell is going on? Who are you people, anyway? And what's all this got to do with me? I've been dragged from my bed in the middle of the night, threatened with a knife and I haven't a clue what any of it's about.'

Glancing his way, I realised that I could actually make out his aggrieved face. The night was almost done and dawn was spreading pale fingers between the trees. On the thought, the first bird called the news to its mates and a regular chorus followed. I said, 'We met before, back in April. We're Ben and Emily, looking for my cousin, remember? You weren't exactly straight with us then, were you? Anyway, I'm afraid it's my fault that he'—I pointed at Tetrill—'brought us here. I told him it's where we found the diamonds. He thought you might have collared the rest of them, you see. I'm sorry. It's all I could come up with at the time.'

The chopper was definitely arriving, the noise loud enough now for the distinctive whup of the rotor blades to be heard. The machine came in low over the trees, its searchlight a sudden artificial sun highlighting the huddle of dwellings. It circled above us once, then set down at a little distance in a tornado of flying dust and grass stems. Half-dressed people came tumbling out of their shelters to gape at the unholy racket it made.

Poor Kil looked more bewildered than ever. 'Diamonds? What bloody diamonds?' Anger seemed to be overtaking bemusement. 'I'd like to know what right you've got—'

The chopper blades had slowed and its passengers were getting out, stooping low under the still-turning rotors. The cop put two fingers in his mouth and gave a shrill whistle, cutting off the rest of Kil's outburst.

Eventually it was all sorted out. The youthful-looking cop was Constable Gary Wickhill, who introduced us to the other two, Constable Marlene Jones and Sergeant Geoff Rustin, and had both Ben and me tell the tale of the night's work. He then led Tetrill, complaining bitterly about his broken elbow, over to the helicopter and presumably secured him within it.

'Are you going to charge him with the attempted murder of my wife?' Ben asked. 'Because although he mightn't have lit it himself, he was behind the fire, and the knifing, you know. Not to mention the attack with the vehicle.'

Rustin grinned nastily. 'Oh, yes. Mr Tetrill is in a world of trouble: theft, smuggling, attempted murder on three counts, abduction, assault on a police officer . . . I daresay we could get him for jaywalking too, if we tried. You'll both have to come back to Darwin and make a formal statement. We need to impound Tetrill's vehicle, so Gary can drive it and you back to Bloodwood Creek to await transport. Don't touch the back. What happened to the switchblade the hippy was on about?'

'I kicked it under the vehicle,' I said. 'If we can't open the back, then how do we return Sam's bike to him? He'll be stranded without it.'

'Nothing we can do about that, I'm afraid. The forensic evidence has to be protected. Perhaps a local can give him a lift out to retrieve it,' Rustin said dismissively.

It seemed shabby treatment for one whose generous action had probably saved our lives. I said as much to Ben, who shrugged. 'I know, Em. Though actually you were doing pretty well with that wheel brace. Better than Kil, anyway. He won't get far in his back-to-the-caves crusade if he doesn't develop a bit of spine. Nature's ruthless. He ought to've learned that by now.'

Constable Jones, meanwhile, had crawled under the vehicle to retrieve the knife and, with an impatient hitch of his head towards her, Rustin set off for the encampment. He would need to interview Kil, I supposed. I said, 'We could drive ourselves in the station wagon and Gary could take the bike, but I don't suppose the boss cop would hear of it.'

'No,' Ben agreed. 'God, what a night. Remind me never to let you volunteer for anything ever again.'

'As long as you remind me of the same,' I agreed. 'I can't get over that Gary, though. At the pub I'd have sworn he was no more than seventeen! The pout and the hair, I guess, and the slouchy sprawl of him – not to mention the attitude. He still looks young but not boyish in the least. You know what I mean?'

'He's just got one of those eternally young faces, and the rest is acting,' Ben said. 'A cinch for undercover work, I'd say. They probably sic him onto drug dealers, posing as a tearaway kid looking for trouble. And furthermore,' he added, sounding thoroughly fed up, 'now we have to go back *again*. Darwin must have some fatal bloody attraction for us. We can't seem to stay away from the place.'

33

Sergeant Bader arrived at the Bloodwood Creek pub, riding with the transporter dispatched to retrieve Tetrill's vehicle. We'd been back for some hours by then, long enough for showers, breakfast and some sleep. We could leave for Darwin at once, Ben had offered over breakfast, or stay the extra day for which we'd booked and rest up. His face was a little swollen and bruised and he still moved his head stiffly, so I had suggested we stay put. The aftermath of the fear and adrenalin in my own system, coupled with a sleepless night, not to mention all the aching muscles from being tossed about in the back of the vehicle during our midnight trip, had exhausted me.

'The state we're in, you'll fall asleep at the wheel and I'm no better. The world can wait a bit, Ben.'

'You're on.' He covered my hand with his larger one, his eyes searching my face. 'Are you okay, Em? Really, I mean. It's not so long ago you were at death's door – I should never have let you come. I don't know what I'd do if I lost you again.'

'You won't,' I assured him. 'And you know, I wasn't lost before. Just waiting for you to come to your senses.'

He raised my hand to his lips, kissing it tenderly. 'Well, thank Christ I did!'

A yawn slipped out. I couldn't help it. 'Oh dear. Sorry.' Another one followed and I stood up, saying ruefully, 'It's lovely to be appreciated but I can't keep my eyes open. You must be dead beat too. A couple of hours' sleep will do us both good.'

Once in our room with its untouched bed, I paused only to remove my blouse and jeans before pulling up the sheet and, barely conscious of Ben's presence beside me, falling asleep. It was like a gratifying slide into the softest, deepest cloud that cradled my body, inviting it ever deeper into slumber, and I don't believe that I so much as twitched until the shrilling of the bedside phone woke me.

'What is it?' I mumbled into the handpiece, feeling Ben stir beside me.

'Mrs Grier? Sorry to disturb you.' It was the front desk. 'There's a police person here wanting a word. Could you come to reception, please?'

I groaned and agreed, then pushed myself up, feeling groggy and disorientated.

'What time is it?' Ben croaked. 'And what idiot rang us? I told them we weren't to be disturbed.'

'It's the cops. Apparently they want a word. And it's three-thirty.'

'Oh, God!' Wincing, he pushed himself up. 'I feel about ninety. Did you sleep?'

'Like a mummy – the Egyptian kind,' I said. 'I'm hungry. We missed lunch. I wonder if we could get a coffee and something to go with it?'

'Let's find out.' He stood up with a groan, still fully dressed save for his shoes. 'I'll just splash my face first.' He headed for the bathroom, grumbling, 'What the hell can they want with us now?'

I had been expecting the 'police person' to be Gary, but it was actually Corrie Bader who rose from a cane chair to greet us, and congratulate us on a good result.

'You woke us up for that?' Ben asked. 'Let me tell you, if it hadn't been for my wife's resourcefulness, you could very well have been hunting for our bodies about now.'

She raised her hands. 'Yes, I'm sorry about that, but plans are nearly always the casualty of action, you know.'

Easy for her to say, I thought dourly. Ben must've been of a like mind. He said, 'Funny, I don't remember that bit coming up when you were making them. Did you wake us just to pass that on?'

'Look,' she said, 'I'm sorry about what happened, but despite what I'm sure was a very frightening experience, you are unharmed. Now, what I wanted to see you about was this cousin of yours, Mrs Grier. We need to interview her, but Gary said she wasn't among the commune members and nobody there seemed to recognise her name.'

'No, well, they wouldn't – she'd forgotten it, remember?' I said. 'And they don't live in the actual commune. The other people are Rick's . . . tenants, I suppose you'd call them. He owns the land, so I imagine they respect his wishes. The idea was to hide her, so of course they played dumb.'

Bader frowned. 'Well, it won't do. I'm not saying she'll be charged for things she can't remember she may have done. But she'll need to be questioned and have a medical assessment, for her own good. Untreated head injuries are frowned upon by medical people, in case you didn't know it. And this man, Rick – he failed to report an accident and held on to goods he either knew or suspected were stolen—'

I sighed. 'We've been through this. He was protecting her. Is that so wrong?'

'That may be so,' Bader said. 'Look, they'll probably both just get a non-custodial sentence, but either way I need to interview them. So will you tell me how to find them?'

Ben took my hand and answered for me. 'Drive out to the actual Jump-up – it's a sort of sheer bluff face and quite unmistakable. Leave your vehicle and walk around to the other side of it. It's maybe a kilometre. You'll find the house there. There may be another way in, but that's the only one I know.'

Bader rose. 'Thank you,' she said. 'You've been told to return to Darwin to make your statement?'

'Yes.' Ben sighed. 'We'll head back tomorrow.'

'Are you taking them in – Aspen and Rick?' I asked.

'Yes, of course.' She looked surprised that I should ask.

'Then I'll see them there,' I said firmly. 'Please tell Aspen so.'

The following day found us again at the same hotel in Darwin, booking in once more.

'Back again?' the girl on the desk quipped. 'You just can't stay away, can you?'

'Believe me this is the absolute last time.' Ben handed over his card and collected the room key, then we headed for the lift. 'I'll fill up the vehicle as soon as we're through at the cop shop,' he said, selecting our floor. 'First thing tomorrow we're out of here and not even a damn tidal wave is gonna stop us.'

I crossed my fingers superstitiously. 'Don't tempt fate. Can we get a coffee or something first, before the cops? Lord knows how long we'll have to hang around if we want to see Aspen and Rick.'

'What else could we do?' Ben asked reasonably.

'At least my conscience is clear.' I sighed. 'I did what Aunt Fee asked, so her shade ought to be happy, and Dad can now get on with his duties as executor. I wonder if Aspen's worked it out yet that the man she can't remember, the one who hurt her in the night, was her own father?'

'Best not tell her if she hasn't.' Ben used the card on the door, strode in and tossed the bags onto the bed. 'Well, here we are again. Let's go find that coffee.'

At the police station, the man at the desk had obviously been told to expect us. 'I'll just ring through and let Sergeant Bader know you're here.'

A few moments later we were being ushered into her office. Corrie Bader was working through a pile of reports but put them aside and rose to gesture at the two chairs facing her desk. It took much longer than I had thought it would to go through our stories, keeping everything in place and omitting nothing. She constantly stopped us to clarify a point, wanting precise times, or as near as we could guess them, and making the distinction between what we had assumed and what had actually occurred. Gary's supposed family being a case in point.

At some stage I said, 'Are you recording this? Because I'm not sure I can remember it all again to put it on paper.'

She nodded at a small black box sitting on the corner of her desk. 'Yes. It'll be typed up for you to sign. We're way past handwritten statements, thank God. Just make sure that your signatures are legible.' She tapped the end of a biro against her front teeth. 'So, I'm curious. Telling him you got the stones off his dead mate – wasn't that a risk? Supposing he'd heard about his death on the news? He'd have known it wasn't true.'

I raised my hands helplessly. 'I hoped you had suppressed that bit. Anyway, it was all I could think of. Ben was out of it and Tetrill was waving that knife around, threatening to use it. It bought us time. An extra hour – that's everything when you think you're going to be killed, and,' I added waspishly, 'when your so-called protection is trussed up like a Christmas turkey on the bathroom floor.'

'But at that point you didn't know that Gary was a police officer?'

'All we knew,' Ben weighed in, 'was that your famous plan had gone tits up and we were on our own. Emily saw a chance to delay matters and took it.'

'I'm not criticising your wife's actions.' Bader smiled apologetically. 'Actually you did pretty well for a couple of civilians. Now, if you'd like to wait a bit, I'll have copies made for you to sign, and there's someone who wants to speak to you before you leave.'

'Aspen?' I said hopefully but it turned out to be the station's superintendent, a tall, long-nosed man with an impressively decorated uniform, who came in, followed by a constable with a tea tray. We took tea together while he thanked us for our contribution to the cause of justice, then left with a hearty handshake and the expressed wish that our experiences in the North hadn't turned us off the Top End.

After that, a constable brought us our statements, which we duly signed.

'Where is Sergeant Bader?' I asked, returning the pen. 'We're waiting to see my cousin.'

'The sarge is interviewing the suspect now,' he replied. 'Shouldn't be too much longer.'

It jarred to hear Aspen spoken of this way, but of course to the police she was just that. It didn't bode well for her future, I thought uneasily, despite all Bader's assurances. However, eventually the door opened again to admit both her and Rick, the latter looking more surly than relieved. Aspen herself seemed lost and uncertain. She wore a dress slightly too large for her that emphasised her slender frame, and her hair was pulled forward on her brow to minimise the effect of her scars, rather than in the chignon she had previously affected, which had been perfect for showing off the beautiful line of her neck and jaw.

Somewhere she had got hold of some make-up, but it couldn't wholly disguise the fact that the scars were still some months away from fading, if not into invisibility, then to something less noticeable than at present. I rose to hug her, something to which she submitted, though with a faint puzzled look in her eyes.

'I'm Emily,' I reminded her, 'your cousin. I was at your place the other day.'

'I know. But'—she hesitated, her diction careful as if she was anxious not to offend—'that doesn't make you real to me. Like I know you, I mean.'

'But I told you about the farm, remember? And me coming to sleep at your house?'

'Yes.' She almost snapped the word. 'But it means no more than if I'd read about it. Remembering is *knowing* what happened, not what somebody tells you did.'

'It's all right, dear,' Rick said. 'Your cousin's trying to help.'

'Nobody understands!' Aspen said despairingly. 'They think if I just try hard enough to remember it'll all come back. Or they're like that cop – *she* thinks I'm just pretending to have forgotten. You should all try it sometime! It's . . . it's horrible. Your whole life wiped out. You don't know who you are, or what's real and what's not—' Her voice broke and Rick put his arm around her and led her to a seat.

'So what's happening?' Ben asked.

'We go before a magistrate on Tuesday,' Rick said. 'We can't leave town before then. You really dumped us in it, mate.' He sounded bitter.

'It was my wife's life that was at risk,' Ben said coolly. 'And *she'd* done nothing wrong.'

Rick sighed then and some of his surliness lifted. 'I know. Not your fault. I shoulda got rid of those bloody stones the moment I found them. Or left them in the car. The wreck was stripped quick enough. Somebody would've taken the diamonds too and we'd have been well out of it.'

But the moment he learned I was looking for his missing courier, Tetrill would still have come after us, I thought, then the sense of his words caught up with me.

'The wreck – do you mean that shell of a red sedan on the side of the road south of Bloodwood Creek?'

'Yeah. That's it. Only takes a day for somebody to come along and strip them. Tyres, brake systems, the lot.'

I shook my head. I'd driven past without a thought for who its driver might have been. I sat down next to my cousin. 'Aspen, when this is all over, why don't you come south for a visit? There's your inheritance to sort out, and—'

'Her name is Marie,' Rick said, bristling.

'Sorry, I forgot. Well, as I was saying, there's bound to be a process to go through with the will. Her parents were quite well off, you know. You could come and stay with us, and'—I took her hand—'you could see a surgeon while you are down. Maybe they could help with your scarring. Not that it is terribly noticeable,' I lied, 'but if you wanted to, you could well afford to have plastic surgery, you know. There's your parents' house too. You might want to sell it, or you could live there, but either way, seeing it again might help you regain your memory. The experts say it's all about association.'

She pulled her hand from my grasp and looked at Rick. 'No. I don't want to. I don't have to, do I?' It was painful to see her so dependent, she who had taken foreign cities in her stride now as panicked as a child.

Rick glared at me, placing a protective hand on her shoulder. 'Of course not. You don't have to do anything you don't want to, dear,' he soothed. 'Emily's just being kind. She doesn't understand.'

'What? What don't I understand?' I was a little nettled by the abruptness of her refusal.

Aspen hesitated, biting her lip, then burst out, 'I don't want to go back, or to remember. I know I took drugs. Rick explained that to me. But I don't know what else I did, or who that man was in the night or – or if there was more than one. But I think there might have been, later.' She swallowed a sob. 'I don't want to be that person any more, and if I remember everything I might want to forget again, and I think that's why I took the drugs before.' Her eyes were haunted by the fear of things unknown.

'It's all right, sweetie, I understand.' I touched her bowed head, the black hair still a jarring sight. She had been so golden before, an angelic beauty that drew every eye. 'It was just a thought. I'll get a postal address from Rick and I'm sure Dad can mail you any legal papers and take care of the rest for you.' I looked at Ben. 'We should probably go, but we'll keep in touch, Rick.' I scribbled out our address and added that of the farm, then handed him the pen and got a post bag number at Bloodwood Creek in return. 'Mackay,' I said, reading it off. 'Rick and Marie Mackay – it has a ring to it. It's been'—I paused—'interesting. I wish you luck with the court hearing. Let us know what happens, won't you?'

He shook my hand, then Ben's, and Aspen submitted to another hug from me.

'Thank you,' she murmured like an obedient child, but her actions resembled the air kiss of a stranger with no feeling behind the words, or in the touch of her arms around my body. And after all, I reflected, without the memory of our shared past, that's what we were – strangers who happened to share familial blood.

34

With nothing further to hold us there, we left Darwin for the final time.

'We'll be called back for the trial,' Ben observed.

'But that won't be for months,' I said airily. 'Maybe years. Generally by the time criminals go to trial, the public's almost forgotten what they did. Except for those involved, of course. But he was arrested in the act – it'd be a waste of time for him to claim he didn't do it.'

'You have such a refreshingly simple way of looking at things,' Ben said. 'You'd be an asset to the High Court.' I thumped his arm and he grinned. 'You need to hang on to that nailfile. It could become Exhibit A for our kids in the saga of our escape.'

I leaned back, stretching luxuriously. 'It's just so wonderful to have it all behind us. No more worrying, no more fear. In hindsight, we could have saved all that money we spent on the alarm system for the house.'

'It's a good investment. Who knows, we might win the lottery someday and buy art. We'd need a secure venue for it, if we did.'

'Oh, yes.' This was a new departure for Ben. I'd never heard him mention the subject. Teasingly I said, 'We could always start our collection with Exhibit A. We'll buy a frame and mount it for the ages.'

'Why not?' he replied equably, swerving to avoid the carcass of a roo that hadn't quite made the verge before it died.

'It'd make a great story,' I said, wondering absently where the item actually was. Had I dropped it in Tetrill's vehicle or thrust it back into its hiding place? I hadn't used the tampons yet . . . My thoughts snagged on that fact and my mind did a slow loop, bringing up the old woman's face on the park bench. Ever since finding Aspen, her words had been pushed to the back of my mind but now I looked across at Ben, at his handsome profile and dark hair, and felt a dizzying rush of delight.

'What?' He skimmed his gaze sideways, then returned it to the road.

'Nothing. I was just thinking my hair's a bit long. I might get it cut in the Alice.'

And visit a chemist – just to be sure, before I told him. But in my heart I was already certain.

We spent three days in Alice seeing the sights, but by the end of the third one I was so tired of Ben's fussing over what I shouldn't climb and where I shouldn't scramble that I told him I was missing Mia so badly I was more than ready to head home.

He agreed at once, his brow wrinkling. 'Are you feeling okay, Em? You don't want to rest?'

I sighed. 'Ben, I'm not sick. I'm pregnant and perfectly well. If you keep this up, you'll be a nervous wreck and no use to me at all when the baby gets here. Relax! You're not going to be one of those fathers who pass out in the delivery room, are you?'

'Very likely.' He grimaced. 'I've never seen a birth.'

'Really? Not even puppies or kittens?'

'Our cat was spayed. And Dad's allergic to dog hair.'

'I didn't know that. Well, come down to the clinic when we get back. There are always bitches and cats in trouble with their young, or mares foaling – you can see how it's done.'

'I think I'd rather not,' he said hurriedly. 'Sometimes you can have a bit too much reality.'

'Oh well.' I patted his hand. 'You'll just have to wait for the big day then.'

The flight home was uneventful but it was late when we alighted from the taxi at the farm. I had vetoed Ben's suggestion that we have my parents meet us, as I knew Mum didn't like Dad driving at night and we had left our vehicle at their place.

Mum had dinner waiting and a bed made up for us. 'Of course you'll stay,' she said even as I stooped to pick up Mia, busy rubbing her face on my ankles. 'We'll hear all about the inquest and how your trip went tomorrow – save on the phone calls.'

I smiled and thanked her, knowing she was going to be thrilled about the real news I had to impart. Of course she already had grandchildren, but the chances were that they would be grown before they returned to make their home here – if they ever did. Ben took our bags up to the room and I followed my parents into the kitchen's welcome warmth; the late August evenings were still chilly. I put Mia down and she immediately climbed back up my jeans, apparently ecstatic to have found me again. 'My, you've grown.' I rubbed her chin while she purred like a dynamo. 'It's so good to be home,' I said, looking around at the familiar space. 'And we have had adventures to relate. After dinner. For now, Dad, I'll just tell you you can stop advertising for her, because we've found Aspen.'

It was a late night by the time we had talked it all out, Ben and I taking turns, telling them everything that had happened. Mum was predictably horrified by what had befallen us at Bloodwood Creek. She gasped at the thought of her niece ferrying illegal diamonds about the country for criminals, and tutted her sympathy over Aspen's resultant scarring, though it didn't stop her interjecting, 'Well, that's very sad, but you were nearly *killed*.'

'I think it could be worse for her,' I said gently. 'The scars are really bad, Mum. Sal dyed her hair black, which doesn't really suit her, but perhaps she doesn't remember her beauty, which would be a blessing. And she really seems to love Rick. I tried to get them to come down once everything's been sorted with the police, but she wouldn't hear of it.'

'Won't she go to prison?' Dad asked. He sounded pretty unforgiving. 'It's not like she's innocent. She presumably chose to do this.'

'We don't know that,' I protested. 'She was an addict. She was probably coerced into it by need.'

Mum exclaimed at the thought. 'Fee would turn in her grave!'

'The one who should be in prison is Uncle Rich,' I said forcefully, in defence of my cousin. '*He* started it all. Thankfully the police – at least the sergeant we dealt with – seemed to think that both Rick and Aspen would end up with non-custodial sentences. Rick didn't really do anything, anyway, except protect her. Aspen's clean now and she's got a life she seems content with, and a solid sort of man to care for her. If she goes inside, it will very likely push her back onto drugs.'

'So he's a farmer, this Rick?' Dad asked. 'He can't be all bad then. What's he grow?'

'Fruit mainly, veggies – it's sort of like a smallholding. Subsistence, not commercial. He has a small flock of goats, and chooks. He told me they fish in the creek and eat the goats as well as milk them and make their own cheeses. He's self-taught, but getting there. Builds his own furniture, loads his own bullets . . . That sort of thing.'

Dad nodded. 'A survivalist. Good for him. No wacky weed or any of that sort of nonsense?'

'No way.' I thought about it. 'I think you'd like him. He's different, but he's genuine enough. They all are really, some just less suited to living their beliefs,' I added, thinking of Kil.

'Well, she could do worse by the sound of things. Poor lass. If only we'd known . . . When the will's been probated, the money will be a handy back-up for them.'

'Yes,' I said, 'but I honestly don't think it will make any difference to Rick. He won't throw in what he's made for himself for a life in town. He despises what that tends to do to people's environmental ethics.'

Mum nodded thoughtfully. 'I can respect that. There's too much of the me generation these days. Everyone intent on grabbing what they can for themselves and damn the consequences to the planet. So, back to work Monday?' She rose to wind the old-fashioned mantel clock that as far back as memory took me had sat on top of the china cupboard. It was the last thing she did every night before bed.

'Depends on how the changeover's gone,' I said, 'but it's our re-opening day if everything's worked out. Anyway, we have another piece of news for you both.'

Dad raised his brows. 'Thought we'd just heard it all.'

'Not this bit.' Ben beamed and put his arm around me. 'We're having a baby.'

Mum gave a glad cry and, forgetting her purpose, turned back to me. 'Oh, Emily, that's wonderful!' Next thing I was enveloped in a fierce hug. 'Oh, you don't know how much I've hoped for this,' she said. 'A child we can watch grow.' Her eyes were misty as she planted a kiss on my cheek.

Over her shoulder I saw Dad congratulating Ben as they shook hands, his weather-beaten face split into a grin. It would mean the world to them both to have a grandchild they could spoil, and teach, and host for holidays and long weekends, and I suddenly understood how much Stephen's decision to live and work overseas had cost them.

'When's the baby due?' Mum eyed me up and down. She was back to being practical and, with a pang of the heart, I suddenly noticed how much grey now showed in her hair. My fierce, plain-spoken, down-to-earth mum was getting on in years.

'Early next year. February maybe? I'm not quite sure. I'll make a doctor's appointment tomorrow.' I couldn't stop a sudden yawn. 'Oh, sorry. Lord, look at the time. It's been a long day. I'm falling asleep where I stand.'

'Yes, you need your rest. You must take care of yourself now, lovie. Off to bed with you. I'm coming up too, so I'll just make sure you've everything you need.' She followed me from the kitchen, and for the first time ever the clock remained unwound.

Later, lying spooned beside Ben, feeling sleep waiting like a comfortable carriage in the wings of my mind, I said sleepily, 'We did it, didn't we? It took a while but we found her. Aunt Fee would be pleased.'

'We found something much more important.' Ben's arm came over me, pulling me close. His hand felt down the length of my arm until his fingers linked with mine, his breath warm on my neck as he kissed the back of my head. 'We found each other again and that's worth all the diamonds in the world. And'—I could hear the smile in his voice—'I think your mum's starting to like me.'

'Dream on,' I murmured, lying safe within the compass of his arm, emblematic of the circle of love in which, after all the lonely years and against all odds, I had finally come to rest.

Acknowledgements

With many thanks to my publishing, editing and cover designing team at Penguin Random House. I'd be lost without you – or at least unpublished, so thank you!

Also by the author

By the bestselling author of *The Missing Girl*

KERRY McGINNIS

Gathering Storms

*Nothing stays
hidden forever*